The Heights and the Moors

D. M. CLARK

LifeRich PUBLISHING

LifeRich Publishing is a registered trademark of The Reader's Digest Association, Inc.

LifeRich Publishing books may be ordered through booksellers or by contacting:

LifeRich Publishing
1663 Liberty Drive
Bloomington, IN 47403
www.liferichpublishing.com
1 (888) 238-8637

Because of the dynamic nature of the Internet, any web addresses or links contained in this book may have changed since publication and may no longer be valid. The views expressed in this work are solely those of the author and do not necessarily reflect the views of the publisher, and the publisher hereby disclaims any responsibility for them.

Any people depicted in stock imagery provided by Getty Images are models, and such images are being used for illustrative purposes only. Certain stock imagery © Getty Images.

Interior Image Credit: D. M. Clark

Scripture taken from the NEW AMERICAN STANDARD BIBLE®, Copyright © 1960,1962,1963,1968,1971,1972,1973,1975,1977,1995 by The Lockman Foundation. Used by permission. www.Lockman.org

Scripture quotations designated (NIV) are taken from the Holy Bible: New International Version®. NIV®. Copyright © 1973, 1978, 1984 by International Bible Society. Used by permission of Zondervan. All rights reserved.

ISBN: 978-1-4897-2928-6 (sc)
ISBN: 978-1-4897-2929-3 (hc)
ISBN: 978-1-4897-2927-9 (e)

Library of Congress Control Number: 2020913716

Print information available on the last page.

LifeRich Publishing rev. date: 07/21/2020

THE GRAND SWEEP

ALPINE FOREST

FOREST OF ANDIA

ARENGARD

BLUFF

MITHRENDIA

OF ODIN

THE MARCHES

DONEGAL'S RANGE

WOLF'S HOLLOW

THE MOORS

MT. HELGA

O'FLANAGAN RANGE

BLACK MOUNTAINS

N

W   E

S

HARFAGR'S LANDING

PART I

INVASION

CHAPTER I

A Lecture and
an Episode

On Tuesday, the thirty-first of October, in the year of our Lord 2017, at precisely 7:36 a.m., Mary Augustine's eyes were opened.

First-period class had begun in a large assembly hall at seven fifteen, and thus it was well under way when Mary wandered in through the faux-wood-paneled double doors in the back of the auditorium. She was fixated, not on class, but on her cellular device. As a consequence, she failed to notice a momentary glare from Professor Thomas Morley. And how could she have done otherwise? The social media site bore an enigmatic message from an equally cryptic sender: "Today, on All Hallows' Eve, your life hangs in the balance."

This formidable greeting was from someone calling himself

or herself Nostradamus2017. Mary had dealt with cyberbullies before but not of this order of magnitude.

She reflexively swept away a wave of shimmering black hair, revealing a beautiful olive-skinned face that had turned pale and was contorted by acute emotional pain. She could feel the tiny hairs on her arms rise, and droplets of sweat coursed down the small of her back.

"As I was saying before being interrupted by yet *another* tardy student," growled the professor, "humankind repudiates superstition with sound reason and scientific evidence. Our senses—sight, smell, sound, taste, and touch—are useful tools, but sometimes they err. Our rational minds? Yes, they can also err. Therefore, our sensory observations and reasoning must be corroborated with factual evidence, and this evidence must be weighed by our scientific peers.

"I was born and raised in St. Louis, Missouri," continued the professor. "You might ask, 'Well, why does that matter, and why should I care?' It is precisely this: I come from the Show Me State. Don't tell me about your bigfoot encounter or the angelic presence who visited your room last night. Show me the evidence! And it had better be good, for the burden of proof is on those who claim to be the source of such nonsense.

"And with that," he added, raising his hands with a theatrical shrug, "fairies, goblins, and ghosts go flying out of the room."

The audience of a hundred or so sleepy faces awoke to express their amusement as Mary took her seat in a middle row of the center section, some thirty feet back from Morley's lectern. This old college auditorium with its raised dais and can lighting system had once staged plays and musical performances, but its charming ambiance seemed of little consequence to her now. Nor did she take much notice of the flamboyant-haired maestro who conducted his pupils with a scientific eloquence that demanded unilateral attentiveness. Out of the corner of her eye, Mary could see Morley's shoulder-length locks of peppered gray flinging about in frenzied animation, but she paid little attention to this habitual practice.

"Skepticism, you see," said Professor Morley, "is the hallmark of a scientist. Belief is based on that which is proven, what is testable, and what is repeatable."

Mary had not yet closed the cryptic message on her phone when Jen, a stentorian-voiced sophomore sitting just three feet behind her, squawked, "And what about singularities?"

Mary surged up in her seat like the arched back of a startled cat. This peculiarity amused the undergraduates sitting around her. She grimaced with embarrassment before powering off her phone.

"Singularities," repeated the professor with a note of intrigue as he rested his elbows upon the lectern. "Hmm. I think I know where this is heading. However, for the sake of our audience, we'll need to define our terms."

"I mean something that is uniquely extraordinary," said Jen.

Mary turned and caught the loud-voiced young woman out of the corner of her eye. *And coming from one with such a petite figure,* she thought. *Am I overreacting?*

"Go on," replied the professor.

"Something that happens on a rare occasion," said Jen, "and is personally witnessed by few. Say, a miracle of God. How is that testable and repeatable?"

Jen's voice ceased to be a distraction when Mary noticed the sudden appearance of two orbs of light. Each was a little smaller in diameter than a tennis ball. They appeared from her right, traveling through the demising wall as if the brick masonry had no solidity or boundary. They swept left across the auditorium, and then the lights dimmed as they began to manifest in the shadows behind the lectern. One of the apparitions, who looked humanlike save for obscuring billows of smoke, dribbled a miniature misty gray basketball toward the lectern before passing it to the other. A flaming hoop appeared above the professor's head. The taller apparition rose above the rim, caught the pass, and dunked the ball. It ricocheted off the unsuspecting professor's noggin and into the ethereal grasp of the smaller ghost, who surged above the dry-erase board, turned, and grinned at the assembled host of young academics.

Mary sat in shock while the professor swept a hand across his scalp as if putting to right those shifting gray strands that had been displaced by a slight breeze.

"Do you see that?" shrieked Mary.

"See what?" asked Morley, whose heavy cheek lines, running from nose to lip, knitted in moments of consternation. "Oh, it's Ms. Augustine interrupting us once again!"

"Are you kidding?" she replied. "Look!" Mary pointed at the two apparitions, now hovering near the outer left wall, who seemed to relish the spectacle of their spectral realm and its camouflage effects on the physical world.

"What?"

"Two ghosts!" Mary replied.

"Ghosts? Yes, I see them," said a young man in the front row. "They're from *Hamlet* and *Macbeth*."

"They're here!" said Jen, quoting the little girl from the movie *Poltergeist*.

A din of laughter erupted as if the amused yet dubious audience had been watching a charlatan's comedic act.

"Someone forgot to take her antipsychotic meds this morning," a young woman to Mary's distant left said, sneering.

"But didn't you see?" asked Mary again. Her words trailed

off as she watched the apparitions salute her with mocking triumph. They broke toward the left wall, with the lively commotions of Chestnut Street echoing just beyond, before abandoning this path and returning to the demising wall from whence they came. *What caused them to turn?* she wondered. She strained her neck so as to follow where their movements indicated they might have gone had they exited through the double-paned window. It was difficult to make out anything. Even now the dreary sunlight was fighting to awaken from its nightly slumber.

"Well, this is quite divine," said Morley. Each uttered syllable brimmed with sarcasm. "A little abnormal psychology posing as belief in the paranormal. I've been distracted during my lectures before, but never like this."

With the departure of the apparitions, Mary sat back down in her chair and began to take stock of her flesh-and-blood surroundings. The shock of the cryptic message and her observance of the apparitions were overwhelming enough. She even wondered if she was in the midst of a lucid dream rather than waking reality. Nevertheless, her sensory observations were all too palpable, and she soon recognized her situation to be a rather awkward and real social predicament. All eyes, it seemed, were fixed upon her.

"And you have nothing further to say after entertaining us with such lively observations?" the professor asked her.

Mary could not determine if she was more embarrassed or scared. She fought back the tears that were begging to cascade down the contours of her cheeks. As a sensitive, she often felt emotions more acutely than others. Nevertheless, she would not give Morley or her peers the satisfaction of seeing her deeper emotions exposed, even if they remained ignorant of what she had perceived. She therefore answered the professor with a stare of silence.

"No? I see then that our little performance has reached its conclusion," said Morley.

Morley returned to his lecture as Mary sat in her seat, picturing a room devoid of all her detractors. With some strength of mind, she was able to regain a sense of composure. Jen squawked again about some topic or other, to which Mary devoted none of her attention whatsoever. She crossed her arms about her fair form as her exotic green eyes did a little welcome navel-gazing. Though she was a little on the short side, Mary's shapely legs were just long enough, allowing sneakers to firmly grasp the barren concrete floor in spite of others' attempts to pull the floor out from under her.

And then yet another distraction, in a morning somehow full of them, caught Mary's attention.

A swirling darkness entered the auditorium, once again from her far right. Mary could not discern its features, but it was about seven feet tall, draped in opaque swirls of shadow. Blacker than black, it seemed to her to possess a maniacal evil.

She checked herself. How could she know this? There was something inhuman about it, and she could feel its hate.

And what of the earlier apparitions? The most obvious clues pertained to their humanoid form and their willing reenactment of a great American game. Those orbs seemed to her like harmless punks pulling pranks before an unsuspecting audience.

The black swirling mass moved toward the lectern. This darkness was like a raging wicked entity—possibly of immense power—conveying an odor of putrefaction. Mary was once again about to jump out of her seat, but she maintained her resolve and watched the lectern. A look of involuntary repulsion appeared upon the professor's face.

"Where is that smell of sulfur coming from?" asked Morley.

For the first time this morning, the self-assured academic seemed to Mary to be a bit perplexed. "Something must be wrong with the ventilation or plumbing system."

Mary could see students in the front rows corroborating the professor's olfactory perceptions with scrunched and upturned nostrils.

"Well, this is intolerable," said Morley. "The custodial staff and building maintenance people must be alerted immediately."

The entity seemed to linger in the classroom as it drifted between the professor and the first row. Though she could not tell what they were thinking, Mary could see anguish in their contorted faces. Even Morley looked a little on edge.

"Until then," said the professor as he shuffled away from the lectern, "I'd say our work is done here for the day. Class dismissed."

The black mass swept across the room and, unlike the ghostly orbs, exited onto Chestnut Street.

Morley did not seem to notice. He wasted no time in exiting the auditorium. Mary heard him say, "Well, this has certainly been an odd morning."

Had the man of sound reason gathered all the facts? A slight breeze against his hair. The smell of putrefied sulfur. Was that all he had noticed?

And what had the students noticed? Just the foul odor?

And did Morley just say "odd"?

Mary sat there in one of the middle rows, quiet as a mouse, as the students filed out of the lecture hall. Some laughed and pointed at her. Despite her embarrassment, she chose to ignore their jests.

Two apparitions, and then a dark, swirling tornado of malevolent intent. Nobody seemed to have noticed them except her. That, indeed, seemed odd.

CHAPTER 11

Further Developments
of an Odd Nature

"That is really creepy," said Benjamin Cranmer as he perused his girlfriend's smartphone. "'Your life hangs in the balance'? What kind of weirdo would send that?"

"And that's not all, Ben," said Mary. She informed him of the three paranormal visitors to the Alfred P. Bias Lecture Hall, that is, three visitors to a packed auditorium that no one else had happened to see. Her fingers wrapped around the wooden armrests of her chair in a knurled contortion. She grasped and stroked them as if she were trying to twist the armrests off.

"Maybe that was from the shock of the message," said Ben. "What?"

"Well, you might have been seeing things."

Mary had already witnessed her fill of devil's advocates in the lecture hall earlier that morning. She hardly needed another, and yet her boyfriend seemed to be heading in that direction. An exasperated frown distorted the graceful, narrow arc of her eyebrows, and her pouty lips curled in peevish irritation. "Are you insinuating that I was delusional?"

Although she glanced away, she could sense Ben's eyes roaming over her and taking stock of the situation.

"Do you see anything unusual now?" he asked.

"No."

His steady hand placed the cell phone beside her on the corner of his slipshod work desk, which often wobbled at the least provocation. There in the subterranean bowels of the Newman Liberal Arts Building, the departmental budget seemed to leave off. Not that the history department was overlooked. No, not quite. The ancient Egyptians, Greeks, and Romans were afforded preferential status on the ground floor. So were the second-floor offices of the Enlightenment, 1960s counterculture, and postmodern studies with their historical reinterpretations through secular modalities. But there, below ground, not a glimpse of natural light was afforded to illuminate the offices of medieval studies, the Reformation, and early modern Europe. Those frequent power outages, therefore, required the use of flashlights or, better yet, candles and tapers. After all, the Dark Ages were better studied in an ambiance of monastic shadow, or so thought the departmental higher-ups from their sun-drenched office spaces above.

Mary, of course, would never have known to venture into this secret lair had it not been for Benjamin. Her boyfriend of two years worked as a research assistant for Professor Nicodemus Porter, who had been inconspicuous as of late.

The basement consisted of a meager secretarial chamber

with the professor's office just beyond. Mary appreciated its relative privacy, tucked away from the clamor of campus activity, but its accommodations were lacking. A musty smell permeated the two rooms as a lingering reminder of the need for constant ventilation. Ben flipped the switch of the portable dehumidifier, which sat upon a concrete floor littered with peeling paint.

Mary glanced over at him, subconsciously seeking a sense of reassurance. Ben stood an inch above six feet, and he possessed wiry arms and legs like those of a cyclist. Dark eyebrows and hazel eyes contrasted with a shock of blond hair that arose from the crown of his head and stood of its own accord. He wore midlength sideburns, which complemented a long slender nose and high cheekbones. The articulation of the latter accentuated his facial expressions when he spoke, a fact not lost on Mary when she dabbled with romantic sentiments.

"I think you will be safe here," he said. "There are few who even know of this office's existence."

"Not even the history majors?"

"Dr. Porter and I hold our posted office hours upstairs. A little hole-in-the-wall. Room 306."

Ben sat down in a dilapidated chair beside her and tossed a blue racquetball in the air.

"Nobody has ever bothered," he said between tosses. "We're in our own element down here."

Mary watched as he bounced the ball off the floor and against one of the walls, which was finished with a wood-paneled wainscot, with warpage and discoloration attesting to a long-term disagreement with the humidity. Above the wainscot, an aged coat of off-white paint was cracking in zigzag patterns, which tended to distract from the hanging artifacts of history: a battle scene of Henry V at Agincourt;

an artist's rendering of the city of Augsburg from 1493; and a medieval world map detailed with questionable precision.

The chamber may have been dated and deteriorated and neglected by the departmental budget, but its isolation felt comfortable to her, so when Mary heard a loud rap at the door, she erupted from her chair.

"You were saying?" she asked sarcastically.

Ben's raised eyebrows betrayed a sheepish expression. Puzzled by the disturbance, he eased his way to the door.

"What say you?" Ben asked in his best medieval tongue. Mary noted his quick recovery, which by now she was used to anticipating. No awkwardness or embarrassment kept him ill at ease for long; in this case, the duration of its effect was one of mere seconds.

"Um ... what?" replied the stranger.

The voice was that of a young male, who was taken a little off guard by the question.

"Identify thy person," said Ben.

"Yeah, okay," said the stranger, clearing his throat. "IT services. Someone posted a repair ticket request for a desktop that keeps crashing."

"That would be me," said Ben as he opened the door.

Mary observed a short, pudgy dude with a skullcap, stainless rimmed glasses, and a heavy dark beard. Hairy forearms protruded from short sleeves and, along with the cap and beard, managed to add a wildness to the geekiness. An unbuttoned collared shirt revealed a graphics tee of a superhero character that had accumulated a couple of holes. His camouflage shorts failed to conceal squatty legs that were a little bowed, and his weather-beaten sneakers looked like a carryover from high school.

"Your name, good sir?" asked Ben.

"Matthew," answered the stranger with yet another clearing

of what might have been a tickle in his throat. He surveyed the room with a quick glance about that seemed to show his dissatisfaction. "Are you guys on probation or something?"

"Sure," said Mary as she leaned against the wall with a sense of relief and reassurance. "We're the rejects of the history department."

"Um ... that was actually for me to say," said Ben. "Being that you are not actually a history major?"

"And yet I speak your language," said Mary.

With the formalities out of the way, Matthew trudged in between them and sat down before Ben's computer. "What does she mean?"

"Mary is a polyglot," said Ben.

"I'm a linguistics major," added Mary.

"And yes," said Ben, "she can speak and read a bunch of languages." He strode into the professor's office and returned with three hardbound books. "So when I go to a primary historical source, say fifteenth century, and it's written in German, I go to Mary." He deposited the first book, an archaic Bavarian text, into Mary's hands. "When it is written in French," said Ben, holding up a Parisian exhibit, "I go to Mary."

Matthew glanced up from the desktop screen at the final exhibit, which bore an inscription with the word *Dominus*. "Latin?"

"Yes," replied Ben. "When it is written in Latin ..."

"You go to Mary," answered Matthew.

Ben nodded.

Mary smiled at the acknowledgment of her indispensable qualities. "One day," she said, "you're going to have to pass that foreign language requirement to complete your master's degree."

"I know, I know," said Ben. "Simple steps. Baby steps."

Mary remembered that Matthew, as an IT guy, was yet another resource. "Say, did you see anything weird on social media this morning?"

"I see something weird on social media every morning," said Matthew, not glancing away from the computer screen.

"How did you find this place?" asked Ben. "Besides us and the professor, there are few who know of its existence."

"I helped Professor Porter with some printer issues a while back," said Matthew. "And even then, I think we met upstairs before coming down to this dungeon. So, yeah, I think you could run a house of horrors down here and no one would notice."

"But did you notice any kind of disturbance on Chestnut this morning?" asked Mary as she moved toward Matthew.

That question piqued Matthew's interest enough for him to look at Mary with a contorted brow. "Um … should I have?"

"When did you pass by?"

"Maybe seven thirty."

"You just missed it," said Mary. "By about five or ten minutes."

"She thinks she saw something paranormal heading in that general direction," said Ben.

"Paranormal?"

"Ben!" shouted Mary. "That is not the type of lead-in statement I would have chosen. Now he knows that about the history department rejects who dwell in an obscure basement, read weird social media, run a house of horrors, and believe in ghosts."

"Um, I'm not that judgmental—or nosey for that matter," said Matthew, "but I must admit, it's been an odd morning."

"There's that word again," said Mary.

"What word?"

"*Odd.*"

Matthew's blank face betrayed his late arrival to the conversation.

"You might believe this," said Ben, handing him Mary's phone with the threatening message.

"Oh yeah," said Matthew. "I saw that. It's probably a prank. You know, just someone getting some kicks out of trying to scare people."

"I saw much more than a prank this morning," said Mary with a tense earnestness.

The room fell silent, other than the occasional clicking of keyboard and mouse and the bounce of a certain blue ball.

Matthew broke the silence. "Not to depart from our theme of weirdness this morning, but there's something funky going on with your operating system."

"Great," said Ben. "I hope haven't lost my files."

"More than likely, yes," said Matthew. "Did you save a backup?"

Ben's shoulders slumped. "Nope."

"How odd," said Matthew.

Mary stared at Matthew in irritation, her emotion having nothing to do with Ben's files. She felt as if she were living in another dimension than those around her. Certainly someone, anyone, in this great wide world had seen the type of things she had witnessed earlier this morning?

"Actually," added Matthew, "a lot of people forget to save their stuff to a backup."

Ben stopped bouncing the racquetball. Mary saw him look back at the professor's office.

"And you know what else is odd?" asked Ben.

"What?" asked Mary, not really wanting to know.

"I haven't seen the professor in a week," said Ben. "No messages. No emails or texts. No nothing."

CHAPTER III

The Descent

Catherine Latimer sat at an outdoor table, sipping a mocha concoction that eclipsed her nominal breakfast budget.

She was enjoying a fine, cloudless day, and the birds, where found among the sparse urban vegetation, were spiriting the environs with well-rehearsed notes of song. Her solitary tranquility, however, was soon vanquished by the conclusion of first-period classes, which emptied hundreds of occupants onto Chestnut Street. Campus traffic came to a near standstill as lethargic students walked into the street and veered in all manner of directions.

Catherine opened her purse and gazed in the pocket mirror at the shoulder-length waves of natural blonde hair to which violet highlights had been added just last week. The highlights, rather generous, predominated over her natural color. She checked the purple eyeshadow, applied in a wide swath before tapering off at the corners of her baby-blue eyes. Thick mascara and dark eyebrows completed what would have been the look of an ancient Egyptian princess save for her pale alabaster skin. College, she found, was an experimental age, and such fashionable choices would never have been allowed in parochial school back home.

In the space of two weeks, Catherine had left a foster child's upbringing and entered adulthood as a first-semester freshman on scholarship at Rhymer University. She was beginning to get to know her roommate and a few others in the dormitory, and her parochial school had placed her in touch with Monsignor Lewis at the local Saint Anne's parish. Save for these somewhat familiar faces, she was settling into a land of strangers. But for an orphan, such circumstances were not entirely new.

A cold front had dispelled the last of the hot weather, leaving mild temperatures. Catherine felt ample warmth in her black leggings that hugged and yet muted the petite contours of her body. She wore a sable jacket with a reflective sheen, which, other than the highlights, attracted the most attention from those passersby who turned to look at the beautiful young woman.

Catherine was prepared to embrace the collegiate existence with boldness, and yet she was not one to take herself too seriously. Comfortable sneakers expressed her amusement about the whole ensemble, for she liked to project an idiosyncratic air that kept others from forming a clear picture of her personality.

These, of course, were externals. She was also aware of her inward qualities, including advanced powers of perception, a contemplative mind, and wisdom well in advance of her nineteen years.

She watched from her café seat as a symphony of

orchestrated chaos flooded her environment with humanity. Alpha male types with jerseys of emblazoned Greek symbols barked instructions about some keg party to one another as clusters of young women chattered among themselves. Distracted students wearing earbuds almost fell over one another retrieving their bicycles and scooters, while an absentminded loner blasted a loud video on his cellular device.

Nevertheless, something of singular interest took Catherine's attention away from this din of activity, something overwhelming and perplexing, and utterly inconsistent with a lifetime's accumulation of sensory perceptions.

The air was rent asunder, like the violent prying apart of the seam of a stage curtain stitched from a colorless fabric of glasslike transparency. Beyond it, the morning light harbored an arresting darkness. There, some thirty feet from her table and opposite the general commotion, the natural world parted to expose another dimension, like a pockmark on the face of the space-time continuum. It appeared to be a localized disturbance, but within this otherworldly dimension, Catherine observed the most overwhelming and hideous of figures.

The figure had scalelike skin of a black-green hue, tautly drawn and covered with dangling clumps of what looked like filth-laden moss. The skin appeared as if it had been scorched by a furnace, yet the epidermis was mired in a greasy sweat. Long ears swelled bulbously about the ear canal and then pinched into a point well above the creature's head. Eyes like smoldering flames were fastened within deep-set sockets, and a pointed nose ended abruptly with an upturned snout. Rivulets of a dark smoky essence rose and fell around this figure, similar to the convective swirls of hot summer gases on a highway.

"Fools!" she heard it exclaim as it scanned the crowded

street with menacing intensity and ominous awareness. Catherine looked on in horror as spittle flew from its roast-burnt lips. The tips of her fingers erupted into spasms, and she felt the blood drawing away from her cheeks and mouth.

Despite her fears, Catherine's eyes remained riveted upon this diabolical presence while it studied the passersby beyond her. There was something strategic about its sudden appearance, as if it knew something that the general public did not.

But even such a demonic being can be surprised on occasion. For while the fiery fiend surveyed the scene without being seen or heard by the masses, it did not appear to notice Catherine at first. She watched as it studied the harmless and unsuspecting people moving along Chestnut Street for some moments, before realizing that its presence was not completely cloaked within the spirit realm.

Catherine sat at the extreme end of this panoramic vision, and it was not until the last of this survey that the fiend turned its hellish countenance toward her. She felt almost naked before its cruel gaze. She surmised that, like a predatory beast, it would sense her fear. Nevertheless, she would not allow her dread of it to overcome her. Her intensity of expression bespoke of resiliency and hidden strength.

"She is one of them!" she heard the fiend say as it gazed into her striking eyes with intense hatred.

The fiend looked as if it had decided to show her something. It opened the other-dimensional curtain wider and wider, like a well-stretched canvas, until it revealed a landscape beyond. She peered within this apocalyptic curtain and saw fire, rock, ice, and torrent. It seemed a distant northerly land of a former era with smugglers scouring the sandy coast of its furthest latitudinal reaches; beasts of humanlike form preying upon peasants and merchants within a great-walled city; and a religious purge, waged by Church and State, to strike fear into the heretical mind and set the body aflame.

This eagle-eye view from below the clouds ascended into a distant vista from the stratosphere. Catherine could see a large mountain-rimmed island north of the Scottish Highlands and west of the Faerøe Islands, a staging point for seafarers on the voyage to Iceland. It was a land of the far North Atlantic with a great-walled city and a heartland of lawless moors. It was a realm filled with hardy folk, the offspring of Vikings and Gaels, yoked in strife.

Catherine watched as the fiend's chapped and serrated lips parted in a grin of heinous contempt. She recoiled from its carnivorous teeth: grossly enlarged incisors and blood-soaked canines.

After some tense moments, she gasped as the creature wrested its attention from her to affix its gaze on a dark swirling mass. This mass was like a compact cyclone, a raging dust devil that had infested Chestnut Street. Something, however, was unnatural about this black mass. Rather than harboring the ferocious winds of a weather event, it carried the stifling stench of putrefied sulfur. Catherine began to feel a distinct chill not unlike the immediate arrival of a cold front. The electric signage above the café flickered as if the mass were drawing away the energy.

She could see the crude outline of a tall, goat-horned being manifest within the black swirls. When it stood upright on two legs in the midst of the shroud, the face reminded her of a graffiti image of a goat man embedded in the intersecting diagonals of a pentagram. She watched as the fiend and the goat man seemed to communicate with another, perhaps telepathically, for nothing audible was uttered.

Catherine struggled to discern their scheme as a wave of dread permeated her thoughts. Some diabolical plan was afoot, not just in the apocalyptic scenes shown to her but in the here and now at Rhymer.

Thirty seconds seemed like an eternity, but the communication appeared to reach an end. The other-dimensional curtain was closed with tremendous force, leaving no traces in the air, not even a seam. The fiend was gone, but the black swirling mass remained.

Catherine faced north from her table as this blacker-than-black entity swept from right to left in a westerly direction some ten yards north of her. It had moved from a lecture hall into the street, and now it appeared to be heading toward a multilevel parking garage northwest of her position. She could not understand why the mass of students had failed to recognize its presence as it projected a fierce negative energy, and it seemed devious and intelligent.

As the swirling mass moved into the garage, there was the deafening noise of an explosion as something of immense strength and continuity ripped apart. The upper parapet on the fourth level launched chunks of concrete like an avalanche of boulder-sized debris. The garage shook as parked cars lurched over the edge, their front tires bearing upon bent steel reinforcing bars.

The force of the blast knocked Catherine off her feet, and she took a hard fall upon the sidewalk. She ignored the bruises and lacerations on her arms as a surge of adrenaline helped her rise to her feet. She could hear bloodcurdling screams amid the dust-laden air and dense smoke. Pandemonium broke out. Pedestrians rushed back toward the campus buildings. Students crashed into one another on the entrance stairs, pushing and pulling at those whose presence at the doors interfered with their instinctual will to survive.

As Catherine observed the aftermath of the explosion, she swung around to see if she could see locate the goat man. To her surprise, a human emerged from the undulating cover of smoky vapor. The face was shrouded in darkness by a hood of blood-red satin. The eerie figure grasped a placard that bore the following inscription:

Your name is known to us.

The turmoil was too much for Catherine to contemplate. She surveyed the carnage of the asphalt-laden street and noticed that fewer people were fleeing southeast toward the Newman Liberal Arts Building. It was another twenty yards down from the nearest enclosure, but there was enough room at the doorway for folks to enter unencumbered.

Just as she arrived at a plan of evacuation, her senses were overwhelmed as glass exploded from a restaurant storefront some fifty yards to the south. This was a popular burrito joint, frequented by the students of Rhymer University. It was too early for lunch, but pedestrians nearby sped in opposing directions, running away from the exploding glass shards.

A similar hooded figure emerged from the evacuated glass. It bore a large sign with this inscription:

Where you live is known to us.

Catherine looked north. The hooded figure from the garage was moving toward her.

She glanced south. The hooded figure from the restaurant was making its way in her direction.

A third hooded figure had been leaning against one of the campus buildings on the east side of the street. It also raised a placard, reading as follows:

WHAT YOU HAVE DONE IS KNOWN TO US.

The third hooded person began to walk into the street.

All three figures seemed to be converging on Catherine. She did not know if she had been singled out, but this was no time to deliberate.

It was time to run.

She launched into a sprint toward the southeast, toward the liberal arts building. Her choice of sneakers that morning had been most fortunate. She swept across Chestnut Street, sped onto the sidewalk, and leapt up the monumental stairs two at a time.

Three sets of double doors gave access to the building. Another student had thrust open the nearest door and managed to get inside. The door was still halfway open when Catherine burst through and jumped behind the granite doorjamb. She could hear the glass door shatter beside her.

One of the robed figures was throwing smooth river rocks at the entrance. She remembered that there was a bedding of hardscape outside the lecture halls.

Catherine looked around. She had taken a few classes here in previous semesters and knew the basic layout of the building. The length of a rectangular vestibule ran parallel with the front doors and emptied left and right into narrower corridors. She moved to the far left to keep out of the pursuers' line of sight and turned abruptly into the corridor. Students, faculty, and other staff members ran toward the stairs and elevators, while others searched for unlocked offices. One professor signaled for others to come inside his office, before securing the door and barricading it with what sounded like a desk and a bookcase. Catherine tried the door handle, but she was too late.

As she ran down the corridor, she glanced back toward

the vestibule. Another hooded figure emerged. This one bore a sword.

Catherine decided that the hydraulic elevators were too slow for an escape. Someone could race up the stairs and meet those exiting the elevator door.

She spotted the stairway at the end of the corridor.

The sword gleamed from about ten yards behind her. Whoever it was moved fast, even in those blood-red robes.

She decided to abort her plan and darted into a side hallway. It contained offices on both sides, but all the doors were locked. She was about to pound on the last of the office doors when she noticed a janitor's closet at the far end of the hallway. She tried the door, but it gave way only a fraction of an inch. The doorframe had shifted, from foundation movement, and it was causing the door to stick.

She heaved again with all her might, and the door moved just enough for her to enter. She flipped the light switch and shoved the door back.

The closet was larger than she had anticipated. There was the usual assortment of mops and brooms and chemical cleaners, as well as a floor drain and a sump. Behind the sump were several rows of shelving, stacked with parts and tools from floor to ceiling. But where could she hide?

Despite her best efforts, the closet door was still ajar by an inch, enough for pursuing eyes to peer into the room. Would the pursuer keep to the corridor or turn this way?

Her chest heaved up and down in hyperventilated fervor. Her mind flew into a flurry of disjointed scenarios.

Something, however, that was counterintuitive to her body's natural fight-or-flight response spoke to her. It was like a quiet internal voice, almost imperceptible, a whisper. In fact, she had never noticed this voice before.

Don't go back to the door.

If she had managed to wedge it open, then surely that large, robed person could push in the door. She felt as though she were trapped.

PVC.

What? That made no sense.

PVC.

She looked at the shelves. Nothing at first.

Her eyes continued to scan the rows of shelving. Light bulbs. Door hinges and locks. Wrenches and sockets.

There at the far corner of the closet was a middle shelf with a tray of PVC pipe fittings. She found the fittings and fingered the space behind the tray. There, behind these objects, was a doorknob. She turned the knob, and a door swung out. The shelving pivoted out with it.

She took a deep breath.

Inside was what looked like a mechanical chase, about four foot square, but it was fitted with an aluminum ship's ladder. A stray light bulb illuminated a fifteen-foot descent to the basement.

She wasted no time in descending the ladder. At the base, there was a door, which was ajar. Catherine walked inside.

She felt momentarily safe, but she was not alone.

"Who are you?" asked a tall male in an annoyed tone. "What is that in your hair?"

The violet highlights?

"She's covered in dust," said a dark-haired female.

This was no time to be concerned with cosmetic effects.

"Chaos!" said Catherine. "On Chestnut Street! Explosions and mysterious robed people throwing rocks and carrying swords."

"See?" said the female. "I thought I heard something, Ben. Didn't you feel the ceiling shake?"

"Yep," said Ben.

"I told you something bad was going to happen," said the raven-haired young woman. "It was that black tornado thing ..."

"What on earth are you talking about, Mary?" said a bearded male who was seated before a computer. "What does this have to do with tornadoes? There isn't a cloud in the sky today."

"I saw it too," said Catherine.

"See, Matthew? Somebody believes me," said Mary. "That's what I saw in the lecture hall."

"But the swordsmen," said Catherine. "One of them came through the front entrance. I think he, or she, might be headed this way."

A shot rang out from somewhere above.

"Gunfire!" said Ben.

Several more shots were fired.

"I should have called in sick today," said Matthew.

"Is there another way out?" asked Catherine.

"Yeah," said Matthew. "Back up that ladder, in the direction of bullets. And assuming that you're right, there's some psychopath with a sword up there too."

"That's not the only exit," said Ben, nodding toward the professor's office.

"You're kidding?" said Mary.

"Let's barricade the door, and I'll show you," said Ben.

Catherine watched as Ben shut the office door and fought with the rusty dead bolt before securing it. He then enlisted Matthew's help as they deposited the computer monitor and keyboard on the floor and shifted the wobbly desk over to the door. Catherine and Mary helped. They all stacked the desk high with books.

The four of them moved to Professor Porter's office and secured his door.

Catherine looked around. It was a modest office, about twelve feet square. The walls were completely covered by bookcases, and there was one cubbyhole housing a model of a galley ship in a bottle and a framed map of the Emerald Isle. Behind the professor's desk, however, there was a recessed closet stuffed with coats and a well-worn umbrella. Ben pushed the coats aside and slid the operable wood paneling at the back of the closet.

They all peeked inside.

Beyond was a another darkened chase, somewhat larger than the other. This one, however, was equipped with a spiral staircase of perforated steel.

"This way!" said Ben.

Catherine had never questioned her footing inside a built structure, especially something made of steel, but four persons trudging in simultaneous discordance up a perforated staircase produced in her a disturbance of equilibrium. The stairs lacked sufficient bracing against the walls and wobbled under the vibrations. Catherine strained to concentrate as she placed each foot on the wide portion of each pie-shaped tread.

The residual light emanating from the professor's office waned as the four ascended some fifty feet into the unknown.

"Is there no other access?" asked Matthew.

"Not from the classroom and office levels," said Ben. "This goes straight up to the roof hatch."

The wall cavity echoed with their rhythmic exhalations as they progressed up the stairs.

"Here it is," said Ben, fumbling with the latch.

The roof hatch opened into a mechanical penthouse, which reverberated with the sound of machinery. It was a brick enclosure with rusty metal framing overhead, a leaky roof, and the stench of mildew. Ben found the overhead light switch and opened the side door, which swung out onto the main roof.

They made their way out and began to look around.

Ben pointed to the left. "There's a fire stair on the south wall."

It took Catherine a moment to get her bearings, but she soon realized that the roof ledge in front of them faced Chestnut Street. The architect had designed the roof without a protective parapet wall, which allowed the stormwater to drain into a decrepit gutter and downspouts. But an unforeseen effect was that it left the roof exposed to the four-level parking garage across the street.

Yes, the garage with the missing parapet.

Catherine, Ben, Mary, and Matthew moved toward the south fire stairs, when a red laser swept across the roof in a full panoramic.

Catherine spotted the laser first. "Get down!"

Bullets began to pepper the roof, pinging against metal air-conditioning units and defacing the brick at the penthouse. Catherine dove behind a large chiller unit that rested on a concrete curb. The others crawled on their hands and knees toward her, minimizing their profiles to the shooter. They finally dove behind the protective curb.

"What now, Ben?" said Mary as the chiller, some twelve feet high, came under fire.

"The penthouse stairs!" said Ben. "It's the only safe place."

"But it's a dead end!" said Matthew. "That other psychopath may be down there by now!"

The piercing sound of gunfire rendered it almost impossible to concentrate, but Catherine forced her right ear against the grimy mineral-surfaced roof membrane. She listened for some sense of direction as before.

Use the spiral staircase.

"Yes!" said Catherine. "Ben is right."

"Are you crazy?" asked Matthew.

"We can't go back that way!" said Mary.

"It's our only way out," Catherine said.

Catherine looked back at Mary. "I saw what you saw in that lecture hall."

"And?"

"And I saw something else, out in the street. It seemed to be from another dimension. Like it was pulling the strings: a puppet master."

Another cascade of gunfire rained overhead.

"So what should we do?" said Mary.

"Follow Ben," answered Catherine. "It will work out."

"Somehow," said Mary, studying the sincerity in Catherine's face from a prone position, "I believe you."

"Believe what?" said Matthew. "I'm not going back that way."

"Suit yourself," said Ben. He began to crawl, with Catherine and Mary close behind.

Ben found a hex-headed bolt lying beside the curb. He picked it up and flung it at an air-conditioning unit opposite their direction of travel. It ricocheted off the unit with a loud ping.

"Now!" said Ben, leaping toward the door of the penthouse.

The others followed close behind and were within the enclosure about five seconds later.

The bolt had proven to be an adequate diversion as the shooter was distracted from their movements for a moment. By the time the enclosure was being pelted with bullets, they had begun their descent through the roof hatch.

Catherine could hear Matthew as he dove through the door. "Ow! A bullet nicked my ear!"

"Hurry, Matthew!" shouted Mary from below.

Matthew seemed to be talking to himself. "Why did I have

to be the one to take this work order to Hellfire Hall and its dungeon basement? Oh right, because the other IT guy called in sick. Far better to be yacking in a sink at home than taking live ammo."

"Come on, Matthew. Don't linger," said Catherine.

Matthew seemed oblivious. "Bullets on the roof! Bullets in the basement ..."

"There weren't any bullets in the basement," said Ben, from way below. "Get your butt down here!"

"We're not going back to the basement," said Catherine.

"What?" said Mary, stopping her descent.

Matthew, despite his impairment, raced to catch up with them on the spiral staircase. "So we're just going to hang out on the stairs while those wacko shooters roam about?"

"You'll see," said Catherine.

"See what?"

"Shut up, Matthew," said Mary.

Catherine knew that the lives of her newfound friends were in her hands. But her convictions were strong, and her faith was growing. As to the source of this faith, she was not yet certain.

Trailing Ben some ten feet from the bottom, Catherine saw it. "It's here."

"What is it?" asked Ben.

"Another route. Look below."

The chase echoed with the collective gasps of the occupants. At what had been the base of the stair, the concrete slab was now gone. In its place was a stone staircase leading down to depths unknown. An emerald light seemed to hover, like a beacon obscured in a dense fog, from the depths.

"That was not there before," said Matthew. "No way, no how."

"This cannot be possible," said Ben, upon reaching what

was the basement level, where the professor's office resided. "This was solid concrete."

"So what do we do?" asked Mary.

They heard gunfire from somewhere beyond the professor's office. It sounded like the chase beyond Ben's office.

"Bullets in the basement," said Matthew, with a knowing smirk.

"You just have to be right, don't you?" said Mary.

Catherine descended the stone steps into the emerald-lit mist. "This way."

The steps hugged the common wall shared with the professor's office and then broke left at a corner. The open side was devoid of railing and dropped off into the depths of imperceptible darkness.

"Careful," she whispered.

The steps descended even farther, wrapping corner to corner about a square-like chasm until they had lapped the perimeter twice. The staircase finally terminated on a moist stone floor that felt slippery, and yet it echoed with every footfall.

"How deep is this?" muttered Ben. "Maybe sixty feet below the basement? How is this possible?"

Catherine observed that the emerald glow had sustained their navigation. It was ever present, and yet it was never seen to be in motion. It illuminated just enough for safe passage, but not enough for careful scrutiny of the surroundings.

Matthew pulled out his phone to use its flashlight. "That's strange."

"What's that?" asked Ben.

"My phone isn't working down here."

"Maybe it's the moisture. I don't think I have ever been in a room this humid."

"My glasses are completely fogged up," said Matthew. "I can't see jack."

"Here," said Mary, grabbing his hand. "Stick with me."

Catherine felt along the wall at the stairs' base. Her fingers glided onto what seemed like a corner, which turned into a narrow inlet with an arched ceiling. Even here, as they exited the stairway into this narrow vault, the emerald glow resonated.

The corridor was some twenty feet in height and extended thirty yards beyond the entrance. Catherine could see its end, where what looked like an oblong mirror stood. It was about the width of two persons, but its height extended to the vaulted ceiling.

"What is that?" asked Matthew.

As Catherine crept closer, she found no evidence of a reflection. The outline of this oblong enigma formed a woven frame of gold. Curvilinear strands circled about in patterns along the border and tucked back through the braids like a maze of Celtic art.

The chamber air was stale and motionless. Along the gilded frame, however, matter seemed to possess a hyperkinetic energy. Eddies of a clear gaseous substance washed along the frame and into the unseen beyond like a flowing current over a rocky riverbed. These eddies swept off to some obscure destination—for the space between was as black as a starless night.

Catherine watched as Ben extended a hand across the vertical plane of this inexplicable boundary. "Whoa!"

"What?" asked Mary. "What is it?"

"I don't know."

"Well, that's helpful."

"That's just it," said Ben. "I don't feel anything, except that the air is much colder beyond."

The others tried the same motion and marveled over the tactile sensations.

"What should we do?" asked Mary.

"I don't know," said Ben. "I certainly don't think we should head back. Maybe we can just linger here, at least until the authorities are able to stabilize the situation up above."

"I think we should go through it," said Catherine.

"What?" replied Ben. "No. I don't know about that."

"You were right, sister," said Matthew. "You were right about coming down the stairs."

"Thank you," said Catherine.

"But going through that thing," he said, pointing into the cold, black space. "That's pushing the envelope a bit."

The emerald glow began to fade, and darkness began to pervade the corridor.

"What's happening?" asked Mary. "Why is the light fading?"

They could hear footsteps upon the stairs behind them.

Catherine could sense that the air was rife with nervous palpitation. No solution was without risk, whether to stay, to retreat, or to move forward.

The inner voice had told her to use the spiral staircase. Since then, there had been no further direction save for the emerald glow in the depths. That glow had since become faint and stationary.

And yet the footsteps were getting louder.

"Perhaps the answer is obvious," said Catherine.

"What?" said Matthew.

But Catherine had not awaited his response. She stepped into the cold darkness and disappeared.

CHAPTER IV

The Moors

The cold wind whistled a shrill dirge as it swept across the heath. Swirling dust devils formed like a spontaneous gathering and buffeted the undulating landscape with an abject recklessness. They jostled and twisted the low-lying plants, most ankle deep, that carpeted the moors in an unending vista. These plants' moody greens were awakened here and there with hues of red and yellow or by an oblong stone set on end to memorialize some antecedent race of a past millennium. There, on a distant hill, resided a lone tree; it was haggard and listing. How its roots had found earth amid an outcrop of craggy rocks, only nature knows. Curt and blunt, the rocks startled the visitor, like the ragged jowls of a crusty and cantankerous old man.

The foursome looked around in dismay. They had not come prepared for this, any of it, not the chill, the landscape, or the remoteness of this place. The most prevalent impression they had was that it seemed a foreign land from their past that none of them could recollect. Perhaps there was some fragment of a memory from a dream or a book or a long-forgotten movie, but nothing tangible enough to take hold of. The only point of familiarity, then, was the portal. And now that they had passed through it, their link to a familiar world, such as it was, had vanished.

The pursuit, at least, was over. The footsteps had not followed them here. Wherever here was.

Catherine shivered as she felt the turbulence of the wind. She crossed her arms as best she could, but what body heat could be preserved was insufficient for her comfort.

None of the others had brought sufficient clothing either.

"What should we do?" asked Mary. "I'm cold."

Ben drew her to him. There was warmth in a lover's embrace.

Matthew, having observed this, glanced at Catherine with an unspoken query: *Want to?* She sighed and shook her head. The shivering was preferable.

Matthew, seeming to be embarrassed by this subtle romantic gaffe, turned away. Catherine watched as he conducted a visual survey of the landscape, observing everything on the horizon save for that which lay in her immediate surroundings.

"I'm not getting a signal," he said after a rapid draw of the smartphone from his front pocket. "No sign of a cell tower anywhere."

"That's strange," said Catherine, not wishing to be unfriendly after rebuffing his advance. "Mine's not picking up anything either."

"Same here," said Ben.

"Nada," said Mary.

Catherine's life, as was the case for her peers, had revolved around communications technology. It had been her high school history teacher, a baby boomer nearing retirement, who pointed out an obscure notion: somehow, over 99.9 percent of human history had transpired and had survived without emoticons, apps, texts, selfies, online games, internet searches, and social media. Of course these curious ancestral types had never heard of such things as a global positioning system, or heard of the ability of a handheld device to locate itself, generate a map, and even provide verbal guidance for its irretrievably lost owner. For Catherine's peer group, such an existence was beyond comprehension.

Not all, however, was lost.

"There is some juice left in the battery," said Matthew. He modeled a goofy grin, and with thumb and pinky extended in opposite directions as if to say *Call me*, he snapped a memorable portrait against this isolated windswept backdrop.

"A selfie?" asked Mary. "Really?"

"Yeah, I guess," answered Matthew. "It offers some proof of this bizarre day."

"But you can't upload it or send it to anyone," said Catherine.

"Nope."

Ben looked perplexed. "What is this forsaken place?"

"I believe this type of landscape is called a moor," said Catherine.

"Yeah. But where are we?"

"I will do a search for moorlands if we can ever get a signal," said Matthew.

Catherine noted that they were now standing upon a modest hill. While there was access in every direction, the landscape all looked the same. In the prevailing confusion, none of them had yet moved more than ten feet. It was like twirling in place, to the point of dizzying nausea.

"I'd wager there's no place like this within two hundred and fifty miles of campus," said Ben. "How could we possibly have gotten here?"

"Would you care to explain our descent from your basement and that weird portal we walked through?" asked Matthew.

Catherine observed the agitation on Ben's face. He seemed like the type who kept his bearings in most any situation, but here and now he was at a loss. Mary, too, appeared to be confused, to the point of grief. Matthew continued to fidget with his phone.

Is this the land that the fiend showed me? thought Catherine. *Where then are the sandy beaches?*

"In a single day," said Mary, "I've seen ghosts, a dark swirling mass, human target practice, and a strange portal. Now we have landed who-knows-where with no idea of what to do or where to go. It's cold, and I'm hungry and tired."

"Still no signal," muttered Matthew. Catherine watched as he pocketed his phone, only to reach for it again.

"Dude, I think you have a love affair with that thing," said Ben, a note of annoyance in his voice.

"What?"

"What would you do if I confiscated your prized possession?"

Matthew gasped. "You wouldn't!"

Ben shrugged. "I might. Just for the sheer entertainment of watching you squirm."

"Don't do it, historian," warned Matthew.

"Guys! Is this really necessary?" asked Mary.

Catherine was concerned about the escalating tension between the young men. Ben fashioned a cocky smile, lunged forward, and dexterously swatted an arm to confiscate the handheld treasure. Matthew, however, twisted away with the device pressed against his abdomen.

Ben undercut his target with a jab below the elbow. The blow grazed a kidney before latching onto a forearm.

Matthew groaned.

Ben clutched the device and was about to pull it away.

"Enough already!" said Mary.

Catherine thought about retrieving the phone herself, but Matthew and Ben's roughhousing was fast-twitched and chaotic. For the first time, she observed Matthew's elongated fingernails, which were smudged in what looked like fast-food grease and dirt. He played *Phantom of the Opera* with the organ keys, that is, his assailant's hand, until Matthew's fingernails punctured the epidermis.

Ben howled in anger before wrapping strong arms around Matthew's torso and lifting him off the ground. The pair collapsed in a heap upon the heath, where the grappling and grunting continued.

Catherine looked on in dismay.

"Guys! Stop this!" said Mary, attempting to disentangle her boyfriend from the man pile. "This is ridiculous."

The boys, sweating, bleeding, and heavy of breath, had reached an apex of exertion. They separated at last, exhausted, and sat upon the ground in a stupor.

"Whatever we're going through, wherever we might be," said Mary, "we must stick together."

Catherine watched as Matthew's arms encircled his knees. He dropped his battle-weary head in between them. Ben, meanwhile, lay completely prone on the heath. He seemed to study the sky for some sign, something he could recognize. Only the rhythmic flexing of sternum and rib cage signaled his conscious presence on the moors.

"Mary's right," Catherine said. "We've had an exhausting day. And yet there seems to be no end to it in sight. We're lost, and we need food and shelter. We're only wasting energy by fighting. We need to figure out what to do."

The two young men, still breathing hard, said nothing. Whatever pondering and scheming that was taking place in the machinations of their respective minds remained unstated.

Some minutes later, Mary glanced toward the horizon to her left. "Is that a road?"

"Where?" asked Ben, awaking from his quietude.

"There," she said, pointing. "That earthen-looking trail."

A small, squinty ribbon of beige lay in the distant horizon.

"Maybe," said Ben. "But that must be a few miles from here."

Mary placed her hands firmly upon her hips. "And do you have a better plan?"

"Well," said Ben, turning a full circle in a fruitless search for one. He strained his eyes in every direction without obtaining any enlightening observation. "No."

"Then we have one now," said Catherine. "Judging by the position of the sun, it is probably early afternoon. That should give us plenty of daylight to reach the trail. The exercise will at least provide some warmth. If it's this cold now, imagine what it will be like tonight."

"Sounds like a plan, ladies," said Matthew, after yet another confirmation of an absent signal.

His dissatisfaction with the absence of signal, however, seemed trivial in comparison to the triumph he felt for having retained his handheld device. In fact, judging from the grin on his dusty, disheveled face, he seemed quite pleased and contented. "All right. Let's get going."

The party moved west in the direction of the trail. The terrain was passable enough, but soon they found they needed to be on their guard for sudden outcrops of rock. The larger ones were easily discernible, but some formations protruded from the ground no higher than the surrounding vegetation. Matthew, in particular, was prone to tripping, especially as he stared into the recesses of his phone. Catherine marveled at this habitual behavior.

"That is most certainly a road," said Mary, gazing at the dusty band lying a half mile or so ahead.

"It seems to run north and south," noted Catherine.

"And yet there's no sign of anyone anywhere," said Ben. "No dwellings or cars."

For the past hour of their journey, Catherine had seen the terrain flattening out somewhat. This, however, proved to be an anomaly. In the direction of the road were foothills, and in the distant haze some leagues beyond, she could begin to make out the rough outline of snow-peaked mountains. The heath gave way to tall grasses, which swayed in oscillatory form like an enthusiastic welcoming committee. Shrubs, and even a few aspen trees, dotted the terrain and beckoned them forward.

Their collective mood had improved with the confirmation of anthropological evidence, even if it had come in the form of a mere trail. Civilization, and with it the opportunity for food and shelter, might be near.

Nevertheless, Catherine registered these changes with a heightened concern as an eerie sense of foreboding clasped upon her like invisible chains and fetters.

The ground and its vegetation, she noted, were parched. Desiccated soils opened like small fissures, and the shriveled vegetation had browned almost to the point of wasting away. And on a personal note, her exposed pale flesh, after hours of walking, was reddening to the point of discomfort.

The four walked up the crest of a small hill and then

down into the dale—a crater, more like, as the depression was encircled by higher ground.

"Anybody have a bottled water?" asked Matthew. "I'm parched."

His query was met with irritated silence.

"Spring water? Rainwater?" he announced with a raised voice. "Creek? Stream? Canteen? Reclaimed and boiled clean?"

Nothing.

"Anyone? Anyone? Actually, I would prefer it ice-cold in a Yeti."

Catherine could not help but wonder if Matthew's publicized query had reached ears in the hidden terrain beyond.

She did not have to wait long to find out. Fireballs like dragon-breathed cylinders of flame appeared at the crest of the hill above them. Slow of movement at first, they tantalized the eye with blazing spokes of ferocity.

These formed a violent assault upon Catherine's senses: the intense and searing heat; the noxious smell of burning pitch; and the sounds of wind-fed flame as it gorged on the vegetation with a ferocious appetite.

The fireballs began to pick up momentum and roll down the embankment, five miles per hour at first. Then fifteen. Then thirty.

"What is going on?" yelled Ben with frustration. He and Mary grabbed hands and broke left. Catherine and Matthew dove right as the mass of spoked heat rolled past them.

Catherine turned her head upon the ground to see the parched vegetation serve as natural kindling. It swelled into a red carpet of flame wherever the mass traveled. The fire grew in proportion, sprouting like low-lying shrubs and then surging into hedgerows of frightening height.

"What now?" asked Matthew.

"Look!" said Catherine in dismay as a band of marauders appeared along the crest of the hill and sprinted toward them. A quick visual summary registered the eight members of this party as people of uncouth appearance with an intention bent on violence. Their manner was rough: long coarse hair, shaggy beards, and a fierce countenance. Bloodied hands, chafed by the cold, wielded club, ax, or sword. These men wore cloaks of fur, which swung about their torsos in rhythmic animation as they ran. Woolen pant-like garments clung to their shins with thick crisscrossed strings that wrapped around stocky calves.

Catherine identified a point along the crest with the widest gap between the pursuers, and she and Matthew scampered up the embankment, followed closely by Mary and Ben.

Another ruffian, however, appeared at the ridge and charged. His eyes bore the clear signs of rage, and his beard was both braided and bushy.

"Aieouf-duh!"

"No, Ben!" screamed Catherine just as Ben surged forward to meet the assailant. The historian landed a crossing right against the bearded chin, and a left jab landed on the leathered chest. Another right struck the mouth.

The ruffian spat bloodied saliva upon the ground and grinned at his opponent.

Ben took a step back, shocked and somewhat disheartened.

Surely, thought Catherine, *he had landed some good blows, but to what effect?*

Ben's adversary rammed his broad forehead into the historian's brow and struck him with a club against the temple. Ben's knees buckled, and he collapsed upon the ground, unconscious.

"Ben!" screamed Mary. She lunged forward to reach him, but Ben's attacker seized her by the arms.

Catherine and Matthew rushed to assist. The ruffian

stank of drink and decayed sweat, as did another, who had caught up to them.

"Wait," said Catherine, seeing the momentary stoppage in violence. She and Matthew eased up some ten feet away as they studied these strange adversaries, who seemed captivated with their captive.

Although the presence of these ruffians seemed revolting to Mary in every way, they studied her dark skin tone and unusual clothing as if observing an exotic beauty. One wove fingers through her jet-black hair as if it were a loom, noting its smooth texture.

This only seemed to anger her.

"Mary, no!" yelled Catherine, to no avail. Mary struck the attacker and bloodied his already bent nose. The other assailant laughed as he delivered a retaliatory heavy blow from his forearm. Mary dropped like a leaden weight to the ground, beside her fallen boyfriend. She was apparently conscious yet stunned. Catherine watched as she slogged mindlessly into a slumped position, neither awake nor asleep.

Catherine thought about what could be done as the men turned their attention to Matthew.

"Now wait a second!" Matthew said, holding up his arms. "We're all reasonable, civilized people, am I right?"

"What are you doing, Matthew?" asked Catherine. He grinned like a greasy politician, trying to win over his adversaries with a disingenuous face.

"Glenne holt maite!" responded the man with the ax. He gave Matthew a hard shove to the chest with the dull end of his weapon, and Matthew too fell to the earth. He looked stunned, but he was conscious.

Catherine watched as the marauders erupted with laughter, exposing mouths riddled with decayed or missing teeth. One of them wagged a black tongue.

As these events transpired, she also saw something out of her peripheral vision. There in the distance, along the band of earthen beige they had been chasing, she spotted a horse-drawn carriage traveling north. She contemplated its relative speed and slipped her hoodie on. Darkness fell across her face.

The marauders advanced upon her.

She drew two oblong objects out of her backpack just before one of the ruffians ripped the backpack from her grasp.

As they studied the strange bag and played with the zipper, she stooped down and grasped one of the objects. She twisted its end and began to paint her face and lips with the darkest violet.

"Matthew," she whispered.

He looked over toward her, but his eyes were not quite connecting with her hooded face. "Yep?"

"Your phone. Take it out."

He looked surprised, even while disoriented. "What?"

"Trust me."

Catherine felt one of the attackers seize her shoulders in a merciless grip and raise her to her feet. She observed his roving eyes as he studied her protruding violet highlights and dark purple face paint with engrossed perplexity.

Matthew turned his phone on and held it up for the marauders to see. They stepped back, all of them save the ruffian beside Catherine.

She watched as he raised his hand to remove her hoodie. But before he could take it off, she turned her phone on and held it up to his dirt-smattered face.

He recoiled for a brief moment in fear.

Catherine took advantage of his hesitancy, dousing him with the contents of the second object: mace.

He howled in pain as the mace interacted with his skin and eyes.

She struck off the hoodie.

The other marauders turned toward her. They seemed shocked by the painted dark hue on that otherwise beautiful face.

"Unhva!" said one of their number.

"Unhva," answered another as they backed away.

Catherine waved the phone around while sounding the deepest, darkest invectives of the English language that she could think of.

Her foreign tongue added to their confusion.

As their initial fears appeared to ebb, however, a few of them crept closer, only to be doused with mace. The ruffians dropped to their knees in clear submission to her witchcraft or, rather, her canned weaponry.

Notwithstanding this victory, the others were proving difficult to dispatch.

Catherine could hear the pounding of hooves getting closer.

Four of the marauders encircled her. The can of mace was almost empty, and waving the phone no longer proved effective. Behind her shoulder, she caught sight of a club rising to strike her down.

Rather than a dull thud, however, Catherine heard a gun blast. She looked about to see four Clydesdales pulling a large wheeled enclosure—a cargo carrier. Indeed it had veered east off the trail in what amounted to a cavalry charge in pursuit of the enemy. The driver wielded a leather whip, which he lashed upon the back of a fleeing ruffian, as another dove away from the thunderous hoofbeats of the horses. Those remaining grabbed their mace-infected comrades and took off, fleet of foot, for the moorlands from which Catherine and her friends had come.

"Aye, and a good riddance!" howled the driver with a blast from the other harquebus in his possession. "Bandits! Marauders! A pox on the lot of them! Methinks thou be the dregs of the commonwealth!"

"Finally we meet someone who speaks English," said Matthew as he labored to pick himself up from the ground. Catherine swept her hand over the back of his shirt, which was covered in grass.

"Early Modern English," said Mary, who had recovered somewhat from the blow of her fall. She rolled her head around from shoulder to shoulder as if rehabilitating her neck muscles after the pain of the blow. "Or a dialect of close resemblance."

"Whoa! Whoa, my friends!" said the driver as he coaxed his magnificent horses. The great carriage lumbered to a halt, revealing a middle-aged man in a green jerkin and overcoat, feathered hat, purple stockings, and leather boots.

Catherine ordinarily would have been amused at such an appearance, but for this strange person she felt only a sense of gratitude.

"Hark ye! Aye, ye young persons, what have we here?" asked the driver. He had large projecting eyebrows, a patch of reddish-brown hair, and welcoming eyes of olive green. "I'd say our services are needed. Aye. It is meet that we arrived at this time, noble Theodus, Orwin, Bliny, and Donegast. What say you?"

Theodus whinnied his assent.

"What would such persons of strange dress be about in these evil lands?" asked the driver. "This be a lawless place, mind ye."

"We've lost our way," said Matthew. "Where is the nearest town?"

"North, young sir. Some seven leagues. 'Tis a long journey by foot."

"Thank you," said Catherine, eyeing the wagon, "for aiding us." She though it looked large enough to accommodate them all.

"You're heartily welcome, lass," said the driver as he stepped down from his carriage. "Me name's Carter. Finnaeus Talcum Carter, at your service."

"I'm Catherine. This is Matthew."

"And I'm Mary. My boyfriend Ben has taken a fall."

"Aye, so he has," said Carter. "Let's have a look at him, shall we?"

Carter seemed to Catherine a joyful man with a ready smile and an adventurous air. Nevertheless, he had a paunchy belly, and his bowlegged aspect was rendered even more obvious in tights.

A full beard helped obscure the residual markings of the smallpox, but his countenance was pleasant. He carried a ready tune at the lips, first by whistling and then by song, which he sang in a melodious tenor:

> This day, this day,
> I left me maid some leagues away
> To ply me trade in foreign lands
> And send me wages home.
> Unyoke the oxen, store the plow.
> When work lies abroad, there shall I go,
> Tending the miners' needs in alpine wood,
> Places ordinary folk shudder to know.

"Are you a merchant?" asked Catherine. "You sing beautifully ..."

"Aye, lass," said Carter. "Thank ye. Me keeps the miners well stocked. Foodstuffs and tools and weapons."

"Where?"

He nodded to the west. "Up in the O' Flanagan Range."

"You sang of danger ..."

"Bandits, of course. You've already caught a notion of that. But there are more sinister things in the highlands."

Mary had rushed over to attend to Ben as the rest of the party made their way at a moderate pace.

"Such as?" asked Catherine.

"Berserkers under the power of the draugr," said Carter.

"Who are they?" asked Matthew.

"The berserkers are shape-shifters, me lad," said Carter. "Fierce fighting men, Norsemen, of long ago who fought battles in a raging frenzy. They were tempted by the wealth and the ways of the draugr and were bewitched by the black arts. Having sold their souls to the devil for power and conquest, they roam the alpine forests as part man, part beast. Ever young, they do not age ... but they can be killed."

Matthew laughed. "What is this? *Grimm's Fairy Tales*?"

"I know nothing of Grimm," said Carter with a serious countenance, "but this tale is no myth. The legends are true; I have beheld berserkers, and even the draugr from afar, with me own eyes. Aye, I have seen their kind and lived to tell about it."

"Then how do the miners survive among these berserkers?" asked Catherine. "And how do you protect yourself from them?"

"The miners do not go outside of their fortifications at night, nor do I. We work by day, we travel by day. It is by cover of moonlight that the berserkers scour the earth. And at the full moon, their strength is greatest."

"Who are the draugr?" asked Catherine.

"Revenants. Vampyres arisen from the dead. Fully empowered and indwelt by devilry. Their abode is in the high places. The miners dare not ascend to the great heights of their domain."

"Vampyres? Devilry? What kind of medieval madness is this?" asked Matthew.

"Mid-ee-val, ye say?" replied Carter. "I have not yet heard its reckoning, but this is no madness, me lad. Ignorance of the beserkers and the revenants is the true madness."

Catherine also struggled to comprehend this new reality. "What is this place?"

"Ye know not where ye are, lass?" asked Carter. Catherine observed him surveying their dress. "Aye, ye do look strange, and ye sound like foreigners. But how could ye not know this is the kingdom of Northmoorland?"

"Northmoorland?"

"That's where?" said Matthew, scratching his head.

"Don't, Matthew," said Catherine as he reached for the phone in his pocket. "It's north of Scotland."

"Aye," said Carter. "Kingdom is a loose term, though. The Crown's reach does not extend more than three leagues into the moors or the mountains. Say ... how did ye get here?"

Mary looked up from her convalescent charge, who was still lying on the ground as the others approached. She seemed relieved that his external wounds were not severe. "We came through a portal ..."

"Port of call," interrupted Catherine. "We came by ship."

"Ye are a long way from port now," said Carter. "Ye sound English, but the accent is strange. Are ye shire folk? Norfolk? Essex?"

"Where are you from?" asked Catherine.

"Me pa was an Englishman," said Carter, "a transporter of

goods in Yorkshire. Ma is from the Orkney Islands, northeast of the Scottish Highlands. Near Skara Brae, if ye must know."

They didn't need to know, but that did not keep Carter from continuing. "Mum, ye see, was a Sinclair, a cousin of the Earl of Orkney. Sinclairs, she said, are descended from the Norse royal family. Yea, among me ancestors are Halfdan the Stingy and Eystein the Fart."[1]

Matthew exhaled the entire pneumatic contents of his nose and mouth with an obnoxious laugh.

Carter, bearing a wide grin, didn't seem to mind.

"We're from Cornwall," said Catherine, choosing a location far southwest of the Orkneys and Yorkshire, and perhaps unknown to Carter. Matthew and Mary glanced at her with peculiar expressions.

"Cornwall," said Carter. "Odd accent, have they?"

Catherine looked over at Ben. Mary sat with him as his cheek twitched a little.

"Master Ben looks put out, if ye don't mind me saying," said Carter.

"He took a hard blow," said Mary, cradling Ben's face in her arm, "but he'll come around."

"Aye." Carter glanced around the landscape. "Methinks we have lingered here long enough. Horse wagons like mine are rare in these parts, as are firearms. Frighten them, we did, out of their wits, but those bandits may double back with greater numbers. Let's get Master Ben inside and ye folks to town."

Catherine knew almost nothing about wagons save for what she had seen in movies. Carter explained that the wagon was the work of a master carpenter and wheelwright. The timber had been planed smooth, and horizontal planks were jointed with small dowels. A hinged door opened in back, revealing a roomy enclosure with storage millwork and a bed. Bundled meats and cheeses dangled overhead from a line. A countertop held a bread box stuffed with rudimentary utensils, and a jug of wine, bundled in linens, had been stowed in an adjacent crate. These containers had been nailed to the woodwork to prevent their jostling around. A longbow and quiver of arrows were mounted to the opposite wall, and a bit of gunpowder was kept stored in a small barrel. Storage bins below contained the goods he traded with the miners. At the center of the floor, Carter had laid out a down pillow and a mattress stuffed with straw. He and Matthew lifted the dead, drooping weight of the historian and placed him on the mattress.

Catherine and Matthew joined Carter outside on the coach seat, while Mary stayed inside with Ben and helped herself to some bread.

Carter took the reins. "Walk on!"

The horses needed little encouragement. There was something unsettling about this place, even for the animals.

"They kept calling Catherine an *unhva*," said Matthew.

"A witch!" said the driver. "A dangerous position to be in, aye, in these parts. They burn witches in Mithrendia."

"Burn them?" said Matthew. "Whatever for?"

"I am no witch!" said Catherine. "I only pretended to be one to frighten those brutish men."

"Indeed," Carter said, winking at her. "A resourceful one then, are ye? Your secret is safe with Carter."

Catherine returned a thankful smile as she began to wipe the lipstick from her cheeks and forehead. Although she could not say, she suspected that they had landed some five hundred years in the past. As they learned about the culture, it might be better to blend in rather than to stand out—for now anyway.

"What is Mithrendia?" asked Matthew.

"The great-walled city, home to the lords of Tröndesund. The king is the eleventh of their dynastic line. But this traveling party, me lad, is going to the Marches."

"What are those?"

"Borderlands, where the clan folk dwell. They protect the southern flank of Mithrendia from the lawless moors."

Carter explained that the Marches stretched like a narrow band from east to west, with its clan folk populating the hills and dales, flatlands, fens, and riverine territories between the coastal mountain ranges. From the foothills of the alpine Forest of Odin in the east to Donegast's Range in the west, the Marches provided a protective zone for the king and his walled city. In exchange for this perpetual service, and in recognition of their tribal-like ways, the Marches were granted certain political freedoms such as limited self-government and low taxes.

Carter explained that *Clann*, the Gaelic word for children, consisted of blood relations as well as the people's close associates and tenants. Ruled by a chief, each clan developed a *tartan*, a distinctive pattern of plaid with colored stripes and bars in a square-like pattern as displayed by plaid shawls and kilts.

These clanspeople were the sons and daughters of the ancient Celts, who called themselves Gaels—a hearty people who, many centuries ago, mixed it up with the Roman legions on the battlefields of Continental Europe and Britannia. They were an earthy people who loved nature, artistry, and artisanship, having an appreciation for unmatched expertise in metalworking. They were a lyrical people who had mastered the fiddle, flute, drums, and bagpipe.

"Me finds an affinity for dyes of verdant green with the Irish, while the Scottish Highlanders, their wools bear the blood red of their battles," said Carter. "Here in Northmoorland, they favor the fierce eyes of the Norsemen, and ye can identify the clans of the Marches by their blue tartans."

"So what happens when these fireball idiots attack the Marches?" asked Matthew.

"Bring out the wee heavies!" shouted Carter with some gusto.

Catherine jumped in her seat, but the horses seemed used to their master's outbursts and stayed on course.

Carter explained the meaning of this boisterous call, saying it was a public summoning of a particular type of athlete: burly, broad-chested men, some of a cantankerous nature, who took their aggression out on objects of flight. Inanimate objects such as hay, stone, metal, and timber were rendered animate by muscular exertion. Whether such objects were tossed, heaved, or spun about, these maneuvers became popular contests in distance or height.

These spectacles served as a tantalizing prelude to the main event: the caber toss. A tree trunk, or caber, of about fifteen feet in length was raised upright by men initially in a crouching position. Then it was carefully balanced and heaved over with a decisive thrust of the hips, thighs, and arms. Flipping it over was a tremendous feat, and if the maneuver were properly executed, the timber would land dead ahead, in a straight line from the launching position of the athlete.

Such execution took much practice. And here in Northmoorland, the women participated in these athletic contests as well. For a hearty folk were the product of the homes and the fields.

"The women perform in these games?" asked Catherine.

"Aye, indeed," said Carter. "For the objects of an athletic contest are exchanged for weapons of war, and those who wield them are formidable. The men take to the battlefield as the women guard the home with unparalleled ferocity. That is why the lawless ones often keep to the moors, where they prey on the unprotected."

"Like us," said Catherine.

"Aye."

"That is, until you arrived."

"Methinks it fortuitous ..."

Catherine sighed and looked over at her rescuer with a weary smile of sincere gratitude.

"Hear ye, thank ye," said Matthew. "But where to now? I mean specifically?"

"Ye have a purse?" asked Carter.

"A purse?" replied Matthew with surprise. "Not where I come from. Perhaps Catherine does."

Now Carter seemed confused. With one hand on the reins, he lifted a pear-shaped satchel from an obscured pocket. The stitched leather sagged under the weight of its contents. "Coinage, my boy."

Catherine had lost track of her purse during the garage explosion. She shook her head as Matthew searched his pockets. She watched him pull out a key to a bicycle lock, a faded student identification card, and of course his phone. Fortunately, Carter's eyes were distracted by the horses and the earthen road.

"Nay?" replied Carter. "'Tis no great matter. Me old friend Marley runs an inn and a tavern. He could use some hired help, assuming ye require room and board."

Catherine and Matthew looked at one another with helpless acquiescence. She was exhausted, too exhausted to object, and his usual sarcasm had struck a mute tone. There were so many questions to ask. What was this place, and why were they here? What had been the outcome of the disaster at Rhymer? Was her roommate at school okay?

For now, however, the necessities of life held sway. All she needed at the moment was a safe place to eat and sleep.

CHAPTER V

The Blue Griffin

"Down from the hills again, eh, Carboni?" said Marley, the proprietor of the Blue Griffin.

"When supplies are at an end," replied Carboni, "it is time once again to visit the Marches. Ye do well, I see."

"Thank ye," said Marley. "Business is good, and we are no longer short-staffed."

The innkeeper was a gangly-armed fellow with a widow's peak bulging from the middle of a dark recessed hairline, the hair at the back of his head standing on end. Carboni always found the proprietor's businesslike frown to be at odds with an otherwise hospitable nature.

"Eh? Is it Carboni I hear?" asked Allister, who, caked in froth around his fluttering lips and bulbous nose, wheeled about in his seat to see if it were true. "Indeed, Friar Draugr is here."

"Draugr?" replied Carboni. "Rather it is the berserkers I

see on greater occasion. As for the draugr, I merely observe their movements and alert the miners when I can."

"Don't be so modest, Carboni."

"Carboni," echoed Seamus, speaking to another table of patrons. Even between boisterous outbursts, Seamus's flame of red hair stood out among the three dozen or so patrons of the Blue Griffin. "They say his very breath is an outflow of garlic!"

Carboni was curious, and even perplexed, about his ever-growing legendary status. "Me means and ways are quite natural, I assure you."

Seamus did not appear to be listening. "Could fell a vampyre with a single breath," he said to the rabble-rousers at his side. A contagion of laughter spread throughout the half-timbered beer hall as patrons pounded the tables. Guests staying the night left their rooms to peer over the balcony at the commotion below.

Carboni walked over to show them his index finger. "Truthfully I often cook with garlic, and there is a variety I have been cultivating that is about as long as this forefinger."

He nodded at Seamus. "Try it on for size."

"What?"

"A handshake, really." He gave Seamus a knowing wink. "In the mountains, it's taken as a sign of luck."

Seamus shook the friar's finger, and from his posterior, Carboni emitted a sound not unlike a trumpet.

"It's what I call a backdoor variety," said Carboni.

This, of course, sent the tavern into yet another state of silly uproar. Along with it, Carboni succeeded in reducing his fabled personality to their level of ordinary humanity—which had its uses and abuses.

"O'Carboni!" parroted O'Gregory. This curious elder with

his thick white beard seemed far too slender for a consummate beer drinker. "Where's your tonsure, ye fat friar?"

Carboni was well aware of the notoriety of his stout stature with large limbs, long unwashed locks falling about the shoulders, and an enormous beard of the darkest brown. He wore a coarse beige tunic, which was tied at the belly with a gnarly belt of rope. Despite such rustic features, his beige eyes and ready smile were full of mirth and wit.

"The essential fact of the matter," replied the friar, "is that God gifted me with a full head of hair. Would you expose a bald cap to the icy-cold alpine air?"

"To be of a mendicant order," observed Allister, "ye surely eat well."

"Beggars cannot be choosers," said Carboni, who seemed not the least bit ruffled, "and my palate is accepting of all offers save for moldy bread."

Carboni felt the effects of his words as he answered all comers and naysayers with a gruff boldness in a voice audible to the far corners of the hall. And well that he did, for he knew that his name had become something of a hot topic among the raucous clientele of the Blue Griffin, especially with the great oaken barrels of ale having been tapped, and the home brew free-flowing into greedy pints and goblets. Indeed his absence of several months had caused the general populace to adopt an amused bewilderment, which of course was accompanied by a groundswell of gossip.

"I'll take a pint, good sir," said Carboni as the bench bowed under his buttocks.

"And how, mind ye, are ye to pay for it?" asked Marley.

"Put it on my tab!" said O'Gregory, who settled in beside Carboni. "I've got him."

"Thank ye," said Carboni, though he knew there was a price to pay, namely, constant badgering.

Catherine and her Rhymer companions were in the midst of their serving duties and overheard the noisy particulars concerning Carboni's arrival. They found the local dialect coarse and strange, and the ways of the people rather medieval and bellicose. Nevertheless, the passage of some homesick months allowed for quick study of this Northmoorlandic culture, a study undertaken by full immersion.

Finnaeus Carter had left them in the capable hands of his friend Marley. Next only to that of the legendary friar, their American accents were an ongoing source of amusement to the patrons and also a means of bolstering their popularity.

"What is a tonsure?" asked Matthew. Catherine caught him once again grasping his breeches in a vain search for an operable cellular device.

"Ever seen a 1980s headband?" answered Ben.

"Yeah, like for exercising?" asked Matthew, wiping a beer-stained table clean.

"Yep. Now picture a headband of hair just over the ears. Everything above and below that line is shaved bald. That's a tonsure."

"What's the point of that? It would look ridiculous."

"That is the point," said Ben. "It's a means of expressing humility."

"But why?"

"To better focus your life on spiritual matters rather than worldly ones," answered Catherine. By now she had traded her gothic experiment for a simple handmaiden's dress of cobalt blue, fronted with a white apron adorned by embroidered runic patterns.

"That's ridiculous," said Matthew.

Catherine looked over at Carboni's dark mane. "I'd think that he would agree."

Catherine, like the others, was now capable of having

extended conversations in the local dialect, which was a mixture of Norse and Gaelic highlighted by the occasional colloquialism. Mary, of course, had caught on to the Northmoorlandic language within weeks, and from there she had disseminated the fruits of her linguistic skills to the others. Catherine found this to be the only cure to their stodgy servants' quarters, where they spent their late nights talking to one another before a meager fire. Here there were no earbuds blasting music or pixelated screens demanding the attention of the eyes. Even reading materials of dried ink on parchment were few.

It was of no surprise that Catherine found this stark transition from modernity to be hardest on Matthew. He seemed to struggle with an attention deficit disorder, and he fussed and fidgeted amid the tedium and monotony of his new environment.

Strangely, however, these frustrations could be washed away with a torrent of water. Matthew forgot himself at times. When on work breaks, he strolled over to the waterworks. Waterfalls, dams, sluice gates, and Archimedes' screws stimulated some latent longing that he was at a loss to explain. Catherine nudged him sometimes to give an account of his sightseeing tours, and once aroused from his lethargy, Matthew would erupt into animated conversation. He liked to linger beside the public fountains as they sprayed geysers, the wind capturing some of the skyward mist and dampening his face. He watched the gurgling torrents beat against short-walled terraces, the water cascading ever downward to a pool below, where sculptures of mercurial sea gods spat arching streams at unsuspecting passersby. Matthew had already befriended one of the city engineers, and as his knowledge of the indigenous language improved, he became familiar with this peoples' technology and practices.

Catherine made no such effort to engage Ben and Mary as

they were a social force unto themselves. The spats between the lovers were of a regular variety, and when Mary was angry, the entire tavern knew about it. Catherine felt sorry for Ben being the brunt of the patrons' jokes. They called him henpecked and suggested that an ominous fate awaited him in his future marital life. Ben, for his part, never tarried in the dumps for long. Like a submerged buoy, his mood always rose back to surface, and with the particular fervor of a historian, he immersed himself in the details of Northmoorlandic culture like a scholar given a special assignment. He used his wages to purchase ink and parchment, and he kept copious notes of his observations.

"What year is it?" Ben asked absentmindedly as he stuck a quill in a short bottle of ink.

"Never met a scholar before who worked for the Blue Griffin," said Marley. "Never met a scholar before who did not know what year he lived in neither. What ye be about there, boy?"

"It's called a brain fart," said Mary as her boyfriend's face reddened.

"A what?" said O'Gregory, rousing the attention of the men at the far tables.

"It's when you say something stupid without thinking it through," answered Mary, which precipitated a boisterous reply by the patrons.

"A scholar and a fool, ye say?" shouted Seamus.

Mary gleamed from the attention. Catherine was well aware of Mary's burgeoning status as the tavern favorite.

"A brain fart, eh? I've had those before," said Carboni, who had come up for another pint. "And in answer to the question, Master Benjamin, the year is 1526."

"Ye foreign folk are strange in ye manner of speech," said Marley. "Harmless, mind ye, but strange."

Matthew finished servicing an adjacent table and collapsed upon the bench next to O'Gregory. "I'm bored," he said as Catherine walked by.

"What? Tired of this place already?" asked O'Gregory. "Haven't seen the fights yet, have ye?"

"What fights?" asked Catherine.

"'Tis place has been at peace of late come to think of it," said O'Gregory. "So much that one might think there is an excess of charity in our hearts. No cantankerous individuals to speak of."

"Here, here!" said Allister.

"Why, there's been nothing remarkable of late save for Friar Draugr's arrival," noted Seamus.

Catherine was anxious to learn more about this itinerant dignitary. "And what does a lone friar do in the mountains?"

"Preach to the miners," said Carboni. "Hunt and fish for food. And keep an eye out for the movements of thine enemies: the draugr and the berserkers."

"Do ye hear that, boys?" said O'Gregory. "Carboni really is a vampyre hunter!"

"And a stain upon his order!" said a stern stranger who had just come in.

"And who, sir," asked O'Gregory, "might ye be?"

"Canon Pious," said Marley. "What would one from the Great Cathedral of Mithrendia be doing in these parts?"

Unlike the others, this stranger scared Catherine. Pious cast a slender-like figure, with deep-set eyes, withdrawn into his black habit. Though she would later learn that he was about forty-five, he looked well advanced in years with rigid lines drooping between mouth and cheek. He had a hooked nose full of vein-riddled flesh, and his thin lips guarded a contemptuous voice that screeched when he spoke.

"I've come to sup at the notorious Blue Griffin," said the

canon. "And I can see, Marley, that the riffraff thrive in your establishment. I will not, then, suppose that the food will be of a fine quality."

To Catherine, Marley seemed to frown even when he did not intend to. But at this point the twitching veins in his forehead bore the signs of a man seething with anger.

His antagonist, however, appeared to have other prey. The canon glanced over at the longhaired friar seated upon a bench.

"Friar Carboni," said Pious, "have you been declared anathema yet?"

"Anathema?" asked Mary.

"My dear," replied Carboni, turning toward her, "the canon is asking in his usual honey-sweet manner whether I have been damned by the Church." He lowered his voice to whisper: "Which, of course, is his special wish."

Mary looked perplexed. "But why?"

Catherine watched in agitated suspense as Pious sat down and was served a plate of mutton. He took a large bite and wiped his greasy mouth upon a clerical sleeve. "You are staring, girl, at a disgraced monk. Married a serving wench against his vows, did he not? Whatever happened to monastic celibacy?"

"In your case," whispered O'Gregory, observing the gargoyle-like canon and seeming to imagine his nuptial prospects, "celibacy would not be hard."

Catherine, having overheard this commentary, covered her mouth.

"Tell me, Canon, do you think that a monk is incapable of falling in love?" asked Carboni.

"With a serving wench!" roared Pious.

"With a beloved woman," answered Carboni. "My wife."

"She was with child, was she not?"

Carboni seemed to be tiring of the inquisition, but he nodded his agreement.

"Your child?"

"Of course."

"Boy?"

"No."

"A wife and daughter then," said Pious. Feigning ignorance, he uttered, "Do they not live?"

"The sweating sickness took them from me five months past."

Catherine could hear a low murmur filter through the ranks of the tavern—a low murmur that bespoke of pity for the man the patrons lovingly harassed.

"It is God's judgment then," said the canon, standing to address the entire assembly. "For such persons not sanctioned by the Church are clearly anathema too. They will spend eternity in the fiery pit!"

Catherine watched in frightened awe as the seemingly affable friar exploded from the bench, leapt across the table, and caromed into the cleric.

Marley shouted, "Matthew! Ben! Help me!"

The two hurried over to pull Carboni off the canon, who had caved under the larger man's momentum.

With some coaxing and an allowance of some moments to collect himself, they convinced Carboni to sit back down, well away from his instigator. Mary brought some clean linen to wipe his face, which was flushed with perspiration.

Catherine sensed an evil not unlike that of those hooded figures on Chestnut Street, the ones bearing ominous placards rooted in some sadistic web of terror and self-righteous judgment. She gasped as Pious stood up, shaking, but with the purity of his hatred untouched.

"Even the friars, who took in a drunkard," roared Pious,

"knew not what to do with this scoundrel! And here he is cast off with the devil's minions, those bloodsuckers of the Black Mountains! I see that the Blue Griffin has aligned itself with this son of perdition. Beware, you fools!"

"Ye have said enough for one day, sir!" shouted Marley. "I ask ye to kindly take your leave."

"Your alignment with such heathen filth is well noted, tavern keeper," replied Pious.

And with that, the cloak-like extremities of Canon Pious's habit ruffled with violence as he threw down some coins and exited the premises.

Catherine watched Marley's enraged eyes dart across the room, seeming not to notice anyone. Marley wandered around the tavern muttering to himself without her hearing anything substantive.

Nevertheless, her perceptions were accurate. She surmised that the canon's remarks had a greater purpose than to serve as a personal attack.

"We cannot have this kind of trouble here," Marley said as he tossed down a soaked piece of linen. "Nothing that would attract the archbishop's attention. We have, as it were, an uneasy truce with Mithrendia here in the Marches."

"I understand," said Carboni. "The fault is me own."

"You cannot be serious," said Mary, "After what that awful man said!"

"The canon has an agenda beyond a personal vendetta," said Catherine.

"Believe me, Lady Mary ..." said Carboni. "Lady Catherine ..."

"Catherine is right," said Marley. "We must be on our guard."

"One does not, or should not, make vows binding one to a monastic order without a conviction to keep such vows," said Carboni. "These are lifelong vows, including celibacy. I, however, was not strong enough."

"You are too hard on yourself," said Mary. "You cannot help your natural inclinations."

Carboni emptied a pint of ale in a single gulp and reached for another.

And then another. And another.

He told Catherine and Mary of his family history. An absent father. A mother who died of smallpox when he was a wee lad, leaving him with no other close relatives. After some wretched years as a wandering vagabond, he developed a knack for being an alpine scout. Having also found that he possessed a ravenous appetite for knowledge, he consumed what books could be had with the profits of his business. Notwithstanding the fact that he was employed, his new trade only fueled his loneliness, and he searched for some sense of community. The friars, he thought, were like family, among whom he might find order to and purpose for his life. He complied with their strict rules of submission to authority and hourly observances of prayer, including the long, unendurable periods of silence. That sacrifice was worth the rewards of studying the copious volumes within their library, including books on theology and treatises on ministering against the dark arts. He even learned of the draugr and their ancient ways. But still his heart was lonely, until one day, beyond the confines of the cloister, he met Viera.

The friar became incoherent with an overconsumption of ale, but Catherine learned thereafter that those who knew Carboni well had seen his drinking draw to a trickle during his brief marriage.

His wife Viera was gone, along with his lovely daughter.

As the days went by, Catherine observed a change. Now the drinking was back with a vengeance.

CHAPTER VI

A Rendezvous

**The Burgomaster's House, Hautebourg,
on the West Bank of the Rhine
AD 1235**

"A boy to see you, sir," said a servant, poking his head in the doorway.

A careworn middle-aged man staggered about the sequestered confines of his office on a cloudless afternoon. He worked at a frenzied pace, tossing parchments, perusing contracts, and signing writs. He swiped a nervous airborne hand to banish the intruder.

The servant lingered. "Sir?"

"I have no time for this sort of thing!"

"I cannot make him leave, sir."

"Who is it?"

"I'm not for certain, but I think it may be Master Evelrood."

The fleshy bags under the man's bloodshot gray eyes hung like crescent moons, seeming to beg for just one carefree night's sleep. Such a visitation could not possibly help matters.

The burgomaster sighed. "Send him in."

A ruddy youth, no more than eighteen, entered the inner sanctum of the burgomaster with an emboldened step. He carried a nobleman's bearing and a certainty of purpose, yet his manner also hinted at desperation.

The boy's impressive height stood in contrast to his gangly shoulders, but these modest proportions would fill out in due time. For now, his searching green eyes peered out from beneath vibrant locks of the curliest black. His narrow jawline and Grecian nose bore a handsome aspect that, when flared with emotion, appeared quite unyielding.

"Eleana is not here, Master Evelrood," said the burgomaster. "And as you can see, I'm quite busy at the moment. I suggest that you be about your business. Good day."

"I must see her," said the lad, grabbing the man's forearm in what seemed like a gesture of angst.

The burgomaster unclasped his arm stolidly. "This scheme of yours will not pass."

"Do you know where she is?"

"I said no, my lord!"

Although he could hear the man's peevish tone, Evelrood's attention was fixed upon a single purpose. "Tell me that you have not sent her away! Tell me she is not with her aunt in Metz!"

"And what if I had?"

"You would not lie to me, sir. You would not lie, for you are a man of your word."

The burgomaster sighed again and dropped his quill nervously. He glanced at the boy and then through the fenestration, looking into the street of busybodies jostling about.

"Then tell me," said the boy.

"Yes, she is in town. But I cannot permit you to see her."

There was an art to accepting a firm, if not unkind, refusal, yet Master Evelrood was not prepared to exercise self-restraint. His passion drove him. The youth swelled with anger. "I demand to see Eleana!"

"Demand?"

"Demand!"

"Bah!" shouted the burgomaster.

"Do not ... test me, man!"

"You should learn to respect your elders!"

"And you should learn to respect your betters!"

The burgomaster gathered his papers, all that his arms could engulf, and heaved them upward. Writs and contracts flew about as if scattered by the four winds, animating the wisps of graying hair about his temples that constituted the lone adornments to a central bald scalp.

The lad stood back, astonished at this demonstration. Somehow the outburst seemed to liberate the older man's frustrations.

"I'm sorry, burgomaster," said the boy at last. "I mean no disrespect. My mind is desperate."

The burgomaster settled back into his chair. He studied the lad with a scrupulous, though hardly indifferent, air. "Do you love her?"

"Yes! With all my heart."

"If you love her, lad, then I implore you to let her go."

The young man bore a facial expression of great pain. "But why?"

"This match can only end in tragedy. Your father the marquis would never allow such a marriage."

The boy, for the first time, fell silent.

"You know this," said the burgomaster. "And it is wise to know it. Yes, we Trautweirs have risen in status along with the recent success of the trade guilds, yet no noble blood flows through these veins."

"Then I will forsake my inheritance."

"A rash, romantic gesture. Yes?"

The boy said nothing.

"Ah, well," said the burgomaster. "You may be surprised, but I once felt as you did. I loved a young peasant named Marie. I wanted to marry her. But my father thought otherwise. So instead of wedding a pauper, I was married to a wealthy shopkeeper's daughter. Did I love her? No. But we have lived comfortably, and over the years we have grown to embrace one another."

"What happened to Marie?"

"Well, well. How should I know?" replied the burgomaster, whose pensive frown seemed at odds with any lingering romantic nostalgia. "She married some woodsman or another. I lost track of her and her kin years ago."

The boy felt certain that his feelings toward Eleana were not rooted in such shallow pretenses. The despondency he both felt and bore upon his face was hardly noble, but it was nobly transparent. Those ruddy cheeks flushed with vibrant color; he was about to burst.

His pragmatic elder, however, ignored the signs and gestured to his displaced papers. "We all have our duties, eh? Mine is to serve as this town's chief official. And yours is to continue your family dynasty."

Duties. Acceptance. Love dies a slow death. The boy, no longer able to bear these thoughts, left abruptly.

"Master Evelrood?"

For the first time all day, the burgomaster left his office

and wandered into the foyer. The servant was closing the front door, which had swung open with violence.

"Gone, eh?"

"Yes, sir."

What sympathies he felt for the lad gave way to fresh irritation. The burgomaster took this abrupt departure as another sign of disrespect. And the boy's certain intention to disobey his wishes? This was a matter of insolence. The son of the marquis might outrank him, but the trade guilds were growing in power and stature. As they rose, so did the office of burgomaster.

"That noble vermin! Metz it is then. We will have to pack her off to Anna's house, for that boy will comb the town and countryside till he finds her." The burgomaster looked back at the servant as his upper lip curled with vehemence. "Summon my men!"

Master Evelrood dashed out into the street. He momentarily thought better of leaving and glanced back at the burgomaster's house. The imposing edifice was three stories tall with blackened timbers in linear and diagonal patterns, and whitewashed panels wedged in between.

The window to Eleana's room on the second floor was open, though there was no sign of her presence within. He figured she could be visiting one of the guild houses, a friend, or a relative. Might it be better to leave her a message here? But how?

A peasant boy of ten stopped Evelrood in the street. "My lord, there is a holy man here to see you."

"Me?"

The boy nodded.

"Well, he picked a poor time to pay me his respects. He'll need to come back another day."

"My lord, he says it's urgent."

"And my business is not?" scoffed the young nobleman. "I'll tell you what. Fetch me a quill, some ink, and some parchment." He gathered some coins from his leather belt pouch and tossed them. "Take this with you, and be quick about it."

"To where, my lord?"

"There is a scholar residing at the inn. Tell him that I will pay for his accommodations if he will loan me those materials."

When the boy returned with the writing materials, Evelrood saw that the holy man had accompanied his young charge. This rough-clad elderly fellow with a tunic of coarse wool was unknown to him. The hood of his habit was down, revealing long, unkempt strands of gray that cascaded down his chest and upper back.

"I thought I told you that we would meet at another appointed time," said Evelrood with some heat.

"The boy answers to me," replied the holy man calmly, "and I told him that I must come. For the Lord spoke to me."

"What lord?" jested Evelrood. "The marquis?"

"No."

Evelrood was used to some form of obeisance, like a bow or the drop of a knee upon the earth, but this old man, plain and unadorned, stood firm like a person of some authority.

"Turn, my son, from your present course," said the holy man. Despite his coarse appearance, there was a radiance emanating from his azure eyes. "Before some evil befalls you."

"What evil?"

"Be obedient in this, and I will show you another path. For He has great plans for you."

"You mean God?" asked Evelrood with some surprise.

The elderly man nodded.

Evelrood thought of Eleana and how he desired her. "And why should I believe you? What could that burgomaster possibly do to me?"

The holy man said nothing as he remained standing there, observing the eldest son and heir of the marquis.

His silent scrutiny aroused Evelrood's ire, and the young man folded his arms in contempt. "Perhaps God spoke to me as well," he said in a tone that mimicked that of the elderly man. "About a different course."

The holy man looked at the noble youth not with condemnation, but with a gaze of sad acceptance. "Behold," he said, "you will come to a distant land in the far north. An island nation will be your home, where your life will no longer be your own."

"My place is here, in my family's dynastic lands," answered Evelrood defiantly. With a wave of the hand, he dismissed the holy man and his young charge.

Evelrood found a bench behind the tanner's shop and sat down to scribble a note. Once done, he rolled up the letter and tied it with string.

He needed to be quick about it. The burgomaster's house was situated in a busy part of town where the residences and shops parted to form a populated square, one that invited the scrutiny of a public official.

Evelrood lingered about in a quiet alleyway, waiting. Some wildflowers would be nice. He procured those from a field outside of town. Stuffing the stems down the hollow of the parchment scroll, he went back to his spot to wait.

He found his opening when a heated argument arose from the far side of the street. The attention of curious shopkeepers, loitering bystanders, and eavesdropping wives was now diverted.

Evelrood slipped the scroll into his belt and began to climb the front of the house. The projecting timbers were not easy to grasp, but years of climbing trees and rocks had led him to develop strength and dexterity in his fingers. He reached the windowsill of Eleana's room and flung his delivery inside.

The drop to the ground was not a pleasant sensation, but he gathered himself and was soon out of sight.

By early evening, in a communal barn on a hill just outside of town, a rendezvous had occurred. There, in the cruck-framed enclosure, under its dinosaur-like rib cage of timbered wishbones, the tired old sanctions of the elder generations were cast out of the minds of the young.

Evelrood paced about, thinking only of her arrival, when a beautiful form appeared in the enclosure. Her soft blue eyes were enhanced by broad, dark eyebrows, and long braids extended like rivulets to her slender waist.

"Abelard?"

"Who calls me by that name?" answered the young nobleman in jest.

"One whom you love."

"And one who would possess you, though the schemes of men are arrayed against us."

"Father, of course," said Eleana. "The marquis. Am I forgetting someone?"

Abelard frowned. "Just some strange holy man whom I've never met before. But they will not deny our love."

Eleana questioned him about this meeting, as well as his confrontation with her father, but Abelard soon assuaged her concerns with loving reassurances.

"I will never forsake you," he said.

The lovers cavorted in the straw-lined loft. As they lay

there speaking softly to one another, he traced a forefinger along the ridge of her cheekbone, down to the dimpled chin, then up and across the fullness of her lips.

"Let's get married," he whispered.

"And who will marry us?" Eleana asked. "Surely no priest around here, under the threat of our parents."

"Let us run away then!"

Eleana was the practical one. "How would we live?"

"I have some gold coins left. And we could sell my ring."

He held up the heirloom of his dynastic line. It bore a ruby, and the gold was embossed with the seal of the marquis: the Black Forest dragon. The lands of the Evelrood family straddled both sides of the Rhine River.

"Sell your family ring?"

"If my father disinherits me for marrying against his wishes, it would hardly matter then."

"What does he wish for you?"

"To marry some old hag in Cologne. A widowed baroness, I think."

"Hag?"

"I've seen a portrait. She's frightfully ugly. But when Father heard of her fortune, he positively swore that she was a beauty!"

Eleana giggled.

"Yet he assures me that I could keep a mistress," said Evelrood. "He says that's how it's done in the nobility."

"I will be no one's mistress."

"No?" he asked in mocking jest. "Then let us revisit my offer."

She gazed into his eyes and seemed to find what she was searching for. Despite the sordid humor, he was willing to sacrifice just about all for her affections, and somehow such foolishness of the heart overrode practical considerations. "Let's."

"Really?"

"Yes."

His faced swelled with rapture, and his chest heaved with the exuberance of one who knew that he was loved, a love that eluded the cold halls and absentee hearts of those within the marquis's castle. "This is the happiest moment of my life."

She began to utter caressing words, but strangely he saw her eyes of love begin to well with fear.

"Abelard?"

"Yes?"

"Look!"

There, through a gap in the wall planks, he saw a scene that sabotaged their domestic bliss.

"Abelard!"

Armed men were approaching.

"Yes, I see them," said Abelard. "Those are not the burgomaster's men."

"And they are not the marquis's men either."

There were six of them on foot, and they looked cunning and savage—outlaws of the forest who had banded together for the sole purpose of dispossessing others of their worldly belongings and, very often, their lives.

"Bandits!" said Abelard. "They must have scouted us from the woods. Hurry, we must leave from the far door."

Indeed, the barn did not afford security, so with great haste the couple descended the wooden ladder, swept across the enclosure, and exited the premises.

Abelard unsheathed his sword with one hand and squeezed Eleana's hand with the other. "Now run, my love! Back to town."

"Abelard!"

"Run!"

She, unarmed, reluctantly obeyed. "I will get help!"

Abelard could hear the bandits circling the barn from both directions. He watched in dismay as one of their number chased after Eleana.

Two approached from the left and three from the right. They hemmed Abelard in against the side of the barn. One brandished a sword, another held an archer's bow, and the others carried clubs or daggers.

"What have we here?" said the sword-bearer, who had a grimy, bloodstained face and wild eyes. He seemed to be their leader. "The foolish heir of the marquis."

This head bandit wagged an index finger. "Dear me," he said, sighing. "And no retinue of noble soldiers about your person."

"Run!" Abelard shouted again. He saw Eleana glance back at the lone vagabond, heftier than the others, giving pursuit. She seemed to outpace him in her flight.

Abelard turned to confront his attackers. He wounded the swashbuckler with a thrust of his sword, and he struck down the archer with a single blow from his fist.

The other three men closed ranks around Abelard, sealing off his escape route. Abelard lunged at the man in front of him when he was attacked from left his flank. A club to the shoulder brought the lad to his knees, and his attackers began to pummel him with their fists. A dagger sliced into his left bicep and incapacitated that arm.

His face already drenched in blood from the beating, Abelard strained his neck to look after Eleana. To his left, he saw the burgomaster's men appear on the horizon. Her pursuer, also having seen this, changed course and ran with fearful agitation back toward his comrades.

Eleana seemed to have an animated conversation with the

guards, who appeared reluctant to do anything other than ensure her safety. She pointed with fierce conviction at the barn, but to no avail.

Meanwhile, Abelard swung his right arm about in desperation. With the wounds and the loss of blood, he was losing vigor, and his mental faculties were beginning to wane to the point of unconsciousness. Wooden clubs battered his rib cage and pelvis as his lower body slumped to the ground. His back leaned into the wall of the barn, which was the only thing that kept him from lying prone.

The lead assailant was still nursing the sword wound to the shoulder that Abelard had delivered. He rose from the ground. "Enough! The young marquis can no longer fight back. And with those wounds, he's as good as dead."

Abelard was gurgling blood and phlegm in a pathetic struggle to breathe as the bandits confiscated his gold coins. His bludgeoned arms were somewhat numbed, but he could feel his assailants yanking greedily at his finger as they removed the noble ring.

"You see, fellows?" said the leader as he held up his stolen prize. "Today we have taken treasure from the dragon."

"Some fire-breathing dragon," said another. "He is a mere boy."

"Nay," replied the leader. "The boy has a stout heart. He wounded two of us."

"I say we finish him off."

Twilight was darkening into night. Abelard's vision was blurry, yet he still had a vague awareness of his surroundings. The five, standing on the sheltered side of the barn, watched as the sixth of their party ran up to meet them.

"There are armed men from the town just uphill," he said, panting.

"Are they heading this way?" asked the leader.

"They came for the girl."

"And not for the son of the marquis?"

Abelard could see the leader gazing down at him with a sudden curiosity and, judging by his wry smile, immense satisfaction. The power to kill the marquis's heir outright or to leave him to the fate of nature was in this outlaw's hands.

Abelard could feel his short-lived existence shrinking into oblivion. He saw movement some twenty yards away, not from uphill but dead ahead, at about the same elevation. Something bipedal yet primal emerged from a verdant copse that had afforded shade and anonymity in the waning light. It must have bided its time with patience and cunning, but now the vegetation swayed with violence.

It elicited a beastly growl, the guttural fiendish utterance of an apex predator. Abelard watched as the bandits looked at one another, their eyes glossed over with fear.

"What kind of devilry is that?" asked their leader. "That is no bear or wolf."

"Are you staying to find out?" asked another.

No response was offered, and none was needed. The bandits took off in the direction opposite the noise, running into the cover of the woods.

Abelard strained his eyes to see what had transpired uphill. The burgomaster's guards were vanishing into the forest with Eleana in tow, held forcibly. He could see the anguish in her face as she kept looking back toward him. He wanted to reach for her, even as a futile gesture, but his shoulder muscles failed him.

All parties had left Abelard to his fate with this strange creature. The boy looked ahead, and for the first time he saw it in full view as it paused to observe him.

It was the size of a man, slender and of tall bearing, and it wore clothing—the clothes of nobility. But its motion was that of a predatory animal with fast-twitched movements that were difficult for the eye to follow. It descended upon Abelard almost instantaneously and fed from the vein of his pallid neck.

A tingling of numbness washed across the boy's face as he felt his life force draining away. Abelard's mind swirled and drifted to the point of blacking out, when he felt the beast pull away. It, or rather he, studied him with a pensive expression as if deciding what to do with his prey.

Through blurred eyes, Abelard saw the dullness of arrested decay, like a revenant that had arisen from its sepulcher. The man seemed no older than thirty, and yet his skin shimmered with what looked like silvery white glitter under the moonlight. His ears were large, folded back toward the head and pointed at the upper tip. The nose was abbreviated and somewhat recessed. His black hair was long and unbridled, while his eyes had an unnatural redness to them. And the teeth possessed a horrific elongation.

"A nobleman's son, I gather," said the vampyre with a tone of eloquence that suggested courtly manners. "In your eyes I see intelligence, refinement, courage, even willfulness. But will it work? After all, it has been fifty years. These things are difficult to forecast, I must say. The last one, that poor foolish soul, was a disaster."

Abelard was too weak to say anything, and his mind bore few thoughts that were lucid.

"I see that I must be decisive," said the vampyre. "For we have but minutes to spare."

Abelard watched as the vampyre procured a small goblet from a pocket inside his cloak. He lifted up his sleeve and drew a line across the forearm with the sharpened nail of his index finger. Blood trickled out and was collected in the goblet. Once this task was completed, the blood coagulated and the wounded skin healed, leaving no trace of scratch, scab, or scar.

The vampyre took the back of Abelard's head in his clutches and waved spindle-like fingers in front of the boy's eyes.

"My name is Matthias. I am two hundred and thirty-seven years old, and I have the strength of many men."

Abelard stared at the vampyre with an incredulous expression.

"Much like you," said Matthias, "love once brought me to the pit of death. Oh, I know. I saw your romance with that beautiful girl from afar. It is such a pity, for you will never heal sufficiently from your wounds.

"Those foolish brutes with their clubs! I can see the brokenness in your bones. Flesh is no obstacle to my sight. Your collarbone might have healed, as would the breaks in your arms and ribs. But your pelvis is crushed beyond reckoning, and now you can never be a husband to that girl in the physical sense."

With the last vestiges of his energy, Abelard uttered a pathetic groan.

"Oh, I know," said Matthias. "But there are other things in this world to hunger for, and I will show you. Broken you may be now, but your healing will come forthwith, and with it the acquisition of powers beyond reckoning."

Matthias put the goblet up to the lad's lips. Abelard recoiled in disgust, but the vampyre forced the entire contents of the cup upon him.

"For the life of the flesh is in the blood," said Matthias. "Yes! My blood I give to you, and with it a lifetime of many generations of men."

Abelard felt like he was suffocating as the goblet emptied what seemed like poison into his internal recesses. He could feel his frail frame rejecting this foreign assault like the invasion of a plague.

"Yes, you will be a new creation," said Matthias. "They will fear you as they fear me. You will hold sway over them by moonlight and enter into the dwelling chambers of their nightmares."

Abelard slipped into unconsciousness as his broken body unfurled upon the moonlit ground with a release of muscular tension and a gradual cessation of breathing.

"But first, my young friend," said Matthias, "you will die!"

CHAPTER VII

The Witch of Hamarjørn

"Where's Mary?" asked Matthew, after delivering a plate of haggis to a patron of the Blue Griffin.

"How should I know?" said Berta, the keen-eyed and quick-tempered wife of the tavern keeper. Her plain face and broad torso bespoke of one who got her ways and means accomplished by strength of will rather than by subtle feminine manipulations. Not surprisingly to those patrons of the establishment capable of moments of sober analysis, she was the real authority at the Blue Griffin. "The girl skirts off the premises every chance she gets."

"And what are you saying, Mrs. Marley?" asked Benjamin in a defensive tone.

"She is an impetuous one, that. Always putting on airs and stating terms like she owns the place."

"Madam," said Ben, "Mary has spoken her mind as long as I have known her, but—"

"Isn't that a fact?" interrupted Berta. "I'd trade her dress for a man's breeches, the way she runs about the mouth. And you tarry in her presence like a whipped puppy."

Catherine glanced at Ben with a knowing countenance that was sympathetic to his plight. She knew that Mary had become the favorite of the tavern regulars, who enjoyed her quick retorts and vivacious ways. They saw her olive skin and dark hair as becoming of an exotic beauty. So on top of their usual spats, Ben and Mary were adjusting to a new dynamic: she had become something of a local celebrity, and Berta was jealous.

"You don't know where she went, do you?" asked Catherine.

After clearing another table, Ben draped a drying cloth across his shoulder and sat down dejectedly on one of the benches. "I haven't a clue."

"You told me that you could take me to see her," said Mary.

"Aye. I did," said the stranger.

"You have half my week's wages. Now take me to her."

"And well rewarded you will be. For none in these lands possess such powers of second sight."

Mary studied this cagey creature. With narrow black eyes, withdrawn and hawklike, he seemed more than just shrewd. The man, about twenty-five, was tall, slight of build, and a bit scruffy with face and hands soiled with the dust of the fields. His dirtiness suggested that he was a peasant, but his eyes hinted at someone with connections: the power brokers, the unsavory, and the nefarious sorts. His subtlety of speech, quick and polished, must have allowed him to outmaneuver many a street urchin. Mary figured that he had done so, securing their money without fulfillment of his obligation.

Today, however, she knew that his gamesmanship would be tested. Mary peered into his eyes with a fierce determination that appeared to put him off guard. His eyes darted about, looking at her and then at the dirty street beyond, with restless animation.

"I hold the other half," said Mary, "which is yours after you perform this service. I also have the means to blind you if you dare to shirk on our agreement. So take heed, sir; I will not suffer a scoundrel. Now take me to the witch of Hamarjørn."

"The name is Magnus, my lady. And quite the bargainer you are. I daresay, I've never seen your likeness."

"Your empty flattery falls at my feet, and I step upon it," answered Mary. She tucked Catherine's can of mace into a hidden pocket sewn into her clothes. "Take me to her."

He feigned a pleasant smile as if uninjured by such direct language. "Right away, lass."

She began to follow him through the crowded streets and the oft-traveled, much-lingered-near town gate, where old men sat about and stared while smoking elongated pipes. As Mary well knew, half the town gossip came from the observations and surmises of these gaffers, whose wisdom and buffoonery swept into the general lore of the Marches as promulgated by the ale-coated lips of the patrons of the Blue Griffin.

Having breached the gate with no worse than the idle talk arising from coarse scrutiny, Mary and Magnus swept across an arched stone bridge that straddled the River Twain.

The town lay behind her, the moors were ahead, and the O'Flanagan Range was to the southwest. Beyond this alpine range, she could glimpse the hazy outline of the Black Mountains.

"Before we go any farther," said Magnus, "we must safeguard our seer's whereabouts."

Mary watched with suspicion as he produced a dark hood. With the subtle dexterity of a magician, he placed it over her head.

Much angered, she grasped the hood and began to remove it.

"No, my lady," he said, halting her progress. "That will not do. Blindfolded, you will find the audience you seek. But unhooded, you must find her on your own. Tell me, does the witch reside in town, on the moors, or in the mountains? That's one in three. But I put your chances of finding her at one in ten thousand."

"No one lives on the moors," said Mary.

She found that talking through a dark hood was disorienting and disconcerting, but she was no less determined to accomplish what she had set out to do.

"Though we walk south toward them," she said, "rather than west toward the mountains. And we've already left town."

"We could go back."

"You fool. You're too eager to make money to waste time walking out here. The witch does not live in town."

"Are you so sure about the moors?" asked Magnus.

"I have seen them."

"But have you seen all of them? The moors are vast in these lands."

Mary did not answer.

"I thought not," said Magnus. "It would take years to scout the moors in their entirety. You are not old enough, and your accent is foreign."

Mary knew that she was but a novice as far as knowing these lands were concerned, and the thought of being less experienced than her guide, though vexing, was indisputable.

"I see by your silence that you take my meaning," said Magnus. "Here. Grasp my hand."

"I will not," she said, batting away his hand. It felt clammy and disgusting to her. She yanked off the hood and squirted a bit of mace in his direction with the canister concealed in her hand.

"Ahh!" he shouted, falling to the ground. "You yourself are a witch!"

"And lucky are you that I directed but a glancing blow," she answered. "But heed me well. If you did not believe that I have the power to blind you, you must surely know it now. Do not test me further."

Mary looked on as Magnus writhed in pain on the ground, twisting to and fro upon the heath. His eyesight was affected by the chemical, but he still saw well enough to rush to the river. There, he doused his eyes with water.

This remedy seemed insufficient. Not knowing what else to do, he became even more scared. He rested upon one knee for some minutes as his body and mind fought with the symptoms.

Mary regarded him from the embankment. She wanted to laugh, knowing how tethered this weasel was to the machinations of her mind. He, the charlatan, was being bullied and outflanked by a woman. It was a far cry from the insecurities of that Halloween morning lecture hall.

Still wincing, Magnus stood up and dusted himself off.

"I must blindfold you, my lady. The witch will cast a spell on me if I don't."

"And I will blind you if you do."

"Then we stand at an impasse," he said. "I cannot take you farther."

She studied his countenance and considered her

predicament. His face was gaunt as if he had not partaken of a hearty meal in weeks. He, of course, needed the money.

He would make a fine poker player, she thought. But now Magnus seemed bereft of cards. He had played his hand, and in his mind's eye he was caught between two witches.

"All right," she uttered. "I will take your advice."

Nevertheless, Mary knew that playing the witch was a dangerous game, even for those living outside the walled city of Mithrendia. She clung to this charade because she had to.

"I have a short rope to lead you with," he proffered. "You need not touch me again."

"Good," she answered. "Lead me on. I will wear the blindfold. But remember who I am and what I can do."

Magnus sighed, as if confounded by his present circumstances. "Aye, my lady."

He tied the rope around his waist and made a loop of what remained, an extension some five feet in length, for her hand. She grasped hold of it, slipped it over her wrist, and then blindfolded herself. A yank on the rope signaled that she was ready.

Their course was anything but direct. She felt the tautness of the rope as he lunged one way and then another like a jackrabbit in flight from a predator.

"Why do you keep changing direction?" she asked.

"Some of the hills in this area are steep," he answered. "I don't want you to tumble."

"And that is appreciated."

Mary doubted his sincerity. This was clearly a means to prevent her from learning the way to Hamarjørn. However, she did not think that such knowledge of the seer's whereabouts was of great importance. She only needed to know the way back to the Marches, which during the day would be evident on the northern horizon.

Nevertheless, Mary explored the terrain with acute awareness. She could see the moors under her blindfold and feel the dew as the heather brushed against her heels. She thought of the marauders. Did they ever venture this far north?

She and Magnus rose up to a modest crest before descending into a wide dale.

"Do the marauders ever venture here?"

"Rarely, my lady. We're too close to the Marches here. Clan forces can be mustered within minutes. To those worthless brigands, the spoils are better exploited in the south. They like to attack stray travelers. Plus, they fear the great witch."

"Are we near her lair?"

"Ha-ha! You wish me to give that away." Even his humor seemed inauthentic. "No, my lady," said Magnus. "We have some ways to go yet."

In this regard, Mary's sneaky, silky-smooth-tongued guide proved a notary to his word. It seemed like hours as they walked up a hill, down into a dale, and up again in an endless rhythm. The dew evaporated, leaving dry plants brushing against Mary's ankles and a cloudless sunlight enveloping their approach.

"How much farther?" she asked, having tired somewhat from the journey.

"Just beyond these next few hills."

They walked another couple of miles, at the end of which Mary felt the rope loosen. She stopped abruptly to avoid crashing into her escort.

"You may lift your veil, my lady."

She lifted the hood. The sun's rays drenched her eyes with a flood of overwhelming brightness.

"You asked and Magnus has delivered," he said with arms

extended in a theatrical welcome. "Behold, the secret lair of the witch of Hamarjørn!"

Mary glanced around at the immense dale. They stood at its bottom. The hills around them seemed like mountains, and the flora, which was particularly beautiful here, consisted of shade-providing plants and trees in a low-lying heath. Flowers tinctured pink, white, and yellow beckoned with unsuspected friendliness, offering repose in the midst of the wild, windswept moors.

"Um … payment please," said Magnus with hand outstretched.

"Not until I have spoken to her," said Mary.

Magnus grimaced, but he acknowledged her sincerity by nodding his agreement to the terms.

"Where is she?" asked Mary.

Amid all this daylight brilliance and vegetation, a dark hollow marked by several blackened boulders announced a cavern buried within the earth.

"There," said her guide.

She swallowed in nervous anticipation. Notwithstanding those hood-adorned moments, she felt vulnerable for the first time all day.

"There?"

"There."

A sinister squall wafted through the entrails of the opening in the earth.

"What is that?"

"How do I know, my lady?" His scheming face, for the first time all day, bore a look of fearful authenticity. "I have never met her in her hellish hole!"

"Then where?"

"She's always met me up here," he said, pointing around at the lush landscape. "Where it's … natural."

"Who comes to seek my counsel?" came a raspy vapor from the hole in the earth.

"No ... no, no," said Magnus, cowering back up the hill. "It was not me."

"I have!" said Mary.

"Descend, girl, and meet your destiny."

Mary glanced over as Magnus scampered uphill. She felt frightened, horribly frightened. But she and her Rhymer friends needed answers, and she was in the best position to get them.

"The deal is forfeit!" he screamed from the hilltop. "Keep your rotten money!"

Barefoot, and devoid of any weapon save a canister of mace, Mary entered the hole and descended into the bowels of the unknown.

The earthen path, which was moist and uncertain, sank under her relatively light tread. It felt like getting stuck in the muck of some primordial wasteland. Vines and branches closed in from the sides and overhead.

Mary could feel a sharp drop in air pressure as some tongue of the devil uttered from the great deep within. The hurricane-force winds bowled her over as she heard a sinister laugh pass by overhead.

"Will you live to hear your fortune, or will you die?"

"I will hear my fortune," said Mary, "and I will not die."

The raspy vapor laughed violently as if gloating over the visitor's ignorant sense of confidence.

"Did you not hear me?" said Mary. "I will hear the portents of my future. And you will leave me unharmed."

Another sinister laugh, a cackling wave struck with a demonic note upon an unearthly keyboard.

"Come forth, my foolish daughter born of men."

And whom were you born of?

With this strange thought in mind, Mary descended deeper into the cave. The branches, as if commanded, receded to allow Mary passage down the mole's path into the earth. The air stank from lack of ventilation, but perhaps more so from the sinister forces at work. The cavern felt uneven. At times she walked, and at others she crawled, yet she knew that some great revelation awaited her.

The darkness awoke with the single lighting of many candelabra. Mary glanced left then right as the tunnel opened onto an immense room filled with the petrified remains of subterranean plants. Mirrors, encapsulated in polished brass, responded to her gaze from four directions. Between them, a great fire arose from beneath the mantel of a marble fireplace.

The witch emerged from the fiery flames, dressed in the drabbest black and smelling of pitch. Her face, a burnished jade, transformed from the hideousness of the fiery pit into the likeness of a Greek goddess, even Aphrodite. In what seemed a mere instant, she appeared covered in white flowing robes, a bathing beauty arisen from some unknown waters of the great deep. Her expression was serene yet sinister, and her scent mimicked that of the colorful flora of the dale.

"What have we here?" echoed the voice, which had shed its raspy tone for one that was clear, powerful, and reverberant.

"I have come to find the source of the portal," said Mary. She felt ill at ease before this strange and powerful presence, who seemed to observe the visitor with an esoteric knowledge of unexplainable familiarity. Nevertheless, Mary's determination was as firm now as when she had first planned this foolhardy venture.

"The secrets of the portals are not for you to know," replied the witch.

"I came through one, and I mean to return home through another."

"Yes, you are a visitor to these times, future dweller," said the witch. "I have seen your homeland from afar. I have also seen the terrors of the day of your departure. Why would you wish to return there?"

Mary had not anticipated this line of questioning. How could the witch know these things? Had Nostradamus been this well-informed?

Perhaps in other circumstances, Mary might have admitted to the cultural failings of her own times. But here and now, she felt defensive.

"Well?" asked the witch.

Mary thought of her gracious new friend Friar Carboni and the irascible and unfeeling Canon Pious. She considered the happenstance gossip in the tavern and streets about dungeon torture and brutal executions, many endorsed by both the Church and the Crown. The spectacles of the executions were a sort of public festival for the people of Mithrendia: a rabid fomenting of blood sport, albeit one with a fixed outcome, but not unlike those that once titillated the pagan spectators at the Roman Colosseum.

"And your time is one of enforced religion," said Mary, "when persecution is in the savage hands of sanctimonious hypocrites. What about your butchers—your headsmen and your dungeon torturers? And you, my lady, live among the moors, a place where unprosecuted bandits roam free to steal and kill."

The walls echoed with the haunting melody of the witch's laughter. High cheekbones and succulent lips formed a countenance of classic beauty that teased of innocence while suggesting one accustomed to the ways of the wicked.

"You have spirit, girl! Few have I witnessed with your willfulness of character. But answer me this riddle: Why return to a place where love grows cold with each passing year and where people lose trust for one another and look to their own affairs?"

"Because it is home," said Mary. "It is what I know. And I miss my family and friends."

"You speak forthright and well."

Indeed, when Mary had first learned of the witch of Hamarjørn by listening to the town gossip, she had heard that the witch dealt in the currency of fear. Rapid heartbeats, nervous palpitations, quivering voices, and unbridled sweat fed her beauty. How she drew cowards to her lair was a mystery, but it was suspected that some of the more fearless marauders kidnapped victims and brought them before her.

Mary, however, was a different case. Her visit had been intentional. Her fears, though present, were mitigated by a refusal to linger upon them in her thoughts.

"Why did you lower your voice, madam?" asked Mary.

The witch glanced into the fire. She seemed melancholy. "You have heard of those who exercise faith?"

"I have."

"The agents of light work wonders when faith is abundant. I have seen it."

"And you do not practice it yourself, my lady?" asked Mary.

"Fear is the opposite of faith, for faith is based on trust," replied the witch. "The agents of Hades wreak their havoc when fear abounds. I am one of their number."

Mary marveled at the admission. "But why?"

"Ages ago," said the witch, "in my foolishness, I made a deal with a demon to assume great powers and preserve my youth. I exercise these powers, but my youth comes at a cost. It must be fed."

Mary's resolve to control her emotions had failed to feed her host, and this starvation with its accursed transformation acted as if on cue. The witch's classic lines of beauty contorted into spasms of pain. Her exquisite splendor was cast away. An outline of burnished jade returned, and her vanity became further incarcerated in stone.

Here then was another soldier, albeit a tragic one. Mary's eyes had recently opened to a war of angels and demons. She had seen a demon in the lecture hall. Since her passage through the portal, she had also witnessed an angelic presence. She had seen one of them during a solitary walk outside the walls of the Marches. The angel was of immense size, much taller than humans. Fortified with almost blinding beauty and strength beyond reckoning, this being shielded an unsuspecting child from the assault of a demon rummaging through the moors.

"Magnus! O Magnus, come forth!" said the jade woman, before her lips hardened into stone.

A few minutes later, the schemer stumbled into the chamber and fell upon trembling knees. It was clear to Mary that some magic was upon him, forcing him forth against his will. He cowered behind one of the petrified plants as the jade woman began to regain her supple flesh. Beautifully toned skin returned to her face and arms, and her lips moved once more.

The witch spoke to Mary: "I will allow you safe passage back to the Marches. But beware! The portal, it materializes when and where it wills. The Lord of the Heights will show you."

"Who is this lord?" asked Mary.

"Look to Wolf's Hollow."

The witch gazed in a mirror upon her classic form, which had returned in full as if nothing had happened. Looking appeased, with a slight upturn to her radiant lips, she glanced at Mary, shouting, "Wolf's Hollow," before she leapt back into the fire and disappeared.

Magnus took off through the tunnel without hesitation

and without one word to Mary. She was left alone in the witch's lair, a remarkable, unblemished survivor.

Mary had found her strength in this foreign land with its slow-footed maneuverings and its antiquated ways. In this solitary quest, however, she had gained nothing more than a vague answer. She faced miles of barefoot travel to the north.

Somehow she felt comforted.

CHAPTER VIII

A Resurrection

From the grave of the undead, the mind's eye roved about ceaselessly, surveying the town from the dual vantage point of time and space. Abelard noted all that had transpired with regard to his person since his violent demise.

A search party formed by the marquis had found the remains of Abelard's broken body the morning following his death. Well in advance of their arrival, the vultures had been seen circling like black gargoyles in the air; but for no apparent reason, they had refused to come down from their lofty position. This was deemed unnatural by onlookers. With regard to this eerie matter, opinions varied. The villagers and some of the burghers took it as a bad omen. However, the more pragmatic-minded had merely surmised that the approach of men had stayed the carrion-eaters' course.

There was a third view.

The marquis saw it as a divine gesture, an open

acknowledgment of his noble family's participation in the Crusades. It was a closeted acknowledgment, repressed and spoken of to no one, but Abelard had heard his father murmuring such effects in his sleep. A difficult situation had been remedied by tragedy. Abelard would be buried with dignity, but more importantly, the sticky legalities of primogeniture had been bypassed.

The marquis had a younger son, Henri, who was his favorite. Abelard had been difficult; his spirited temperament was too much like the marquis's own father, Maximillian, whom the marquis hated. Henri, on the other hand, a compliant lad of twelve, was a joy and would be a privilege to raise up as his heir.

All had not been lost this day.

Eleana, however, saw nothing celestial or fortuitous about this funerary occasion. She had lost the one, the only one, who had ever made her feel alive. Now she was destitute. From inside an interred box, Abelard anguished over her suffering.

Eleana refused every comfort, including food and the consoling embrace of her mother. Her anger burned white hot toward her father, who might have been more accommodating to the deceased and perhaps might have prevented this tragedy altogether.

They buried the young nobleman on a chilly, foggy morning in the family cemetery beneath the recently completed flying buttresses of Saint-Gousteaux. The nave's clerestory had been heightened to admit more light, but today the mist shrouded everything. The mist hovered about the tombstones and darkened the aspect of a crucifix mounted to a small outdoor shrine.

Something unnatural was afoot, but no one could surmise why. The bishop nervously uttered his Latin as if straining against a brooding atmosphere, yet the countenance of the marquise Lady Eloise remained as stoic as ever. Louis, the marquis, though flooded with thoughts of the boy's childhood, shed not a tear either, for to do so would be to stoop to the common level—and above all else he must maintain his noble bearing in public. Expression of grief, therefore, was left to the common class, including the household servants. None of the family knew that the deceased was viewing these proceedings from a restful, although not eternally restful, state some six feet below.

To the burgomaster's house was apportioned the greatest measure of guilt and shame. The burgomaster himself bore an agonized face with many failed attempts at solemnity. His crestfallen family lingered until the last, while the gravediggers waited—not in haste—within the intoxicating confines of a local watering hole. They sipped, gulped, and gossiped while eyeing the distant cathedral from a window seat in order to gauge the departure of those from the departed.

"Never shoveled dirt upon a nobleman before," said Denis, when they finally got to work.

"Yes, well," answered Heinrich, "they all suffer the same fate in the end. A dead nobleman is no less dead than the common folk."

"Every day above ground is a good day."

"You know, Denis, I find it eerily satisfying."

"How's that?" asked Denis as if eagerly awaiting a soon-to-be-divulged secret.

"Consider, my friend, for at this time the marquis's son lies beneath us." He stomped on the loose dirt to compact it.

Denis smiled through his greasy, sweat-laden beard. "And not only is he lower than us now, but also he'll never be our equal again!"

Heinrich, having no beef with the deceased in particular,

but rather with the highborn in general, spat upon the compacted earth. "For the living do not suffer the dead."

Their physical and philosophical work done, the triumphant gravediggers gathered their shovels and marched to their quarters among the living. Abelard had observed it all, seething at their impertinence, while patiently waiting for them to complete their task. He slept a bit as it was still day.

That evening, the wind turned diabolical and blew around and under the flying buttresses. Tree branches tapped on the stained glass portals of the walled cathedral aisles as if to break them. The shrubs and grasses were buffeted, yet the mound of recently compacted earth lay still. Perfectly still.

The undead could sense that the sun had drawn back for its nightly rest. Fissures appeared in the dirt like the desiccated lines of parched earth. Hairline in size at first, the separations grew into fractions of an inch, and then into inches, until the earth rose above the surrounding grasses. The absent gravediggers, had they been there, would certainly have been at a loss for a rational explanation, for how could the subject of a premature burial, unaided, broken-boned, with limited air, and lying prone, lift six feet of compacted earth off the nailed lid of his coffin? It was unthinkable, and yet the feat was accomplished with the tips of the fingers.

The vampyre rose from his interred dwelling with fresh aristocratic clothes covered in dirt.

"It hardly befits the occasion," said Matthias, the lone spectator, "for the resurrection of a nobleman. But as it has been said: *Out with the old man and in with new!* Or shall I say, these fools bury their mortals, not knowing that they will walk this earth again. For it is in the rare individual that the will is too strong to die. Your will is strong, Abelard. I detected that almost at once."

Here Matthias mused for a moment, while Abelard shook off the loose dirt and studied his postresurrection form.

Not only had his body healed, but also his senses possessed an exquisite sharpness. In fact, it bordered on sensory overload.

However, he soon found that by focusing his mind, he could hone in on certain sensations: the whispery bedtime chatter from inside a house a hundred yards away; the smell of the silt-laden river meandering along the opposite side of town; and the contoured sight of every crater on the moon's surface as if tracing a finger upon a pockmarked face.

"What did that gravedigger say?" asked Matthias. "Ah, yes: *For the living do not suffer the dead.* Let me now rephrase that little dictum: *The immortal dead does not suffer the living except to feed upon them!*"

Abelard, however, seemed to dwell in his own little world as he studied the newfound power coursing through his sinews. He gathered a cobblestone from the ground, studied its smooth, hardened texture, and crushed it into fragments in the palm of his hand.

Yes, his hand; it now bore a different aspect with its elongated fingers, which looked narrow. They would not have been characterized as narrow before, but their postmortem extension now made them appear so. And that was not all. He felt along the pointed tips of his ears and the recessed profile of his nose. He sensed the extension of his canines as they poked at his lower lip.

How repulsive I must look.

Indeed, his skin had assumed an ashen hue, and its texture was less supple.

"Step forth from the shadows," said Matthias.

Abelard obeyed. In the moonlight his skin radiated a white

iridescence. He gasped as he saw this strange nocturnal evidence glowing on his outstretched arms and fingers.

"Have you not heard?" asked Matthias with a subtle grin. "Even the devil can masquerade as an angel of light."

"I thirst."

"I'd say that you must by now. Your metamorphosis was costly in the sanguine sense. Come with me."

"Where?"

Matthias seemed almost giddy at the question. "Into town. Oh yes, there will be much to choose from. Look upon tonight as a banquet. Hmm? A wealthy old codger? A beautiful young debutante? A peasant, perhaps? How I love those visits to the bedchamber, whether they be furnished with a four-poster bed or with nothing more than a mere mat of straw! What sweet rapture to give the sleeper a deathly fright! And not just a fright, but a delicious peck and an extraction of their precious life force."

"And then?" asked Abelard with a tone of annoyance.

"And then? My, you're hasty to dispel the notion of such delights. Well, my boy, I'll tell you what: I gorge myself until I am swollen and he or she upon whom I feed gives up the ghost!"

"That is abhorrent," said Abelard, who felt a bit at odds with this new friend of his, this sire of his undead existence.

Matthias feigned a look of shock. "Do you mean to say you have a conscience?"

Abelard did not answer.

Matthias marched about thoughtfully with his hands behind his back. "No matter. I can cure you of that. While the first one will affect you, and perhaps the second, you'll soon grow used to—"

"No."

"If you do not satisfy the thirst, Abelard, you will surely die."

"I will take my nourishment in the forest or beside a stream."

"A hunter and a fisherman, eh?"

"The animals have blood too, have they not?"

"Abelard, you disappoint me."

The young protégé had nothing more to say. The thirst beckoned to the point that Abelard could think of nothing else but how to quench it.

Matthias watched him disappear into the shadows.

"He'll tire of the taste of beast one day," said Matthias. "There is nothing like human blood. For the connoisseur, it is like a finely aged wine.

"And when that day comes, oh, the hilarity of it. I will delight in his moral turpitude. Then he will see that he is no better than I. Then Abelard will see his heart begin to petrify as he abandons his lingering regard for the human race.

"For we vampyres are instruments of the darkness. Yes, we are the right hand of the demonic horde."

Somehow the participation in supernatural affairs brought much pleasure to him. Matthias delighted in the darkness.

"Abhorrent, eh?" said Matthias. "I think I will visit those abhorrent gravediggers."

The wind stirred once again, and a dust devil disturbed the remains of what had been Abelard's subterranean incarceration. The forces of nature bore a malevolent will this night. Matthias studied the unfurling of the windswept earth.

"*Every day above ground is a good day,*" he mocked. "Then this day shall be their last good day."

CHAPTER IX

Overtures

S ome weeks had passed since the interment. Eleana was beside herself. After all that had happened, along with the ongoing and vigorous mourning of her beloved, she had managed to grate even further upon the burgomaster's overstrained nerves. His solution was simple and self-centered, as was his prerogative as head of the household: he packed his daughter off to her aunt's in Metz for a prolonged stay.

There Eleana had brooded without succor, which disturbed the normal tranquility of the home. Her even-tempered aunt knew not what to do, but an uneasy peace had formed when the girl sequestered herself in her room for days on end. Offerings from the kitchen were left outside her door, rarely to be accepted, and often nibbled on by the fifteen-pound tabby named Boris.

It took a fortnight for Eleana to reestablish normal conversation with her aunt, uncle, and cousins. Over the succeeding months, the tension in that household waned, allowing for a rapport that was at first congenial and, much later, convivial. The aunt's long-suffering had paid off.

A full year and a half later, Eleana returned home.

The passage of time had cooled Eleana's passions to the point that her father began to scheme about her future. The burgomaster thought that a surrogate beau might be procured. Though his previous meddling had brought only suffering, he surmised that his daughter's happiness and security could best be provided by his further intervention.

He interviewed young suitors, often a guild master's son, and brought those he favored by the house to break bread with the entire family.

Eleana to be sure was more than a bit irked by her father's maneuverings, but then again, in her world of choice there were arranged marriages and the disinherited variety.

Nevertheless, some things had changed.

Though the burgomaster said nothing to the effect, she gleaned from these lively feasts and the quiet aftermath that the final choice would be hers. And given all that had happened, that was a concession she could live with.

Relations improved within the burgomaster's household, and though her heart had scarce abandoned her lover's memory, Eleana had learned to move on.

That being said, the passion of love had never left Abelard. He was now ageless, a veritable fountain of youth, yet he had been cut off from the joys of being young. He had lost his love as well as his ability to be a man. Vampyres reproduced their kind by the transference of blood, hence the absence of working parts below the belt and the newfound focus on the functions above.

Abelard had also lost his family.

Despite the cold relations he had long suffered in a loveless aristocratic family focused on wealth and rule, Abelard had attempted to reconnect with his parents and brother. This was a grave error, instigated by the loneliness he felt during Eleana's absence from town.

When Abelard returned to his ancestral castle one night, he bypassed the front gate and ascended the ramparts. There he met the night watch without welcome.

"But it is I, Abelard," he declared as he stepped over the ashen-gray stone parapet.

"The marquis's eldest son is dead and buried," said a guard in awe as he struggled to reconcile what he had just seen with a lifetime of rational and defensible observations. "You ... you were suspended in air just a moment ago." He started to shudder. "A ghost! A foul fiend of the night! Go back where you came from!"

Abelard's senses awoke to the outcry of these desperate words. Whispers of rumor invoked chattering about an enigmatic presence. Dark fenestrations in the uppermost story lit up with burning tapers, and many who observed him swore about the fulfillment of their nightmares. The private quarters of the marquis were astir with feverish activity as household servants scattered in a state of terror.

Most fled while a few fought back. With great reluctance, Abelard struck down brave knights he had known since early childhood. These would leave an emotional scar, but not like what was to follow.

In the corridor leading to the family's private chambers, the marquis charged at him with a sword.

"You would attack your own son, sir?"

"You doppelganger!" replied the marquis. "You devil! How dare you impersonate my dead son!"

With one defensive strike, Abelard watched in agony as

the marquis slumped to the floor. His normally stoic mother appeared at the chamber door in hysterics.

"You! You … you stay away," she said, wagging a trembling finger as his brother, Henri, hid in the shadowy recesses of the chamber.

"But it is I, mother! Abelard. I have no desire to harm any of you."

She slammed the door in his face, and her steps receded discordantly, until she stumbled into an armchair.

Abelard listened as Henri approached the door. "Go away, you monster!" said Henri, who then fixed the lock.

For a moment, Abelard was alone. He looked about the corridor and then checked the breathing of the fallen. The marquis would wake up; the guards would not. His eyes filled with the tears of grief, but he would not wallow in it. Abelard was still learning to control his powers, and it was difficult not to overwhelm those who confronted him.

He could hear the shuffling of heavy boots and the jostling of chain mail as other guards ascended the stairs. There would be more carnage unless Abelard left.

His kin knew him no more.

Somehow this ancient family had weathered the storms of life for a millennium. One of their recent ancestors had created the title of marquis, the ruler of the Marches near the western border of the Holy Roman Empire, for himself. Self-appointed or not, this title was well understood among the populace now, and the peasants and burghers dared not contest it.

This had been Abelard's destiny. Now the title would go to Henri.

That night Abelard left his ancestral demesne for the last time. His people would live on without him, as would the sunrise, which he had often arisen to like a welcome friend.

The source of light and warmth and growth had become like a death ray, a blistering, scalding furnace, an object of scorn.

The lesser light, the moon, would have to be his companion now. The distant stars would be his family.

Abelard often returned to the spot of his mortal demise. Bloodstains lingered upon the beaten stretch of grass. Had he been destined to become a monstrous creature of the night? What if he had dispatched those ruffians?

And yet Matthias need not have waited for the bandits to do their worst.

Matthias.

As his mind rehearsed the events of that perilous night, Abelard began to understand why. It was by Matthias's cunning.

Contrary to popular belief, feeding on the living produced a death of eternal rest, not the undead. Nature, it was said, had its checks and balances. Otherwise, with the vampyre's repetitive urge to feed, the population would be swarming with their kind, multiplying well beyond the birth rate of peasant, burgher, and nobility alike. Rather, the unseemly transference of blood from predator to prey was needed to increase their numbers.

This took a willing, or feeble, partner. To turn a strong-willed boy in the prime of his youth into a vampyre, Matthias needed to break that boy's will, and a weakened, disoriented state best sufficed for securing a new pledge.

What a strange friendship with no bonds to speak of other than cause and effect! One vampyre begets another not through birth but in death.

Abelard brushed that thought aside with a passing glance at his beastly hand.

No matter.

Abelard held an uncertain trust for Matthias, but he did

not despise him; rather, his heart burned with anger at the brutes who had destroyed his life. He imagined the sweet, savory revenge of inflicting pain and loss as they had done to him.

The marquis, in fact, had already sought to bring the bandits to justice at the executioner's block. However, armed forays into the forest were unsuccessful.

The father's justice had failed, but perhaps the son's would prevail.

Abelard's wrath had been of such account that when he stumbled upon a freshly dead forest animal, he consumed its blood to fight off the craving for those he would vanquish. He felt an utter revulsion, not only for them but also for their blood.

An alleviated craving also meant a clearer head. When he set upon their camp at the mouth of a moonlit cave, he thought coolly of what justice he would dispense.

The six ruffians sat around a warm fire with a satisfied ease. They had eluded the marquis's men while managing to steal tools and wool from a neighboring hamlet that bordered the dense forest.

Now they were about to satisfy their bellies. Abelard knelt behind a large fir tree, where he could smell their feast wafting into the starry night. The archer in their company had shot a wild boar, which was roasting upon a spit. Abelard relished what it would be like to consume roasted beast instead of something raw.

Their leader, however, brandished their biggest prize to date, which gleamed in the light of the flickering flames.

"A ring like that will fetch a pretty price at market," said one of the ruffians.

"Aye, if you are lucky enough to find a wealthy merchant with the means to buy it," said the archer.

Abelard seethed in the shadows.

"But a market far from here," said the leader. "The insignia on that ring would be familiar to many. Too familiar for purchase. Nevertheless, the marquis has enemies who might desire such an heirloom. We could sell it under cover through an intermediary."

"Or we might melt it down," said the archer. "It would fetch less, but then we wouldn't have the risk of suspicion."

A swift boot sent fiery logs exploding like shrapnel into the night air. A flutter of dried leaves and dirt covered the remaining flames like a blanket.

This violent disturbance aroused the ruffians from their self-satisfied reverie. One yelled as the others grunted. Save for the light from a few burning embers, their vision had been swept into momentary darkness, their anxious eyes straining to adjust to the starlight.

Abelard could see them perfectly as they grasped about in a desperate search for their weapons.

He interrupted their search with a guttural growl that recalled a familiar terror outside that communal barn.

"You would sell my ring?" asked Abelard. "My ring, you say? Fools!"

"The son of the marquis," whispered the leader. "But how?" He looked about, searching in vain for a company of armed men.

"What of that beast?" said the archer.

The other four ruffians converged upon the spot from which the words had been spoken. They swung swords and clubs in a fervor of madness, but Abelard sidestepped their advance with fast-twitched agility before shattering a club with his forearm.

A blade sliced through a small tree branch a few steps behind him. Judging from the unencumbered speed of the swing and the cleanness of the cut, the sword was razor-sharp. Abelard did not fear clubs or even arrows launched in the blindness of night. Any wounds from such weapons would heal. Sharp iron, however, conveyed a sense of permanence: it could dismember or decapitate.

Abelard's hooded cloak hid his iridescent skin, so the bandits hunted him by the sound of his footfalls and the scattering of leaves. Nevertheless, he eluded their death strokes with a propulsion and dexterity that was inhuman, outmaneuvering their sensory perceptions like a magician using sleight of hand. He could not help but feel the thrill of the exertion as his body glided in the air with speed and grace.

The men, by now, were adjusting to the darkness and surrounded him. "We've got you, fiend!" said their leader. "You monster!"

"Answer me this riddle," said Abelard. He dropped his hood as his youthful yet macabre face shone in the moonlight. "How can a monster be the heir of a marquis? For you have my ring."

"What does he mean?" said the archer.

"He has revealed himself," said the leader, "this shade from Hades who impersonates the dead. Kill him!"

They fell upon him with their collection of weapons. Wood and iron swung about as arrows flitted by the vampyre's head.

Abelard grasped one hand after another, each bearing a sword or club. He crushed the wrist wielding each weapon before extending a violent thrust to the head or torso.

For the ruffian who shattered his pelvis, he administered two blows: one above the belt and one below.

In the tumult, an arrow had managed to find its mark. It lodged into Abelard's chest, and he staggered back. Pain shot through his upper regions.

The archer grinned in the moonlight. "So you are mortal."

"Hardly," replied the vampyre.

Abelard seized the archer's bow and snapped it like a twig. He ripped the arrowhead from his flesh and planted it into the man's sternum. The archer collapsed like a felled tree.

Abelard, in his postmortem state, had subdued them all. He had left them a broken heap upon the root-laden floor of the forest.

He surveyed the remains of his conquest. The young vampyre was yet unsure of that fine-tuned threshold that marked the line between a lethal blow and one that merely incapacitated. At his ancestral home, he had checked his family members' breathing against a small metal plate. Here he would leave the verdict unknown.

Abelard confiscated his ring and the remains of his leather pouch. There were few coins left; he tossed them among the fallen.

The depths of the wild forest could be unforgiving. Animals would surely be drawn to the scent of roasted boar. The vampyre could already hear the distant rustling of a pack of wolves, and he welcomed their company.

Abelard looked one last time upon the fallen. "I leave you all to your fate as you once left me."

"And did you taste your sweet revenge tonight? Was their ruffian blood ripe?" asked Matthias upon Abelard's return to the abandoned fortress some three leagues from town. They had been living there in the shadowy ruins with its cobwebbed walls and moth-eaten fabrics for some months.

"Yes and no," said Abelard. He reclined in a high-backed chair with a generous seat, but immediately drew himself up again. He began to pace the cavernous room, which had once been a great meeting hall for knights and their lord. Now it was a repository for rats and ravens.

"Well?"

"I subdued their number, but I dared not taste them."

"No?" asked Matthias as he took a playful bow. "Why, you are a principled man."

"Was a principled man," said Abelard. "You sought an end to that."

"Yes, yes. We have recounted your woes in life once too often. But did you find satisfaction in their disposal?"

"I hardly know."

Matthias picked at the frayed fabric on the arm of his chair. His refined tastes had always seemed at odds with the decay of his surroundings. "You are a strange one, Abelard. To have been granted the power of revenge ..."

"All I know is this: the violence I have wrought upon those bandits does not bring the satisfaction I seek. Only more anger."

Abelard felt the weight of Matthias's gaze. Matthias had shed his teasing demeanor.

"Take care of that emotion, my young friend, and do not let it fester. It does not become you. Such unbridled trait is a marked characteristic of the berserkers."

Abelard did not answer him.

"Remember," said Matthias, "we stand above those four-legged man beasts. They rove about like rabid dogs. One day you will rule over legions of them."

Abelard could not help, even in his anger, but relish the thought of rule. It was in his bloodline. "How do you know this?"

"I have foreseen it."

Abelard knew that Matthias kept some things from

his young charge. Vampyres, especially older ones, had premonitions, but Matthias had once admitted that these were broad, hazy outlines of events yet to come.

"The master told you?" asked Abelard.

Though Matthias had spoken of the master only once, Abelard had yet to meet another of his undead kind.

Matthias seemed to ignore the question by responding with a kindly smile. "These things will come about in due time. Meanwhile, we need to find something else to suit your tastes—a diversion."

"Hautebourg."

"No," said Matthias. "Do not go to her. I have been down that road, and I can assure you that the experience will be most unpleasant."

News of Eleana's departure, and the memory of that disastrous encounter with his own family, had deterred Abelard.

She was back in town now.

"I must know," said Abelard.

"Is there anything I can say to sway you toward another course?"

"None."

"Very well, my noble friend," said Matthias with an annoyed sigh. "You are proving to be a more stubborn companion than the last."

Abelard traveled back to Hautebourg that very night, to that alleyway where he had once waited to post a lover's message.

He could hear the burgomaster's family as they conversed inside. They were planning something, a celebration. Eleana's mother was sewing a fine white dress, and the burgomaster went on and on about the accomplishments and business prospects of the master mason's son. With the combined responsibilities of engineer, architect, and contractor, the master mason was a man of means, and he was building a new fortress for a nobleman along the Rhine.

"Oh, Father," said Eleana, "you make this boy out to be a saint."

"He is, my dear," replied the burgomaster. "Well, sort of; at least he builds the abodes for the blessed saints. I have seen the reliquary he and his father built for Saint What's-His-Name."

"You cannot recall, Charles?" asked the mother.

"Um, well, it housed the saint's knuckle bones," he replied. "And for a modest donation, I hear, those relics cure warts."

Eleana laughed.

Her father continued, "The monks, I hear, can afford to feed their cloister from those funds alone. You would think that warts had become an epidemic. What say you, Hilda?"

"I'd say that there is a home remedy behind this," noted his wife, "and that after viewing the relics, the pilgrims are told to use such remedy to work out their healing."

"Hmm," said Charles. "You are a wise woman, my dear."

"Well said, Mother," added Eleana.

Abelard continued to eavesdrop. Eleana wished her parents a good night before ascending the creaky wooden staircase to her room.

Abelard walked around to the front of the house. With most of the burghers in bed, the busy city street lay quiet and too indisposed to heed the tall figure hovering outside Eleana's room. She had already changed into her nightclothes and was about to blow out the candles when she saw him.

She gasped but somehow managed not to scream.

"Are you really going through with this, Eleana? To marry?" asked Abelard. He had accessed her window as before, only this time using his bat-like wings.

She raised the candle for a better glimpse. "You specter! How dare you spy into my room!"

"Eleana! Do you not know that it is me, Abelard?"

Her straining eyes seemed to deny the familiar voice that had not changed in death. "No, it cannot be," she cried.

Abelard was dismayed. "But it is me."

"No, never. For I saw his broken body. I saw my love buried."

"And yet I live again!"

Her sweet face contorted in confusion. "Do not torture me with those memories, you specter—or whatever you are! I cannot and will not bear it!"

Eleana's voice tended to carry when she was emotional. Her father, hearing her, called from the base of the stairs, "Eleana?"

"I'm fine, Father! I just saw something in the street that startled me. Nothing more."

"Eleana, I am he," said Abelard in a low voice.

He sensed an unveiling of light, and as he looked up into the heavens, he saw that the clouds had shifted. The moonlight shone upon him, and for a moment the iridescence of his alabaster skin masked the decay.

"Abelard," said Eleana with a gasp. She rushed over and leaned into his arms.

Oh to be with her again. His love had been taken from him in the prime of youth. Could it be possible for this nightmare to be blessed?

She stroked his arms and chest with her fingers, but something startled her and she backed away. He observed helplessly as she rubbed her fingers with a probing thumb and as her loving expression turned to one of doubt.

"There is no warmth in your touch," she said. She seemed mesmerized by the iridescent glow that, despite its luster, shed light on the nature of its bearer. "And your skin is ashen and rigid."

"I am not what I once was," said Abelard, "but it is still me, your beloved."

The sad confusion on her face mingled with what seemed like an involuntary repulsion. "And yet you hover there outside my room like a fairy or a specter. It is all so unnatural. This cannot be."

He could feel her pulling away from him emotionally, which registered as pure agony in his soul. "And yet it is."

"You are not yourself," she said, shaking her head while staring in terror at the grave-dwelling figure before her.

"I know. But it is me."

"Then tell me what happened to you that night at the barn," said Eleana.

"I was made this way when my will and my strength were weak."

"What are you?"

"I am a vampyre," said Abelard. "A revenant. One of the undead."

She gasped. "A monster!"

"Yes," he said, sighing. "A monster."

Eleana staggered back, bracing her hand against the post of her bed. "This cannot be, Abelard. You were buried in consecrated ground with the blessings of the Church. You should be in heaven, or purgatory at worst."

"And yet it has happened, my hell on earth. Those men who assaulted me, they left me a virtual corpse. As I lay dying, Matthias gave me a second life, and now I am a creature of the night."

Shrieks burst forth into the quiet of the moonlit streets.

Abelard turned and saw that he had been spotted by someone in the square.

"You must go," said Eleana. "The townspeople will not understand that it is you."

Abelard was crestfallen. "But when will I see you again?"

She began to cry. "I do not know, Abelard. How can we see one another in such a state as this?"

Abelard looked upon her lovingly as if storing up her memory for the many solitary years ahead.

"You must go, my love!" said Eleana. "Please, before they try to hurt you."

It was clear to Abelard that she did not understand his powers, for it was the townspeople who would be harmed if he were to defend himself. Nevertheless, he felt he must leave for her sake and her safety.

"Yes," he answered. "I will go. But let me say this: I overheard your family conversation this night."

"How?"

"My powers are far beyond an ordinary man's."

"What part of it did you hear?" she asked.

Abelard reached deep into his soul to sacrifice what was most precious to him for her sake.

"I want you to know that you have my blessing, Eleana. Marry the master mason's son, my love, if that is what makes you happy. For I cannot marry. Nor can I have children. All that I ask is that you remember me as I once was and how we were once together."

She studied him with the gaze that he once knew, a gaze that could, for a moment, cause him to forget the hellish changes that had come over him. It was a gaze he would remember no matter the expanse of time.

The rancor in the street was rising. Abelard looked down

as men bearing torches were assembling arms—swords, spears, and pitchforks.

He glanced back at Eleana. She looked frightened, and even more so as her father burst forth into the street to ascertain the source of the disturbance.

"Yes, Abelard, of course I will remember," she said. "But you must go."

Abelard wished to linger upon Eleana's face, but the uproar in the square was building. Men and women wildly gestured at the burgomaster's house as the burgomaster glanced back in astonishment. Shock became wrath, and he seized a torch and led the mob as they encircled the front of the house. A spear stuck into one of the vertical timbers just below Abelard's feet.

"Go, Abelard, go!" said Eleana.

He left with great reluctance, pausing to look at her one last time.

"I love you," said Abelard.

As he began to fly away, the angry mob cursed him and threw stones.

The words hurt more than the stones, which simply glanced off his powerful wings. He fought against his impulse to retaliate against this ignorant, bloodthirsty mob. As defensive and as anguished as he was, he wished the people no harm as many of their number were known to him.

He rose ever higher into the moonlit sky. Soon Abelard was out of the reach of their rocks.

The moon illuminated the edges of some cumulous clouds, and now and then he took a dip behind those clouds like an actor stepping behind the curtain. His audience, his people, knew him not, and it was time to retire from their stage.

PART II
MONSTROSITIES

C H A P T E R ✗

The Awakening

I awoke from a long, deep slumber, one of an ethereal quality, like a calming realm of nothingness. The peace of the obscure vision I had been bewitched by only moments before receded, leaving in its wake a growing awareness of things unfamiliar. And with that unfamiliarity came a numbing loss of equilibrium.

The late afternoon rays shone through the diamond-paned glass, illuminating suspended particles of dust in my chamber. *Flakes of gold,* I thought. I waved my hand about. It was fool's gold. The hand dipped in that treasure would take nothing away.

I turned my attention to more pressing matters that troubled me.

The large, drafty room was foreign to me. How I'd gotten here, I know not. Rough-hewn stone rose above me like a massive cylinder, climbing some thirty feet above my four-poster bed to a ribbed ceiling of timber beams. They collected, each rafter, from equidistant points along the cylinder and merged above into a single point like the giant cone of a castle turret.

Even heavier timbers spanned horizontally from the base of these rafters, and from the middle beam an enormous banner was suspended. This flaming-red banner bore a heraldic coat of arms: a shield, quartered, with a triple-mast sailing ship at the lower left and upper right; a pair of crossed scimitars at the upper left and lower right; and a leering dragon in the center.

From my four-poster bed I glanced around at my accessible accommodations. The drafty air had conquered what had once been a roaring fire. Set inside a projecting hearth of carved limestone, the fireplace's hulking linearity contrasted with the curvature of the bedchamber. Here, only the dull red embers remained amid the occasional crack and pop of the last of the vestiges of the sacrificial wood.

I wrapped my arms in a coarse blanket and tiptoed about the foreign chamber. The cold stone floor sent shivers through my legs, which were half covered by a loose-fitting robe.

The tapestries hanging from the wall captured my attention. Scenes of great battles adorned them with cavalry charges of armored knights, lethal sword fights, and pikemen resisting an infantry charge. Siege towers and trebuchets launched an offensive while longbowmen fired flaming arrows from the heights of a moated castle.

My memory still failed me, but somehow I felt like an anachronism, like I was foreign to my times.

I was not merely viewing an aged historical collection from the usual point of view. In fact, my surroundings seemed newer than they should be. Dark and dank, yes, but not yet decayed by the centuries. Here, then, was a clue. The historical longings inside me caused me to surge with excitement.

Some ten feet to the left of the hearth I noted an oaken door with an iron latch. I tried the latch, and aside from the stubbornness of its great mass, it responded to my weakened exertion. Just beyond a square vestibule, the wall opened into an immense hall with a long table. It was lit with tapers emanating from three- and even five-armed candelabras, which sat in the center and illuminated the whole room with a soft glow. The table was large enough to seat perhaps a dozen, but there was a matching chair at each far end, and two flanking each other at the middle. A place had been set in front the middle chair nearest to me and at no other spot. From afar it looked like a Cornish hen, some roasted potatoes, cabbage, rye bread and butter, and a goblet of something from the vineyard. I glanced about and saw that the room was vacant.

I suspect that I had not eaten in days. My stomach responded with vigorous rumbling. Surely they would not mind if I helped myself?

As soon as I sat down, I confess that I lost my table manners. I must have resembled someone of the barbarian horde. I fingered, gnawed, slurped, and chewed until meat hung from my lower lip and there were splotches of red wine upon my robe. It was not like me to do this—I at least remembered that—but never before had I felt so ravenous for a hearty meal.

A long oval mirror faced me from the opposite wall, its length almost matching that of the table. I studied my countenance. Aside from the artifacts of the feeding frenzy, my face looked grizzled and haggard, and my forehead was scabbed over with abominable red markings.

"Herr Hunsdon?"

I jumped in my chair.

An elderly couple appeared in the room. I think they had

come in behind me, in complete silence, from the vestibule. I had noticed another door there, opposite that of my room, but not their approach.

"Herr Hunsdon?"

Was that my name? I could not say, but for now it would have to do. "Yes?"

"Are you feeling better?" asked the man.

"A little, thank you."

The couple appeared to be in their eighties.

The old man's cheeks had receded inward, almost cadaverously so, revealing the bony outline of his facial structure. The skin on his forehead alternated between what I assumed was his true color, now a weathered tan, and spots of pale white. The white areas seemed stretched a bit as if worn thin by the endurance of a hard life. He had an aquiline nose, bushy gray eyebrows, and deep-set olive eyes.

Despite his fearsome appearance, I was struck by the tone of kindness in his voice. It was a deliberate voice delivered in a low-toned lisp, and sincere.

"My name is Constantine. And this is my dearest Anya."

She curtsied. "Hallo."

Her short, broad figure amply filled a peasant's dress, and a blue-green kerchief concealed much of her puffy, lined face. Her kerchief matched her eyes, and her gray bangs spilling out from beneath the cloth retained a glimpse of the dark sheen she had possessed in her youth. That beauty had long since faded away, but there was something about her face that was quite pleasant and reassuring to a stranger, especially one who could not recall yesterday or the week before.

"Hello."

Their German, though serviceable, carried an eastern European accent. We carried on with some pleasantries, during which I learned that they spoke no English. But since I knew German, this was our only practical means of communication.

Nevertheless, there was something about their particular dialect that seemed archaic to me. Once again, I sensed a discontinuity in time.

"What year is this?" I asked in German.

Constantine laughed. "You took a strong blow to the head, ja?"

I nodded. I was beginning to think that my convalescence might prove more of a mental rehabilitation than a physical one.

"The year is 1526."

"Whose schloss is this?"

"Lord Ananias Berbery is the owner of this castle," said Constantine.

I had the feeling that the castle was enormous, and I was anxious to look about. "Is he here now?"

"Ja, Herr Berbery is in residence. But he comes and goes as he pleases. His party was out hunting this morning."

"Has he had dealings with me before?"

Anya must have felt sorry for me, because she sighed and began rubbing her arthritic thumbs into the overwrought sinews of my shoulders. "You must rest now. Our master has appointed these rooms for your use as you recover."

She pointed to the magnificent ornamentation to my right. "His library."

The dining hall, some forty feet in length, opened into an even larger room that was maybe thirty feet high. From my chair I could make out gilded wood paneling, along with upper and lower tiers of bookcases circumnavigating the room. The upper tier was serviced by a narrow mezzanine, and the ceiling appeared to contain artwork of a most intriguing nature.

"The well water is good here," said Constantine, pointing to a silver decanter.

I believe I thanked him, but the mesmeric enchantment of the library commanded my attention. I moved in that direction as they cleared my dinnerware.

There upon the ceiling an artistic genius had captured the Hagia Sophia, the Church of Holy Wisdom. Massive triangular pendentives in this Byzantine cathedral spring from pillars like arches, one at each corner, curving upward and inward to support a circular dome. That's right: at its core is a round dome centered over a square floor plan. One speaks of the incompatibility of a round peg and a square hole, but here it was done by early medieval minds in the sixth century.

The artist had mastered three-dimensional perspective. The vaults seemed to lift the ceiling far above its natural limit, pushing the room higher and higher into the upper reaches of the castle. It was like I was standing in one of the largest churches in Christendom before Constantinople fell, in 1453, into the hands of the Ottoman Turks.

I thought then of the scimitars upon Berbery's crest of arms. These swords with their curved blades were Arabic in origin, but the Turks used them too.

My host, then, was a learned man, and a man who had seen distant parts of the world. That he possessed enormous wealth, I was assured, judging from his personal library alone.

I still felt weak, but my mind was astir, so I perused the lower-tier bookcases to see what else I might learn about my host.

The bulk of his collection was written in Cyrillic script. I chastised myself for not having added this to my former linguistic studies. A few of the manuscripts I perused had illustrations, while a smattering of books were written in German, Latin, Greek, or Turkish. Most were bound, whereas some were loosely tied piles of parchments. A number of these loose leafs had been hand copied.

I remembered that I had learned the classical languages of antiquity: Latin and Greek.

Was I a scholar? a theologian? a diplomat?

I considered my current plight. "Some allowance for recovery will do me well."

English was my natural-born language, but I repeated the sentence in as many different languages as I could recall: French, Italian, German, and Spanish—though I struggled a bit with the last one.

"Herr Hunsdon!"

The intonation and volume of this address was far more forceful than Constantine's. The words were commanding, even domineering.

The man had appeared out of nowhere, a curious feat for one so broad and powerful-limbed. He wore a bejeweled doublet and overcoat. A long, forceful nose met a thick black mustache. A matching beard swept up his olive-toned face in an arc. Wavy dark hair stretched to his shoulder blades; his jaw was square; and his eyes were black and calculating. His large calves looked like they might burst out of his red stockings. Despite his luxurious accoutrements, he smelled of perspiration and the outdoors.

This man of noble bearing introduced himself in a Norse- and Gaelic-sounding language that, to me, sounded like gibberish. Yet his accent seemed to be that of someone from the Black Sea region.

All I could comprehend was something he said about a Lord Dominus Berbery.

I felt a bit naked in my bedclothes to be addressing a person of such bearing, and as a guest in his own house!

I made my apologies for my appearance with pathetic hand gestures.

"Sprechen sie Deutsch?" he asked.

I nodded and bowed.

"You are a man of learning, are you not?" he asked, shifting into a dialect I could follow. "I take it that you like my library."

"Yes, my lord," I answered. "Very much."

"Where are you from? Not from Germany, I would wager. Your accent is nearly English."

His face beamed with hospitality, but his black eyes suggested something far from cordiality. I suspected that neither perception was entirely correct, but perhaps the latter was the closest to being true. His pensive stare bore into me as if he were a practitioner of the dark art of mind control, and it made me uneasy. "I cannot ... remember."

"Do you recall your arrival here?"

I searched my memory, straining to recall something, anything. "I'm afraid to say that I cannot remember anything prior to awaking this morning."

"Indeed. You took a nasty fall upon the cobblestone road just outside my fortress. My guards found you four days ago, and here you have been ever since."

"Then I must convey to you how grateful I am for your assistance in sheltering me and providing for my recovery."

"Rest assured, you may convalesce here as long as you like," said Berbery, "until your memory and physical health return."

"Thank you, my lord."

And with that he departed from the room.

Before the far door of the vestibule closed, I could see two large guards positioned in the outside corridor. One brandished a ring of keys, one of which was used to secure my door.

I tried the handle without success, which confirmed my suspicion: I was both a guest and a prisoner. My host no longer seemed so hospitable, and this worried me.

I began to pace about. My body had not yet harnessed the energy from that delicious repast, and once again I felt weak.

Nevertheless, with curiosity overwhelming me, I rushed to my bedroom window to look outside. I could see a large cobblestone courtyard six stories below, and it was flanked by a long arcaded gallery. This stone arcade, the second of three stories, was a busy thoroughfare of guards and household staff moving from one part of the castle to another. Each bore the distinctive livery with the coat of arms I had observed in my bedchamber.

The colors of these uniforms were bright and audacious. I wondered if additional information about these symbols might be found in the library.

I returned there to study the titles. Fortunately the volumes appeared to be arranged categorically. Along the bottom tier I found works about animal husbandry, agriculture, and peasant management practices. As I walked around the room, I found sections on mathematics, astronomy, and music. No luck so far.

Perhaps what I was looking for was shelved somewhere above.

I ascended the gilded mezzanine staircase to reach the upper tier of books. There I found treatises on military strategy, siege engines, fortifications, and the art of rule, but no sign of heraldry or any genealogical records of the Berberys.

As I worked my fatigued body around the perimeter of the mezzanine, I observed a latticed gate at a far corner. It was sealed shut.

I could see the incarcerated volumes beyond, but not their titles, owing to the lack of light in this tucked-away location.

This only added to my enticement. Those titles, whatever they were, seemed to illuminate in my mind's eye.

Fortunately, as an otherwise unengaged prisoner, I possessed a bountiful amount of time.

The key was missing from the lock, so I looked around. I began pulling dusty volumes off the shelves just outside the gate. Nothing. Where was that key?

There was a desk below with several drawers. I thought of descending the staircase, when I noticed an obscure volume through the latticework, just beyond the locked gate. I'm not sure why it caught my attention. Its binding was black and unlabeled. I had to reach both hands through gaps in the latticed framing to grasp hold of it. It slipped in my fingers and I almost lost it.

Nevertheless, I managed to secure it and fit it through a slot in the lattice.

I opened the book to find that a square hole had been cut into the pages. This pocket housed the key. I tried the gate lock and found that it responded.

The inaccessible volumes, even close up, were too obscure to read. I descended the stairs, grasped a candelabra, and returned to the secured section of the library.

The categorical content in this section had a more sinister portent than the content of the books shelves in the unrestricted areas. These were volumes on poisons, alchemy, and witchcraft; illustrations of capital punishments and sadistic tortures; and manuals of instruction regarding lycanthropy, sorcery, and necromancy. What kind of noble lord was this Berbery?

I grasped a stray volume and returned to the desk below. It was entitled *Mystical Enchantments and the Summons of the Demonic Horde*. I opened the bound volume and gazed upon it under the candelabra.

Groupings of horned figures, goats, and pentagrams converged in diagrams of diabolical intent. With them were words, grisly words of the darkest magic, hailing from the abyss and the spiritual realms of wickedness.

I felt light-headed and nauseous. *Where am I? How did I get here?* I felt like a foreigner in this place and also to these times. How was that possible?

I looked again at the magical enchantments, and for some odd reason I felt tempted to read one of them aloud.

Fortunately my better sense prevailed. I slammed this diabolical book shut and collapsed into the chair.

No, I will not utter such foul things!

The air around me grew cold as the lights of the candelabra flickered. I looked around, but there was nothing to account for this change, no draft or breeze—and yet I was at the point of freezing. Was it a drop in my body temperature? I still felt weak, but I did not feel sick.

How bizarre.

As I continued to take stock of this unaccounted-for wave of coldness, I felt something scratch me across the left shoulder blade. I instinctively looked behind me and then around the room. Nothing. I was alone.

But I don't think I could have imagined this incident, for the flesh in that region of my shoulder ached. I walked over to the dining room mirror to be sure. Yes, a reddish wound was there, and it bore three long marks, three parallel stripes, like the tines of a pitchfork. What could that signify?

I staggered back to the library. As the coldness lingered like an uninvited guest, rational thoughts gave way to irrational sentiments. My mind strayed, and I began to think of nothing but death. My death. I considered that I would never leave this place and would never regain the knowledge of who I was: my actual name, my date of birth, my family, my home.

What was happening to me? I began to panic. I swirled around and around, looking anywhere and everywhere without seeing a single person.

Something laughed. It was a contemptuous laugh.

My nostrils picked up the strong scent of rotten eggs. I could now sense a shadow hovering behind my shoulder, where I had been scratched. This entity, this being of energy, grasped hold of me with inhuman strength and shook me as if my body were made of straw. I felt powerless to oppose its force of will.

It held me upright with the tips of my toes just above the floor. My head fell back, and I glanced up; the heavy ceiling seemed to be moving. Fissures erupted and swept across the vaulted dome of the cathedral. The pendentives buckled, and the last vestiges of the eastern Roman Empire, conquered by the Turks, began to collapse upon me. The Christian images faded, and the sun ceased to pour forth its light.

I felt a wave of vertigo.

"God, please help me!"

The room began to spin, and I fell unconscious upon the Persian carpet in the center of the room.

C H A P T E R X I

A Heart of Stone

"Liars?" said William McCormick.

Adaira, his teenage daughter, sighed. "He's still at the quarry."

"He's been gone awhile," said her father. "Tell Erik to fetch him back. We have to close up shop early today."

Adaira pranced through the back shop, where Erik was poring over plans. Here in the far north, heavy timber held up well against the ravages of time and, hence, remained the construction material of choice. Nevertheless, the wealthier patrons of Mithrendia had recently taken a greater interest in stone and, along with it, an architectural flare for the Gothic that was centuries overdue. Among these late-awakening patrons was the Northmoorlandic Church. A cathedral was to be built west of the royal palace, and McCormick had just been awarded the job. Erik, a handsome freckle-faced youth of eighteen with the ruddy beginnings of facial hair about the chin, studied a drawing of a cross section of the towering nave with great intent.

"Erik, my love?" asked Adaira. "Father wishes you to fetch Lars from the pits."

Erik looked up from his work. "Why do you call me that?"

"My love?"

"Aye. For obviously I am not."

There was a certain luster to her azure eyes when she flirted. "Why do you say such things, Erik?"

"Easy," said Erik. "You speak of Lars that way as oft as you do to me. More so, actually."

Her laugh caught him off guard, but it carried a tone of amusement, like coming from one holding the upper hand in a bargaining situation. "Either of you would do well to marry me," she teased, "for I am Father's only child."

Adaira was right, and Erik knew it. Someone would need to take over the business in another fifteen or twenty years, and a young apprentice could do far worse.

"But you'd better hurry," she said. "Father has been talking to the wool merchant's guild down the street. Jannik's son, Frederik, stands to inherit far more than you can ever earn."

"Frederik looks like a goat," said Erik with jealous disdain, "and he has the personality of a boar."

He watched in irritation as she laughed again in her playful manner; she seemed to enjoy eliciting his facial contortions and heavy frowns. She liked to have her way, which was becoming the common course as she flowered into womanhood. With flowing blonde hair, which fell to her curved waist, and an angelic face, Adaira was easy to look upon. At times, Erik found it difficult to take his gaze off her. Given this fact, the parlay of suitors, jousting at one another for her roving affections, annoyed him to no end. There was something disingenuous about it. Erik grumbled to himself as he arose from his chair.

"What's that, my love?" she asked.

"Nothing. Nothing, my love."

"Oh, you jest?"

He returned a knowing smirk that resembled her own.

Normally Erik was reluctant to engage in this type of capricious give-and-take with Adaira. He preferred sincere conversations about serious things as reflected in his work habits. His steady ways included long hours of studying drawings, editing them, and directing the sculptors with an adeptness that belied his age.

Notwithstanding that, Erik was not some dull draftsman sitting in an obscure corner. His heart burned with an unquenchable fire. He would embrace Adaira's whimsical moods, even for a lifetime, if she would but favor him.

Unlike the guild members' sons, Erik was of modest means, though hardly poor. He was her father's favorite apprentice, valued for his conscientiousness and intelligence. Erik was dependable and trustworthy; Lars was volatile and unpredictable. Lars barely had a coin to his name. But something about Lars drew Adaira toward him like no other could. When Erik sensed her partiality, the air he breathed became thick and wretched, and he felt a leaden weight upon his breast.

Even now he could feel his lungs constricting. It was time for a change of scenery.

Erik stepped outside of the massive stone edifice that served as the master mason's place of business. It was a fine, cool autumn day; the snows had been delayed this year. Passersby busied themselves with tasks that were best accomplished before the next freeze. Erik swept in among the crowd as they walked the narrow street with a series of shops that wound around in chaotic defiance of a straight line. Here in the Merchant Quarter, fullers, tanners, drapers, tailors, cobblers, and wool merchants plied their trades. The half-timbered walls of commerce bulged and sagged, the edifices bearing the artifacts of dust and grime.

As he followed this rambling procession, Erik distracted his thoughts with the details of the cathedral. After all, the royal chapel, when completed, would have the highest spire in Mithrendia. With a job well done, McCormick's reputation was projected to soar along with it. Erik stood to become a beneficiary of these proceedings. Such enticements were well worth deliberating over.

Nevertheless, Erik's thoughts returned almost involuntarily to his affections. He lingered over that beautiful young woman and how she toyed with the heart as if it were some frivolous plaything.

With the success of the cathedral, of course, there would be other prospects. Erik could do quite well; he might even marry a merchant's daughter.

"It hardly matters," he muttered as he made his way to the city wall. "Oh, I know the odds are not very good. But I cannot entertain the thought of anyone else."

Armed guards eyed with suspicion those passing through the gate as threadbare-clothed beggars begged for offerings. Erik was nearing the western edge of civilization. Lars, the favorite, dwelt in the pits beyond.

Erik's province, that is, his occupation, dealt in precision and beauty. It also required refinement.

Given the particularities of artisanship, the ability to sculpt rock into beautiful forms was a later-stage event. Hulking bedrock became what the human mind fashioned it to be at the jobsite, where the foundations of a sky-bound spire were being laid. This melding of physical bulk with artistic precision resulted in exhilarating edifices with ribbed vaults and rose windows, with gargoyles and flying buttresses. And yet these magnificent structures, which arrested the roving of the eye into a prolonged stare, teemed with delicate tracery: stone chiseled to such fine edges and profiles that what was once opaque now almost seemed translucent in the sun-drenched light.

Lars, on the other hand, dwelt low among the shifting shadows. For it was here in the pits that the grunt work began with amorphous blocks of granite. No building scheme, no matter how audacious, could germinate apart from its source. Here a cathedral, a master of the heights, had its humble beginnings in the depths of the earth.

"That's it, men! Wait till Erik's crew sees this one! It will break their backs! Ahoy, up there! Lower the curler!"

Lars belted out a swath of commentary and a string of commands with a forceful voice that resonated in a chorus of echoes. In the beginning, the gray-whiskered laborers had been slow to warm to the cadence of a twenty-five-year-old. But such was no longer the case. Some leaders are made, whereas others seem to be born. Lars fell into the latter category. He asked nothing of his men that he would not undertake himself. Moreover, he dealt with their wages and their grievances in a judicious manner.

Contrary to this, the master of the quarry wielded a savage aspect at times. From sunup to sundown, Lars remained in constant motion, but on occasion his work habits took on a frenzied pace. Darkened moods set upon him. Outbursts of fury kindled fear among the ranks. Those bold enough to study the flustered contours of his face found an enigma: the sky-blue eyes of a Norseman swirling with an incalculable rage.

He had become a man through hard work, but hard work could not contain him. With wild shanks of Northmoorlandic blond hair and a physique that bulged with every sinew in his body, Lars exuded the unbridled willfulness of a northern barbarian. Those foolish enough to test him felt the broadness of his boot upon their backs.

Lars's present mood, however, was more civil. "A draught of mead for all if we raise this mass of stone before dark!"

The men lumbered more than usual today, but his forceful rousing words seemed to drive them out of their listlessness.

"The cornerstone will this one be," said one of the workers, his face caked in dust and sweat.

"Aye," replied Lars. "And several other foundation stones. The curler has nigh doubled production."

Indeed the blocks had become larger. Some Mithrendian mechanical genius had developed a lifting device, which had been mounted to the surface some seventy-five feet above. From pit level, however, all that Lars could see was a short bridge that spanned across two outcrops of rock. In the middle of the heavy timber planks was a large square hole from which an interwoven chain of iron dangled from a massive overhead pulley. The heavy chain lowered until it clanked upon the ground of the pit, spreading dust forcefully.

"That's it, men! Bring the mass forth!"

A team of oxen pulled the block as laborers ensured that it slid upon a series of timber rollers. Whereas these beasts of burden were formerly struggling up an incline, a flat trajectory better suited their backs and buttocks. Their deep-toned utterances betrayed less strain than before as the curler ensured that these animals were not overtaxed.

"Steady! Steady! Ho! Secure the rigging!"

Lars and his men grasped long staffs with hooked ends, which they fed between the gaps in the rollers. They grasped the rigging and pulled the ropes to the opposite side of the block. Then they corralled the block in a myriad of rigging, meeting at a central hook.

Lars cast his fierce face upon the embankment above and gave the signal.

He heard the machinery above creak and groan as it got into motion. Though he could not see the activity above, he recalled it in his mind's eye: There another team of oxen drove a pivoting mass that looked like a spoked wheel laid on its side. The animals' walking a circle turned a central iron shaft, mounted overhead to perpendicular gearing. The mechanical genius had devised cogs, like thick teeth in a mouth that had lost many others. The teeth grinded against one another in the gaps as one shaft turned another. The whole assembly acted like an enormous winch to pull the chain to higher ground.

Lars watched as the block of granite rose against the shadows of the embankment and then penetrated the square hole. A driver and a team of horses pulled a bulky cart under the block, which was skillfully guided and lowered into place.

The driver, appearing to swallow a pair of fingers, sounded a great whistle into the depths.

"Mead it is then, men!" shouted Lars.

As far as this block was concerned, the quarry's work was finished. It was Erik's problem now.

The recipient of this enormous piece of granite had just walked up and watched in astonishment as the driver took the reins. "With what Lars is sending me," said Erik, "we'll have to hire more sculptors."

The old driver shrugged with apparent apathy. "It's no problem for my team, laddie."

"I'm glad to hear of it," said Erik. "It's the work of breaking these down that concerns me."

McCormick must know of this, thought Erik. Sometimes the men at the jobsite got ahead of their supply line. That certainly would not be an issue now.

"Tell Lars that McCormick wishes to close up early today. Lars is wanted at the shop."

The whistler complied with a lengthy composition, and Erik could hear Lars barking out orders to the men. Some ten minutes later the master of the quarry surfaced from a nearby ramp. The sight of him was a little intimidating, but Erik had become accustomed to bullies.

"Come to see how real men work?" asked Lars. "Had enough of the company of your limp-wristed sculptors?"

It was a jest, and not a well-thought-out one. Then again, Lars's jests rarely missed the mark.

"I've already seen what you do," replied Erik, "and the only thing recommending any intelligence was the development of the curler. Which, of course, could not possibly have been conceived in your head."

Lars shoved Erik to the ground with a quick thrust to the chest—if one could call it a shove. The strength of the man's fingers felt like percussive waves against the sternum.

Erik could not help but wonder about the physical power this man wielded. It felt unnatural.

Despite the lingering pain, Erik got back to his feet in short order. He wanted to throw a punch but thought better of it.

"Are you going to snitch on me, boy, for tossing you around?" asked Lars with a malevolent sneer and a voice brimming with sarcasm. "There's always more where that came from."

Lars's eyes had an unusual redness to them. Curiously, Erik had not observed this before.

"Only if you show up for supper," said Erik.

"The master's table tonight, eh?"

Erik did not answer.

"He beds early, does he not?" said Lars. "Which leaves time with Adaira. A little bit of fun to be had there."

Erik conceded to his impulse and threw a shot across the bow. It landed on Lars's jaw.

The next thing Erik remembered was lying prone on the ground with his torso clear off the edge of the embankment. Lars had knelt down and grasped him by the shirt. The workers had all gathered round. None of them would leave, but not one of them dared to say or do anything.

Those red eyes, thought Erik. *Malicious. Unpredictable.* He shuddered at the thought of what Lars would do next.

"So that's it, eh?" said Lars. "A little competition for McCormick's throne. A little competition for the princess. I could end this before it even begins."

"And then the hangman will come to mount you from a gibbet," said Erik.

"With witnesses like these?" said Lars. "They belong to me!"

"You wouldn't survive the inquest."

Lars toyed with his grip. The shirt began to tear. Erik's head and back gave way as the rip lengthened. Erik could feel the sensation, the terror, of a total loss of control. He could feel his legs slipping upon the rock. Thoughts flashed in rapid succession. The completed cathedral, its stones drenched in the noonday sun. Adaira walking with him, her chosen love, upon the moors. She was dressed in an embroidered woolen robe of Northmoorlandic blue, the hue of a sapphire, and her braided hair billowed in the wind. She glanced at him in a moment of joyous rapture.

He uttered a silent prayer.

A hand of inordinate strength caught his shoulder and thrust him away from the edge. He was slapped across the jaw, pelted with enormous fists, and kicked in the back for good measure.

Erik fell face-first upon the earth. He lay there in shock as he heard the men laughing. His freckled face was riddled with dirt, and he coughed up phlegm and spat it upon the moistened ground.

He rested there for some time and dozed off a bit. When he regained his senses, he looked up. The quarry was deserted.

He thanked God for his life.

Erik felt exhausted and lingered there a bit longer. There were lacerations and deep bruises over his face and chest. One eye was blurry and half closed. The left side of his rib cage had suffered a violent blow. He could feel the pain intensify, so he rolled over onto his back. That alleviated the frontal pain somewhat, but at the expense of the area that had felt the thrust of the boot.

Erik studied the sky. It was a sweeping tapestry of pastels with stratus clouds set against a fading azure backdrop. The sun was setting in the west.

He wondered if Lars had gone directly home and how long it would take to get there himself in his current condition. He'd miss dinner, but that would be okay as long as McCormick did not leave Adaira alone with the brute.

Why hadn't he thought of that before? He needed to get there fast. He got up with some difficulty.

Erik tried running, but the sharp pains in his rib cage thwarted the attempt. He walked a bit.

No, no, this will not do, he thought.

Erik broke into a full sprint. He pumped his arms and legs to their utmost capacity. He shouted in sheer agony. A raven burst into flight from atop a birch tree. Its cawing seemed amplified and strained.

Keep going.

As Erik neared town, he could feel his lungs begin to burn. His familiarity with hard work proved to be no preventative as his daily regimen consisted of walking, lifting, and swinging the tools of the mason's trade, not fighting and running. Running after a fight was even worse.

He thought of Lars with Adaira. Anger, like a second wind, rose in him, and he gave chase.

Erik sped through the city gate just as the portcullis was beginning to descend amid the chilly night air. No more strangers would enter Mithrendia this night.

Was this what was meant by the poets when they wrote the heart was aflame?

The streets did not teem with their usual liveliness tonight. People were sparse, and those who did walk the streets were mainly carousers or people who loitered outside the gambling halls.

Erik, despite his exertion, could not maintain this pace for much longer. The Merchant Quarter had never seemed this far away.

"Lord, do not let me be too late."

The shops he'd passed a few hours earlier were all closed. This was not unusual. But the street merchants, even the nocturnal fortune-tellers, had crept back to whatever dwelling or hovel they had come from.

You toy with the heart, Adaira.

The shutters in the living quarters above were all closed tight. Light was scarce save for that from the torches that flickered on the walls of the public buildings.

But little do you know of the harvest it will reap. A bad husband, or worse.

The people seem scared.

Erik looked up. *The moon is full tonight.*

CHAPTER XII

Beyond These Gates

"Where ye going, lads?" asked the curious gatekeeper. "Oh. Four of you, eh? Two gents and two lasses. Unarmed and on foot!" Catherine watched in discomfort as his curious eyes surveyed them. "'Tis hardly safe beyond these walls after dark."

"Our business is a private affair," said Mary.

"And my business is the clans' business," pressed the gatekeeper as his gaze from a squinty left eye lingered upon their features. The complementary eye was an orb of freakish size that seemed to swell like an optical illusion. Catherine's discomfort grew under the man's gaze, leaving her to wonder about his eye's powers of perception or if it communicated lecherous intent.

"I cannot let you pass as you are," said the gatekeeper.

Portions of the Marches were bereft of fortifications, leaving hardened, battle-scarred clan members to provide their own security in response to any threat upon the moors. The Blue Griffin, however, was not positioned near those naked breaches; it sat snugly behind town walls, allowing its residents the opportunity for a peaceful night's sleep. Here protection of the whole was paramount, and it was at rare moments like this one when an inquisitive gatekeeper seemed at a disadvantage.

"We'll escort them," answered a husky voice, "for a price."

Trackers and mercenaries lingered around the fortified gates, waiting for opportunities to line their pockets. Catherine had overheard a discussion among tavern-goers at the Blue Griffin, many of whom suspected that schemes and machinations were at play because the gatekeepers seemed to live above their means. Furthermore, the swelling of their leather purses attested to the funneling of spare coinage they received for aiding and abetting armed men in being hired.

In this case, there were three such armed men. They were long-shanked and long-armed, clad in leather hauberks.

"We need no help, thank you," said Ben with a brash coolness.

"To the moors, are you?" asked the husky-voiced knight. "Or perhaps to the western foothills? You would not last the night out there, not without our help."

Catherine studied the men-at-arms, who cast rather intimidating shadows in the torchlit night. Their negotiator wore a ribbed iron helmet with a thick noseguard. His grizzled beard camouflaged, yet could not conceal, the scarred remains of a long-ago knife wound. Swipes of pale mottled flesh ran down his right eyebrow and across his left cheek.

Catherine had not been sure if her friends would be willing to go through with this ill-conceived venture. Having seen their resolve at the gate, however, she realized that common sense must prevail.

She whispered to the others, "If we are going to do this, we cannot go alone."

"Yes, I agree," said Matthew.

Matthew had always been fidgety, at least in the months when Catherine had known him. But he became more animated when nervous, and his arms twitched about as he studied this trio of armed men, including the width of their shoulders and the length of their broadswords. "But how do we know we can trust them?"

"The name is Darrig, man-at-arms," said the knight, before Catherine could answer. "My men are Roald and Bjorn." He produced a folded parchment. "Here are our qualifications."

The parchment, which attested to his authorized conduct of trade, was signed by the local magistrate. To it were added several references with various signatures.

"You know this magistrate?" asked Catherine.

"Aye," said the gatekeeper. "All about town know of him."

Catherine glanced at Mary. She had seen a sense of determination in her friend after that improbable trip to Hamarjørn, a sense of confidence that proved infectious. Without Mary's newfound outlook, this journey, even to the town gate, would have been a nonstarter.

"What is the fee?" asked Mary.

"Ten yørn," said Darrig.

"Why, that's a month's worth of work at the tavern for the lot of us," declared Matthew, checking the meager assemblage of coins in his pocket.

"Your price is steep," said Ben.

"And yet that is the price," said Darrig, leaning upon the head of his war ax.

"Can you put a value on your life, lads?" asked the gatekeeper. "I for one won't answer for it if ye were to run off and do something rash."

"Like what?" asked Matthew. "Scale down these walls unassisted?"

"Not on my watch, laddie!"

Seeing the gatekeeper's luminous eye fixed upon them, the Rhymer Four turned their backs and huddled.

"Did you get a load of that circus sideshow?" asked Matthew. "He looks like Canon Pious's cousin."

"But does he speak truth, or is this some deceitful scheme?" asked Mary.

"Probably both," said Ben. "We've seen evidence of the danger out there, and that was before nightfall. No doubt, though, this is how they make their money. The question is, can we afford to go through with this?"

"Can we not?" replied Mary. "I refuse to believe that we came through a time portal for this and nothing more."

Catherine nodded. "If we don't go, what else is there for us? Our youth wasted in the company of tavern men who address us as 'wench' and 'lackey'?"

Ben, seeming to deliberate the conversation, was attempting to discern what its tone meant. "Okay, ladies," he said after a moment's pause. "I'm in."

They all looked at Matthew.

"And I'm going to say no?" he asked with a shrug. "I'm outvoted as it is."

Having decided this course of action, they pooled their resources and produced the requisite funds.

"This had better work," said Matthew. "Or we'll have nothing but the uneaten vestiges of food from the tavern and stale bread for the next month."

"Hardly a consideration when our mortality is at stake," said Catherine. "After all, this is a deadly quest we're on."

"Aye, a deadly quest," echoed Darrig. "Where would you have us go?"

"West," said Ben. "Into the highlands."

Darrig rubbed his beard with subtle hesitation as if deciding if the yørn were worth this type of adventure. He looked at his two companions, seeming to take their measure, and nodded at the gatekeeper.

"Aye," said the gatekeeper as he grasped the spoke-handled winch to open the portcullis. He wound the hesitant winch as the chains reverberated against the heavy oaken door. The door rose up into a fitted slot amongst the grime and dirt that coated the stonemasonry.

Catherine watched as the knights secured saddled horses from a nearby stable for their four clients. Apparently ten yørn wielded ample purchasing power.

Ben and the two young women took to their saddles with little effort, but Matthew, the shortest, had to be assisted onto his mount by one of the knights.

With the gate now open, the group of seven exited the relatively tranquil town, going into the unknown beyond.

Catherine conducted a brief survey of the others. Mary had ridden on her family farm in South Jersey and proved a suitable rider. Catherine herself had once ridden for multiple nights at a county agricultural fair. The two boys, however, were first-timers.

Catherine listened to the knights as they provided a crash course on horseback riding, talking about riding both through the gate and into the unprotected night beyond it. They barked a cache of verbal instructions in the moonlight and resorted to grabbing up the reins with a free hand when needed. Still, the armed men proved to be capable instructors, and the steeds were of a compliant disposition. After some anxious moments, the novice riders settled down into a more comfortable rhythm.

This provided an opportunity to contemplate the surprising

enlargement of this expedition from a party of four to a party of seven.

"How did they sneak up on us?" whispered Matthew.

"They must have seen us in the courtyard as we passed the entrance to the magistrate's chamber," said Mary.

"Rather, heard us," said Catherine with a sarcastic glance toward Matthew.

"Some thief in the night you'd make," said Roald, who had been listening. "Kickin' rocks into the waters of the gully. A bit o' rattlin' and a-splashin' ... waking up the whole bloody household, of all those around."

"Okay, so I tripped," said Matthew.

"And let that be the last of your distractions," said Darrig. "Stealth is a worthy substitute for strength of arms after nightfall. Particularly where we are going."

"And where do you think we're going?" asked Ben.

Even in the moonlight, Catherine could see the crease of Darrig's weather-beaten lips as they rose up in subtle jest. "To Wolf's Hollow. You said westward, did you not? Or has your foolishness abated?"

Ben scowled but did not answer.

Catherine had read about the traditional feminine practice of riding sidesaddle, but in Northmoorland, the women rode astride the steed just like the men. Here pragmatism won over foolish propriety, much to the astonishment of Europe: noblemen with mouths agape upon hearing that Northmoorlandic women knew how to shoot an arrow while on horseback.

Catherine had not yet managed to achieve such a feat. Neither had Mary. But here they rode astride like the native women. The peer pressure was daunting. Ben and Matthew had no choice but to fill their respective seats with as much false confidence as they could muster.

Their journey began well enough as they passed over grassy meadows and short, shrub-covered hills. An hour later as they entered a copse of birch and aspen, Catherine saw what looked like small beacons through gaps in the branches. There was luminance rising amid the distant darkness.

"That can't be Wolf's Hollow?" asked Ben.

"No," said Darrig. "That is Edelburg, the last outpost, the westernmost town of the realm. This is the last safe haven from the evil beyond."

They came upon an arched stone bridge, which served as an ideal vantage point of the walled town. To Catherine, this area seemed to lay upon indecisive ground, sequestered among the surrounding wilderness and rising foothills. Weather-beaten buildings squeezed together in a cramped allotment between fortified walls as if huddling before an oncoming storm.

"We are between mountain ranges?" she asked.

"Aye," said Darrig. "Donegast's Range to the north. O'Flanagan to the south. Wolf's Hollow lies in a deep gorge between them."

"The depths of Hades, they say, in that gorge," added Roald.

"Aye," said Bjorn. "The Devil's Gap."

"That sounds inspiring," muttered Matthew.

Catherine seemed unsure even of this so-called haven Edelburg as they approached its solemn walls of rough-hewn rock. The gatekeeper offered minimal hospitality while peppering the traveling party with an array of impersonal questions, followed by several of the personal variety. Somehow, amid this bewildering interrogation, her company had passed for decent people, and they entered the town gates.

"That was worth two yørn right there," said Darrig, "dealing with that prickly fellow."

Hoofs clopped against the cobblestone road, rendering stealth something to be saved for the countryside. Windows opened as curious townspeople arose from their slumber and looked about. Catherine felt like the center of attention as sentinels looked out from upper-story windows. From their secretive perches, they peeked and surmised, before whispering to their wives in a mysterious manner as if wary of something ominous being afoot. Those few stragglers upon the streets stopped their progress to stare at and ponder the mounted passersby.

Most of the buildings of Edelburg stood three or four stories. There were a few constructed of stone with gables rising like ponderous stair steps above the roofline. Others were half-timbered with posts, beams, and diagonal braces with the gaps filled in with wattle and daub. Ben had told Catherine about this curious earthy process. Thin branches called wattle were interwoven like wicker before being covered in daub, a curious mixture of moistened earth, straw, and dung. Mercifully, and for the sake of one's nostrils, the final product was whitewashed with lime.

Catherine noted that nearly all the buildings possessed enormous brick chimneys with flues poking out like the tubes of a church pipe organ. The upper floors were cantilevered over the lower floors, making them top-heavy facades that resembled a burly-armed man with thick shoulders and skinny legs.

At ground level were the places of business. Brackets of curvilinear iron jutted forth, from which lanterns or hinged signs hung and swayed in the breeze. Some brackets were composed of wooden sculptures in the image of lions or dragons to chase the evil spirits and bad customers away. Flowering plants, now devoid of their spring glory, adorned a few windowsills or dangled from the brackets, as Catherine had seen in the Marches.

Despite its residents' distrust of strangers, Edelburg looked much improved the longer a visitor observed it. After all, this town was the last safe haven before the untamed lands. Catherine thought of down pillows, a thick blanket, and a roaring fire at the inn. Part of her wanted to stay.

Still, her heart beat with the excitement of facing the unknown. The destination of this troupe lay not in someplace comfortable but in the highlands beyond with their coniferous alpine forest carpeted with a mysterious, low-lying mist and populated by such creatures as described by the lyrical folklore of the peasantry. Catherine had heard a few tales in the Blue Griffin, but her friends remained largely ignorant.

Just outside the comforts of town, her company turned onto the neglected trail leading to Wolf's Hollow. The rolling terrain shifted in the direction of the heights. Open grassland sprang up with rocks like large roots, and copses of aspen, birch, spruce, and fir appeared to the left and then to the right. The pace of the horses slowed, yet they seemed ill at ease. The screech of an owl and the distant howls of wolves caused a nervous Nellie to spring into a gallop. Some minutes later the group caught up to the knighted rider, still coaxing his steed with calming reassurances.

"Bjorn?" said Darrig. "What is it?"

"I've never seen Baymoor spooked like this, sir."

"'Tis this place. Few ever go this way, and for good reason."

The riders took turns holding lanterns. The rough patches of earthen road had been eroded by gullies of stormwater, exposing large tree roots that the horses had to step around.

What crept upon them seemed anything but subtle. They were engulfed in forest and in an eerie, ethereal mist that hung in the air like the cold-drawn breath of something old and otherworldly. The vapor lingered everywhere, not just in their line of sight but also in the moistened touch of the fingers, the stagnating stench in the nostrils, and the languishing torpor of the mind's eye. One's very thoughts seemed encroached upon by a bewitching presence.

"We were fools for coming here," said Bjorn.

"Aye," said Roald. "The mist, it whispers to you. Foul things. Awful things."

"Oh, what superstitious nonsense," said Matthew. "It's nothing more than a thick fog. Your minds are playing tricks on you."

Catherine disagreed with Matthew, but she quietly kept watch on the hired escorts, who continued their pace without threatening to abort their mission. The men were right. She could feel a strange presence in the thick night air.

Matthew's verdict did not remain unchallenged. Fortune favored a macabre motif. Vultures, defying their diurnal curfew, circled overhead and swooped down some fifty yards beyond where they were traveling. The vultures perched upon a stone-walled enclosure about six feet high that opened at an iron gate. At each end of the wall opening, a bedeviled gargoyle sat upon a globe-like mound of stone and glared at the strangers. Rather than warding off evil spirits, these stone objects seemed to be the embodiment of their presence.

The vultures took to flight as the horses approached. Catherine saw Ben dismount before sweeping his lantern in a slow arc to observe the monument. The sculptures and wall were besmirched with mildew, but the original carvings, still visible, had been the tinkering of a master artisan. Emaciated torsos revealed the bony protrusions of the rib cage, and upon each sternum rested a long, pointy beard. The beard slipped through the clawed vise of a hand, if one could call it a hand. Scaly fingerlike appendages captured an angular chin in a moment of demonic contemplation. Thin arching eyebrows swept over vacant eyes. Prominent teeth of unnatural length protruded through the lips in a reptilian way, yet a pair of horns were mounted on the forehead in the manner of a satyr save for their length. The horns rose in a linear fashion for three-quarters of their length before bending about a radius.

"Early thirteenth century by the looks of it," said Ben.

"And how do you know this?" asked Mary.

"I studied art history. The detailing is High Gothic."

Curiosity seemed a momentary cure to the brooding enchantment of their environs. Part of the wall was a spindle-topped gate with an array of fog-piercing spikes. Ben attempted to swing the gate for a better view, but the hinges had rusted in place. The gate was suspended in an open position, and apparently had been so for some considerable time, as if it were permanently beckoning the foolhardy to enter.

"Yo! What is that?" asked Matthew, pointing.

Catherine looked at the object of his gaze. Just beyond the gate was a wooden stake impaled in the earth. It rose up six feet, and from it hung a type of sign. The sign consisted of a gable roof in miniature. No more than an arm's length, this canopy shielded something below.

"It's an Orthodox cross," said Ben.

A long vertical leg was intersected by three crossing members, two at top and one at bottom. It should have been a crucifix with an image of Christ's body, but it was covered with the corpse of an animal.

"No," said Matthew. "I mean that."

Just below the miniature roof, a sculpture of a wolf's head seemed to be placed, out of context with the religious imagery. Except the head was too textured for stone. Ben walked up to it and touched the coarse fur and canine teeth.

Ben glanced back at the others. "This is taxidermy."

"Creepy," said Matthew.

Perhaps the fog is settling in on Matthew as well, thought Catherine.

"This," said Darrig, "is the entrance to Wolf's Hollow."

Catherine surveyed the faces of her friends in the moonlight and found a sudden lethargy in the expedition's momentum.

"Remind me again, gang," said Matthew. "Why are we seeking one of the inhabitants of this place?"

"Um ... to get back home?" answered Mary with a sarcastic tone. "The witch said that the portal is known to appear at a nobleman's house in the hollow."

"What nobleman would live up here?" asked Matthew.

"I was thinking the same thing," said Ben.

"What witch?" asked Darrig. "We burn witches in Mithrendia—the very enemies of Holy Mother Church."

"Aye!" said Bjorn. "Smoke 'em, roast 'em like a boar on a spit, till nothin's left but ash."

"How barbaric," said Mary.

"Where does this witch live?" asked Darrig.

"I cannot say," she answered with apparent relief. "I was led to her lair blindfolded. The others here have never met her."

Darrig seemed doubtful as if Mary were hiding something. Catherine could sense some hesitancy mounting in these men for hire. The realities of Wolf's Hollow were weighing upon them all; she feared the knights might abandon her and her friends. Her party had been stubborn and foolish at the first, but warriors such as these were an asset to have alongside.

"And what of this portal that will take you home?" asked Darrig. "It sounds like witchcraft."

Catherine exchanged glances with Mary.

"The portal leads to unspeakable riches," blurted Mary.

Great, thought Catherine. *Mary speaks without thinking*

things through sometimes. Now I must say something, anything, of substance to bolster Mary's subterfuge.

"Riches? What portal?" asked Roald.

"What are you talking about?" asked Matthew.

"Have you not heard of the riches of Wolf's Hollow?" asked Catherine. That part was true, if one believed the legend spoken of by the patrons of the Blue Griffin. Evidently Matthew had been out of earshot during that conversation.

"No," said Matthew.

"I did not ask you," said Catherine, turning toward the knights.

These men-at-arms, of course, were thinking of a treasure trove. But what if there was none? What if the legend had no veracity?

"Its place is marked by blue flame," answered Bjorn. "At least that is what the legend states. Corpse light, it is called, for Wolf's Hollow is known as a place of the dead."

Catherine had not expected this type of revelation. Her lips began to move, but they uttered nothing. She glanced blankly at Mary.

"And the witch spoke of blue flame in the hollow," said Mary with a wink. With catlike dexterity of her intellect, she seemed to land on her feet.

"Well, well," said Darrig with a lustful look of greed. "Some hoarder has left an ample supply of wealth, and all we have to do is find it. Lead on, fair ladies."

"Where to?" asked Matthew.

"The nobleman's house," said Roald. "Wager you six pints of ale, this road will lead us straight to it."

Catherine could once again see the skeptic at work in Matthew thoughts. "And I would wager that there is no nobleman to be found this night," said Matthew.

Roald rode up alongside him, spat into a hand, and extended it to Matthew.

Catherine saw Matthew glance over at the saliva-coated palm and wince. Before he could decide, the warrior clasped his hand in a firm, lubricated grip.

It was only when Roald rode on ahead that Matthew used the horse's back as a personal handkerchief.

Catherine rode between the men-at-arms as they made their way up a steep grade for another three miles. The trail cut a swath into the mountainside, leaving a precarious drop to their right. The hovering mist stretched its way across their path, rendering Catherine's peripheral vision unreliable, and thus it was difficult to ascertain where the shoulder of the road transitioned into the shadowy depths.

She joined the other riders as they cheated toward the left edge of the trail. This choice was precarious as well, for wolves howled from somewhere behind them, on the steep embankment above. No matter how fast the horses galloped, the wolves made haste and seemed to find a favorable path for gaining on the riders.

As the horses picked up the pace, the pursuit took on multiple fronts. Catherine sensed that something was in the mist and that, whatever it was, its influence was one of bewitchment. It seemed to settle in during a momentary absence of communication; it seemed to thrive on fear. It whispered to her, not as an audible transference, such as the tickling of vocal chords upon the wind, but like prying fingers in her mind.

She did not immediately comprehend—how could she?— that her thoughts were not always her own. It—whatever *it* was—possessed a subtle power to contaminate, to coerce. The quiet voice said that her life as she knew it would soon be forfeited, that her will would be subjugated to the will of another.

Her emotions flooded with thoughts of abject helplessness. She fought them while attempting to focus on externals, but the howling did not allay her fears. She was being attacked from within and from without. It was difficult to concentrate. Memories of abandonment, of loveless foster homes, resurfaced.

"Nobody ever wanted you," it whispered. "Nobody thought you would amount to much. You were merely a means to your foster parents' compensation. A check in the mail."

She wrestled with this sudden onslaught of despairing thoughts. How could this be anything other than her own mind? Who could possess such information about her personal history, particularly here in Wolf's Hollow? And yet why would she be bombarding her mind with thoughts like these in a circumstance such as this? Why attempt self-sabotage in a flight-or-fight situation?

Catherine felt overwhelmed. The reins shook in her hands. She began to lose control of mind and body.

"Bloody wolves!" said Bjorn.

The audible sound of the mercenary snapped her back to attention. She sat upright and jostled the reins before reengaging them. Catherine realized that a battle had erupted in her mind. With a dogged, diligent focus, she fought back and reclaimed self-mastery.

She felt herself again, at least for the moment. Her enemy, however, was cunning. A silent force wrapped its misty fingers around her shoulder and pulled her toward the deep ravine.

She shrieked.

Darrig reached over and grasped her left arm. "Whoa! Steady!"

Catherine gathered herself in her mount.

The horses, however, were spooked. They exerted their

massive sinewy quarters in a life-preserving gallop and begrudgingly slowed at their masters' incessant beckoning. Two of their number leapt off their front quarters, jabbing their hooves at the menacing night air.

"You were about to go broadside, girl," said Darrig as he glanced into the fog-laden ravine.

"Something in the mist grabbed me," said Catherine.

Darrig had fixed his attention upon adjusting the reins of his horse, but a brief stare communicated a lack of faith in her report.

"Much about this place is difficult to explain," added Catherine.

The wolves sounded louder now.

"Can we go? Now?" asked Matthew as he struggled to master his steed. Roald rode over to assist as Mary coached Ben in the particulars of equestrian mastery.

"Look!" said Bjorn. Some forty yards behind them, on the ridge of the embankment, a pack of wolves appeared.

Catherine glanced back as the wolves snarled and salivated, slobbering over elongated enamels that, even in the distance, looked as if they had been filed to a sharp point.

"I have never encountered this breed," said Darrig.

With pointed tufts at the ears.

"Nor I," said Bjorn. "Much bigger than the lowland wolves."

And a grizzled beardlike growth under their snouts.

"A dire wolf, perhaps?" said Roald.

And wielding wicked bloodshot eyes that bespoke of fiendish intelligence.

The horses continued to whinny.

"Let's get them moving again," said Darrig, apparently realizing that the bestial sense was one step ahead of the master's.

Catherine had little trouble in rousing her horse to a

life-or-death gallop. The road gnarled and twisted around the extension of the mountainside, covered in alpine forest and the occasional outcrops of snow-crested dolomite. It rolled around the embankment, hiding from view their immediate destination.

The wolves followed along from above, just a bit off pace of the steeds. Catherine glanced back with greater frequency. Circumnavigation of the winding road gave the wolves a shorter radius to work with. One of the pack, perhaps braver than the others, jumped from the ridge onto a boulder of dolomite with the sure-footedness of a mountain goat. From there it sprang down upon the riders, knocking Bjorn off stride and sending him reeling to his right.

The knight had chosen the studded leather of a hauberk without the accompanying chain mail, presumably for ease of movement. This left his neck exposed, where the wolf buried its teeth. Bjorn groaned at the acute shock of pain and attempted to swivel his right arm back to grapple with the animal. This wolf weighed nigh as much as he did. Bjorn's legs fought to remain in their stirrups.

Catherine struggled, like the others, to master her reins while surveying the shocking scene before her. The ferocity of the animal appeared to surprise even this hardened fighter. The wolf gnashed and gnawed its teeth into the man's flesh with seemingly little regard for its own safety as its entire body swung about his torso. Bjorn reached for his dagger, but it was sheathed at his left hip. As he twisted around on his mount, his boot lost contact with the left stirrup. He tumbled off the terrified horse, which continued to surge forward along the trail. Bjorn collapsed onto the wolf, dislodging its grip upon his neck. A quick thrust of the dagger into the animal's underbelly elicited a raging shriek. The beast surged toward his neck again. A second thrust drew a dying whimper.

"Bjorn?" called Roald from well beyond.

Catherine felt an instinctual pull to help, but her horse would not respond to her attempts to corral it. She swung back on her mount to see Bjorn lying sprawled out upon the trail, his arms and legs splayed in a helpless manner. He appeared to teeter on the brink of consciousness.

"Bjorn!" she said with heartfelt sympathy for her comrade, whom she had scarcely known.

Fifty more wolves, their eyes filled with a peculiar look of hate, were making their descent from the ridge. Encouraged by their pack-mate, they had found a path down to the trail.

This time the horses refused to slow down, even to a canter.

"Leave him!" said Darrig with a desperate shout.

"Leave him?" Mary gasped. "How could we?"

"Have mercy," said Catherine. "Roald?"

Only Roald's horse slowed a bit, to let the riderless horse catch up. Roald grasped his ax, shifted his shoulders as much as his mount would allow, and hurled it. The ax struck its target, felling a wolf. But where one fell, others were present to refill the ranks in overwhelming numbers.

"Darrig's right," admitted Roald, whose long sword was too unwieldy to throw from a mount. "We cannot save him. There are too many."

Catherine looked back with grave sadness. Several wolves descended upon their fallen prey, who was soon rendered a corpse. The rest of the pack continued to track the horses, which by then were a hundred yards ahead.

The riders rounded the bend, and then the trail forked off from the mountainside. It narrowed into a thin strip of land not more than thirty feet wide. A left embankment emerged, giving way to a valley. Snowy, windswept treetops could be seen in the depths below.

"There! Ahead!" shouted Ben.

Some five hundred feet beyond, they could see a stone tower crowned with a reddish double-pitched roof. It crested in a steep ascent at the peak, where two finials, bulbous at bottom but tapered to a fine point on top, perched as a permanent rebuke of the thunder gods. A timber hoarding cantilevered out from the top of the wall's perimeter to meet the lower roof. From this vantage point, guards had a secure place to view the trail, and if necessary, they could fire a volley of flaming arrows or drop boiling pitch upon the unwelcome visitor. The lower half of the hoarding, almost chest high, was fitted with vertical clapboards. These opened above to a gallery of posts, and between posts sprang a series of ornate Romanian arches.

To Catherine's astonishment, the wolves were gaining on the horses. They were a mere fifteen yards behind now. It seemed inconceivable. She had never heard of a canine outrunning a horse.

She began to scheme, and hope, about the sanctity of their mysterious destination. A large stone vault breached the tower at its base and formed a tunnel. As the riders approached, she could see that it was wide enough for three rows of cavalrymen to pass through with ease. The portcullis had been raised, perhaps some time ago. Spiders had added their own elaborations between the timbers above, and an overlay of fungi covered the stone where water had collected and dripped down the edifice. In fact, the gloomy guardhouse appeared to be deserted save for the light from the torchlight sconces mounted on the walls. As the party rode into the arched vault, the only audible sounds were the clip-clops of hooves and their own nervous mutterings.

Seconds later, the party exited the vault onto a short-walled causeway. It appeared to be a bridge of considerable length.

"The wolves!" shouted Ben. "Can you believe it?"

Catherine glanced back.

"They're slowing down."

In fact, the pack had slowed to a deliberate gait and meandered around the front entrance. The wolves, for some reason, refused to enter the vault.

"They won't enter," said Roald. "But why?"

"Just be grateful," said Catherine after a long exhale.

The horses, sensing that they were out of danger, slowed to a canter and then to a trot. The riderless horse kept up with the company and marched in stride with Roald's steed.

Catherine sensed a general relief among the party, mingled with grief for the loss of a comrade in arms. Darrig maintained a stoic demeanor. Roald's face, however, shook with the ravages of despair. Catherine could only pretend to surmise what adventures Roald and Bjorn had had together over the years and what battles they had fought together.

Nevertheless, she could share in the grief, even if for other reasons. She and her friends had chosen this perilous adventure, though they had been ignorant of what awaited them. Still, the guilt was palpable. Catherine could see it on her friends' faces, especially Mary's. She wondered about Bjorn's family and if they were awaiting his return.

Catherine glanced back and saw that the wolves still would advance no farther. Her mind swirled with one thought after another.

The shock of seeing a human being killed would have remained an unequaled traumatic experience in her brief life if not for that deadly disturbance on campus. Murder had previously been somewhat of an abstract concept—something *there*, not *here*. And whether analyzed ad nauseam on a cable news outlet or simulated to gory effect in a movie, it remained *there*.

Catherine imagined that this was the experience of her friends as well. Now the concept of having one's life taken through violent means had become a personal matter of extreme poignancy.

The Rhymer Four had witnessed loss. All of them. Loss of home. Loss of family. Loss of contemporary society. However, to witness a premature death in person was a life-altering event, a mental point of no return. It shocked Catherine's senses; it grieved her soul to its core.

Now it had happened twice.

Catherine felt terrible about her helplessness and having abandoned the fallen knight. It added yet another chapter to her overburdened heart, still grieving the loss of anonymous peers on Chestnut Street. The accumulation of her thoughts and sensory perceptions felt like a blur. In this momentary jeopardy of oblivion within the foreboding lands of Wolf's Hollow, she wondered if this was but a waking dream.

"Look!" said Matthew, pointing back toward the gatehouse.

Catherine could see smokelike eddies around the vault entrance, in a manner strangely reminiscent of the portal. Beyond, the wolves continued to linger, for some reason refusing to move forward. They had been in ferocious pursuit only minutes before.

"How can this be?" asked Matthew.

Catherine surmised that everything in Matthew's mind had to have a natural explanation. He'd rather doubt his own senses than believe otherwise.

"My word!" said Ben. Rather than watching the gatehouse, he seemed to be staring at the path ahead.

"What?" asked Mary. "Oh ..."

Catherine turned from Matthew's vantage point to see what the others were looking at.

There was a faint blaze of torchlight suspended from something dark, something massive.

CHAPTER XIII

A Decisive Set of Circumstances

awoke once again to the gnawing awareness that I was still a stranger to my memory and a prisoner to my host. My last recollection was my collapsing upon the Persian rug in the library. Someone had carried me to my room, and here I lay, staring up at the coned ceiling high above my four-poster bed.

"Ah, Herr Hunsdon," said Constantine, who had just come in with some linens. "Back among the living again."

I sat up in bed. "Tell me, my friend, how long have I slept here this time?"

"Two days since we found you passed out on in the library."

"Who moved me?"

"The guards helped me."

"I failed to ask you before, but how did you first learn of my name?"

The old man went away for a moment and soon came back with a scroll. Formerly sealed, it now lay open. It appeared to be some type of contract written on parchment and, judging by the inkblots, the product of a quilled pen. At the bottom of the document, the signature bore the name of Herr Hunsdon.

"We found this document in your possession when you hit your head outside," said Constantine. He lifted a finger to his lips. "And we also found these."

He handed me some keys, a handkerchief, and a leather wallet.

Constantine whispered, "I confiscated these items before the guards could discover them. Otherwise you might not have seen them again. The master knows only of the parchment."

I thanked him profusely, but I was curious as to why he had done this.

"Anya and I know that you are here for a reason."

"What reason?"

"Only God knows that answer," said the elderly man. "Meanwhile, we are here to help you get back on your feet."

I nodded my appreciation and unfolded the wallet. It contained what appeared to be paper currency and some forms associated with commerce. These included three pieces about the size of playing cards that were made of a curious material. It was strong, flexible, and thicker than ordinary paper. Two of these pieces were embossed with lettering. Only I could not make heads or tails of any of these items—not the embossing and not even the currency. The lettering and images had been damaged beyond all recognition. It was odd how these items had been defaced. It was not from water or even acid. I contemplated these findings but could not find a rational explanation.

"You are English, ja?"

Again, my token identity would have to serve for now. "Yes. Where are you from?"

They had come a long distance from their homeland, which was along the western edge of the Black Sea. Traveling west along the Danube and north via the Rhine, their master had first settled in Germany.

They stayed there some years. Then their master realized that better profits, lower taxes, and less bureaucratic oversight could be afforded in the far northern climes. And so the lord's entourage had landed in Northmoorland eight years ago.

"Lord Dominus Berbery?" I asked. "Does he not know that his Christian name is a Latin reference to the Lord? Does he make himself out to be a god?"

"His real name is Ananias," said Constantine.

"He has taken to using that other name as of late," said Anya, who had just entered my chamber.

"He is an evil man," whispered Constantine as his bushy eyebrows knitted in consternation, "a blasphemer."

"He made his start by raiding the fishing villages along the Black Sea," said Anya. "Poor folk."

"Why target them?" I asked.

She started with a derisive exhalation as if the answer were condemningly obvious. "Easy prey."

"What did they have that he could possibly want?" I asked. "Certainly not money."

"Religious icons," said Anya. "With gilded frames. Despite their worth, the people will not sell them. The icons get passed down from one generation to another."

"Thereafter he got involved in the spice trade, and silks," said Constantine. "You know, to appear respectable. Once he became rich, he bought the two of us in the underground slave market in Varna."

I looked at them in amazement. "And you have served him faithfully all these years?"

"The rain falls on the good and on the evil," said Constantine with a shrug. "We are fed and clothed well enough. So we tend to the domestic needs of this man's house."

"Cooking and cleaning mostly," said Anya. "When Ananias was a young man, we used to hold out hope that he would change. But with the passing years, his evil has only grown."

"Have you ever tried to escape?" I asked.

"Never," said Constantine. "This fortress is always under heavy guard. I have seen others slaves try, only to be recaptured and tortured."

My heart sank at this revelation—for Constantine and Anya, of course, but also for me in my current situation.

"Why did he relocate here," I asked, "so far away from home?"

"He ran afoul of those with whom he had once traded prosperously, the Turks," said Constantine. "The viceroy placed a price on his head."

I felt restless. I shifted to the edge of the bed, and as I began to stand up, my undershirt fell to one side, revealing my wounded shoulder blade.

"My goodness," said Anya. "Look at what you have done to yourself!"

She came over and examined the three red marks.

"Oh yes, that happened to me in the library before I fell," I said.

"Before you fell?" asked Anya as she rubbed her fingers over the wound.

"I know," I said. "It doesn't make any sense. I don't recall stumbling into anything. And nobody was in the room with me at that time."

Perhaps it was some type of skin irritation. Yet how had it flared up all of a sudden?

"You were tempted by the forbidden section, ja?" asked Constantine.

I nodded like a sheepish child and confessed what had happened. I recalled my ethereal visitor and the awesome power it wielded.

"You were attacked by a demon," said Constantine. "You should have never taken something from the forbidden section of the library. It is full of witchcraft and sorcery. I had to seal that book with holy water."

"How do you know this?" I was incredulous.

"The three parallel marks," said Anya. "It is a mocking of the Holy Trinity."

Constantine did the sign of the cross across his head and chest. "God the Father, God the Son, and God the Holy Ghost."

The sincerity of these people, and the faith they placed in their convictions, left me in awe as I wrestled with my own skepticism. Nevertheless, I was at a loss to explain by some other means what had happened to me. I simply could not recall any physical object brushing against my shoulder.

Constantine and Anya left my bedchamber with a promise to return with an ointment for my wound.

I pitied my new friends for having to work for this Berbery. For their part, they seemed to carry on about their daily duties as if guided by a secret hope. I marveled at this as they performed their work with a heartiness that belied their condition as serfs.

My restless mind remained a slave to these ruminations, but I ate well that morning. My strength was returning. Today I would get a better feel for my surroundings.

From the shifting position of the afternoon sun some days ago, I had been able to guess that my accommodations had a northwesterly aspect with my bedchamber on the far north end. There was a large window at the south end of the dining room tucked in a corner, before entering the library. From this vantage point, I gathered that the castle sat upon a high cliff. I learned from my friends that a river ran along the base, hundreds of feet below. Across this deep ravine an old cathedral was set among the forested terrain of a mountainside. Its facade had three tiers of Gothic arch windows with the uppermost tier rising to a gable end wall flanked by twin spires. Unlike the other fenestrations of stained glass, the central window of that gable had been infilled with stone save for an opening in the shape of a large cross.

There were other buildings surrounding the cathedral. I wondered if this complex might have once been a monastery. I say once because it now seemed uninhabited and long forgotten. It was a misty, overcast day, and the stones of the cathedral appeared dark and damp. No light could be spared to penetrate the abandoned cross.

I stepped away from the window and entered the library. It was a windowless room save for a central oculus—a disconcerting all-seeing eye of translucent crystal in the center of the frescoed ceiling. I did not like this eye, and after the events of the other day, I no longer cared for the fresco either. Despite the library's immense size, I felt constricted by the shadows, though Constantine and Anya kept this room supplied with an abundance of candlelight.

There was something about the restricted section, however, that tugged with an insatiable will upon my thoughts. I knew that I had promised not to return there, but I must admit that I walked up to the latticed enclosure to gaze within. *Just a peek,* I rationalized. *I won't go in.*

I was startled not by what I saw there but by what I heard:

deep agonizing moans. The restricted area bordered the east wall, and sounds were coming from some unknown chamber across this barrier. Amid these human utterances I could hear the rattling of iron fetters and the metallic clanking of a large gear. Oh, those poor souls. I had not noticed their cries until now.

At that moment, there was a commotion outside to the west.

I ran back to my bedchamber window, where I heard the sound of hooves prancing upon the cobblestones. I looked out of my window to see that a host of cavalry had assembled in the courtyard about seventy-five feet below. The horses seemed anxious, and the courtyard swelled with their whinnies and snorts. Above the horsemen, along the second-floor gallery, dozens of foot soldiers bore halberds and held them aloft in a show of warmongering. Many of their chain-mailed number had already marched out through a distant drawbridge at the western edge of the courtyard.

Berbery was assembling an army.

I knew nothing of his plans, yet I could only think that they had some evil purpose. Should I escape and warn somebody about this army and about those moaning prisoners? But how? And whom would I talk to?

That evening, over a dinner of roast beef, I peppered my elderly friends with questions about the fortress.

"Have you considered that our master may let you go free once you have fully recovered?" asked Constantine.

I thought it unlikely. I was a foreigner, and he suspected something. I must find a means of escape.

"Herr Hunsdon, please remember that Lord Berbery has placed you in our care," said Constantine. "Therefore we are responsible for your security and well-being."

I had not thought of that. He would hold them accountable

if I somehow managed to depart from this place. Whatever momentum I had to execute a stratagem of escape seemed to dissipate.

Anya, who had been quiet throughout, was stooped over more than usual. She managed a smile but seemed to be in much pain. I asked after her health, and she raised her hand to dismiss my concerns. She rested against the west corner near the window.

I stood up from my chair and began to walk her way.

Constantine arrived first as was meant to be. He extended his arms, and husband and wife met in an embrace that signaled the many years of their mutual affection.

"We are old," she said. "But we still love."

In the window beyond, I could see the setting sun cast its expiring glance across the great ravine. The cathedral was bathed in the shimmering pageantry of the westward horizon, and that dull, dreary cross awoke with the lively illumination of golden rays.

But that was not all.

A bronze shield of concave design was mounted to the outside wall of the library. It reflected the waning light and angled the rays toward the window. The light fell upon the aged couple with a power that defied rational analysis. For a moment—it could not have been longer than a few seconds—I saw what I can only describe as a vision. They were clothed in phosphorescent robes of dazzling white, and a golden sash spanned from shoulder to hip across their torsos. Age and infirmity were no more; these had been replaced by a reflowering of youth and vigor. The tortured expressions of arthritis gave way to joy and serenity.

Before me was a handsome couple of no more than twenty-five. The old man's chest and shoulders leaned to the right side, but now I gazed upon an athletic build with a robust symmetry. His previously sparse head of gray was covered in a wild shock of dark brown curls, and his age spots had vanished in a youthful wink. Similarly, the deep crevices lining Anya's forehead had extinguished, becoming mirages of the past. Sagging skin about her chin and neck once again looked supple and cleansed. Her beautiful blue-green eyes shone the better for it, and rivulets of raven braids cascaded down the length of her perfectly formed back.

I was so transfixed that I had neither the time nor the notion to process the significance of this scene as it occurred.

In the next instant, however, the light was extinguished, and the dining hall was swept into shadow. Elderly Constantine and Anya, after a brief rest, carried on with their work as if nothing had happened.

I, the skeptic, knew that I had just witnessed something akin to a miracle, but was it merely a vision in my mind's eye? Was it a delusion or a fantasy? Perhaps I saw them as they once were or, more precisely, a vision of who they are and what they will become when the ravages of time no longer hold sway in the afterlife.

After some moments of contemplation, I told them what I had just witnessed.

"May God be praised," Anya said.

"Young man?" said Constantine. He seemed struck by my account.

I must admit, it felt good to be middle-aged and still be called young. "Yes, my friend?"

"We can no longer live in fear," he said. "When we do, evil wins. Come, I will tell you."

We walked back to the dining table, and he sat down beside me.

"Lord Berbery is not the original owner of this castle," he

whispered. "It was built some centuries ago, and there are hidden passages that not even he knows of."

"You know them?" I asked.

"Some, but I think not all."

"But something relative to these quarters?"

He nodded.

"Remember what you just saw through the window?" said Constantine.

As if I needed reminding. "I saw you and Anya."

Constantine's bushy eyebrows leaned in toward me. "Not just us. What else?"

"The cathedral," I said.

"Ja. Now look to the mosaic."

"The mosaic?"

"It is concealed by Persia. Set it free. Let it shine forth again."

I looked to the window again. Night had set in, and with it had risen a full moon. The vision of light had been swept away by darkness.

I could hear heavy bestial breathing just outside the vestibule door, the door that Constantine and Anya normally came in through and left from.

Constantine got up to leave.

I tried to stop him, but he held up a finger to stay me. He withdrew from his inner garment a silver amulet attached to a leather necklace. This he placed around his neck. Anya did likewise with her own necklace.

They both embraced me.

"Go in peace," said Constantine.

"May the angels protect you," said Anya.

And with that, they departed from my presence. The bestial breathing ceased for a moment as I heard their departing footsteps along the corridor. But as I crept close to the door, the breathing started again, followed by a hellish snarl that reverberated in the corridor.

I jumped back like a frightened cat and retreated into my bedchamber. Within a moment I had secured the door and stood before the fire. There I did nothing but listen. The sentinel snarled a bit more, but finally its lumbering resonance died down. I could hear the crackling of the fire, but behind me there were shouts outside my window. I walked over to see about the commotion.

A foul smell emanated from the courtyard below. The stench of beast. An army of men had been replaced by a company of wolves. Werewolves. Shape-shifters. Hundreds of them. Wild, uncontrollable, and howling into the cold night air. I shivered as if buffeted by a cold blast.

The yapping and howling was like a sensory overload of discordant sounds, a cacophony of unrestrained anarchy. And yet when Berbery walked in their midst, the wolves made way with the discipline of soldiers before their commanding officer. His form was something between that of man and beast, burly and stout as before, but his fingers were elongated, and his mustachioed face was covered in stalks of the blackest hair. He looked up, I think, but I darted away from the window to avoid eye contact. For I did not want to arouse suspicion.

Was I too late? Curiosity got the better of me, and I looked again.

There was no doubt now. Berbery glared at my window, as did some of the other werewolves. Berbery saw that I knew. But what would be his response?

Time to act.

I left my room, and I could again hear the unnatural rhythms and guttural outbursts of my gatekeeper beyond the vestibule. I turned into the dining room and then the library.

The Persian rug lay under the broad legs of an oaken desk.

I rolled it up from one side and discovered the mosaic tile floor, little square pieces, hundreds of them, about an inch in length, arranged into beautiful patterns in many colors: turquoise, white, red, gold, and brown, as well as many shades in between. The floor's design was of the Byzantine style, and it appeared to depict an assembly of the saints. These persons were attired in body-length robes, and their faces gazed at me with a peaceful solemnity as if quietly delighted at being recognized after many years of solitary confinement. They stood before a baptismal fountain, but I could only make out its lower regions. The rest of the mosaic lay under the desk.

My sentinel's erratic behavior was escalating. It was beating on the door as if it wished to come in. Either it did not have a key, or in this crazed animalistic state it did not know how to wield it. I knew not which, and had no time to deliberate upon it.

I had noticed before that the door, when opened, swung into the vestibule rather than the corridor. I ran into my bedchamber, where I had seen an iron poker by the mantel. The narrowness of the vestibule was to my advantage as the poker was of sufficient length, owing to a deep-set fireplace. It was also thick and heavy, which made the chore of stoking a fire difficult unless one had muscular arms, but was advantageous for my intended use. I closed the bedchamber door, raised the poker up laterally, and jammed it into the outside face by the doorknob. From there I lowered the opposite end to brace against the vestibule door.

My would-be assailant's thumps and knocks made it psychologically and physically difficult to complete the work. However, the beast seemed to be affected by the close proximity of my scent. As it sniffed and snorted, it gave the pummeling a moment's rest. This was my opportunity. I wedged the end of the poker tightly into a grooved edge in the door paneling. With that done, I fled into the library to complete my investigation. The beast, sensing my distance, erupted into a commotion of guttural spasms, which if not for the awful ruckus in the courtyard might have awakened the entire castle.

The desk was heavy and covered with books. Even with my rush of adrenaline, it proved too difficult a task to move it, so I began transporting the books to other parts of the library. With this done, I tried once more. The strain was almost unbearable, but with a last gasp, I managed to lift the desk and twist the position of the legs off the rug. Once this was done, I set the desk down with the delicacy of a brute.

I dropped to my knees and rolled the carpet. What was I looking for? I tried to recall Constantine's words about the cathedral. I must admit, in my agitated state it was difficult to think clearly.

I looked into the mosaic. I saw no cathedral, though perhaps the saints were standing inside one. *What was Constantine talking about?*

It was even more difficult to concentrate with those ongoing guttural spasms in the corridor. *I must tune it out somehow.*

There above the baptismal font was a cross mounted to a wall of stone. Of course! Like the monastery wall! I felt along the vertical and horizontal segments of the cross. They intersected at a single mosaic tile of pearl white. The joints of this one particular tile were missing the setting grout that the others had. I pressed it with my thumb, and it lowered.

The depressed tile activated some hidden mechanism near the base of the mezzanine stairs.

Something shifted.

I had not noticed it before, but below the bottom steps, box paneling of some species of fir tree ran parallel to the stairs and stopped abruptly. This transition was fronted by a short bookcase, maybe thirty inches tall, that ran under the width of the stairs and provided an interesting nook for short people or those fond of kneeling.

Certainly I had noticed the quaint low-lying shelving before, but the paneling had been painted to blend in with the bookcase. It was only upon close examination that I noticed a small joint, a narrow gap between the back of the case and the paneling. I saw darkness within this gap. But there was a depth to the darkness.

Unlike the desk, the short bookcase was not very difficult to move. I slid it away from the paneling. The hidden side of the paneling, which had faced the back of the bookcase, had given way. The tile mechanism must have folded it back. I saw a rectangular hole in the floor. It was half the width of the stairs and little more than the breadth across my shoulders. A musty smell emanated from the hole, the smell of prolonged disuse and poor ventilation.

I grasped a candelabrum from a nearby table and returned to the hole. The light illuminated a circular stone staircase below.

I turned back toward the direction of my bedchamber. The beastly eruptions near the vestibule were increasing. It seemed that other beasts were assembling in the corridor. And they sounded ravenous.

There was but one choice. I fought my claustrophobia and slipped into the hole. There was no time to hide my tracks, so I descended onto the stone steps. These cold stones formed a staircase, like an unending array of pie-shaped wedges, orbiting about a central pillar. I had to watch my footing to avoid the bones of rat carcasses. And lest I fixate upon my feet, there were large spiderwebs to dodge overhead.

Four, five, or perhaps six times I completed a full circular revolution in descent before I heard the sound of water. But I knew that this place was too high in elevation to be level with the riverine valley.

What was it?

Something about this stone staircase jogged a memory. I recalled a portal.

The circular staircase emptied into a tunnel. Though ample in width, the tunnel was low overhead. It was about chest high, and the gradient was steep. I could not see where it led.

I could hear the echoing howls of the shape-shifters overhead. Surely they were in the library by now, if not on the circular staircase.

I stepped, or rather bent down into the tunnel. My feet stumbled into the shallow, freezing cold water. This was shocking enough, but I had not expected the stones to be slick—as slick as ice. My feet gave way, and I landed with a thud on the side of my pelvis. The waters doused the last light of the candelabrum, and I slid cleanly down into the depths of darkness. My torso tilted one way and then another in a helpless abandonment of self-control.

What was worse, shape-shifters giving chase, utter darkness, claustrophobia, freezing waters, or a descent approaching free fall?

I slid with great speed down into the depths of the watery tunnel as reflexive shivers coursed up my spine. I could see nothing and could discern nothing other than the sound of rushing water and the echoes of my heavy breathing.

The steepness of the grade leveled out after some moments. The tunnel wove to my left, and my body careened into the wall. It took a hard shove to move off the wall of rock just before the bottom seemed to fall out. I slid, or nearly dropped, for several seconds. I could feel my stomach as if it had surged into my chest.

Then the grade curiously reversed. Momentum pulled me uphill, but I was slowing down. Where was the summit? Would I reach it, or would I become stuck in the pitch-black tunnel?

Meanwhile, I had lost track of my pursuers. I doubted the wolves would immerse themselves in a flume ride to nowhere, but if they shape-shifted back into human form, who knew what they'd do.

Though the water ran unabated, I lost momentum on the ascent. The implication was petrifying. If I fell back to the bottom, I might never get out of this blind, watery tomb. I reached out, swinging my arms into nothingness, until at last my fingers grasped hold of the rock on tunnel's left side. I pulled with all my might and crawled to the top several feet beyond.

I succeeded only to slide headfirst, on my belly, down another descent. This seemed like minutes but was probably mere seconds. With the speed at which the water was moving, I could not have stopped my progress by any means.

The tunnel at last gave way to the cold night air. I managed to flip my torso over and move onto my back, but my trajectory was still headfirst. Ironically, this gave me a view of what I was leaving. Far overhead in the heights, I caught a momentary glimpse of the castle, awash with torchlights and surely that raucous assemblage of beasts I had witnessed before my departure. I worried for my elderly friends. *May those silver amulets keep them safe.*

I must be crossing over the river now. The knee-high walls on either side were sufficient to prevent my fall from a prone position, but they were built for the continuous supply of mountain water rather than human transport.

I slid upon the smooth stones of an aqueduct. I could

imagine the tiers of arched vaults rising from the riverbed and forming a magnificent bridge to civilization. Could it be near?

To my profound dismay, the aqueduct reentered the darkness of the abyss. I was back into the depths of the rock, but this time, or so I presumed, on the south side of the river, well under the monastic ruins that lay perched atop the cliff.

Adrenaline helped me fight off the contagion of the cold wetness, but I hyperventilated from the shock of reentry: a return to darkness, a return to claustrophobic encapsulation. I was back inside a tunnel. One of the worst aspects of torture is the recognition that it will resume.

Nevertheless, the reentry triggered something. Snippets of memories about another subterranean experience began to flow through my mind. I wrestled inwardly with myself, trying to retrieve anything that spoke of my past life.

I began to focus less on this never-ending watery transport into the great unknown and more upon any vague memory that materialized in my mind's eye. This effort bore little fruit at first. Still, the linkage of thoughts was like an interconnected chain, requiring intense focus on each successive link.

I started with the obvious: the subterranean tunnel reminded me of a portal. I had descended to it from a musty forsaken basement that housed my office—an office on a university campus with lecture halls and with students making their way on foot, by bicycle, or by motorized vehicle. My office had a desktop computer, and I remembered the nameplate on the office door.

There was no letup to my descent through the icy-cold waters of the tunnel. Nevertheless, my breathing slowed. I remembered it now, the office of one Nicodemus Porter, professor of history of medieval and early modern Europe.

The portal!

The year 1526, eh? Why, I'm living in these times now!

Europe slumbers in its medieval robes and awakens to an early modern sunrise. The authority of the Church, dreamily unquestioned in its restful sleep, is shaken out of its corrupted complacency by the dawn of a reformist era: the Reformation. I'm living it! If only I can endure this torture, this watery conveyance from rock, to see the day, then I will be able to observe the transformation, to witness history in the making, to interact with the men and women who charted its course.

At long last, the watery darkness was alleviated by the cover of night. I exited the mountainside and pressed on, hopeful but with soggy fingers swelled like a prune, to the welcoming arms of civilization. Unless you have tread in my shoes, it is not possible to comprehend the joy of trading one form of darkness for another. Darkness is darkness, but dark confinement is worse. The moon, even a full one with its lustful eye for mischief, gives its light to wayward souls.

And such am I, a wayward soul.

I see it! A large town spread among the foothills. Can I escape this conveyance? Will this place provide shelter for the night?

I raised my head to have a look over the side wall of the aqueduct. The farmers had assembled these towered bells of hay. They stood ten, even twelve feet high like helmeted masses, giant works of art upon the grassy land.

My timing had to be right. Rather, it must be impeccable, as the drop is enough to shatter bones.

I could see the top of another hay bell mere yards away as the watery conveyance carried me forth.

With a decisive thrust, I grasped the wall of the aqueduct and free-fell off its side.

CHAPTER XIV

The Terrace

Berbery, the builder of a lycanthropic army, sat breakfasting upon a sundeck overlooking the river valley.

Unlike the coarse revelry of the night before, there was a renewed calm to the morning.

Berbery's keen senses missed nothing. Squirrels scurried along evergreen branches, their needles of green uplifted to the heavens. The branches flourished in a light breeze and danced pleasantly to the delightful compositions of birdsong. The stirring of cool air brought a soothing, meditative aspect to the lower terrace of the castle.

Despite his acute powers of perception, Berbery thought little of such things. Rather, he pondered his next strategic moves while indulging a voracious appetite.

"Dominus?"

"Eh?" asked Berbery between bites of a meat pie, meat

that had been undercooked on his express instructions. It still bore the hallmark of blood, which squeezed through gaps in his half-rotted teeth and stained his chapped lips. He smacked and chewed and then slurped his wine, depositing the remains upon the rare silken fabric that clothed his upper arm.

Berbery motioned to his personal guard. "Bring them here, Svein."

Berbery knew that this brutish reincarnation of a Viking, with a long, coarse beard of scrubby blond and a flowing mane, was ever vigilant, keeping an eye on his master. Whether it be saboteur or assassin lurking from flank or rear, an intruder's presence would be known before an attack. Berbery, of course, could well take care of himself; still, with such a trusty subordinate, the lord could afford to relax and focus on more important matters.

Svein, prone to extreme violence, had been rescued from execution in one of the villages. Berbery needed loyalty, and nefarious lords far too often employed a motley band of like-minded schemers and scoundrels. These types could be controlled by fear, but only to a certain point. But a man saved from the headsman's ax, now that gave rise to an exemplary form of gratitude.

The blond giant towered over the elderly couple, who needed no such intimidation as they had long served the master well. This the giant knew. Svein ushered Constantine and Anya into the lord's presence with a respectful bow.

"Ah! My old friends from Varna," said Berbery as he gnawed upon half-cooked flesh. "Tell me, have you ever been baptized?"

Their faces bore the evidence of surprise at this line of questioning.

"Ja, my lord," said Constantine. "As infants."

"And yet I hear that some are practicing this sacrament at an age of consent," said Berbery. "At least in these breakaway sects that the Church has failed to eradicate."

"You mean, my lord, when one is old enough to make the choice for himself?"

"That is exactly what I mean," said Berbery. "What do you think of it?"

"Well, my lord, I suppose my parents meant the best."

"I'm sure they did. And yet wouldn't you like to make that choice yourself?"

Constantine looked back at his wife with a quizzical expression. "We belong to the Orthodox Church, my lord. We are not Catholic, and we know little of these German protestors."

"But if you had the choice ..."

"Then ... I suppose so, my lord."

"And where, pray, is the best place to do this John the Baptist activity?" asked Lord Berbery.

Constantine once again looked at his wife. "In the river, my lord?"

"Should Svein be baptized too?"

Master and guard offered a muffled chuckle.

"If he wishes to, my lord," said Constantine. "Ja, I see no harm in it."

"Then consider this my gift to you and Anya for your long years of dedicated service."

Constantine and Anya bowed, although with their physical ailments, this proved difficult and slow.

Berbery looked over at Svein.

Svein paused for a moment and looked back at his master. The guard's large mustache twitched in the gentle breeze.

"Do you have a priest in mind, my lord?" asked Constantine.

Berbery stared into his guard's eyes and nodded.

"I do indeed," said Lord Berbery. "Your priest is … Svein!"

The giant grasped the husband and wife, one by one, in the viselike grip of each massive hand. The backs of their clothes fitted into his grasp like large knots. He surged forth across the terrace, which was an unwalled pavilion of stone, and thrust them from the ledge.

The ledge was hundreds of feet above the river basin. They tumbled head over heels into the breezy air that whipped through the gorge. Far below, the turbulent waters of the river coalesced into a foamy tirade between outcrops of rock.

Berbery could not help himself. He had risen from his seat and darted over to the edge of the pavilion for a better view.

Constantine, wild-eyed, reached out with a feverish determination to touch his wife as their bodies sailed in the hapless insecurity of a free fall. Her face was one of inordinate shock, but he managed to find her hand and secure it.

They made impact in the turbulent, foam-charged waters. All was over.

Berbery grinned with savage delight. He had executed his vengeance over the assisted escape of Hunsdon, but his perceptions were limited. His true hostages, his long-suffering servants, had been set free. Their ailments, their infirmity of age, they knew no more.

CHAPTER XV

A Reception at Wolf's Hollow

Roald seemed too troubled to celebrate winning his wager, and Matthew was too distracted to remember that he had made one. Having dismounted, Catherine watched as they just stood there eyeing the castle walls, which towered into the great heights. Beyond the gatehouse, at the end of the causeway, a nobleman's fortress was revealed.

"This place makes Castle Brygge look inadequate," said Roald.

"Aye," said Darrig, "but don't tell the duke that. He'll suffer no rival of lesser rank."

"How do we know that the owner is of lesser rank?" asked Ben.

"There are only two dukes in the realm," replied Darrig.

"The master of Castle Brygge and the Duke of Donegal. None outrank them except for the royal house."

"If this were my place," said Matthew, "I would not suffer the king."

Darrig and Roald stared at him.

"Aye," said Roald as he appeared to size Matthew up and find something wanting. "This place would make even you a pompous arse."

The company, for the first time that night, enjoyed a little levity at Matthew's expense.

"But who is guarding it?" asked Mary. "I see no garrison."

"Aye. If someone lives here," said Darrig, "they seem brazenly secure."

"Look," said Catherine. "The fog is lifting."

The passing of the fog was like the lifting of a veil, revealing the monstrosity in front of them. The dark stone edifice rose six stories high, but its asymmetrical array of turrets ascended ever higher: fifty, seventy, and even a hundred feet above the battlements.

Catherine took the opportunity to scout the terrain beyond the walls of the causeway. Indeed, an assault from any direction was problematic. The castle was situated on a vertical outcrop of granite that rose up from the depths of the dale. This dale, which was actually a wide gorge, appeared to surround the entire perimeter of the castle.

"The rugged mountains that surround us must be inhospitable to the movement of artillery," said Ben.

"And?" said Mary, as if anticipating more.

"The approach of an advancing army, then, is limited to this narrow causeway," said Ben. "Which, to this point, is unmanned and unsecured."

"Except for the wolves," noted Matthew as he glanced back at the gatehouse to reassure himself again. The wolves had ceased their howling and were resting upon the parched ground.

Ben nodded. "They could handle a cavalry charge."

"It is peculiar," said Darrig. "All of it."

"I've never seen anything like it," said Roald.

Catherine surveyed the edifice of the fortress, which gave an impression of possessing anthropomorphic features. The turrets were crowned with thick beards of corbels and machicolations. Course by course, stone by stone, they crept out like stair steps beyond the main wall in defiance of gravity. On top of the machicolations, carpenters had framed dwellings like aerial stations for sentinels and longbowmen. The towers wore these artifacts as grim masks with talon-like timbers fitted tightly against the stone. The turrets also bore a helm. The roofs rose into a double pitch, at first short and squatty like the brim of soldier's helmet, but then rose in a steep ascent to a ridge. The timbered masks were perforated with lids of darkness, where eyes could rove unseen.

"We're being watched," said Mary.

"How do you know?" asked Ben. "I can't see a thing up there."

"Shh!" whispered Catherine. "Listen."

There was a heavy sigh from somewhere within the castle, then another. An unnatural breathing, slow and rhythmic, it sounded not human but rather like the wind manipulating the creaking timbers of a large galley ship.

"What is that?" whispered Mary.

"Got to be the trees," said Matthew. As he looked over the ledge of the causeway, Catherine followed his gaze. There in the great deep, she could make out the rustling and swaying treetops, but the sounds had not emanated from the depths.

There was another heavy sigh, almost a groan.

Catherine looked back at the others, who were studying

the massive front door ornamented with gnarled spikes of iron. The door seemed to be slightly ajar, and the interior torchlight crept through a small gap at the jamb. But the exhalations had not come from the direction of the door.

There was yet another sigh, this time followed by an awful groan. The voice seemed archaic and disturbing as if this fortress were communicating ... something.

They all gazed up at the great stone edifice.

Catherine could hear a loud thump. A pulse emanated like a flash of lightning from one of the upper chambers, from a projecting oriel, consisting of a pair of pointed arch windows gazing outward with doubting arched eyebrows. The sculptured stone tracery surrounding the fenestrations wove upward in a knobbed helix like a boa constrictor twisting its swollen length around a slender tree trunk, squeezing, suffocating, and yet unable to cordon off ...

Another flash. The accompanying thunder sounded like the pumping of a large heart. The pumping was slow, forceful, and rhythmic.

"That's not lightning," said Roald. "It's coming from inside the castle."

"I see blue flame," answered Ben as he looked up at the oriel.

"The treasure is not buried in some plot of ground in the hollow," observed Darrig. "Rather, the place of the dead lies within."

"Inside the fortress, you mean?" said Ben.

Darrig nodded.

"Let's go in," said Catherine. She was determined, motivated not by greed but by a desire for answers, as the witch had spoken of the Lord of the Heights.

The mercenaries, seeming to marvel at Catherine's

courage, made their way toward the door to comply with her request.

"Wait!" said Ben.

A curious script adorned the transom above the entrance:

ÎNTRA TUO PERICULUM.

A mildew-like substance fed upon the crevices of the deep-chiseled Latin words, and stringy cobwebs bridged over the letters. Nevertheless, the letters were legible.

"What does that mean?" asked Ben.

"It means," said Mary, "to enter at your own peril."

"Could this explain the unlocked door policy here?" asked Ben.

"If the wolves keep a distance," said Matthew, "might that be a cue not to go in?"

"And stand on the bridge all night?" replied Mary. "I'm going in."

Roald handed his torch to Ben. The iron spikes proved problematic, but the knight adjusted the placement of his calloused hands and pressed upon the heavy door. It did not respond, not even for this well-muscled man, so Darrig had to help him. The pair of them exerted and strained. The hinges creaked, and the door dragged against the stone floor. They managed to gain enough separation for passage through the portal.

The unnerving recitation of rhythmic exhalations and thumping swept through the passage. The visitors concealed their reconnaissance as best as possible. Only the flickering of the torches and the tapping of boots upon the stone floors signaled their presence. The torchlight cut wide swaths against the oval-shaped walls, which were festooned with decrepit portraits of long-forsaken ancestors. The air smelled old and rotten.

As most of the group passed through the gallery of portraits, one of their party lingered behind. The historian was engrossed, and not for scholarly reasons.

"Ben?" asked Catherine as she walked back to see who held his gaze.

His attention was fixed upon a raven-haired beauty, and not just for the artistic quality of her rendering. Catherine marveled as the portrait came alive in his presence as if awakened from a hibernating slumber. A heaving bosom signaled a palpitated respiration. Riveting tresses cascaded and bounced over alabaster shoulders. Wide, wild eyes of dark sapphire seemed of a design to allure, and thick, pouty lips were an irresistible provocation. She teased her male admirer with coquettish eyes, a coy smile, and curls wrapped around an outstretched finger.

"She's gorgeous," said Ben.

Catherine said nothing, but his admiration had been noted elsewhere. For his merits, Ben received a swift punch to the rib cage from Mary, much to the amusement of the portrait, which gleamed at the preferential treatment.

"You're a fool to prefer the dead to the living," said Mary. "She's long decayed in her grave."

Catherine looked back at the woman in the portrait, who stiffened with the serious resolve of a rival.

"She's bewitched you," added Mary. "Your roving eyes would rather latch on to a Gothic fantasy."

Despite the lecture and the poke to the ribs, Ben stood motionless, gazing into the portrait.

Darrig, Roald, and Matthew seemed to pay little attention to such dalliances. Their focus was upon the gallery or rather whatever lay within its adjoining rooms. Just left and beyond the favored raven-haired portrait, the corridor opened into a side room. They wandered into it, followed by Catherine.

It was a reception hall of some sort. Inside, a fire, fully ablaze, appeared below a marbled mantel as if summoned out of the dead air itself. Its suddenness was matched only by its overwhelming heat, causing Catherine and the others to back away. From the flickering, lapping flames of light swept a greenish mist. Catherine thought it might be an apparition. As it glided toward them, this ethereal form developed an anthropological aspect.

"It's the lady in the portrait," whispered Catherine.

The apparition glided into the hall, entered and exited Mary's torso, and flew into the portrait. Mary appeared to be unharmed, but her facial expression was one of bewilderment.

Ben had not moved in the interim. He stood there like one who would have to be physically pulled away for his own good.

Catherine noted at least one additional reason for his mesmerism. The face in the painting seemed to twitch about, not without some consternation. The woman's skin, once a smooth alabaster, took on an ashen hue. Her full-figured lips bespoke of rotted flesh, and those dark sapphire eyes sank into the depths of the dead, leaving nothing but hollows in the bone. Her raven hair grayed into thin wisps and disintegrated.

Ben groaned as the exuberant glow of youth settled into a ravaged, cadaverous likeness. Unadmonished beauty yielded to the unrepentant spectacle of the grave.

"Look at her now," said Mary. "This specter of death is practically a hag, and yet here you stand, riveted to her portrait."

Catherine wondered if the cause lay elsewhere. Certainly there was something to be said for the visual stimulation of men, who could not resist the sight of a beautiful woman, but this place seemed to harbor enchantments.

Mary placed her hands upon Ben's cheeks and forcibly turned his face toward her own. His eyes bore a look of shock and guilt.

Neither, however, had seen what Catherine had noticed in the portrait: the embers that lingered in the eye sockets.

The air around Catherine felt charged as if saturated with static electricity. She stood at the doorway to the chamber from which the ghost had sprung. Gilded armchairs, tables, and candelabra began to levitate a few feet in the air. Plates and knives rose up as well, before crashing into walls. Flames burst from the fireplace and swirled about the room before heading for the corridor.

Something was angry.

Catherine fled with the others down the corridor, which ran some fifty feet before opening into a vast atrium. The atrium featured a grand staircase that wrapped along the outer wall, floor by floor, overlapping itself and vanishing into the indistinguishable heights above.

"Let it pass!" yelled Darrig.

They all dove onto the floor of the chamber as the tunneled flames roared overhead. The fiery mass turned upward, flooding the upper reaches of the staircase with its fury and disappearing into the distant contours above.

"Is it gone?" asked Mary.

"Yes," said Ben. He lowered his voice to a whisper. "I don't know what came over me back there."

"Well, I do!" said Mary loudly. "Men are dogs!" Her angry voice echoed throughout the vast chamber.

"We're all obliged, I'm sure," said Roald, looking back at her with an annoyed glance.

"What are you talking about?" asked Mary.

"What he means is that if anyone had not previously

noticed our arrival," whispered Darrig, "they certainly have by now."

Ben appeared to lack the appropriate words, whatever those were. Catherine saw him try to help Mary up from the floor, but she swatted his hand away.

A knocking sound well overhead distracted Catherine from further observation.

"What is that?" whispered Matthew.

Cracks appeared as fingerlike fissures in the vaulted ceiling above the staircase. Sculptures lining the landings shattered with a sudden burst. The staircase reverberated as if the recipient of seismic shock waves, while fragments of ash and rock coalesced into larger objects. The atrium took on a noxious air. Fiery yellowish stones gathered into a torrent and rained down like an indoor hailstorm.

"Get back!" shouted Darrig. "Get back against the outer wall!"

They backed against the far wall of the staircase, which afforded some protection because of the stair framing overhead.

"What is that stench?" said Matthew.

"It smells of sulfur," said Catherine.

"What?"

"Brimstone, Master Matthew!" said Darrig. "From the quarry pit of hell itself."

Fiery projectiles lit up the stairwell floor like dozens of flaming torches that had been cast aside in unison. The flames leapt up a stair step, and then another, kindled by some powdery contaminant on the floor.

"Up! With haste! Make haste!" said Roald.

"Keep to the wall," said Darrig. "We'll exit onto one of the upper floors!"

The stairs shook from the torrential impact of the rock.

Dodging this shower of spontaneous combustion required a rhythmless form of tap dancing as each step offered varyingly a terrain of cold stone and burning ember. The party kept to the outer wall, which afforded lateral stability against any wayward loss of balance. The inside edge of the staircase, however, offered an unimpeded path to a violent end: death by free fall upon the smoldering stone below.

Catherine stepped out upon the second-floor landing, away from the flaming hailstones, to gaze down the corridor. Sconces of torchlight burst aflame, dimmed, and rekindled. She saw spectral masses like wisps of monochromatic permutation—one an arterial red; another, a veinlike blue. Still others fashioned themselves in the hue of yellowy jaundice, greenish bile, or even a corpus gray. These entities of the netherworld lingered and meandered along the corridor in a most unwelcome manner.

"We must stick to the staircase," Catherine said.

"Why?" asked Matthew. "Where we can get picked off at any moment by one of those flaming hailstones?"

"Be my guest," she answered with an outstretched arm in the direction of the hall.

"Matthew! Wait!" said Darrig.

Matthew, however, had already taken several additional strides into the hallway. He seemed intent on exploring it in full, but his pace slackened when he saw the flickering torchlights.

"Don't like what you see?" asked Catherine.

"There must be a natural ventilation system somewhere," answered Matthew, "to make those lights flicker."

His words echoed through the hall as the disembodied wisps of color shifted about.

"And what of those specters?" asked Catherine.

"Some type of light projection through multicolored glass?"

replied Matthew in a tone that grasped at certainty but in truth revealed an anxious mind. "Perhaps a stained glass window."

"And where is the window?"

"I don't know."

Indeed, the stone corridor admitted no such light source. Nevertheless, amused, Catherine admired Matthew's tenacity and his stubborn skepticism.

"And what of the indoor hailstones, that portrait downstairs, and the levitated objects?" she asked with a sly grin.

Matthew seemed to hesitate as sweat cascaded down his pensive face. He stood there in what appeared to be a state of limbo without taking another step into the corridor. "If I survive this night, I'm going to wake up tomorrow with the conviction that something hallucinogenic was placed in my supper."

Catherine laughed. "Oh, so that's it."

Mary shook her head. "You're incorrigible, Matthew."

"You realize that we all share in this delusion, right?" asked Catherine.

Matthew seemed annoyed at this response. He took another step into the corridor, when something skeletal and ethereal darted toward him and moved through him. He moaned and reflexively grasped his chest.

"You're not injured, so get over it," said Mary. "The same thing happened to me downstairs."

The specters must have overheard the conversation. Catherine watched as they encamped around Matthew. The evidence for a supernatural world swept by his face one by one.

"I see wispy monochrome colors," said Matthew as he fingered the air. "Faces, even! They sneer at me."

"The last one we encountered started that hailstorm," said Darrig. "We have lingered too long."

Matthew glanced at the staircase and then nodded at Catherine. "Our path is upward."

The flaming hail, with its putrid odor, continued to fall as they made their way up the steps to the higher levels. Their passage grew more treacherous with each level as the safe patches of cold stone shrank with each step. Catherine observed the knights kicking the flaming brimstone away with their thick boots to create a navigable surface, and others followed suit.

The sudden strokes of a keyed musical instrument startled her, but Ben felt its worst effects. The historian lost his balance and rolled down several steps, until his left hand crashed into the outer wall. The young man howled, his sleeves wreathed in flame.

Mary shrieked as the two knights rushed down the stairs. Roald threw his cloak upon the fallen lad. After suffocating the flames with violent strokes, the knights raised Ben to his feet. The back of his clothes had been singed by an ember of sulfur. Mary swept the loose debris away with her gloves. Earlier, Catherine presumed that Mary wanted to punch him, but now she watched as Mary embraced the lucky fool from the depths of her heart.

"You are a fortunate one," said Darrig, "to have fallen into the outer wall. These steps are never ending, and to fall over the precipice of the opposite ledge means certain death."

The sounds of a keyed instrument began in earnest again, and the eerie melody flooded the staircase. This time Catherine was relieved to see everyone hold their ground. The musician engaged in the plucking of strings from a far end of the sixth floor. It carried a light, dainty air, more so than the dense, vibratory sounds of a pianoforte.

The brimstone ceased to rain down.

"What is that?" whispered Ben.

"A miracle," said Roald in answer to the cessation of the lethal hailstorm.

"Yes, I suppose. But that music ..."

"I believe that is a harpsichord," said Catherine.

"Oh, you didn't know?" asked Mary. "For a historian, you are certainly losing your touch."

Ben appeared to take the slight with some irritation, but Mary's desire for his safety had been apparent. This was merely part of the punishment process, Catherine presumed, which for now was open-ended.

The staircase flooded with additional keyed notes from above. Even to Catherine's untrained ear, the harpsichord music sounded like an accomplished performance played by adept fingers. The melody confirmed the light expression of keys, rendering an archaic yet beautiful composition.

Ghosts responded to the soulful melody and flooded the staircase to welcome the guests. Catherine could see them enter the landing at each of the floor levels. Specters of every macabre color imaginable painted the atrium, still smoldering from the hail, with an eerie composition that only heightened the dread of the unseen maestro.

The musical composition reached a crescendo and then came to an abrupt halt.

Catherine and her party stood at the top of the stairs and waited. For a few moments, which seemed to languish in unendingness, the castle slumbered in an uneasy silence.

She heard a loud thump such as the one they had discerned when they were outside the castle. This sound was accompanied by a hellish breathing, sick and bestial, like the burbled waters of a dank, deep primordial well.

She heard another loud thump. It triggered a flash of blue like a strobe light set at a very low frequency so that each flash carried its own measure of poignancy. She felt disoriented by its presence.

There was yet another thump and a pulsating movement with an abrupt swiftness of acceleration that was decidedly unhuman. The breathing and sucking sounds came from one location, and then another, as if the mode of transport moved the source from place to place in breathtaking succession.

"Can we possibly treat with this ... presence?" asked Darrig. "Would it give us a safe audience?"

"It is what we came for," said Catherine. Though fear held her in its grasp, her resolve had its own momentum.

"Can the witch be trusted?" asked Ben. "What if she has sent us to meet our demise?"

"I'd rather know than regret not trying," said Catherine as she stepped down the corridor.

"And I refuse to believe that it has been a wasted journey," said Mary, following after Catherine.

With the men just behind them, they made their way down the corridor, where the depths of darkness gave way to a candlelit room. There they found the harpsichord with the seat of mahogany before it vacated. Handwritten sheets of music were haphazardly scattered about the floor and furnishings. Matthew swept up one of the compositions and studied its handwriting.

"Who dares to enter my lair?"

The voice carried an echo of past centuries and had the forcefulness of a regal character.

Catherine noticed the knights staring at one another as if trying to discern where the voice had come from.

With his broadsword in hand, Roald attacked a place rather than a target as his target was still unknown and still hidden from immediate view. The sound had originated from a dark corner opposite the instrument, but the stroke severed nothing but musty air.

"Swords down!" said Darrig. "We would treat with our host in peace."

Catherine heard an internalized cackling that seemed to reverberate in the throat. The fiend seemed to be laughing.

"Will you not speak with us?" asked Darrig.

From the next chamber, which remained unlit, came the strange sounds of a tongue rasping and licking its teeth. Catherine could not see this entity, but she had a vague notion that it saw them. She would soon learn that it saw through darkness, and through skin and bone, charting the course of their beating hearts as they pumped that sanguine substance through the highways of artery and vein.

"I seriously doubt, captain," said Roald, still gripping his sword, "that this foul creature can be reasoned with."

Catherine felt the pulse of her own heart beating in rapid succession as the anticipation of some dreadful action overwhelmed her senses in the darkness.

"Will you not treat with us?" repeated Darrig.

Catherine saw a whirr of blue light stir up with eddies of high propulsion. She saw the beast in the blue light as it surged forth. Its recognition preempted any motor coordination, for prior to her reflexive instinct to retreat, it had arisen from the recesses of darkness and descended upon its prey.

Catherine gasped.

The beast had attacked one of the knights. Roald's broadsword fractured into shards in its grip, which, now freed, seized about the victim's neck. The battle-hardened warrior choked and gurgled like a helpless child, overwhelmed by a being far superior in power and speed.

"You disturb the lair of a vampyre—a vampyre of old!"

raged the beast. "I am the Lord of the Heights. My powers have swelled with the centuries."

Darrig, abandoning diplomacy, turned to help his comrade. Catherine watched in terror as he lunged toward the vampyre, which grasped the knight and thrust him some ten yards in the air. Darrig careened into the far wall. The force of the blow knocked him unconscious.

"For this transgression of trespass," said the vampyre, "your lives are forfeit!"

"Is this how you treat your guests?" demanded Catherine as her three friends gathered beside her. She knew that this was the moment of no return. There was no escape through strength of arms or flight, but perhaps they could stand on principle.

"I did not summon any guests here to Wolf's Hollow," said the vampyre. "You came of your own foolish accord."

"The witch of Hamarjørn advised us to come here," said Mary.

"Did she, eh?" replied the vampyre. It released its iron grip from Roald's neck, and the knight collapsed upon the floor, his legs splayed about in an awkward manner of abject helplessness. With Ben and Matthew unarmed and retreating from its presence, the vampyre did not pursue them.

"Would that not constitute a suitable reason to visit your lair?" asked Catherine. "For we do not come here for ill purpose."

She stood there in the full resoluteness offered by her petite frame, observing this monstrous perversion of humanity with its sunken, blood-red eyes and leathery-textured ashen skin; with its recessed nostrils and high pointed ears; with its long fingers and protuberant teeth. A living corpse, a revenant, it was the fearsome combination of life and death.

"You are a brave one," replied the vampyre as it moved

toward her, "but I need not look into your eyes to ascertain fear. For there are other signs. Your heart pumps at three times its normal rate. Your lungs strain in a rhythm of swelling and collapse to sustain your heavy breathing. Yes, I see your internal organs just as plainly as you see my face."

She just stood there motionless. This being seemed omniscient and omnipotent.

"You must wonder, and shudder, at such knowledge," continued the vampyre. "At such unwanted intimacy. Yes, I am the lover of your blood, your life force." It paused for a moment as if marveling at her courage. "And yet you do not run from me ..."

Her instinct, of course, was to flee from this beastly presence. Yet Catherine sensed an inner notion, which flew in the face of instinct, to remain still.

Catherine had once read the story of a camper who settled down for a well-earned night's rest in a sleeping bag. The camper soon had a visitor, a serpentine visitor. A rattlesnake had slithered inside the sleeping bag, cozying up next to the warmth of his body. The nearest hospital was remote from this place. Any sudden movement might prove lethal. The man remained as still as a statue. Minutes seemed like hours. They tortured the mind. He fought off every desire to twitch, to scratch, to alleviate the discomfort of lying still in an uncomfortable position as an agent of death clung to him. He managed his breathing with slow, dull, steady exertions.

And then the serpent slithered out.

The vampyre grasped Catherine's smooth chin with its bony fingers. It turned her lovely head to reveal a sensuous neckline.

"But we are your guests!" shouted Mary.

Catherine watched in horrified awe as those protuberant

canines erupted from the upper lip and honed in on her jugular vein. She screamed, "Please, no! Do not do this!"

"I cannot escape the craving," replied the vampyre. "It is my curse."

The vampyre sank down over her neck. She could feel the tips of his teeth settle upon the surface of her supple white skin. The vampyre was about to puncture the epidermis when its gruesome eyes lifted from her neckline and glanced into her face.

At this moment of peril, one overwrought with fear when she felt at her most helpless, she noted something in its gaze. It seemed to recognize some point of familiarity and pulled away from her neck. From there its inquisitive eyes roved upward. It studied the curvature of the jawline, the dimpled cheeks, the crested summit of the lips, and the smooth bridge of the nose.

Like the camper who had a serpent in his sleeping bag, Catherine struggled against every notion to squirm in the vampyre's unyielding grip. It lingered like a man, even a lover, for some moments over her wise, knowing eyes.

Then it noted her short blonde hair, now shoulder length and beautiful to look at, but somehow foreign, and the anthropomorphism extinguished. Once again, she saw an abhorrent beast as it began to lean down toward her neckline. She could hear Mary screaming and the men shouting as she considered a last reprieve.

"You don't want to do this, do you?" said Catherine calmly, as if talking in an intimate manner.

The vampyre lifted its head, and she could see the tiny vessels in its bloodshot eyes constrict, revealing white corneas, irises, and pupils that seemed human. The protuberant teeth shrank away, and the ashen skin for a moment bore the hue of a young man.

"Eleana?"

The serpent, ever so close and lethal with its bared fangs, had slithered away upon the sand, leaving a man in its wake.

But only for a moment.

"Nay, it cannot be," said the Lord of the Heights, answering his own question.

Centuries of emotion seemed to sweep across the horrid countenance of the vampyre, and he turned his face away from her gaze. He knelt on the floor, dwelling upon untold thoughts.

Catherine stepped back from the vampyre.

Ben grasped a halberd hanging from the wall and closed in on the vampyre. He swung the weapon at the creature's exposed neck.

At the last moment, the vampyre thrust an arm up, grasped the halberd, and snapped it like a small twig in his palm.

Yet the creature did not retaliate.

Ben seemed to consider what else he might do, but Catherine answered with a subtle shake of the head. Their foe was too powerful, although he appeared to suffer from some untold misery.

They stood there staring at the crouching figure, who seemed lost in contemplation. No one spoke of what to do.

And then it happened.

The vampyre darted across the room with breathtaking speed and thrust himself through a sealed window. Shards of glass flew into the night air. The creature descended into the forested valley.

Roald awoke some time later and, with Catherine's help, managed to revive Darrig to consciousness. The knights were startled to be alive and alone.

When once again on their feet, they found the others staring into a blue-lit room two chambers away. There

Catherine found thirteen treasure chests wreathed in blue flame that stood open upon the floor. Gold and silver, though abundant, were overwhelmed by the sparkle of sapphire.

"There is more wealth here than the Crown could conceive of," said Darrig.

"You live!" shouted Mary, embracing the knight as if a long-lost friend.

Darrig, seemingly shocked at this momentary display of affection, embraced her in return.

"Shh," said Matthew. "Who knows what else might linger about the castle."

"I think we're a little late for clandestine activities," said Ben. "Anything and everything in this place has to have been alerted to our presence by now."

"But of course!" answered a regal presence. The vampyre had returned with bloodstained lips. "Nevertheless, I am master here, and you need not fear me now. The thirst has abated."

Catherine, like the others, was astonished to look upon him. The beast who had left them but a short while ago possessed pale, leathered skin, parched and cracked like a dried riverbed of clay. A hoary mane of aged gray coursed from his head as similar tufts forested his beastly forearms and even the creviced lines of his palms. Now refreshed, however, the centuries-old vampyre looked not a day over twenty: a strange synchronicity of monstrosity and youth. He licked the remaining droplets from sickly blue lips that had been rendered ruddy in complexion.

"How?" asked Ben.

"I hope you will forgive me in time," replied the vampyre. "I fed on your fallen comrade."

"Bjorn!" said Roald with a grimace of disgust. He appeared

to be on the verge of violent action, but upon consideration of his target, Roald stood his ground.

Darrig tried to calm him. "Remember, he was already dead when we left him."

"But the wolves—" said Mary.

"Are subject to me," said the vampyre, "and fear my power."

"Who are you?" asked Mary.

The vampyre swept away his black cloak, revealing regal furs and a shoulder-width band of woven gold, fronted by a centerpiece of a wolf. "My name is Abelard, Lord of the Heights."

"You are no lord. You are a monster!" roared Roald. "You fed on my friend like a common vulture!"

"The life of the flesh is in its blood," answered Abelard with an eerie calmness. He seemed poised and philosophical, even in the midst of such confusion and rage.

"Aye! Blood that you took by your own admission!" said Roald.

"It is written," said Abelard, "'You shall not eat flesh with its life, that is, its blood.'[2] Furthermore, 'Whoever sheds man's blood, by man his blood shall be shed. For in the image of God He made man.'"[3]

"He condemns himself with these words," said Darrig, looking at the others.

"Aye," said Abelard. "I know that I am accursed. My sustenance condemns me. And yet my sustenance has also kept me alive these three hundred years."

Catherine was astonished, as were the others.

"Why do you speak these words, knowing how you stand before them?" asked Mary.

"I was made what you see before you," said Abelard, "against my will."

Catherine was beginning to understand that an internal

war had been, and continued to be, fought between a man and his accursed nature. "Eleana?"

"Aye," said Abelard, "you bear much likeness to her. We were to be married, and then I was attacked and became the creature you see before you. I cannot help but wonder if you and Eleana are related."

"I'm afraid I do not know," replied Catherine.

"Given this edict about blood payment," interrupted Matthew, "wherever it comes from, why aren't you already dead?"

Mary tugged on Matthew's sleeve, to no avail.

"Before arriving at this strangely civil conversation," continued Matthew, "host and guests were poised to kill one another. And yet with your powers, you seem almost invincible. Surely this judgment, or whatever it is, has passed you by."

Roald's eyes flashed with fury. "Then Bjorn will become an accursed vampyre like you!"

"Nay," said Abelard. "Your friend is dead. One must partake of my blood to become like me."

"I thought victims became vampyres just by being bitten," said Catherine.

"What strange legends are these?" asked Abelard. "You must remember that blood is the life force. To drink is to weaken. To drain is to kill."

"Drained or not, you left Bjorn's body to the bloody wolves," said Darrig.

"Nay. He lies safely in the crypt below the castle. You may gather his remains as you wish."

Darrig was astonished. "But we cannot possibly transport him home."

"Then I will make the arrangements for transport."

Darrig, perhaps not wishing to convey a sense of gratitude, merely nodded.

Abelard turned toward the gilded chests that lay open to all. "Ah. I see that you have found the renowned treasure of Wolf's Hollow. Only foolish ruffians and thieves have sought it before."

"Without success, I gather," said Ben.

"They forfeited their lives."

"Do they lie in the crypt as well?"

"After I was done with them," said Abelard, "their bones were gnawed and chewed to oblivion by the wolves."

"Hence the warning sign out front?" asked Matthew.

Abelard offered a sinister grin.

Although the present conversation carried a civil tone, Catherine had no assured sense of security while in the presence of their host. A lion, even one with a full belly, was still a lion. She whispered to the others that they dare not take of the precious gemstones and coins.

"Your entourage is unlike the others," said Abelard as he observed the two warriors and the four young people. "Your motives, though mixed, include some higher purpose."

"We seek a portal," said Mary.

"Indeed?"

"Can you tell us of it?" asked Catherine.

"Aye," said Abelard. "Witches and alchemists and sorcerers have sought for it for centuries. Sought it in vain. Lunar cycles and fiery masses in the sky and mathematical algorithms proved of no avail. None, at least none of flesh and blood, know where the portal will appear next."

"But the witch said that you would know," said Mary.

"Did she now?" replied Abelard with astonishment. "The beautiful witch of the moors?"

"Aye."

"She gives me a great compliment," said Abelard with a knowing smile.

Catherine felt despair. It had been a life-threatening journey, and to what end? "Please, Lord Abelard. Is there anything you can tell us?"

"My lady," he replied, "your presence has revived a hope within that was all but extinguished. Do not seek the portal. It is folly. Find your high purpose. You are here on this northern isle for a reason. When the time is nigh, the portal will find you. That much I know."

Catherine felt relieved. In a sense, they had found what they had come for. Hopelessness had been replaced by faith—faith that they would one day return home.

However, her protectors Darrig and Roald held no interest in portals, not with a glittering array of gemstones and precious metals to lust after.

"Take as much as you like, my friends," said Abelard. "Whatever you can carry. I have but little use for it now."

The warriors seemed to be astounded at so generous an offer. They wasted no time in gathering up all that they could carry.

Catherine, however, was not astounded. She sensed that there was decency in this accursed man, this creature of the darkness.

Abelard looked to the diamond-paned fenestrations that pierced the east wall. He could sense the imminent unveiling of the dawn.

"And now I must leave you for my diurnal rest. The chambers, even the crypt, of this castle shift about every twenty-four hours. It is but a maze to a stranger. I go where none can find me, where ancient incantations would snare the most adept of vampyre hunters.

"Depart from this place. 'Tis safer in the woods than when

you found it. The wolves of the hollow slumber. They will not bother you by day."

"Sir?" said Matthew. "One last question. What is that thumping sound that we heard? It was a throbbing echo, like a thundering pulse."

"Do you believe that a habitation of stone can live?" asked the vampyre as he glanced around the chamber. "That a house full of memories has those of its own?"

"I had not considered it," said Matthew. "Nor do I think that I am capable of believing it."

"Believe what you wish, young master," said Abelard, "but the generations of people who have inhabited this castle comprise its personality."

The vampyre looked over at Ben. "I take it that you have already met Sonya. She was flirtatious in her youth, but she is ever protective of this place. Many men fell for her charms. Bewitching, is she not?"

Catherine knew what was coming. Ben, his fingers spilling over with coins, looked down sheepishly as Mary glared in his direction. There would be hell to pay.

"The castle breathes. It whispers. It pulsates with a stout heart," said Abelard. "And it will purge itself of any unwelcome guests.

"Now go! You have my protection as you leave Wolf's Hollow. Look for me again upon the Night of the Draugr, when the prophecy will be fulfilled. The reckoning will occur when the lawless undead reconvene with their master."

CHAPTER XVI

The Lunar Cycle

Last month Lars had been in one of those moods. They came upon him with little warning. The blackness. The hunger. This scourge of rage. Savagery met volatility in a primordial way, primordial in the sense that it predated him. This *other*, somehow it had fused with him. He knew not what to think of it. It was something sinister and dark and reeking of an old decay, yet it was energized with frenzied animalism, snatching him like a violent seizure.

Social mores and employer restrictions had meant nothing that night. He had started well past his curfew at a tavern, where he had flattened an older man who dared to look upon him for a blink of an eye too many. From there Lars moved to the gambling hall, only to squander most of his modest pay on frivolous card play. He then visited the closest brothel to exhaust his last coins. Nothing quenched that feverish thirst. The anger, the disdain for the human race, would not dissipate. The moon hid behind a colossal shifting mass of cloud cover, yet it threatened to reveal an earthly rage.

Lars barely remembered his mother. His father? Not even a fragment of a memory.

Anyway, he remembered mother in sparse snippets like vague scenes. One stood out above the others: tapers lighted and carefully arranged upon a musty earthen floor. A string extended upon a linear path and then abruptly turned about a stake. It coursed across the floor until bending around another stake and weaving in a different direction. And another. And another. And then another. How could a young boy recognize the symbol of a pentagram?

Mother, attired in loose linens, her dark hair splayed wildly, sat in the center and chanted bewitching words that made no sense to his youthful ears. Something seemed to stir, and his little head twitched here and there to see. Nothing was visible to account for the stirring. Yet he heard an archaic breathing, which his nervous ears registered as close by. Mother's frenzied chanting continued. He rubbed his moistened eyes, unremitting in their release of unrestrained fear, and strained to watch Mother. She seemed not herself but a crazed person, swirling and contorting like a serpent upon the earth. She scared him, and yet somehow, despite her odd behavior, she remained his mother.

He stood there, riveted, watching, listening to her crazed chants. When his anxiety finally exhausted him, he fought the urge to sleep, but those eyelids seemed like droopy, leaden weights. His curiosity succumbed to fatigue, and he slumbered upon his straw bed.

Sleep proved a dubious partner. That night he awoke in terror as a spectral hand reached from the outer darkness like a manifesting mist of gray. It touched him upon the shoulder. It tapped its spectral fingertips along his soft neck, leaving a trio of parallel scratch marks that rendered him a shrieking, inconsolable youth in his spasmodic mother's arms. Something was marking him; something was claiming him for its habitation.

At some point, much later in life, Lars had been bitten. By a wolf or a wild dog maybe? He remembered not, but it had happened on one of his drunken binges through the Merchant Quarter. He had awakened prone on a ditch-lined street laden with the filth tossed by chambermaids from the windows. Gross teeth marks penetrated his flesh, the blood clotting into a scabby mass at the base of his neck.

It had not been a vampyre, that obscure revenant known as the draugr, though rumors of this hideous cult abounded. These demonic beings were thought to dwell in the distant Black Mountains, far south in the forbidden regions. No law-abiding Mithrendian dare stepped in that direction without express, written permission from the Crown. The fortified city walls kept the civilized within, whereas the barbaric and beastly were kept without. At least that was the protocol.

Lars's head droned on and on in a dull ache. Feeling sickly, he upchucked the remains of a meal within his stomach upon the cobblestone street. Somehow this ejection proved relieving; lucidity returned after the purge. He surveyed the wound with his fingers. His flesh had scabbed over, and the loss of blood had not been extensive. But if his assailant was not a vampyre, what was it? Some animal? Rumors of shape-shifters abounded. Yes, from the west and south, but also from the east.

There was a reason that Mithrendians celebrated the breadth and depth of the city's wall defenses like a hallowed saint on his or her feast day. Mythology, or at least its earthbound creatures, had proven a disturbing reality on this island of the far north. It was the duty of the Fifth Garrison to protect those within the walls. In turn, those who kept watch from the towers were held in high regard by the inhabitants.

A month had passed since the infestation of Lars's wound. Tonight was Allhallows' Eve. He was able to recall the incantations of his mother from years past. Not the words per se, but the tone of her voice and the fierceness of her conviction. He knew not the source of her anger, or upon whom she desired to avenge herself, for someone or something had wronged her. Somehow this angst had been passed down to him. The motives of his mother remained an enigma. He knew very little of her save that she was wild, unbroken, and misunderstood.

As was he.

Not that Lars was the type to dwell upon such things. He was no dreamer or thinker, and he lived mainly for the present. Nevertheless, something haunted his memory. Something lingered there. Yes, one of her words had stuck, and he could recall it clearly from his youth: *lycanthrope*.

The shifting cloud cover revealed the lunar mass. The master of the tides was a late arriver, but it shone in the dark night like a monarch holding court among countless celestial courtiers. The pristine northern air, such a rarity to modern urban dwellers, brought those courtiers, the stars, into clear focus. This vision was the last pleasant memory Lars could recall.

It began with growing pains, excruciating pains that accompanied years' worth of physical growth in mere seconds. Bones and sinews stretched and bulged, creating an optical illusion of receding sleeves and pant legs. The ankles broke off in agonized spasms and ascended the lower leg, only to be reattached to a reconstituted plantar structure. The moderate patch of hair on muscle-laden forearms densified into a thick black forest. Fingernails, normally bearing the dust of the quarry, expanded and curled another two inches beyond the tips of his flesh. The nose broadened into a raspy, moistened snout that breathed like an aerated, dripping pipe. The ears unfurled, lengthened, and converged into fine-tipped tufts well above the head. Enamel glistened with a luminance that reflected predatory expansion and sharpened extremities. The eyes, the windows of the soul, assumed a reflective sheen in the illuminated night that darkened the creature's anthropomorphic origins. The skeletal structure was now a canvas, teeming with a palette of fast-twitch muscle.

Lars felt empowered, even unstoppable, but at the cost of self. His thoughts dulled. As he lost control of his faculties, terror arose from within. All the frustration and all the pain of life coalesced into a blind rage.

It was then that he blacked out. His cranium had shifted, and the frontal cortex reasoned less like a human and more like an animal.

"Lars? Erik?" yelled McCormick as he peeked up the third-floor stairs, soon returning to his fur-laden seat before the fiery hearth.

"They have not yet returned, Papa," said Adaira.

Adaira knew that McCormick required his hired help, namely, the two apprentices and two household servants who dwelled above the shop, to be home by sundown. By now it had been dark for some time, and the master grew restless.

"It is not like them to be late. Well, I say that of Erik. But Lars ..."

"He is not so heedless as you think, Papa."

"I beg to differ," said McCormick as he stroked his thick, salty-red beard. He was a stocky man of forty, a veteran of the army, and still of robust build. "To be plain, the man is an enigma. He seems hardly fit to dwell in domestic quarters, let alone inside the confines of the city walls."

Adaira glared at her father with those pursed lips, which amounted to her version of a contradictory position.

"Oh, I know, I know," said McCormick. "The favorite, 'tis he?" He lowered his voice to a mutter. "Not by my reckoning, but a fine quarry master."

Adaira had stopped listening and returned to the west wall, roving from window to window as she looked down upon the deserted city street. She had hardly touched her supper, leaving her father, a widower, alone at the table. The wasting of his culinary talents seemed to irritate the surly cook, Markus, who marched straight up to bed even faster than was his usual habit. Adaira's concern for placating Markus paled in comparison to the strange absence of the young men of the household.

"I could send Markus to look for them," mused McCormick.

"And awaken the beast?"

"He's gotten rather stout. The fresh air and exercise would do him well."

Adaira often enjoyed her father's humor, but it was difficult at a moment like this. She had just entered puberty when McCormick took in the two apprentices. Now she was a beautiful young woman, the desire of men, but neither of her household suitors was presently accounted for.

Gilda, the housekeeper, checked the fire as her master rose from his favorite chair. "Will you be needing anything else, sir?"

McCormick seemed fidgety. "Are all of the openings secure?"

Adaira knew the regular nocturnal practice well. Here in the Merchant Quarter, the shutters were fastened from the inside, and doors were secured with a broad timber beam fitted through slots of iron.

"Yes, sir," answered Gilda.

The oaken front door below reverberated with a desperate knock.

Gilda, a sharp-eyed spinster, had done her best to be a surrogate mother to Adaira. "Shall I answer it, sir?"

"Nay, that would be my duty after dark," said McCormick. "However, I will ask you to summon Markus."

"Aye, sir. But I daresay Markus will be a wee cranky for he dozes off as soon as he's abed."

"On this night," answered her employer, "I daresay we'll take that chance."

McCormick had served in the army in his youth, and he still housed the weapons of that trade: pike, broadsword, and dagger. Adaira had not seen him practice in recent years, but he spoke of the old maneuvers of offensive and defensive movement. She followed him to his war chest, from which he seized a dagger, for use at close range.

She could hear the dogs howling from somewhere as her father carried a torch downstairs. The moon's light filtered through the slits in the shutters.

She could just make out the tips of a pair of boots from beyond the door. The left boot was smothered in bloodstains.

"Stand back, love," whispered McCormick as Adaira retreated up the stairs—but only a few steps.

The pounding resumed upon the door.

"Aye? It's late!" shouted McCormick. "What do you want?"

She could hear heavy pained breathing.

"We'll take no vagabonds here!" shouted McCormick. "Go! Show yourself to the Augustinian monks down the street. They may take you in, even on this dreadful night."

"It's me ..."

The voice sounded faint and weak.

Markus was half asleep and mumbling Norse curse words when he appeared with Gilda at the top of the stairs. The housekeeper tried to restrain her young charge, but Adaira escaped from her grasp and ran down to her father.

"Is it Lars?" she asked.

"No," said the voice outside. "It's me."

"Erik?" asked Adaira.

"Aye, it is Erik," said McCormick. "The poor lad sounds awful. Here, hold my torch."

McCormick removed the board from its slots and cracked open the door. The young man, who had been leaning upon it, collapsed upon the cobblestones.

The full moon illuminated the lad's fallen profile. His clothes were torn, tattered, and drenched in a disturbing concoction of blood and sweat.

"By the Black Mountains!" said McCormick. "What has happened to you, lad?"

With some assistance, Erik arose and sat upon a knee. His chest heaved with pained convulsions, and he struggled to speak. "Lars ..."

"Lars?" shrieked Adaira. "What has happened to him?"

Spittle poured from Erik's lips. "Not ... here?"

"Of course not," she answered. "Where is he?"

"Cannot ... trust ..."

McCormick knelt down to examine the wounds on the boy's chest and arms. The bruising and lacerations were severe. Adaira covered her mouth when she saw that one eye, half closed, had swollen and taken on the appearance of a deformity.

"Did Lars do this to you?" asked McCormick.

Adaira grew defensive. "They have always disliked one another, Papa. Maybe Erik deserved it."

"Tut-tut!" said Gilda. "Coarse words, my lady, and none of them friendly."

"Such heartless sentiments will hardly serve a daughter of mine!" exclaimed McCormick.

Adaira looked away in shame. Her instinct had been to protect her heart's desire as Lars was not there to speak for himself. Nevertheless, had Erik earned such a pitiless affront? She strained to fight back what was welling in her eyes.

"Why, we haven't the faintest as to the circumstances," continued the housekeeper, "not as of yet. Let's get Erik inside. We can sort this affair out later."

"Indeed," said McCormick. "Markus! Help me."

McCormick grabbed the boy's torso, and Markus grasped his legs. It was no use carrying him up two flights of stairs, so Gilda prepared some bedding within the shop. Some tapers were lit, the boy was laid upon the bedding, and Gilda returned with water and a washcloth.

Despite Gilda's best efforts at nursing, Erik's face and arms moistened with uncontrollable perspiration. Adaira felt his forehead, which simmered to the touch. His sickly face swayed in grave discomfort to one side and then to the other.

"I fear he has been struck with a fever," said Gilda. "Let us pray that it is not the sweating sickness."

Erik, only half conscious now, spoke in garbled tones. "Eyes ... raging ... coming now ..."

"The lad's hallucinating," said McCormick. "Talking nonsense."

"He needs a physician," said Adaira in tears. "Please, Father!"

"Aye," said McCormick with a depressed sigh. "I will fetch one."

"And I will go with you," said Adaira.

"It is too dangerous."

"I must go, Father."

McCormick looked upon his daughter with renewed affection. "You have the strength and will of your mother."

She returned his glance with a pained smile.

McCormick handed her his dagger and grabbed the broadsword for himself.

Somehow we will make it, she thought. They turned toward the door.

An unrestrained howling vanquished the momentary tranquility of the street, and a rustling wind stirred what had been a still night air. The howling sounded near—too near.

The door slammed before father and daughter could test their mettle.

Markus moved well for a stout cook. He stretched a fleshy arm to bar the way. "That is no dog, sir. You'll never find a physician with that racket going on."

The city fortifications had been built to keep the beasts at bay, but shape-shifters were like an elusive vagrant. When in human form, they found society to be a veritable camouflage. Few could discern the monster within, even when closely acquainted with the host. Only a subtle reddening of the eyes before twilight of the full moon foreshadowed their transformation. Lars's solitary witness lay in a deathly state of fever.

The Merchant Quarter lay in a restless slumber like a thousand fatted calves, not knowing which ones would be selected for slaughter.

"Otto! Otto! Son, come away from that window," said a nervous burgher, who slammed the shutters shut and slipped the timber through prefitted slots of iron.

The werewolf was attracted to the noise. It bounded into the wall of the house and embedded its crescent-shaped claws in the wood casement. Glass shattered as it pressed against the shutters. The timber beam bulged a couple of inches from the impact. It seemed on the verge of splitting. Sniffing and snarling, the wolf heaved throaty breaths as the burgher and his family cowered in a corner of the back bedroom.

The werewolf reared its arm back to punch the shutters. With a single thrust, the timber beam snapped in half and the shutters swung open.

The children inside began to scream.

"Look here, you foul beast!" cried someone from outside.

"Send that monster into the abyss!" shouted another.

The street filled with a flutter of arrows as a team of archers had answered the call. Their best archer, who doubled by day as a tanner, blew upon the feathered tail of an arrow and positioned it in the bow. He bent the bow into a wide arc and aimed, but his unkempt mane like that of a sheepdog fell upon the line of sight. The werewolf was on the move. The archer adjusted his mark, blew aside the wayward strands, and fired. The arrow punctured the lower back of the werewolf.

The beast howled in obvious pain; it seemed poised to jump down from the second-floor window. However, with that course of action, the barrage of arrows would only increase.

Though the werewolf's mind was structured like that of a canine, it retained remnants of the man's thoughts. It strategized and schemed, and at times it was capable of overcoming its instinctual pulses.

As another arrow found its target, the werewolf scanned the area for a place of retreat. Something about this place seemed familiar.

The volley of arrows continued. The wall of the burgher's home looked like a dartboard.

The target, however, had ascended the roof, where it spied something familiar a mere five houses down. It smelled the cold night air, teeming with fear, and let loose a throaty howl.

"What is that ruckus?" asked McCormick as he glanced out his second-floor bedroom's window.

"Something is moving along the rooftops," said Markus. "Close the shutters, sir!"

"Oh, Lars!" shrieked Adaira. "Where could he possibly be?"

The werewolf ravaged the wood shingles, those lining one Mithrendian roof after another, as it traveled a zigzagging path that left its pursuers below in a state of bewilderment and disconcertion. It leapt over parapets and even chimneys with ease. When it looked back, the arrows had ceased to flutter.

"Lars can fend for himself, I daresay!" shouted McCormick. "Did you check on Erik?"

"Gilda is with him," said Adaira.

"It is coming, sir!" said Markus. "Be on the ready."

The werewolf, able to hear such domestic conversations, settled upon the roof of a familiar abode. The beast remembered that the family slept on the second floor; the apprentices and servants, on the third.

It toggled back in its memory: *The girl sleeps on the second floor.*

Adaira. Blonde mane, alabaster neck.

The beast tore through a weak spot in the roof near Markus's room.

"Get my pike, Markus!" shouted McCormick.

The werewolf ravaged the wood shingles as it worked to enlarge the hole. Precious seconds elapsed, taking with them the element of surprise. The werewolf had once seen McCormick's prized chest with its weapons of war, but it did not fear sword and dagger.

"Keep well back!" said McCormick from well below. "I'll skewer this foul beast!"

The hole was large enough, and the werewolf was about to leap through. It saw McCormick raging up the stairs with an infantryman's pike. With its awkward, abnormal length, it seemed an obscure weapon for domestic quarters.

Markus and Adaira assembled on the stairs behind McCormick. McCormick's eyes glared with a fiery rage. He seemed almost like a man possessed, shouting curses as he surged upstairs with his long weapon.

The beast was not distracted from its intentions. It sighted the young girl and surged from the roof.

"North Legion, ho!" shouted McCormick.

The werewolf was met midair by the pike. It felt the tip of the weapon penetrate its abdomen and push through vital organs. The werewolf had been impaled, but in its momentum, it descended on the assailant, knocking McCormick halfway down the stairs.

The red-maned master mason grunted coarsely as his thick shoulder blades, rather than his head or neck, struck the steps.

The werewolf collapsed onto the landing, splitting the planks and howling with hellish savagery in a rage of pain.

"Father!" shouted Adaira as she surged to meet him.

"Markus! Gather my sword from downstairs!" said McCormick as he struggled to get back to his feet. "Adaira, you must keep well back."

With it prodigious strength, the werewolf grasped and pulled the pike, removing it from its body. The creature howled with tortured fervor, a ferocity that spawned agonizing screams from otherwise unharmed burghers up and down the city street. Then it felt a subtle change in the night. The beast glanced up, overhead, at the hole in the roof. There was a shift in cloud cover, and for a moment the moon was veiled.

The beastly form remained, but the werewolf's eyes became those of a man—familiar eyes of sky blue glaring down the staircase, captivating eyes that had bewitched a certain young woman as of late.

"Lars?" said Adaira. His were eyes that betrayed her trust and affection.

"It cannot be," said Markus.

Lars's eyes beheld her as an object to be consumed and disposed of.

"By George!" said McCormick. "'Tis he!"

The moon's veil lifted, and the vestiges of a man vanished in an impenetrable reflective sheen. The beast seemed to surge with new rage, but its wounds sabotaged any attempt it might make to wreak revenge on humankind.

In a single leap, the werewolf exited the roof.

Shock turned to relief. Relief turned to shock.

"Lars! He tried to kill me!" said Adaira.

"Aye," said McCormick as he held his daughter in his arms. "A beast of hell living under my own roof! To think of my foolishness ..."

"You cannot blame yourself, Father."

Markus raced upstairs to greet them. "Well done, master!"

McCormick felt the surge of victory along with the remorse of not having heeded a broken voice.

"Good and faithful Erik," said McCormick as he held his daughter close. "The poor boy was trying to warn us."

Adaira began to cry. "But why did this happen, Papa? Why Lars, when we have been nothing but good to him?"

"There was always a dark element to his character," observed her father. "Dark and obscure and tucked away from our notice." His eyes widened. "Now we know how dark."

Gilda returned with news. The fever was of a malicious sort, but the boy was fighting back vigorously.

"He wrestles with something," she said. "Some kind of predator in his mind. He will not let it win."

Despite her insight, Gilda was unprepared for the news upstairs.

"Lars?" she asked. "Are you sure of this, sir?"

"Aye," said her master.

"Well, well," answered the housekeeper. "A scoundrel 'tis he."

Lars had left them.

Only the putrid smell of beast remained.

CHAPTER XVII

Into a Foreign Land

I had learned a little about Northmoorland from Constantine and Anya, but I was unprepared for a cultural immersion. Not that I had a choice.

My dreaming atop a haystack was almost instantaneous. The prior chapter of my life, one of incarceration, had been followed by a jailbreak via a watery flume. I abandoned my means of escape and leapt into the darkness for a chance at a free life. Exhaustion followed exhilaration. What had absorbed my impact had also become my bed in the great outdoors.

I did not awake until the following morning.

When the sun's first rays fell upon me, I rolled over as if on my mattress at home and fell nearly twelve feet to the bedewed grass. Middle-aged knees, let alone young ones, were not equipped for this type of landing. Thankfully the twisted ankle I sustained in the process of tumbling was the worst of it. I stood upright and swept myself off to the best of my weakened and bruised ability. My back and shoulders were covered in loose straw.

I had no friends—well, except for the elderly couple in the castle. I wondered, with grave concern, how they had fared in the aftermath of my departure. Something aggrieved my heart as I considered their prospects, and a reflexive shiver ran down the length of my spinal cord.

Nevertheless, no matter what had happened to them, I needed to move forward. It would have been their wish.

Though I longed for the comforts of my bachelor existence back home, I had a curious sense that I had been placed here for a reason. Maybe it was a spiritual purpose as my elderly friends would have described it. Whatever it was, I determined that it was my duty to discern this purpose and to fulfill it. Meanwhile, the historian in me decided to make the most of this opportunity, which was like stepping into the well-worn pages of an archived historical document.

Farmers and milkmaids stared at the curious stranger with tattered clothes and disheveled hair as I limped my way through the fields. They seemed to be simple folk, clothed in plain-threaded woolen garments and living in modest stone abodes with thatched roofs. I watched them as they watched me, neither party quite sure what to make of the other. Meanwhile, my ankle bore the brunt of this procession and was throbbing as I arrived in town.

I had no money.

The urge to consume the necessities of life cared not a twig about my current state of poverty and acted of its own accord. My mouth salivated as if in rhythm with a rumbling stomach. A shopkeeper hung dried meats, which dangled from the ceiling of his store with tantalizing effect. In my mind's eye,

I had already eaten them when I reached into my pockets, hoping for a miracle, and retrieved only lint.

I tried to distract my thoughts from the pain by listening to the locals as they went about their daily business. My conversations with Constantine and Anya had, of course, been in German, so the Northmoorlandic language was completely foreign to me. In short, I understood not a word of it, but it seemed a curious mixture of Scandinavian and Gaelic.

Context clues would serve best in this situation—gestures, facial expressions, tone of voice, and eye contact. I looked about for signage. Spying a projecting wood bracket with a dragon head upon it, I surmised that here was the town inn.

My guess was correct. I saw strangers with trunks of luggage descending the heavy-timbered stairs. On the bottom floor was a busy public house serving both food and ale. Servers and scullery maids scuttled about like drones in a beehive, speeding slabs of roast beef, carrots and potatoes, loaves of bread, and sliced cheese to hungry recipients.

The hungriest customer of all dropped with exhaustion into a secluded booth, where I knelt and placed my forehead in my tired hands. The smell of food was almost a torture. Try as I might, and though I usually could master my perspective on a given situation with positive thinking, I repressed a sob. I was at the brink of mental exhaustion.

"God help me," I whispered.

"Ever heard of a Lord Berbery?" asked someone loudly from an adjacent booth.

He had his back to me, so I could not see his face, but his animated reddish-brown hair jumped about from beneath a cap of fine cloth. I'm unsure of the type of hat, but it looked like a broad, flattened beret with thick, sagging folds of velvet.

"Why wouldn't I?" answered his associate with a gruff voice. This man seemed somewhat older with a thick gray beard that converged at a point well below the neck. "The gossip about town usually centers on Berbery's escapades."

"He's making raids on the neighboring villages," said the younger man with some heat.

"We know well about that."

"And?"

The older man shrugged his shoulders. "What can we do about it? He's a powerful lord, and our spies tell us he is building an army."

I was overjoyed, not because of the news, but because I understood what they were saying. It was an older dialect of English, no doubt, but one I was familiar with from years of reading historical documents. I strained my neck forward to hear more.

"Who then has power over him in these lands?" said the younger man.

"No one really ever comes about here," said the elder. "These lands do fall within the demesne of the Duke of Donegal, though he seems to care not for such affairs. Always up in his tower, they say, he is poring over books and concocting potions in a crazed search for the secrets of alchemy."

I was struck by the recognition. The first voice, the younger one, betrayed a Scottish accent. The second seemed to be one of a Welshman. They appeared to have settled on a common language to speak anonymously in a foreign land, suggesting that they were educated men and well traveled. This familiarity encouraged me. I stood up and addressed these two men.

"Excuse me, gentlemen," I said, "but I could not help overhearing your conversation. You cannot know how much it means to me to hear a familiar tongue."

The two well-dressed men looked at me with countenances that bespoke of bewilderment.

"Oh," I said, "I see that you observe my manner of dress and the state of my condition. Forgive me. My name is Nicodemus Porter. I am a scholar who has escaped incarceration in the castle whose master calls himself Lord Dominus Berbery."

"How is this possible?" asked the Scotsman. He had impassioned green eyes and a thick goatee that drooped for a brief moment from his astonishment.

"Castles, as you know," I said, "have hidden passages. I was alerted to one by certain members of the servant staff. From there I descended the mountainside and traveled across the river by a conveyance of water, an aqueduct."

The two men seemed to marvel at this account. They appeared to scrutinize my shabby attire as well as my manner of speech.

"Sir, your accent is one I have never heard," said the Welshman. "May I ask what it is?"

"American."

"American? Why, that applies to the New World."

"Aye."

"But we have not known of that land until recently," said the Scotsman. "How could a white man have lived there and acquired such an unusual accent?"

I chose to avoid any talk of mysterious portals permitting time travel. As a rule, I abhorred deceit, but a slight fabrication was needed here.

"My father was an adventurer," I answered. "I was born and spent my youth in foreign places."

"And what brings you here now?" asked the Welshman.

"I was searching for certain documents that can only be found in Northmoorland," said Porter. "I found them in Berbery's library."

"And what documents are those?" asked the Scotsman.

"Ancient accounts of lycanthropy."

My two-member audience looked at one another as if taking a stoic stance in response to what must have been a stunning revelation.

"Furthermore," I said, "I've seen his legion of werewolves assemble in the courtyard below my rooms."

"Shape-shifters!" gasped the Scotsman. "So the peasant rumors are true ..."

"And what, dear sir, is this Berbery planning?" asked the Welshman, with a surprising steadiness of composure.

"War," I answered, "though I have not learned of the time or place. He seems little concerned with the local nobility, and therefore my suspicion is that the target is Mithrendia."

"Treason against the Crown!" said the Scotsman as he pounded the table with a strong fist. This, of course, caught the attention of many strangers who sat near us, but they seemed to understand not one word. One man raised his pint of ale and nodded as if enjoying the passion of this outburst.

"Aye. I need to alert someone," I said. "Someone of political consequence who can counteract this schemer."

"The Duke of Donegal is a fickle man," noted the Welshman. "Except, of course, when it comes to his own interests."

"Aye, there he is consistent of purpose," said the Scotsman with a magnanimous laugh. "He'd sooner admit a charlatan of the dark arts than grant us an audience."

A serving girl brought their plates of roast beef. My nostrils swelled with envy.

The Welshman took a hearty bite, which did not prevent him from speaking. "I daresay that Berbery's priorities align with our own in one sense, and only one: the petty earls and barons of these northeastern lands are not worth your time. All they do is quibble and warmonger with one another."

I was almost in agony. "Then where might I go? I escaped with my life, but I have no money."

"We were planning a westward voyage, were we not, Morfaddyn?" asked the Scotsman.

"Aye, McCollister."

"Then let's visit the duke."

I was in shock. "But, sir, I thought you said he was not worth appealing to."

"I did," said McCollister, with a wink.

I knew not what to say. Meanwhile, the beef and the carrots and the potatoes were insufferable enticements. It was all I could do not to reach for them.

"What my business partner means," said Morfaddyn, "is the Duke of Mithrendia."

"Ah," I said as I snatched my imaginary extended hands back.

"But we cannot bring this man to the duke's attention in such rags and derelict condition," said McCollister, again with great heat.

"Aye, we cannot," observed Morfaddyn.

McCollister slapped a fistful of coins upon the table. The serving girl spotted the gleaming coinage and rushed to the table.

"Feed this man," said McCollister, pointing to me, "with the heartiest meal from the kitchen. And send for a tailor! We must get him outfitted immediately!"

CHAPTER XVIII

The Monastery

Twilight faded into darkness, casting black shadows upon long-forgotten stones. In had been many years since the cloister had fallen into disrepair, but Abelard remembered its abandonment. Arched colonnades, roofless, stood like upright dominoes waiting to fall. The refectory also lay in disuse, as did the cells where quiet monks once slept after whispering their prayers.

At the northern edge of the monastery lay the cathedral, founded upon a great outcrop of rock. Its long forgotten facade seemed fixed upon one object as it gazed at Berbery's castle across the gorge.

The same fixation could be observed in its visitor that night.

Abelard stood leaning on the northwest corner, oblivious to the sheer drop-off into the distant river valley. He had flown under cover of ominous clouds to Vindegaard in the alpine

Forest of Odin. Here, autonomous warlords, owing barely more than lip service to the Duke of Donegal, played their own games of life and death with the villagers as their pawns.

Abelard knew the history of this place. Centuries ago, this thriving monastery, by the power of the cross of Christ, had vanquished the Norse gods to the hinterlands. Now, however, those warring entities had returned with anger and designs of vengeance. They had returned to Vindegaard and found it wanting. The old Viking settlements were now filled with the domesticated descendants of ancestral raiders, living peacefully with Scots and Irishmen. The spilling of blood had reached an ebb.

Abelard knew that these so-called gods were demons, as he could see into the spectral realm. They had bided their time with cunning and patience, and the results of their return were obvious. Monasticism was waning, along with the local wool market managed by the abbot. Abelard remembered that the monks had grown quite wealthy from trade and the rents of their tenants, including farmers and shepherds. This gave rise to petty jealousy among the populace, including the poor, who also gave their tithes to the monastery. Meanwhile, the monks had grown lazy, selfish, and indulgent.

Bitter anger was stirred up afresh, and an arsonist set fire to the cathedral. The practice of civility and common courtesy faded. Neighbor argued with neighbor over the most trivial of matters, and corrupt officials could be bribed. Foreign profiteers arrived, and power mongers arose among the privileged class. The noblemen mustered standing armies and built siege towers. Berserkers abandoned their posts in the distant south and rose up to fill the ranks. Violence surged and the monastery was pillaged. Few monks survived the raids, and those who did abandoned the region. A coldness of heart had settled in Vindegaard to outlive many a winter.

Abelard remembered all those winters when he had been a mere soldier following his master's orders. He too had shared in the coldness, but tonight those memories brought him an anguish he had not felt in many a year.

"When I saw her," he uttered, "I remembered what I had lost long ago. I remembered what I once was, and the rage of the centuries departed from me."

He studied his arms and elongated fingers in the moonlight. The cadaverous hue shone with a white iridescence that seemed almost beautiful, apart from knowledge of its true color.

"What am I, a monster, an agent of evil? Can the heart, what is left of it, break the bonds of allegiance to a cruel master?"

Standing upon the forsaken ruins, he was brooding but no longer giving voice to his thoughts. This proved fortunate, he thought, as some moments later Abelard realized that he was not alone.

"Are you abandoning me, Malsadus?" he asked with his gaze still fixed across the forested gorge on Berbery's castle. Despite Abelard's aversion to this creature, he feared the consequences of insubordination.

"You have grown intractable in your old age," uttered a deep guttural voice.

Abelard did not have to behold this hideous fiend to sense its presence. That voice was like no other. The hairs of Abelard's arms raised as the air was torn asunder like the seam of an invisible curtain to another dimension, through which the arch-demon stepped. Here was the master Matthias used to speak of, one Abelard would not meet until after Matthias's death, one whom Abelard wished he had never met.

"Have I?" replied Abelard.

Here was that puppet master, that agent of devilry, whom

Catherine had seen on Chestnut Street. After her visit to Wolf's Hollow, Abelard had scouted Catherine's place of residence in the Marches and began a habit of correspondence via his mail carrier, a raven named Bartholomew. Through the medium of pen, parchment, and a wax seal, Catherine had grown to confide in her strange new friend.

"There," said Malsadus, pointing his foul scalelike appendage, draped in something like decayed seaweed, left toward the western horizon. "I know of your habits: perambulating endlessly through your grand halls; staring at the stars from your alchemist's tower; hording boundless chests of precious stones and goblets of gold. There in Wolf's Hollow you pine away, year after year, brooding and ruminating about the decay of your dynasty."

"Decay?" answered Abelard. "Death more like."

"But you could always make more. I've never taken that opportunity away from you."

"More vampyres?" asked Abelard. "To what end? We are a race of parasites. There is no sentiment among us. Though we transfuse the same blood from creator to creation, the other vampyres are not my relations. There is no loyalty. The same could be said of those forsaken creatures who dwell in the Black Mountains. Barbarous hordes! None of them are bound to me, just as I was never bound to Matthias."

"Though Matthias shared your exquisite tastes," said Malsadus with a mocking grin. "Yes, the sophisticated refinements of a cultured nobleman."

"That was all we shared in common," said Abelard. "We could agree on almost nothing else."

Abelard remembered little about Matthias that provoked any fondness. Oh, Matthias had shown him a way of living as far as the vampiric means of subsistence was concerned. That perhaps should have caused within him the sense of a debt of gratitude. Abelard, however, tolerated his existence as a vampyre, whereas Matthias reveled in it. One brooded over his misery while the other enjoyed the destruction it wrought.

"It was you who killed him," said Malsadus. His accusing eyes smoldered like the flames of hell.

"That is a lie," replied Abelard with anger. He hated these engagements. Malsadus was shrewd. The master liked to stir things up, only to arraign with charges later. "I left Matthias to his destruction in the year 1265."

"Is it?" said Malsadus. "Rather, you abandoned him as the stake-bearers drew near the crypt."

"Why should I protect a mass murderer, hmm?"

"Because I assigned him to you," said Malsadus.

"The lower latitudes had become too warm for someone of my sanguine temperament," said Abelard, knowing it to be an ineffective jest.

"It is perhaps fortunate that I have found use for you in these cold climes," said Malsadus. "Remember that fact. For hell calls, my friend, at a moment's notice."

Abelard did not consider Malsadus a friend. A vampyre, especially an old one, reigned supreme over the natural world. Humans were no match for the powers of the old vampyre's strength, or for the wisdom accumulated over many generations. Berserkers could be a threat, especially in great numbers, as could the draugr, a type of vampyre unique to the North Atlantic. Nevertheless, there was only one lord who dwelled in the hollow, a central and strategic location between Mithrendia and the Black Mountains. It was a position well suited to the formidable son and heir of a marquis.

Abelard sighed. A friend would not threaten him with a one-way trip to the outer darkness with its eternal torments and its weeping and its gnashing of teeth. "A threat that you like to leave hovering about me."

"Then you must remember your place," answered Malsadus.

Abelard had been given a special commission and, with it, more-advanced powers than his rivals'. He was the wisest and strongest of the vampyres of the North Atlantic. Nevertheless, in supernatural parlance, Abelard's powers were limited. True, he could do battle against the lower demons if he were forced to, but above him a diabolical hierarchy existed. The arch-demons such as Malsadus wielded unimaginable powers and, within this hierarchy, were answerable only to the devil himself.

"What would you have me do?" asked Abelard.

"I would have you devote yourself to my affairs," said Malsadus.

Devilry in its truest personification inspired the confidence, loyalty, and worship of a rare individual. The fiend was incapable of any enduring bond of relationship, and the machinations of its mind abandoned notions of fair play. Abelard knew well that friendship with these beings was an illusion.

Abelard also knew something of the demonic saga. In the primordial past, before the reckoning of human history, Malsadus, like Lucifer, had been an archangel. The two had been companions from the beginning, when Malsadus was known by another name, a noble and good name, now lost to the ages.

Lucifer, however, shone with a special luminance, a radiance above the other angelic hosts. The blessing of beauty and wisdom, however, became a source of conceit, and conceit spawned an unholy ambition. Lucifer made a prideful play to be like the Most High God, his Maker, and sought the highest of heavenly thrones. Other angels, including Malsadus, followed his lead.

For this vainglorious affront, the celestial sky lit up with flashes of lightning beyond reckoning. Abelard could see it in his mind's eye, a third of the angelic host cast down from heaven in slender ribbons of light. They had been banished for rejecting their calling, for rejecting the loving authority of the Father of lights, with whom there is no shifting shadow.[4]

With the coup thwarted, the war of the ages was just beginning. The fallen angels coalesced around their leader. Their lightness of bearing dimmed into darkness, and their identities became those of the demonic horde. What was once beautiful was now a scourge and a horror, a monstrosity of evil, a perversion.

Abelard began to mark their ways, ever since the day his eyes were opened. Demons have always hated humanity because it is humans, not angels, who bear the image of their Maker, whom the demons rejected. Even shape-shifters and vampyres retained a faint coding of their original authenticity. They walk the earth, where demonic spirits need assistance to carry out their strategies. But who would trust them save for the gullible?

Loyalty, therefore, had to be secured some other way. A substitute was needed, a temptation, some type of trade, bargained and negotiated, with the principal signatories engaged in an eternal contract—a desperate desire sated in exchange for a forfeited soul.

Malsadus specialized in the whetting of appetites. Once the compulsion was honed, he swooped in with an enticing offer of fulfillment. Fame. Power. Sex. Greed. He knew intimately the lusts of humankind no matter what form they might take. The passage of millennia had allowed the demons ample time to study human nature.

Abelard knew well that Malsadus's strategic operations did not require his human targets, his puppets, to give a thought to the arch-demon's existence. In fact, anonymity often aided the demonic strategy. It left the humans with the notion that they were in full control, that they were the apex beings on terra firma.

"Have I not fulfilled my obligations?" Malsadus asked. "Did I not make you the lord of your demesne? Did I not grant you powers beyond measure?"

"I was forced into this standard of being," said Abelard.

"Not that you were deprived of some free will."

Indeed it was an unusual contract, thought Abelard, *like one signed by someone who was not in his right mind at the time of the agreement.* In addition, he, broken-bodied and dying, had no idea who Matthias was or whom he worked for.

But again, devils do not play fair.

"I succumbed to my own weakness, my own brokenness," said Abelard.

This was the guilt that Abelard had long borne. Every night he remembered that night like a live rehearsal in his mind. He had lost the light of love and had acquired dark powers, thereafter being romanced by the moon.

"That holy man was sent to warn you," said Malsadus with a self-satisfied sneer. "Had you listened to his words and obeyed them ..."

Abelard attempted to compose himself, but the shock of this remembrance by his demonic accuser overwhelmed him. So Malsadus knew. Of course he knew.

Abelard had often wondered what might have happened had he obeyed the holy man, and he had spent the loneliness of the decades hashing out various scenarios in his mind. Such considerations had been missing in his knuckleheaded youth, when he had arrogantly dismissed the old man without sufficient heed of his words. In those foolish days, Abelard had been so certain of his own purpose.

Indeed, the holy man had come to save him from himself.

Perhaps God loved me once, Abelard thought, *before I became cursed.*

Abelard gazed out into the gorge and for a time said nothing.

"Will you attend to my affairs?" asked Malsadus once again.

"The world has changed," said Abelard as he surveyed the ramparts of Berbery's castle. "The order of things has been subverted."

"Precisely."

Abelard looked back at his master. "A shift in strategy then, my liege?"

"Unlike you," said Malsadus, "Berbery knows nothing of me. Though I have visited him often."

"With the cloak of invisibility, you practice this subterfuge?"

The arch-demon sneered. "As you have already said, Abelard, the world is changing."

"But why Berbery?" Abelard hated this upstart.

"His plans, for the most part, align with my own."

"What does he seek?"

"To eradicate the kingdom of Northmoorland," said Malsadus, "through death or conversion."

Abelard was surprised by the sheer scope of this man's ambition. "Conquer Mithrendia, and turn its inhabitants into crazed wolves to do his bidding?"

"Yes," said Malsadus, "but he means to conquer from within. A coup. He's already become a Northmoorlandic citizen, even a scheming warlord of vast power, yet through the enchantments of his witchcraft, he is ignored by the quarrelsome nobles of the Forest of Andia."

Abelard surveyed the width and depth of the castle's ramparts. "By the looks of it, that castle could accommodate a garrison of not more than three hundred."

"He's building a vast army of berserkers," said Malsadus. "They dwell in the towns, the hamlets, the forest, and even the mountain caves."

"Why have I not heard of this before?" asked Abelard. "I am lord of the shape-shifters of the north!"

"You have been too busy brooding. Berbery is no respecter of authority, and he's arrogant enough to think he can control the powers of darkness. But the occult, in its fullest sense, is beyond the reckoning of mortals, even those of his lycanthropic kind. His necromancy and his witchcraft and his divinations bring him power, but he has not yet realized that they are a snare. For the dark powers he meddles with are possessed of ancient wisdom, a wisdom that is cunning and shrewd."

Abelard considered his adversary whom he had not yet met. "I detest this Berbery."

"Precisely."

Abelard sensed that yet another plan was afoot. "What, my liege, do you want of me?"

The fiend flashed his false smile once more. "When Berbery completes the work I have for him, I will call on you to destroy him."

"It will be my pleasure."

The fiend nodded.

"The shape-shifters and the draugr have abandoned Wolf's Hollow," said Abelard, "but they will kneel to me once more. And I will resume command of the legions."

"Upon the night of the prophecy, you will wield an army unmatched by man," said Malsadus. And with that the fiend disappeared into a hidden seam in the night air.

Abelard was once again alone.

He surveyed Berbery's troops, watching their movements on the battlements across the gorge. They appeared in human form on this calm night.

Abelard stepped off the ledge of rock. The vampyre crossed his arms over his cadaverous chest as his body went headfirst into a state of free fall. He dropped hundreds of feet before wings, approaching the size of a pterodactyl's, unfolded from behind his shoulders. They deftly maneuvered the momentum of the free fall, and he swooped upward from a diving arc. He surged up, past the diagonal slits that had naturally formed in the mountain rock, and rose above the castle walls with his blood-red eyes aflame. He circled the castle, studying the turrets and ramparts.

Abelard saw the guards on the watchtower shudder as he swept off to the west.

CHAPTER XIX

The Grand Canal

Matthew had taken one of his rambling strolls. He had wandered farther afield into Mithrendia, where his perusals of the great city drifted into the night. He had done this before, wandering until well after the city gates had closed, which forced him to seek shelter in obscure places for the night. He always awoke in the wee hours of the morning to return to his post with the others, Catherine, Mary, and Ben, as lackeys and wenches of the tavern trade. At least that was how they were viewed by the patrons of the establishment.

The four had some money now courtesy of Wolf's Hollow. Unlike their hired protectors, however, who carried satchels on their horses, the four had not brought the means to convey much of their treasure back. Neither could they, in good conscience, argue for their fair share with armed men, whose number had dwindled from three to two in the cause of their quest and in the protection of their lives. Nevertheless, the four could afford their own accommodations now, and the thought of an independent existence, if not a leisurely one, was tempting.

Matthew, like the others, could not forecast the duration of their stay in the Marches, nor could he surmise their purpose here. He was bored with his job, as was Catherine. At night Mary and Ben related to them the escalating insults by their employer's wife, Berta, which caused Matthew and Catherine to take the lead in scouting out a better means of living for them all. Meanwhile, Catherine had cautioned them to save what money they had. Matthew had found a perfect hiding place, behind a loose board by his bed, and there they hid their modest treasure.

Matthew could now afford to take a day off here and there, which allowed for a little temporary amnesia regarding the Blue Griffin. The people-watching on these sojourns was always a source of entertainment, but he had heard of the repairs under way at the Grand Canal and wanted to see it. The engineers had diverted the riverine waters from the stone-lined canal, which wound like a crescent around the Glenhorne district, the core of the city. When operational, it was fed upstream by the Olan River southwest of Glenhorne, where the white-walled royal palace and ancillary government buildings stood, only to return what was given to that same body of water northeast of the district. In the interim, the waters were siphoned, at specific intervals, from the canal into various waterworks serving the needs of the local people.

Along this crescent, the Helsborg district fronted the canal's east flank. Here, Matthew leaned upon the stone guardrail, which rose like a parapet from the wall of the canal. He studied the embankment some thirty feet below. The canal was devoid of the usual violence of the turbulent waters, yet as twilight eased into night, the air was disturbed. Men were shouting and arrows were flying from Cuidaffe Green, a verdant, tree-lined area on the west side. State executions by the hangman and headsman were carried out on Cuidaffe Green, but four corpses lay in the canal.

Corpses in the canal? What were these archers about?

Matthew followed the course of their arrows, and when he saw it, he shook like a madman. He saw the foul beast, a werewolf, as it sprang across the canal with bloody footprints and headed toward him: a lone, solitary soul without protection save for the projecting wall of stone barring him from the depths below.

Amid this fear, however, Matthew tried to steady himself with a resolute focus. He strained his eyes in the darkening shadows of the canal. Two of the corpses had been felled by arrows. The others, however, had been gored and gutted with a savagery beyond reckoning.

Matthew considered the logistics of his plight. Could this thing surmount the curved thirty-foot wall of the canal? He did not know, but it sprang with an unnatural gait that defied reality. No animal could leap like that, and its claws might cling to the joints in the rock, allowing it to climb.

Matthew could see the teeth and the claws and those hellish eyes. They seemed to gaze upon him with hatred. He thought of running.

Before he let go of the railing, Matthew looked left to what ordinarily would have been the upstream direction. There, some fifty feet away, was a fifteen-foot-diameter hole. The hole was angled into the wall of the canal such that it was almost parallel to the embankment.

Matthew charged south, uphill, running alongside the stone guardrail.

There was a secondary waterworks nearby.

He could hear the howls echoing off the wall of the canal as he reached the entrance. Here the earth had been dug away, revealing a doorway that had been carved into the bedrock. It was presently unguarded. He went inside and descended a ramp.

Just beyond the base of the ramp, Matthew observed a circular opening. It was the top of a massive cistern, which had been cut from an existing cave in the bedrock. He had seen one of these before. In the winter months, an underground furnace heated water pipes that fed into the cistern chamber. In the warm months, the cistern was replenished by inlets from the Olan River.

Small outlets near the base serviced a network of pipes providing fresh water to the populace, but there was also a large outflow to the canal—the outlet he had seen from outside. Matthew needed to find the winch that controlled the sluice gate to this outlet. But even if he were to find it, he knew that these devices were seldom operated by a single person.

"Hey! You can't be down here," shouted a strange authoritarian voice.

It was a guard, average-sized, yet one still exceeding Matthew in height and build. He carried a thick wooden club.

"You can help me," said Matthew.

"Leave now before I am forced to subdue you and summon the gaoler!"

Although the threat of arrest scared him, Matthew was more concerned with the claws and teeth that shone in the moonlight. "Did you see that thing outside?"

"Aye," said the guard. "'Tis a werewolf."

Matthew wondered if the guard had abandoned his post outside.

"And did you see the carnage it left behind?"

"Aye. Four dead."

"It will be worse if it escapes the canal. Think of all the innocent people on the east side of town."

The guard studied Matthew but said nothing. There before the torchlight sconces of the ramp wall, the man's eyes glistened in fear.

"Listen!" said Matthew. "I have toured the waterworks of this city extensively. I am an engineer."

Well, that was a fib. An engineer major, yes, but hardly a registered professional.

"I know how the waterworks function, sir," continued Matthew, "and this cistern could save many lives. Will you help me?"

The guard hesitated.

"Think of how you will feel after that beast surmounts the east wall of the canal," said Matthew. "What regrets might you have?"

To be sure, Matthew did not know where the beast was right now. He did not even know if the wall could be surmounted, but if anything had the ability, that beast would be the one to do it. Memories of the portal, the moors, and Wolf's Hollow flashed through his mind.

Now this. Matthew felt a strong conviction to carry out his speculative idea.

"Well ..." muttered the guard.

"Sir, there is no time to waste!"

The guard nodded and beckoned him over to a half wall of rock that lay just outside the perimeter of the cistern. Behind the wall was a winch.

"Help me," said the guard. "From the top, turn it left."

They both grasped the spokes of a wheel that controlled the winch.

"Now!" said the guard.

The required initial effort was beyond what they could muster. The wheel would not budge.

"You do not possess sufficient strength?" asked the guard. "I cannot do it alone."

It did not matter that this question pertained to the both of them. It felt individualized. This was a question that struck Matthew at the core of his soul. He had never been an athlete. He had never been regarded by others as bearing the physicality of a man.

The wheel stood before him and taunted.

The mocking memories of the past flooded his mind. Matthew burned with anger. "I have not come down here to fail."

The two of them grasped the wheel and heaved. Matthew strained with all his might, until the veins surfaced like slithering serpents upon his neck.

The wheel began to move.

"That's it!" shouted the guard as his biceps twitched into convulsions.

The initial movement was the hardest part. The wheel moved more freely now, though it still required a concerted effort.

The pressurized flow of water could be heard far underneath, at the base of the cistern. It was leaving the cistern with ferocious intent.

The two men twisted the wheel a couple of revolutions until it would budge no more.

"We have spun the wheel as far as it will go," said the guard. "The outlet will discharge at full strength soon."

"Let's go see the damage," said Matthew.

They raced up the ramp and down to the spot along the canal where the werewolf was last seen. Matthew hesitated a moment and then looked over the embankment.

A hairy arm reached up from the unseen deep and swatted a claw-laden paw at Matthew's upper reaches, but the instinctive withdrawal of his head saved him from decapitation.

"Upstream!" shouted Matthew.

The pair raced southward toward the massive hole in the wall of the canal. The circular lining below reverberated with the rapid torrent of an approaching outburst. The watery outflow, initially a trickle, gathered in size and ferocity. The hole became a quarter full, then a half. It sprayed the east side of the canal with new rapids.

Matthew glanced downstream, direly hopeful of his plan's success, but the beast had not been swept up by the flow.

"Dammit!" he said. "Where is it?"

"I dare not look over the ledge," said the guard.

Matthew considered the outflow, which was at about three-quarters' height now; it possessed a hydraulic power that could not possibly be resisted by any land-walking creature. Yet there was no sign of the beast.

"Where is it?" asked the guard.

The beast seized the top of the ledge with a single paw. It hung for a brief moment and was about to spring over the wall.

Nothing would stop it once it surmounted the east embankment—no gaolers, no archers from Cuidaffe Green, and certainly not Matthew and the guard of the cistern.

There was nothing more they could do.

Matthew took several steps south of the werewolf's position and mounted the stone guardrail. The guard followed but remained on ground.

"What are you doing?" asked the guard.

Matthew decided that he would leap to his death before getting mauled by this murderous beast. Still, he needed to be sure of his plan's success. He surveyed the werewolf's position as it struggled to disengage its claws from the rock.

Right below Matthew's position was a residual mass of boulders. This debris had been deemed too impractical, he thought, to be cleared away after the original construction of the canal. Water flowed around it and shot through gaps between rocks.

The archers on the west side had adjusted their position, and arrows were flying against the precipice of the east embankment. The werewolf writhed about, dodging arrows as it fought to find a firm grasp on the guardrail. An arrow found its mark in its back, but its ferocious attempt at an ascent only increased.

"It will be upon us in a moment!" shouted the guard. "We'd better run!"

The guard ran back toward his underground post. Matthew, however, moved southward along the top of the guardrail, away from the onslaught of arrows. He was now on top of the outflow, and he could see that the discharge of the cistern operated at full speed. The rapid flood of water gushed at the rock, spraying outward and upward.

Matthew could hear the torrent as the water surged at the beast's legs and torso. The claws pressed into the jointed rock of the embankment. It dug into the rock, seeking a secure fitting.

Matthew could hear the creature's dense, foul breathing and could see the condensation rise from its snout. Fear overwhelmed him. He could see the end nearing and leapt.

Rather, he leapt to the ground behind him, where he picked up a palm-sized rock and jumped back up on the guardrail. He aimed and released the missile. It struck the beast on the shoulder, and it gave way, falling into the developing rapids. It howled in misery.

Matthew saw the werewolf tumbling, striving to gain air, as it cascaded into the farther reaches of the canal, where it would rejoin the river.

And then it was gone. Matthew was once more alone. For a moment, anyway.

The guard returned, and Matthew recounted the climax that he had missed.

"Halt!"

A mounted cavalcade of gaolers and soldiers surged toward them as thunderous hooves clopped upon the cobblestones.

"Halt in the name of the king!"

The horses stopped about ten feet before them.

"Aye, sir," said Matthew, as he beheld the mounted men with a mystified glance. "I was just enjoying the spoils of satisfaction at a certain beast's departure."

"I am Constable O'Malley," said their leader, a tall man with a long, thick mustache. "Dare I say that you were the ones who opened the east cistern?"

"Aye, we have," said Matthew as the guard tried to shush him. "And we're unequivocally proud of it too."

"And your names?" asked O'Malley, who mirrored no such sentiments.

Matthew looked at his partner in this watery affair and shrugged. "My name's Matthew Kirkpatrick."

"Dawson, sir," said the partner. "I am a guard of the east cistern."

"What were you doing, guard?" asked O'Malley. "That was half a month's supply of water."

"Well," answered Dawson.

"You were saying?"

"What's with this line of questioning?" asked Matthew. "Without us, you'd still be dealing with a werewolf. And I daresay it would offer more mayhem than you are capable of defending against."

The cavalry drew out their weapons—broadswords and bows and arrows. Matthew found several arrow tips pointed at his head and sternum.

"And why," asked O'Malley, "did you waste the king's water?"

"Forgive us, sir," said Dawson. "We were only doing what we felt best to prevent this beast from assailing those who live near the east embankment."

O'Malley lifted his arm, and those about him lowered their weapons. "Did you not think the constable of the tower had this matter well in hand?"

Matthew laughed. "No."

"Ah," said O'Malley. "The short one."

Matthew always hated that type of retort. He looked up at the constable, seated high on his mount, with a resolute countenance. "Short or not, my reach upon this east embankment extended farther than yours."

"Well, well, my brave little one. And what will say for yourself in a court of law?"

Matthew relaxed into a wide grin. "I was washing the dog."

PART III

DISSENSION

An Assault from Within

"Traitors? Heretics?" muttered King Alfarin. As he leaned forward on his mount, he pictured his arctic white fur cloak as a shield, and his delicate crown of Celtic woven gold as a helm.

"My liege?" asked Queen Toriana in a voice far more audible than her husband's.

The king was lost in thought, even in midst of this ruckus of humanity. Nevertheless, he heard his wife's measured delivery, a brazen yet smooth intonation, which always made her sound as if she were in firm control of her surroundings.

The king glanced over with a subtle smile of admission. How keen she was to observe his peculiarities, even amid the din and clamber of the public eye. Alfarin loathed these processions, but Toriana, he could see, was enjoying the spectators' enchantment with the royal couple as their horses trotted along the promenade paralleling the Lingenthorne battlements. Here in the Norsetown district of northern Mithrendia, the city's defenses stood arrayed against all those of ill intention who might come by sea.

That, however, was not what worried him.

"Your lips flutter, and yet I cannot tell what you say," said Toriana, amid the trampling of hooves and the festooning of ribbons by mesmerized commoners. "Can you be lost in thought in this company? Among your subjects, who delight in your presence?"

"You disarm me with your attentiveness, my dear," said Alfarin. "By the love of the saints, I cannot fathom such powers in the hands of my enemies."

The queen appeared to enjoy the compliment. Twenty-five years younger than the king, Toriana's flaming-red hair had yet to entertain any vestiges of gray. It tossed about the length of her back like an advertisement of vitality with further embellishment provided by her adept handling of the steed. Her emerald eyes with a mystical quality akin to the aurora borealis, or northern lights, provoked a great many stares from passersby.

Alfarin indulged her, such as he once did himself. He had been quite robust in his youth, but time, it seemed, had not served him well. The worries of state compounded by an excess of drink had overtaken his good looks, leaving indelible marks. His gray shanks in and of themselves mattered little, but his cheeks were hollowing, rendering a once ruddy face weathered and gaunt. He felt tired, almost perpetually so, and after a long day he sought the privacy of his domestic quarters.

"I long for my armchair and a roaring fire," said the king.

But the king could not escape his duties, which most of all included the protection of his people. Its remoteness and inaccessibility had allowed Northmoorland to pass unscathed as carnage went on around it for centuries. That being said, its northernmost province, known as the Grand Sweep, had long been the kingdom's geographic point of vulnerability. Navigation of the frigid swales of the North Atlantic was surprisingly tempered by calm waters as one approached Northmoorland's northern coast. Sandy beaches fanned out eastward and westward for leagues, permitting an endless array of entry points for raiders and opportunists.

"We make this journey so seldom, my liege," said the queen, "and yet it is vital that we come."

Following Alfarin's entourage was a double-file line of knights and liveried servants, all on horseback. The latter group included heralds, attendants, pages, minstrels, and even the court jester—because humorous entertainment, to the king's notion, must be portable.

Nevertheless, the king's mood was somber. It was because of the existential threat to the Grand Sweep that a sparse population inhabited the peninsula in huts, hovels, and cruck timber dwellings arranged in small clusters and hidden by the reeds. Here smugglers dwelt among fishermen in meager hamlets. Most of these hardy folk were beyond Alfarin's protective reach.

Nevertheless, the king's forebears had built walled enclaves on the peninsula's southwestern shore. There the kingdom's ports of trade marked the true beginning of civilization. Foremost among these ports was Arengärd, the home of the Crown's navy. The moorings of merchant boat and warship were secured by a strategic alliance of iron and bronze, that is, cannon. These lethal devices were mounted upon fortified seawalls, daring the foolhardy to launch an armed offensive.

Alfarin knew the terrain of his northern peninsula, which, from the battlements, he saw on the distant horizon across the blue-gray waters of the Firth of Jutlanger. In his youth, he had been anxious to see the entirety of his kingdom, and with the road-weary royal court in tow, he completed one daring expedition after another. Some regarded him a fool for October swims in the sea of the northern lowlands, which rose steadily to the south, where a narrow cliff-like isthmus was the only landmass connecting the Grand Sweep to the mainland.

"That was before I married," muttered the king, "when the thunder of Thor ran through my veins. Trader's Gate and Butcher's Gate I inspected personally, questioning those of a slothful or conniving disposition and revealing my wrath when needed."

Trader's Gate, an imposing tower on the north end of the isthmus, housed a querulous garrison and scheming customs officials. Despite its austere accommodations, it provided a means for the ambitious and the unscrupulous to rise from subsistence living to luxury. Alfarin knew that there was an art to collecting customs duties, as well as to withholding what was due. Smugglers made hidden compartments in their carts and paid tariffs on the conspicuous portions of their wares. In return, the oversights of the customs officers and soldiers were rewarded with kickbacks, and yørn flowed both for the Crown and for the embezzler. The sheer volume of trade compensated all involved, and with such means and measures, some trivialities could be overlooked. Passage was granted, and merchants and smugglers streamed across the narrow landmass like an army of commerce, under the watchful eye of the king's guard.

"That isthmus has made us rich, my dear," said the king, pointing to the northeast.

"Yes, my liege."

The vast majority of the Crown's subjects resided on the mainland, where the king's attention usually gravitated.

Mithrendia, the nation's capital and only metropolis, was entered by Butcher's Gate on the south end of the isthmus.

Alfarin knew the stories of his ancestors, who in the thirteenth century fashioned the city's defenses after the famed walls of Constantinople. Their structure consisted of an inner wall forty-five feet in height and a twenty-foot outer wall. The outer wall hugged the rocky coastline, stretching for seventy leagues or so between mountain ranges with the alpine Forest of Odin to the east and Donegast's Range to the west. The sea formed a natural moat to the king's urban castle, and the wall-topped cliffs were its ramparts.

"And it is virtually impenetrable," said Alfarin. He could tell that his wife was half listening as she bathed in the pleasantries and well-wishes of the crowds. Not that she was disinterested in military matters, but she did not revel in them as he did.

The isthmus, as supposed by the king and his advisers, was the only way to bring an invading army to Mithrendia. Rigorous mountain ranges lined the mainland coastal areas like tall sentinels, leaving no strategic access point from sea level. The invading army, then, would assuredly arrive at Trader's Gate, and assuming that this defensive post was breached, the army would be forced to march in a narrow column upon a narrow isthmus. Their reward for such an undertaking? A reckoning at Butcher's Gate, without any form of natural protection from the cyclopean glare of one hundred cannons. The king held a sentimental fondness for his artillery units, and his largest piece, Purgatory, fired fifteen hundred-pound balls of lead upon those bound for the afterlife.

Foreign invasion, then, was futile here, and King Alfarin intended to keep it that way. Every few years he made a grand tour of his fortifications, which he relished, although he disliked the endless parading. Garrison commanders were interviewed, often by him personally, to determine if improvements might be made to the battlements and those who defended them. This had been done to the king's satisfaction, and his entourage was headed back home.

"What troubles you?" asked Toriana as they turned south toward Glenhorne and the royal palace.

"Our defenses are superb," answered Alfarin with a careworn glance, "but I cannot help but wonder about the people."

As a boy, he had grown up with Old Norse tales about combating an enemy army or navy. The warrior king he had become on the plains of battle knew friend from foe, whereas for the political king in the courts of state, stark notions gave way to subtlety. What worried the guileless Alfarin, therefore, was a matter of allegiance. The smiling face of a friend and subject might mask a heretic or seditious upstart—for a cesspool of dissension grew upon the mainland, both within the city walls and without. Rumors, always rumors, ran rampant through the whispering lips of courtiers. Stricken with grave anxiety, the king found little rest these days. Perhaps it was best that he had married someone shrewd with a keen awareness of human nature and its duplicities.

"You worry excessively, my liege," Toriana said. "Archbishop Otta has a plan, and I think it a sound one, to counter these Lutheran rabble-rousers. Remember that he is to join us tonight at dinner."

"One cannot be too careful, my queen," said Johan Otta, archbishop of Mithrendia, between abbreviated slurps of a meaty broth. He sat with king and queen, and Baron Voya, at the royal table: a quartet condensed at one end of a banquet hall like a disproportionate assemblage at the stern of a Viking longboat.

Here, Alfarin had long noticed, words conveyed power, echoing off ashlar stone walls as they rose to meet a vast ceiling of enormous roof timbers. His great-grandfather had seen to their embellishment with dragons' heads, longboats, and runic symbols of Norse mythology carved into the trusses.

"Your Grace, you surprise me," Toriana responded with amusement. She had shed her furs in exchange for a scarlet robe trimmed in gold, and her flowing mane had been plaited. "Should I have been taken to fright if a few heretics were among that outpouring of well-wishers? Do you think an assassin might have been among their number?"

"My wife, if she could steady a lance, would joust in the tiltyard with men," offered Alfarin. "As it is, her boldness is something I find wanting in some of my knights. If only they had your resolve, my dear."

A slight crease of a smile appeared upon her flushed cheeks and full-bodied lips. "My resolve, my liege, is for the sanctity of the Church."

"And yet this pestilence grows," said the archbishop with his usual steady strength of delivery. His deep tone was of accord with his status as the highest-ranking ecclesiastical power in the realm.

Alfarin found Otta to be a stern fellow: tall, overbearing, and persuasive. His linear facial features of nose, brow, and chin appeared as if honed for a single purpose: the preservation of the Church and, along with it, the European states of Christendom.

"These disorders have a way of sorting themselves out," answered Voya as he manhandled a leg of turkey, which he chewed while speaking. "Ye need not meddle."

"That sort of carelessness will not be tolerated," said Otta with outstretched finger.

Voya raised his goblet and smiled a rebellious smile. "Can't have the peasants thinking for themselves, can we? Keep the Mass in Latin, I say, so they remember the sounds of the words but do not understand them."

Alfarin was used to his cousin's antics. Voya, the bastard son of Alfarin's late uncle, never stood on ceremony, nor did he stray from debate. Prior to their five-course meal, Voya had consumed a couple of goblets of wine. Some of it had missed the mark, observed the king, evidenced by the rivulets flowing down his cousin's scraggly brown beard, coating it with a reddish hue. Still, Voya held his libations well, and a sharp tongue accompanied his sharp mind.

"They have neither the knowledge nor the wisdom for God's Holy Word!" thundered the archbishop in irritation. "No," he said with a more composed voice. "It is the task for learned clerics. We must be the caretakers on behalf of the people."

"Caretakers or pretenders?" answered the baron. "Wouldn't want your clerics to be held accountable for their actions, would we? Luther, that learned monk from Saxon Germany," he said, emphasizing the word *learned* in his mocking retort, "merely puts our Holy Father the pope to account by illuminating what the scriptures say. I daresay that the scriptures, being inspired by God and the words of God, are the higher authority."

"Baron Voya! You speak heresy!" shouted Toriana. Alfarin could see embers of fire in her eyes. She seemed to desire a physical means of persuasion in the archbishop's dungeon. That would shut the baron's loose lips, but the king would not allow it.

After a moment's glance at her husband, Toriana checked herself, folding one tightfisted hand inside the other.

"What spiritual needs do the peasants have, Baron?" asked Otta with a high-arching brow. "What spiritual needs do they have that we cannot provide under our papal father's oversight? We the Church lead the people in the celebration of the saints and their feast days. Masses are said in almost unceasing succession for the people to partake in, and our priests offer the holy sacrament of penance via the confessional. Our monks comb the streets, offering indulgences for purchase to anyone desiring the remission of sins, so that their stay in purgatory may be of short duration. I'd say, Baron, we hold their souls in the highest regard."

Voya dabbed his wet lips with his beard. "Indulgences, eh? Sounds like a capital building campaign in Rome to me. Our money flows one way, southward, never to return."

"Do you not hear what the archbishop is saying?" implored the queen. "In one momentous sweep, this renegade monk Luther would diminish the daily affairs of Holy Mother Church and her intercession for those souls who suffer in purgatory. Luther, this heretic, would dare to curtail the sale of indulgences and the holding of requiem masses for the dead!"

Alfarin sighed. He had hoped for a quiet meal upon his return home, but his wife was irate, and Otta seemed much displeased. The king thought of his jester, but the present mood was too dark and religious for such frivolities. He saw a shadow at the doorway beyond, but rather than a whimsical jester, it was a nervous administrator who appeared in the banquet hall, holding documents of parchment.

The king waved him in, and the administrator, clothed in leather and wearing a felt cap, came forth.

"Your Majesty," said the administrator, "a thousand pardons for this intrusion. Your Majesty's secretary thought that His Grace the archbishop would be interested in these three warrants of execution."

"Heretics?" asked the king.

"Yes, Majesty."

"What are they accused of?" asked Alfarin as he read off the names of a tailor, a scholar, and a printer.

"Oh, that notorious trio," said Otta. "They are part of a conspiracy to create a Northmoorlandic translation of Luther's New Testament. I know because I questioned them and found them guilty. Westfall is the center of the problem, my king. The Lutheran heresy has spread like a plague from the high seas, and it has infested Westfall and the western Marches. Word travels fast—by mouth, by broadsheet. We watch the printers closely."

The king cast a wearied glance at Otta and his wife.

The queen scoffed with anger. "Fools! Can they not make do with what their betters condescend to tell them? Why must they conceive schemes of their own?"

The king nodded slowly. "They will die by fire, my dear. Their bodies scorched by flame. Will that not quench your wrath?"

Alfarin could see a faint flicker of a smile appear on his wife's furrowed face.

"And if afforded divine mercy," said Otta, "their souls will be subjected to further purifying pain in purgatory."

"Some mercy," interjected Voya with a subtle grin. "Two prolonged tortures for the price of one."

"It is the only way with these fools," said Otta. "They must be stamped out, utterly eradicated, with fire!"

"We must!" said the queen. "I can feel God's anger being kindled. I fear His wrath."

Alfarin had noticed his wife make a change of late to a more ascetic course. This dinner notwithstanding, she ate little. She spent hours in her best garments, outstretched upon the floor of the royal chapel, facing the altar. She was even beginning to scourge herself at night, laying open her fine alabaster skin about the shoulder blades. Some misguided monk had fashioned a device of braided leather with loose strands tipped with barbs for use as her personal chastisement. The king did not encourage this behavior, but she seemed of one accord with the archbishop these days.

"Only a strict and regular observance of the sacraments will do," said the queen. "As you know, Archbishop, I attend Mass thrice daily. Confession, penance, and almsgiving are also part of my regular habits. For who can fathom the capriciousness of God's mercy? Is not the minor offender's sentence in purgatory a dreadful and prolonged course?"

Otta seemed understanding, but his face bore a stoic expression. "That is why we invoke requiem masses, Your Majesty. To lessen the troubles of the departed. We desire that they reach heaven with minimal delay."

"And so shall it be for the condemned, if they would renounce their heretical beliefs," said the king. Alfarin leaned forward in his chair. "I would advise you, Cousin, to watch your tongue. Your continued safety remains at my discretion."

Toriana smiled as Voya looked down at his unfinished plate and said nothing.

Alfarin turned to the administrator. "Bring quill and ink."

The administrator bowed and left the room, returning moments later with several guards. As a domestic servant cleared his dinner away, Alfarin studied the parchments lying before him.

The king sighed again. "The sacrifices one must make for the collective good of the realm."

He signed the warrants, and the guards parted to inform the royal gaoler.

"Are we not defenders of our Catholic realm?" asked the king. "Are not the Crown and the Church as one, a united front to subdue all who challenge our authority to rule this kingdom?"

"I'm sure, my liege," said Otta.

"Leave us, Baron," said the king.

The queen seemed to delight in Voya's dismissal. He excused himself from their presence, not uttering a word more.

"My spies are everywhere, Archbishop," said Alfarin, "and my informants tell me that yours prove quite active as well. The heretics will be found."

"The heretics will be found and burned!" said the queen.

Otta nodded.

"Meanwhile we must maintain the security of our city defenses," said the king. "Some warlord by the name of Berbery stirs in the east."

"Berbery, I hear, dabbles in black magic," said Otta. "He is a pagan from the shores of the Black Sea who once had dealings with the Ottoman Turks. If the reports can be believed, he is a shape-shifter."

"A werewolf?" asked the queen.

"Aye," said Alfarin with a nervous twitch in his hollowed cheeks. This type of news is what kept him up at night. "We will double the watch along our east wall."

"And what of Westfall, my liege?" asked Otta.

"The duke's receptiveness to Lutheran sentiments troubles me," said the king.

"Why not go after him?" asked Toriana. Her eyes kindled again with a passionate zeal. "Why not seize his assets? He could be made an example of, to deter others."

The queen and archbishop were shrewd and persuasive, but the king was a loyal man. Alfarin sensed that he would need the support of those he trusted in due course. Besides, the duke had never moved against him.

"The Duke of Mithrendia is, and always has been, my friend," said Alfarin. "I've known him since we were boys. We will secretly watch those who come and go from his castle and no more."

"And what of the Marches, my liege?" asked Otta.

"Difficult as they are," said Alfarin, "those Celtic peoples with their ear-ringing bagpipes have proven loyal to me. Not all of them have forsaken the Church traditions. The eastern Marches remain staunchly Catholic. As for the western Marches, consider this: our south wall has never been attacked because the Marches have prevented any incursion from the moors. Truthfully, our defenses are not as stout in those quarters. We need their assistance."

"Surely not from the roaming bands of marauders upon the moors," said Otta.

"No," said the king. "Those barbarians matter little. Our threat lurks in the Black Mountains."

CHAPTER XXI

Harfagr's Landing

Harfagr's Landing, the Southernmost Tip of Northmoorland

"I thought that gale was going to push us eastward to the Faerøe Islands."

"Your men did well, Captain Dunman," said Lord Connaught.

"Obliged, I'm sure. But look at 'em. They're scared out of their wits."

Surely the whites of their eyes shone forth like those of madmen. Weather-beaten forearms shook as did those of a sufferer of delirium tremens as they fumbled with the mooring. The vestiges of their raggedy clothes provided little protection, and they were soaked through to the bone.

How would such a collective outfit be suitable for an expedition into the Black Mountains?

Even now, under the protection of this natural harbor, the

ship listed to port. Its cargo had shuffled about in the storm. Thankfully the starboard mooring would suffice until the cargo could be redistributed inside the hull.

"I've seen my share of gales," said Dunman, a well-dressed yet coarse-looking fellow of fifty with a salty beard. "But something sinister is about, sir. The winds dropped off as soon as the lighthouse was sighted. It's as if our course had been predetermined. It plays with a man's sanity."

"Nonsense, Captain!" said Connaught, his employer. "I'll hear no more of your superstitious musings."

Indeed, the ship's employer had rendered the treacherous journey quite useful in his candlelit quarters. The voyage had given him ample time to inventory his armaments—long swords, pikes, and cannonballs with gunpowder—and even falsified letters of introduction signed by the lord deputy of the Pale, the commander of English-occupied Ireland, which included Dublin. These documents might prove necessary if circumstances were to find Lord Connaught, as he called himself, in the court of some noble or ecclesiastical dignitary.

"Your men merely need a few nights at port, if you take my meaning," said Connaught.

"Aye," said Dunman. "At this point they'd drink the dregs of a barrel of this port's worst, sir."

"Then let them run about town, Captain! A little levity will set their spirits right."

Connaught had heard tales of this port. Its torchlit streets beyond the quay awakened the longings of a seafarer's heart, and whether merchant, navy, or pirate, all were welcome for the fair provision of their coinage. Fresh cod, herring, halibut, and Harfagr shrimp awaited them in the pubs and gambling houses. There was whiskey for the dry palate and cold ale sold in double-pint goblets for the more poignant of thirsts.

Women, of course, awaited the accompaniment of a lonely foreign adventurer.

"Aye, sir," said Dunman. "They can take care of themselves whiles off my watch. It's the pub for me, for a hearty meal, and then off in search of a down-feathered bed—a landlubber's bed, aye."

Connaught was preoccupied with other affairs. "Where is Gustafson's foundry?"

"Just east of the market, sir."

Connaught, a scheming man of thirty, had a determined eye set on things that might further his own ambitions. He bore the dark longshanks of a handsome adventurer, though frown lines were already setting in, as were crow's-feet from an excess of squinting. Though hardened, he was not necessarily a hard man, but he allocated little time for camaraderie beyond the scope of his purpose.

"This port is not affiliated with the kingdom of Northmoorland, is it?" he asked.

"Nay, sir," replied Dunman. "Harfagr's Landing is too far south of the Crown's reach for now. The king sets his mind on Mithrendia's defenses, leaving this place to govern itself. Besides, the moors are cut off from this port by the Black Mountains, and no one in his right mind would linger there."

Connaught looked about himself at the City of Ships with its great masts soaring like steeples. In the twilight, to the distant north, he saw the foreboding peaks of dark rock that Dunman spoke of, whereas the place here on the coastal plains was a virtual oasis. A narrow strip of land projected into the sea like a bent finger, protecting the harbor and beckoning the seaward traveler forth to enjoy shelter and respite.

"It seems hospitable enough," observed Connaught.

"The mountains?" replied Dunman, seemingly transfixed in his gaze at the northern horizon.

"Nay, sir," said Connaught with a mild grin. "This harbor."

Lord Connaught stepped down from the moored ship onto the quay and glared at the torchlit town. It seemed a curious place with timbered buildings of colorful siding and slotted spy windows. At the roof ridges, wooden beams crisscrossed, bearing the images of dragons. Here, he supposed, people were welcomed for their money and yet suspected all the same.

"That's a mighty craft you have moored out yonder," said a stranger. Blond locks defied his age, making this man of perhaps forty-five seem fifteen years younger. "Triple mast with artillery, I see. What's her name?"

"The *Augusta Rose*," said Connaught.

"Nice name for a lethal vessel," said the onlooker.

"She's made more than her share of widows."

"I see," answered the stranger.

"Your name, sir?"

The man, bearing a slumped, pensive posture, straightened at the request. "Øregard, at your service."

"Do you know how many times this port has been sacked?" asked Connaught.

"Well now," he answered with a bemused countenance. "That's an intriguing question for a visitor. Are you planning on doing the same?"

"No. My interest is merely from a historical perspective."

"I'm sure," said Øregard with no pretense of sincerity. "This port was sacked three times before the thirteenth century. But never since. Ole Crookjaw, the famed Baltic pirate, tried in 1434, but—"

"That will do, Øregard. Thank you," said Connaught as he walked past, from the quay onto the mainland.

Connaught could smell the pleasing scent of tobacco. The market was set up in a strategic place among the inns. It offered an eclectic mix of goods while stimulating a din of activity, which included bartering, laughter, and even fisticuffs. He strode by as peddlers offered snuff, dried meats, and candies. Gypsylike voices read palms and told fortunes, while a virtual armory of firearms, knives, and broadswords were available for the right price. At the far end of the market he saw a large ancillary building bearing the name Gustafson upon its walls. To his disappointment, the foundry was shut up for the night. Connaught made an abrupt turn, retracing his steps through the market, in search of a repast to satisfy his seaworthy stomach.

Øregard trailed some twenty yards behind, stepping into the shadows made by signs and building corners to avoid being noticed. *A nosy one, that man,* thought Connaught. With a subtle gesture, Connaught glanced to look back over his shoulder. He saw the raised collar of a cloak vanish behind a wall. Øregard, it seemed, had darted into the harbormaster's house.

He must be the eyes and ears of the harbormaster himself, thought Connaught as he entered a public house with a wind-tossed sign bearing the name the Lubbering Leviathan.

"Prospecting, eh? From what my informants tell me," said Femund, "King Henry is beginning to debase the coinage. You would do well to provide the English with a new source of silver."

"My presence is no longer welcome in my homeland," said Connaught. "I was exiled to the Pale, in Ireland, eight years ago."

The two were seated at a booth with a window offering a view of harbor. Femund, a man of fifty years or so, was known around the port as a master of arrangements. His graying hair looked disheveled and his cloak was a bit scuffed about the fringes, but Connaught saw cunning in his eyes.

"If you play your cards right," said Femund with a gravelly undertone, "you could redeem your value at home, become a peer of the realm, and make yourself rich."

"I prefer a life abroad," said Connaught, finishing off a slice of buttered bread. "Do you know what they do to traitors in England?"

"Let me guess," said Femund. "They chop off their heads and mount them on pikes for the birds to peck at."

"That's the finality of it, yes," said Connaught, leaning forward, "but not before the condemned is dragged to the place of execution on a horse-drawn hurdle. Lying prone, the head and torso feel every rock, every shift in terrain, in that makeshift wooden sled as it slithers and jostles over the road. That," he said in somber exclamation, "is a mere prelude to the pain."

"Aye?"

"Once there, the traitor is hung by rope on the gallows until half dead. Then he is cut down and revived with vinegar or smelling salts. A banquet table is laid out before him, only the table is covered in the executioner's choice of sharp iron instruments. They place him on an adjoining table, and the executioner selects one of the tools. He then cuts open the bowels of the condemned and draws out the intestines before the sufferer's very eyes."

"Despicable!" said Femund, looking away in disgust.

"Finally," said Connaught, "they cut off his head and divide the body into quarters. It is a veritable butcher's table."

Connaught knocked back the remains of his draught of ale

as the Lubbering Leviathan swelled to accommodate the full medley of its raucous patrons. Perhaps it was best that the din of activity mitigated the threat from any eavesdropping ears.

"The traitor's death," said Femund. "A grisly affair, to be hung, drawn, and quartered. Have you seen this in person?"

"Aye," said Connaught with disdain. "And they call themselves Christians. It is a state execution at its worst."

"You'll find no argument here, I'm sure," said Femund. He seized the arm of an unsuspecting barmaid as she walked by. "Wench? Bring me another draught of ale. I need a distraction from the barbarous notions of this conversation."

Connaught mustered a sly grin. "That, Femund, is why I delight in the northern latitudes. There's freedom here. It's a place where a man can do well for himself."

"Aye. And I hear that you are already a man of means."

"What you say is true, but my ambitions are more grandiose," said Connaught. "I mean to make a discovery of great import. Do you understand?"

"I may. What can I do for you, sir?"

The barmaid returned with another round. Femund sampled the heady draught and licked the froth that had gathered across his thick mustache.

"What if I were to say that I was organizing an unusual expedition?" asked Connaught.

There was an abundance of light over the long tables in the center of the establishment, but here about its periphery, a single candle acknowledged the shadows dwelling in each booth.

"To the Grand Sweep?" asked Femund. "It's a smuggler's haven for just about anything, including silver. Plenty of potential for profit there."

"No."

"Mithrendia? There are ways, even there, to bypass the customs officials."

"The walled city?" replied Connaught. He hated anything walled and barred. "Too confining for my purposes."

"Then where?"

"I am a direct man, Femund. When I say that I have a mind for silver, I mean at its source."

Femund gasped. "The Black Mountains!"

"Well?"

Femund pushed his draught away. "Only a fool would venture there."

"Indeed?" asked Connaught with a subtle tone of contempt. "They say those mountains are evil, do they not?"

"Well, yes and no."

This response irritated Connaught. "Do not answer me, sir, with riddles."

"Pshaw! Them mountains yonder?" asked Femund, pointing a thumb toward the north. "They ain't evil."

"Oh?"

"The deeds that have been done there, that's what makes the place evil. And mind you, it's an old evil."

"An old evil?" asked Connaught with a dismissive tone. He had little time for people's superstitions, but perhaps he could extract some nuggets of truth from an embellished legend.

"Ages ago," said Femund, "the first peoples, see, they came in through the Grand Sweep and across the isthmus into what has become Mithrendia. A few settled there, but most of their number moved south through the moors into the mountains, for they were an alpine folk. Lives had previously been lost in futile attempts to climb the Black Mountains from the sea, but then someone discovered an access point from the far north."

Connaught was growing impatient and tapped his fingers on the table in rapid succession. "And?"

"Well, they brought their pagan rites with human sacrifices. They worshipped the gods of the mountains, making pacts with evil spirits and erecting monuments to them in the high places. But these were a wicked people, and their deeds became even darker."

Connaught believed none of this, but he decided to play along. "What did they do?"

"They passed their firstborn children into the fire, and the elders drank the blood of beasts."

"You are going to get somewhere with this, I suppose," said Connaught. "And what became of them?"

"The Most High God saw their evil deeds, but being patient and slow to anger, He gave them time, centuries, to turn from their evil ways. They refused, blaspheming His name with unspeakable curses. Therefore, in due course, they received their recompense, and their dwelling places among the mountains became cursed."

"Cursed?"

"They became what they practiced," said Femund as he emptied his pint. "A mixture of man and beast with a mind bent on the will of their demonic overlords—yes, the very spirits they had long worshipped in the high places."

"Have you seen one of these creatures?"

"Aye. I have seen werewolves. Those wielding the most consummate powers, however, are the draugr."

"The draugr," said Connaught. "Yes, I have heard legends about them. They are revenants supposedly."

"Yes," said Femund, drawing closer across the table. "Their creation is of a special kind of union born of the grave. A man or woman dies only to rise again, to walk the earth once more in physical form as a vampyre. Yet they remain part of the spirit world. They can render themselves a misty vapor, like a dense fog, rendering any attempt at bondage and incarceration useless."

"If they are real," said Connaught with a skeptical tone, "has there been no crusade to stamp them out?"

"Once a battalion of soldiers sponsored by the Church ventured south from Mithrendia into the Black Mountains, never to return. Various motley bands have also tried, but if battle-hardened soldiers failed, you can imagine the carnage awaiting untrained peasants armed only with pitchforks and sickles."

"All massacred?"

"Not necessarily," said Femund. "The draugr, you see, are territorial. If their numbers or those of their minions decline, they replenish their stock by turning humans. They infect their victims with their own accursed nature. Nevertheless, the draugr are careful not to swell their ranks."

"And no human lives among them?"

"It is said that no seed may be sown for a harvest in the high places," said Femund. "There in the Black Mountains, the hunter becomes the hunted. Sustenance is futile. Death is certain. Only black witches and warlocks have been able to coexist with them, because they serve the same masters."

"Come now. Someone is bound to rise above the superstition of such desolations," said Connaught.

"I have seen parties of men vanish into the fjords," said Femund, "never to return."

Connaught was becoming exasperated and slammed his hands on the table. "So they disappeared. The mountains are treacherous. How does that prove that the draugr exist?"

Strangers at nearby tables looked over at them and began to murmur their disapproval. Femund seemed to notice, but rather than betray any annoyance, he summoned his acquaintance forward with a beckoning finger. Connaught leaned over the table.

"If you have a mind for silver and would place yourself at the brink of death to obtain it," whispered Femund, "the lodes are to be found in draugr lands. And if these creatures exist, you will certainly find them there."

"So be it," said Connaught. "I will find my silver, and nothing—no mystical creature born of man who is also the spawn of the devil—will prevent me from achieving my aims."

Femund leaned back. "And you need my help to assemble a team, I gather," he said in a normal voice.

Connaught leaned back as well. "Aye. Sailors do not make mountaineers. I need swordsmen, strongmen, archers, carpenters, and miners who can traverse high ground."

"I know a few local carpenters and mountaineers," said Femund. "But the warriors are found among the transients. Never fear, my friend. Plenty of the foolhardy adventurous type enter our harbor. However, I will need some time to scour the market, the inns, and the public halls."

"I will give you a fortnight," said Connaught.

"Fifty pounds, up front, is my fee," said Femund. "And twenty percent of your haul, if your team returns from its quest."

"Five percent."

"Ten."

"Done!" said Connaught. "But under no condition will your portion exceed one thousand pounds."

"My young English friend, you are ambitious," said Femund. "If you bring me a thousand pounds and are still alive to tell your tales, I will consider myself well compensated."

"Indeed," said Connaught. "You are about to become a very wealthy man, Femund. I will have the contract drawn up tomorrow."

CHAPTER XXII

The Hermit

"Well, young man, what has been done to you?" Lars, barely conscious, could hear an elderly man's voice as bony fingers fumbled with his own.

"Your fingernails are covered with blood," said the old man. "And your back is pierced with arrows. Yet you live!"

Lars felt the agonies of the puncture marks, including a large one in his abdomen, to say nothing of the lacerations and bruises that marked every appendage. A slight tug on the shaft of the arrow sent Lars howling through gnashed teeth. He was fully awake now.

"These must be removed," said the old man, relinquishing his walking stick and bending down. It was a windy day, and his bushy, unkempt beard, which drooped to his lower belly, swung about in the gusts. "And soon."

Before the old man could pull, Lars grasped his forearm. "Leave it be for now."

"But these must be extracted."

"Bring me some food," Lars growled.

The old hermit obeyed, shuffling off to his small slipshod cottage. Its thatched roof sagged from fallen tree limbs, and its wattle-and-daub walls had seen their own share of arrows with some remaining in the half-timbering.

Lars continued to lie on his belly, but the soft grass failed to comfort him in the noonday sun. He thought only of the night with its mystical curative powers.

Minutes later, the hermit returned to the river's shore where Lars had been found floating among the reeds. The hermit spoon-fed Lars with a small wooden ladle from a clay-fired bowl. It was some sort of stew with fish, potatoes, and carrots mixed with herbs. Lars would have eaten almost anything, but the hermit's fare was even better than his last meal at the McCormicks'.

"Your name, old man?"

"Janus."

"They call me Lars."

The hermit hesitated. "And what of your wounds, Lars?"

Lars lay with one cheek upon the ground. "Leave them be." He could feel an insect teasing about his neck, but this was nothing compared to the pain of the arrows, which pointed upward like raised standards without a flag.

"But you will die," said Janus.

Lars closed one eye, the one touching the grass. With the other, he saw a crucifix revealed from between the folds of the old man's tunic. It dangled there in front of him from a meager necklace of leather.

"Let me alone," said Lars, "and you will behold a miracle."

The hermit seemed to look upon him with pity. "I could prepare fresh straw bedding for you. Even here, if need be, by the shore."

"Here I will lie," said Lars as the hermit covered Lars's lower extremities with sackcloth. "You have done enough."

As the moon awoke from its diurnal slumber, Lars began to dream. The fusion of man and beast brought strange thoughts to his mind, and this night, the beast ushered in its recollections: little snippets, no more than a few blinks of the eye, of the wolf's remembrances from its last manifestation.

Arrows fly in the streets of Westfall as he tears open a hole in the McCormicks' roof. Adaira is screaming as her father, in a controlled rage, charges upstairs with a large pike.

The city gaolers in Glenhorne, accompanied by a team of archers, give chase across Cuidaffe Green. The wolf fells some of their number in the empty basin of the Grand Canal.

A torrent of water sweeps him away into the Olan River. The flow carries him eastward, until he is ducking under massive city walls and traveling through Dunleavy's pipe. His enlarged chest, deprived of air, begins to take on water, which thrusts his tumbling carcass against the stone lining. Drowning is nigh, and he blacks out.

He awakens, coughing water, somewhere in the Forest of Andia, where he is unclad and caught up in an outcrop of reeds.

A talkative owl, somewhere high in the trees, wakes the man from his beastly slumber with its screeches. It is the dead of night. Lars glances over in the faint glow of the moon and sees the arrows lying on the ground. With a satisfied grin, he rolls himself over.

No more pain.

"What kind of devilry is this?" said Janus, examining his patient.

"Did I not say you would behold a miracle?" asked Lars.

In the soft light of the early morning, Lars proffered the remains of his wounds for viewing. There were no punctures, scabs, or scars.

"How can this be?" asked the hermit as he grasped the crucifix in his fingers. "And my animals, the birds, the deer who eat out of my hand? Nowhere to be found since your arrival."

Lars stretched his arms as he paid no heed to the man's words. "So this is the Forest of Andia. Peaceful, yes, but I see by the looks of your hovel that it is not always so."

Janus glanced back at his trophies, his spoils of war, that stabbed his walls. "Oh, those?" he said, laughing. "These are prime hunting grounds for Baron Olibard, Countess Neschy, and the Earl of Jelling. Only they make war with one another as often as not. I catch a little of their crossfire now and then."

"Yet you remain here," marveled Lars.

Janus smiled with outstretched hands. "It is my home. I help the travelers, like you, who make their way through the forest."

Lars wrapped himself in the sackcloth and stood up while he studied the crucifix Janus was holding. "You put your faith in such things?"

"I do," said Janus. "And if you would allow me to venture, I'd say that our meeting was providential."

Lars was confused. "Providential?"

Janus pointed up at the sky and placed a hand to his lips as if whispering a secret. "I think He arranged it."

Lars thought about the stew. The beast had not managed to feed, and without nourishment there would have been no healing. Lars also remembered that upon awaking to his wounds, he had been too weak to hunt.

"Would you like to know more about such things?" asked Janus.

Lars did not attend Mass with the McCormicks, and he hadn't done so growing up, what with his mother being a witch. He had no concept of a father, let alone a heavenly Father. *What is that to me now?* he thought. Besides, his stomach was rumbling again. Lars waved a dismissive hand.

"You know what I want?" said Lars as he glanced up at the hermit's dilapidated roof. "That stew. Bring me some more, and I will fix your roof."

Janus nodded.

"Afterward," said Lars, "can we make some clothes from this sackcloth?"

Lars's moods were growing darker with each passing day. The thatched roof had been repaired, and there was little reason to linger, except that he had nowhere else to go. He could not go back to Westfall, of course, and resume his former ways, and he couldn't he stay here with this loner the hermit.

He thought of Janus's necklace with the crucifix. It had not bothered him at first, but now Lars felt an increasing revulsion toward it. The beast within was weakest just after a manifestation, but now its will was growing inside the man's mind. It was taking hold of him, and the beast detested any representation of the cross of Calvary. Darkness was its abode, and it was there that the beast would dwell.

Meanwhile, Lars was becoming acquainted with the Forest of Andia. He had scouted the castles of the warring nobles

Janus had mentioned. Each noble seemed to possess an abundance of land, yet they thirsted for more at the cost of bloodshed, at the cost of the armed men in their employ, like pawns on a chessboard, depleting their own resources in their greed.

Lars had also found that his powers were advancing. He could not yet shape-shift at will, but the frequency of these occurrences was growing. As the beast grew in its ferocity, the man gave way inch by inch. Paradoxically, the utter abandonment of will to the wolf's purposes had an intoxicating effect on the man, and Lars found himself drawn to its effects. Here his rage at the world, and his torment by wicked spirits summoned in his mother's pentagram, found retribution in an outburst of predatory carnage. A man of brutish strength but of modest means in society wielded almost absolute power as the beast. What he needed was an opportunity to display such power before the social institutions that once lorded over him.

One night, fifteen armed men, with nothing more than torchlight, encircled the oak tree where Lars lingered, asleep. At least he was pretending to sleep; his heightened senses had picked up the men's scent from a half mile away. Through squinted eyes, he detected their armaments. They carried longswords, recently sharpened, and their hauberks bore the heraldry of Countess Neschy. Lars kept as still as a statue as some of their number dismounted their horses.

The horses were nervous.

"One of the baron's men, I'd wager, by the scraggily looks of him," said one of the scouts. "There's no fortune to be had here. Nothing worth takin'."

"A deserter then?" asked another.

"They execute deserters."

"Once they find them."

"You think there's a reward for catching one?"

"I dunno. Perhaps."

The creature within Lars's breast began to growl. It resonated with menace and malice. The horses launched about wildly with their forelegs, making it difficult for the riders to maintain their mounts.

"'Tis one of them!" shouted one of the knights. "A werewolf!"

They've seen my kind before, thought Lars. Where then do the shape-shifters dwell, and what are their numbers?

"One of Berbery's men," said another knight. "He is moving his forces west to attack us. Kill him before he changes!"

One threw his sword end over end like a dagger. Its aim was true, but Lars was too fast a climber. He could already feel the change coming upon him as he reached one of the higher boughs of the tree. The pain, though present, was not as acute as before. In fact, it lessened with each change as he was becoming one with the beast. Skin birthed dilated hair follicles, and bone shifted to accommodate a surplus of muscle fiber.

A second knight secured a bow from his saddle mount and matched it with an arrow. He aimed well and fired. The shaft of the arrow was snatched in midair, inches away from the beast's sternum, by the padded folds of a beastly palm, which enveloped the missile and split it in two. The werewolf snarled with an anger akin to hatred.

Down below at ground level, shards of iron were upraised. The beast jumped from the tree without thought of self-preservation.

The horses did not wait for their masters' command and scattered from the base of the oak tree. The werewolf chased from behind as its hind legs pummeled the ground; this allowed for an explosive gait with swift, elongated jumps and brief moments of contact with the earth between. The beast leapt onto one of the mounts, sinking its claws into a knight's protective-leather-covered back and pulling the man off the saddle as the horse maintained its frightful gallop. The werewolf dragged the knight upon the wet ground as if he were made of straw and dug its serrated enamel into the neck of its prey. The man cried out in unrestrained agony, and blood coated the ground like a scarlet blanket.

The werewolf, having fed, looked up at the lustrous moon and gave its howling consent. It studied the lunar object, seeming to discern information from its pockmarked surface. The wolf lowered its head and ran eastward, rather than chasing its remaining prey. It saturated the air with the eerie vapor of its vigorous exhalations, racing as if against time itself. For half an hour it kept this vigorous pace, before making one final leap.

It came to a halt and observed its surroundings. In a clearing just beyond the dense forest, the werewolf saw a fiery encampment flagged to the full with flaming red coats of arms. Each bore a shield, quartered, with a triple-mast sailing ship on the lower left and upper right; a pair of crossed scimitars on the upper left and lower right; and a leering dragon in the center. This army of shape-shifters, like him, worshipped the moon in beastly form.

The encampment caught a new scent and looked due west. Lars stood his ground as hundreds of savage canines surveyed his sudden incursion onto their lands.

Rather than charging, they began incessantly howling.

The beast within Lars understood as they bade him welcome.

CHAPTER XXIII

Arrested Momentum

"It is not like Matthew to stay away this long," said Catherine.

"Well, he needs to get back here before he gets sacked," said Marley, the tavern keeper, as he stacked some mugs behind the bar.

"You don't really mean that, Mr. Marley," said Mary.

"You don't think so, eh?"

Catherine knew that Marley was a sucker for the wants of his girls. He hemmed and he hawed with an assortment of protests and warnings that a proprietor is able to dangle before the hired help. In the end, however, their opinions and requests factored into almost all considerations of their employer, unless Berta was present to pound her husband into submission with one of her sour, jealous moods.

Catherine had observed that the beloved curiosity known as Friar Draugr was struggling. Carboni had lingered about town for nigh a week more than was his wont, and those extra days had not been productive. They had been full of ale. Not for recreational and social enjoyment, but for many hours of continuous and egregious consumption.

Once inspired by drink, Carboni had sung a few mountain dirges to the delight of the patrons. That was before his utterings in the Blue Griffin began to border on the incomprehensible.

"Nay, Matthew's a good lad," said Allister, a frequent patron who had been listening in. "It's that fat friar who needs to be sacked."

"And I'm tired of having to haul him upstairs to an unpaid room," said Marley with a scowl.

"The poor dear," said Catherine as she glanced at the piteous creature slumbering at the far corner table. She noted that his hair was disheveled and that that his tunic was full of stains.

"He smells a bit ripe if you get within five feet of him," said Mary.

Ben finished wiping off a table. "I found him in the horse trough this morning. I walked out there and saw two large dirt-stained feet dangling from the edge and horse muzzles on either end lapping up the water. He just sat there, all wet, muttering something about judgment and being damned."

"He was already grieving when he first arrived," said Catherine, "though he did his best to appear jovial."

"And then that mean-spirited Canon Pious arrived," said Mary. "How could a man of the cloth say such—"

"Aye," said Marley, who, after a heavy sigh, appeared to have lost his scowl. "That was when our friar took a downturn. Look after him, will you, girls?"

Catherine nodded and went to fetch some supplies. She returned with soap, fresh water, and clean linens, while Mary produced a plate from what could be scoured from the kitchen. It took some prodding, but they managed to awaken the friar. He was still somewhat incoherent, but they helped him to wash his face and hands. And then with a clumsy effort, he began to eat.

Carboni's spirits seemed to revive a bit as he filled his stomach. An hour later, Catherine could tell that his words were less garbled. She and Mary let him rest a bit more, and later on, once he could articulate his thoughts, she sat down with him. The odor was only a little less bothersome, but Catherine fought through it. She was determined to divert Carboni's attention away from the source of his depression.

"Now," she said, "tell us about these draugr. You seem to know them better than anyone in the Marches. We've heard that there is a prophecy."

"Aye," said Carboni. "The prophecy of Saint Augustus. The draugr march north from the Black Mountains. The original settlers, who compose their highest ranks of elders, crossed the isthmus many centuries ago. They passed through Glenhorne, before Mithrendia existed of course, and then went south into the moors. From there they entered the alpine lands and desecrated them with their evil religious rites. The draugr will retrace those steps, though in reverse order."

Catherine was curious. "Why is that?"

"It is what they know. The elders remember that path. It is sacred to them."

"When will this be?"

"Soon," said Carboni as he wiped his face with a dry cloth. "Weeks? Months? I cannot say with precision. They will come by night, of course, as they sleep by day. Their movements are difficult to predict. They have their own ways, and sometimes they linger in places."

Catherine placed her elbows on the table and rested her chin in her hands like a child being told a story. Despite his unkemptness, Carboni was someone she felt comfortable being around. She regarded him as someone trustworthy. "Who was this Saint Augustus?"

"Not all settlers dwelled in the mountains," he replied. "Some chose to live here, where Augustus arrived to convert many of their number to our faith."

"Did he utter the prophecy that is named after him?"

"Aye. Augustus knew that the alpine dwellers would always remain a threat to the Catholic settlements in the north. Therefore their safety here would remain dependent on their unity. The prophecy states that the draugr will return from whence they came when the Church turns against its own people."

Since his experiment in heroism, Matthew had been grounded. Rather, he had been placed in the stocks of a public square in Helsborg that doubled as an open market.

It was a strange phenomenon, watching the exchange of agricultural produce, fresh-caught fish, and wool from a prone position. For two days now he had engaged in this unique opportunity.

His judiciaries had provided a wooden seat. But with a forcibly flattened torso, and wrists and neck bound in the narrow holes of a wooden yoke, he found that it had not taken long for discomfort to set in.

The restraints were beginning to rub rashes and abrasions. Any itch of the face, or anything southward for that matter, became a source of torturous, unrelieved discomfort.

Matthew had also been a public spectacle. Shoppers stared at the incarcerated wonder. He knew the reputation of adolescent boys with their nefarious and crowd-pleasing practice of pelting the face of one in his position with a medley of tomatoes, potatoes, and pies.

And yet no such teenager had felt so inclined.

The vanquisher of the werewolf deserved better no matter what legal authority he had thwarted in the process.

Instead of being hit with vegetables, his stationary head had been wreathed with garlands of flowers by the womenfolk of east Mithrendia. Matthew had never known such attentions from the fairer sex, nor could he escape from them. The young women lingered, feeding him, massaging his aching shoulders, and covering his flushed cheeks with preferential kisses.

Am I in heaven? he wondered while incarcerated in the stiff wooden stocks, which acted like a strict chaperone.

"Master Matthew?" asked a deep, stoic voice that did not figure among the new female admirers.

Matthew's ego was swelling with the attention. "Lord of the maidens, you mean."

"A lord of the maidens who cannot lift his head."

He was an older man, fully whiskered, and well-dressed in the livery of someone important.

Matthew struggled with the yoke. "Aye."

"Would you like to lift it again?" asked the man.

"They say that I will be freed from these stocks in three more days."

"What if I let you loose now? Would that be worth your newfound celebrity?"

"What do you mean?"

"The Duke of Mithrendia has heard of your accomplishment. He would like to offer you sanctuary."

"Sanctuary?"

"Safe conduct into his luxurious abode. You need not work at the tavern anymore."

"But the maidens …"

"Suit yourself. Kisses or not," said the liveried man, "the chill of the night air is known to cause a crick in the neck."

Cricks were like muscle cramps, except that an uncomfortable head was a more delicate item.

"I've yet to experience one," said Matthew as he nudged his upper lip toward a slight twitch in his nose.

The man looked about them. "Notice the breeze that has picked up this last hour?"

"How could I not?" answered Matthew with some irritation. The maidens kept their distance as the liveried man outstayed his welcome. "There's not much else to do but sit and observe the minute details of this square."

"A cold front is coming," said the older man. "And with it surely a stiff neck." He leaned down and spoke in Matthew's ear. "Are you too stiff-necked to do something about it?"

CHAPTER XXIV

Wolfsbane

"Erik, my love?" said Adaira. Of late the daughter of Lars's employer had found the other apprentice back at work in McCormick's shop, where he was poring over plans for the new cathedral. This time Erik was studying the narthex with some proposed setbacks in the walls. These setbacks would provide some needed savings in material costs, but they were not unwelcome, for McCormick had found a means to make the architecture aesthetically pleasing.

Adaira's presence was pleasing as well. The two young people had grown close during his feverish convalescence— ever since Lars had revealed his true nature.

Adaira still teased a bit, yes. However, there was true sentiment in her words and no more talk of that goat the guild merchant's son, Frederik.

Or had Erik once characterized him as a boar?

"Yes, my love?" said Erik. This time Erik's response was one that resonated with sincerity rather than sarcasm.

She leaned her head a bit to the left and seemed to study his kindly eyes. Erik knew that Adaira had learned the events of that fateful day from the pit laborers when he had challenged their brutish master. Now that Lars had gone, the laborers had no reason to hush it up.

That brute. That bully. That beast.

Erik had run home, covered in debilitating wounds, to warn her family before collapsing in a fit of fever—an otherwise lethal fever that he somehow had survived.

Erik knew that he was not the physical specimen that Lars was. He was not the spontaneous enigma who had kept Adaira guessing and crooning. Nevertheless, Erik thought he offered her loyalty, devotion, and security. He was already in line to succeed her father as master mason one day. Perhaps she might recognize those advantages in time.

Gratefully Erik harbored notions that there was already some movement in that direction.

"Father wishes to speak with you," she said.

As a rule, Erik did not like to be distracted from his concentration. The sculptors knew when to leave the studious young man alone.

But Adaira was a welcome interruption. He did not avail himself of that impatient look he bore at such times and glanced at her with affection.

"You've regained your color," said Adaira as she walked over and rubbed her thumb over his forehead.

He could smell the sweet scent of a bloom she had placed in her long, flowing hair, which draped over his shoulder. *Let us linger like this a little while,* he thought as she hovered over him.

"I will take you to him," Adaira offered, which he could not, and would not, refuse.

She led him upstairs. Along the way, their hands bumped, and she ran her fingers over his. They clasped one another like wayward souls who had found a mutual affection. However, they instinctively let go of one another as they appeared in the master mason's presence.

McCormick was sitting before the fire and smoking a pipe. The gray strands in his thick red beard seemed more vigorous ever since he'd impaled a werewolf. He had been the talk of the Merchant Quarter, and all of Westfall for that matter, ever since his heroic deed. Nevertheless, the master mason seemed grounded in humility, often responding to admirers that he had done no more than what any father might do to protect his family.

"Been peeking at the drawings again, eh?" said McCormick. "You know that it's Sunday."

"I wondered, sir, why the sculptors were not around," said Erik. "Guess I've lost my bearings a bit as of late."

"I'd say it's no wonder after such an illness."

"Will you be attending Mass with us?" asked Adaira with a subtle eagerness.

"Do you feel up to it, Erik?" asked McCormick.

Now Erik understood why she was wearing her best dress. He wouldn't miss this for the world.

Erik took a deep breath. "I feel that I am ready."

"Spera in Deo, quoniam adhuc confitebor illi: salutare vultus mei, et Deus meus."

Erik did not understand most of the Latin words that the

priest uttered, yet somehow they comforted him. They were foreign yet familiar from years of repetition.

"Gloria Patri, et Filio, et Spiritui Sancto."

That part, however, he understood, and he felt grateful as each member of the congregation made the sign of the cross over their forehead and torso. He was grateful because his prayers, those he uttered as he was clinging to life at the verge of his mortality, had been answered.

The McCormick family sat comfortably in a wooden pew about halfway between the front row and the last. The church floor plan, of Norse influence, was a simple arrangement of a modest narthex and an elongated nave. It was devoid of side aisles and that formal grid-like geometry of arched colonnades. Rather, the trussed roof of the sanctuary rested on four timbered walls with painted wood siding, sequestering the congregation in a familiar space with close proximity to the sculptures and tapestries of the saints. An ample arrangement of fenestrations allowed light to flood in, and the light gave its life to heavenly thoughts of spiritual contemplation and even that unquenchable earthly habit of people-gazing. With the hundred or so families who had gathered to partake of Mass and to look upon one another, perhaps none of them celebrated life on this day with quite the fervor as the master mason's.

Erik gazed upon the large crucifix mounted on the wall behind the altar. It bore the likeness of the crucified Christ, bearing the sins of the world. Those agonies were beyond Erik's comprehension. Still, he had witnessed some of the hardships of life, which matured the young apprentice beyond his years. He had entered such trying times a mere boy, but left in their wake was the countenance of a man.

Adaira's hand had found its way back into his. For the moment, his heart was full.

Erik looked about at the congregants of this two-hundred-year-old church. There was something loving about this place. There were no lords or ladies here, no dignitaries of note. In the Merchant Quarter, the usual attendees were merchant families and their employees. These were hardworking people who enjoyed the traditions and the celebrations of their saint day feasts. They were people who went about their daily business not perfectly, but with a fairness in trade and a concern for the welfare of their city. Many of them did not understand the need for Luther's reforms, though they respected the Duke of Mithrendia. He was known to be a good and fair man.

For Erik's part, he knew little of the circumstances surrounding the duke's position. Neither did McCormick or Adaira. They were no theologians, and yet to them the system did not seem to be broken, at least not here at Saint Michael's parish. No heretics were spawned from here.

Meanwhile, the men of the McCormick household were acclimating to defensive military exercise. The wolf scare had galvanized the master mason, who felt strongly about the pike as a tactical weapon.

Erik, like the others, had heard rumors of werewolf sightings in the east, somewhere in the obscure corners of the Forest of Andia. The duke's bailiff had even approached McCormick about forming a regiment. A month later, about fifty had organized on the north green abutting Castle Brygge, the duke's abode. This company of volunteer soldiers had been swelling in number ever since.

Erik learned from McCormick, who was aware of the tactical maneuvers of the ancient Greeks and Romans. These maneuvers, of course, did not always figure with sixteenth-century weaponry, but the target was a werewolf—or a group of werewolves if the reports from the east could be believed.

McCormick said that a werewolf overpowered. A werewolf could strike and cleave to any point of the human body. The beast possessed athletic powers that dwarfed those of a mere man. Its claws were like daggers and swords, wielding ferocious power. It took skill and courage to fell one werewolf, but what of a horde of their kind?

Erik asked his master this question. McCormick responded that it required offensive and defensive formations. It was best to shield the body while presenting numerous offensive strike points. It was a first-strike opportunity, or else the beast would rip the shields away and expose the torso to a brutal assault.

With that in mind, the phalanx formation of the ancient Greeks was revived for fighting within narrow urban streets. Rows of pikes were set at varying angles, threatening to impale the enemy, as the pikemen marched in disciplined synchronicity.

For defensive maneuvering, the tortoise, or testudo, formation of the Romans was employed. Men hidden behind walls and roofs of convex shields could project spears or pikes through small gaps in their cover. If the wall of shields were breached, then the soldiers had been taught to re-form the lines and surround the enemy with an improvised wall.

Behind these formations, a row of archers would fire their volleys. If high ground or even a balcony or battlement were found for the archers, this proved even better.

"Good!" shouted McCormick. "We've accomplished much this day, men. Go home to your families with pride. Company dismissed!"

The men grunted their approval and began to disperse to

their homes, but Erik walked up to his commander as he stood beside the castle walls. It was a fine cloudless day, seemingly heedless of the dangers that were being prepared for.

"Sir?"

"Yes, Erik?" replied McCormick.

"I wanted to ask you something last Sunday," said Erik with a sheepish tone, "but Adaira was around."

"Oh? I thought you enjoyed her company."

Erik wanted to slap himself. "I do! At all times, sir. It's just ... I didn't feel it was appropriate to ask you a certain question in her presence."

McCormick seemed to understand what his apprentice was getting at. "And you want to ask me for her hand?"

Erik could take on a bully, but here, on this occasion, he was at a loss for words. It took a moment to collect himself. "How did you know, sir?"

"I'm not so preoccupied with the affairs of the shop and regiment to neglect being a father."

Of course, thought Erik. He tried to articulate a response, but in his nervousness he said nothing.

"Well?" said McCormick.

"Sir?"

"I've never known you to be tongue-tied before, Erik. Say what you have to say."

Erik had not thought it would be this difficult to verbalize his thoughts. However, this was a momentous occasion, one he would remember for the rest of his life.

"With your permission, sir," he said in haste, "I would like to marry your daughter."

McCormick seemed to suppress a laugh by clearing his throat. He studied his young apprentice like one who was counting the dwindled numbers of his kin. Adaira was precious to her father on every account, and she was his only child. Erik knew that McCormick would take no less than the best suitor for her present and future security. He also knew that his financial prospects left much to be desired, at least for now. All depended on his becoming the next master mason.

Erik's face was flushed with anxiety.

"Well, my boy," McCormick said at last, "I'll have you if Adaira will have you."

Erik could not help himself. He lunged forward and embraced the burly master mason as if he were his own father.

Of course he would be his father if Adaira said yes.

"Well now, well now," said McCormick with a hearty chuckle.

There would be a second round of nervousness to follow, but for now Erik felt the joy of relief. The McCormicks had been like family to him, especially after he had lost his own. He still had an aunt, an uncle, and some cousins, but his parents had departed this world far too young.

McCormick and Erik walked home talking about any number of things, not least of which were Adaira and the regiment. The streets filled with their words of sentiment, with merriment, and with well-wishing.

If all could live to see such times renewed.

A poison bloomed beyond the city walls. It was a beautiful dark blue-purple, captivating yet deadly. At times of direst need, the city archers were known to tip their arrowheads in these toxic juices.

Indeed the formation of the regiment had been well-timed.

Night was coming, and it would cast shadows upon the meadows of the mountains of the west, where wolfsbane bloomed.

CHAPTER XXV

The Doctrines of Men

Catherine Latimer's Journal Entry
Castle Brygge

Perhaps I have been too cautious in saving our money, but thanks to the duke, I now have an abundance of parchment at my disposal.

There are some who keep a diary. As a habit, I do not. But the horrors of yesterday afternoon overwhelm me. I must put my words to paper lest these dark memories lose their lucidity over the years and in the future I fail to separate fantasy from the reality of a living nightmare.

Before I compose what my hand trembles to write, let me address some recent developments. Matthew, it seems, is a hero. His thwarting of a werewolf at the Grand Canal, and his subsequent incarceration after being convicted of wasting a cistern's worth of municipal water, caught the attention of the

Duke of Mithrendia. His Grace, a kind and generous man, has offered the four of us a place to stay in his castle. Of course we accepted without reservation, though it proved somewhat difficult to say goodbye to Mr. Marley and the patrons of the Blue Griffin. Not that I will miss Berta and her horrific mood swings.

Another event requires my attention. We had always assumed that there were four of us, but that number has been revised to five. Two gentlemen brought a man to the castle a mere day after our arrival. Ben and Mary recognized him instantly as Professor Porter. He was absolutely elated to see us, as we were to see him, even though to me he was a complete stranger.

While we all miss home, the terrorist attack sobers us, tempering our enthusiasm to some degree. The professor had not seen this and was astonished to hear of its occurrence. I think it is easier for me, an orphan, as the others have family whom they long for. I do hope that my roommate and Monsignor Lewis are well.

It seems that the professor was the first to travel through the portal as verified by his conspicuous absence from Rhymer, which Ben asserted was of about a week's duration. The four of us always had each other, whereas the professor arrived alone in Northmoorland, suffering from temporary memory loss. I thought our arrival on the moors was bad enough, but his imprisonment in Berbery's castle seems worse. Nevertheless, he has recounted his tale to the duke and duchess, who have alerted the king and queen. Rumors are spreading throughout the city, I am told, and the inhabitants of Mithrendia sleep poorly at night. Something ominous hovers over us—this threat in the east, along with movements from the south. The duke summoned Carboni to give an account of his sightings of the draugr in the southern alpine regions. The entire household here is on high alert.

There, that diversion has helped. The stroke of the quill has once again found its natural rhythm in my hand. For though the threats from beyond the city walls linger, none of them shake me to the core as the events of yesterday.

They led this man in a somber procession of armed guards and clergy to Cuidaffe Green. I understand that he could not have been older than thirty, but his body was ravaged and broken like an elderly man's. He had to be led out in a wooden cart. What tortures they had subjected him to, the authorities did not say. I suspect that the rack was utilized, judging by his agonized cries when the men lifted his arms to carry him from the cart. Dislocated joints are the usual result, separating ball from socket, when the ropes stretch the arms and legs farther than their natural limits.

Hundreds of city dwellers had gathered around the walled encirclement as if anticipating a festival or grand entertainment. It was some thirty yards in diameter and consisted of a log fence just high enough for adults and teenagers to lean upon and rest their elbows. Small children would swing underneath and chase one another, while in the background vendors peddled their meat pies, cakes, and ales. To the east side, grandstands had been constructed for the clergy and the nobility.

The jovial, carnival-like atmosphere did nothing to allay strong convictions. The notion that this man was getting what he deserved was accepted by many. Among the commoners there were even exuberant shouts of, "Burn the heretic! Feed him to the flames!"

Their shouts were obliged. The clergymen made a symbolic gesture of turning the condemned over to the state for execution. A parchment was passed, and some words were uttered in Latin. The executioner, a stout bearded man with a grisly black hood, bound the poor condemned fellow to the center stake with iron shackles. It was a small knoll covered in meticulously placed logs and kindling laid in a circular arrangement. The spiked ends of the timbers rose up in diagonals like defensive spears placed on a battlefield. Yet the condemned would be engulfed rather than impaled.

I studied the so-called heretic and noted that his undershirt fit loosely. It had once been white, but now it was covered in bloodstains and the filth of whatever dank, dark cell they had kept him in.

I hear that he was once a priest who had been defrocked.

The condemned man had been swayed by the writings of Martin Luther, who argues that one may find salvation, and therefore eternal life, by faith alone—not by good works, not by frequent participation in the sacraments, not by the purchase of indulgences, and not by a lengthy stay in purgatory, but by God's grace through faith in His Son, who died on the cross for our sins and was raised from the dead on the third day.

Tortured as this priest had been, the authorities had failed to obtain a recantation from the condemned. Now they would let the fires purge him of his heresy.

They lit the kindling around his feet. His torso and face shook in tormented fear, like knowing that the burner on the stove is on but you are powerless to remove your hand. His lips moved rapidly as he mumbled something that almost certainly was a prayer. The kindling worked slowly at first, but the agony of the flames soon swept about him.

Somehow, inexplicably, his demeanor began to change. Fear segued into conviction. He spoke aloud the words of John's Gospel in Northmoorlandic for the people to hear. He spoke for as long as he was able, until his digits fell off, the blood and the fat poured forth from his singed body, and his internal organs shut down. The smoke swirled about his head like a swarm of insects.

As I write this, I feel now like I am there again in that present moment. The sun creeps behind the storm clouds and withholds its light. Behold, noon is like twilight. It seems that nature is toying with the heretic. It foreshadows heavy rain, but it does not empty the sky. The rain clouds just sit there like hypocritical spectators.

I see the listless faces of the common people covered in sweat and grime. They were excitable at first, but the slow roasting of a human being takes its toll. Even the air seems languid. The timbers of the surrounding buildings look dull and gray. Soil of a sootlike black has been kicked up by the noblemen's horses. The nobles laugh at one another, sitting there in the grandstand and sipping their goblets of wine. I can see the ruby-red liquid dripping from the Earl of Bergen's lips. Though a devout attendee of Mass, he once bragged that he had never learned a word of scripture and that he never would.

For many in the grandstand, it is just a spectacle, an exercise of state power and an entertainment, a way to be seen with their festooned silks of vivacious colors like peacocks.

Meanwhile, the queen looks sanctimonious, even among her courtiers. I hear that the king despises these spectacles and is off on a hunt. Easy enough for him. He simply signs the heretic's death warrant and washes his hands of the affair. Far better to see a roasted boar on a spit than a human being.

This is beyond my restraint. I, a Catholic, cannot abide this cruelty. I must do something—and soon.

What, however, can I accomplish? My mind wanders.

The doctrines of man.

I cannot help but wonder about divine justice. Are God and His Church of one accord on this matter?

What if God thinks different?

CHAPTER XXVI

The Mother Lode

"The gods must be pleased with us," said Harald the blacksmith.

"Aye," said a sailor. "Someone must have placated them. The waters were eerily subdued this morning and easy to navigate."

"Shush with your superstitious nonsense," said their commander, Leif Magnusson. He was a burly, broad-shouldered man with a thundering voice that seemed to galvanize the lethargic and ostracize the timid. "Are we not seafarers? Are we not observers of the sky? We purposefully selected the back end of a gale to begin our journey."

Leif would not say it, but even he marveled at their fortuitous beginnings. The fjords were a place of awe, a place of fear. The favorable conditions, which started with a confident launch from Harfagr's Landing, were almost unsettling.

Perhaps the references to long-lost pagan gods were fitting.

After all, traditional Viking longboats had been selected over the hulking galleys that served the navies of Christendom. This, however, was a practical matter rather than a religious one. The longboats were better suited for navigation of the narrow inlets, and once ashore, men could not be spared to guard the costly moored ships. Moreover, the longboats could be stored out of water. They would be needed time and again for supplies once a base camp had been established for Lord Connaught's expedition.

Leif did not know, but glacial erosion during the last ice age had carved deep channels in the mountain valleys. And the sea had obliged, swimming into and filling the inland depths with a Nordic blue, which seemed to mirror the sky. The mountains, rooted below sea level, rose to fill the heights along the horizon like a long canyon. Here and there the rugged shoreline pinched inward before expanding outward again like a bloated stomach. At their exposed base, the mountains were capped with a verdant green; they soared above, bare-chested, before finally broadcasting ample deposits of snow.

The longboats had been taken ashore and stowed away some hours ago. The armed contingent, already feeling a bit oxygen-deprived in the heights, struggled up the slippery limestone of Borgund's Pass. Leif counted forty in their number. Adventurers. Mercenaries. Some were from Scandinavia, and others were from the British Isle and the Emerald Isle. Ten were bowmen. Most of the other soldiers bore broadswords and war hammers with barbed ends. The largest, at seven feet and weighing almost four hundred pounds, wielded a Morning Star mace with its spherical bulb and protruding tricornered spikes. Christened by his mother as Olaf, his comrades had nicknamed him Goliath. Once encamped, they would all entertain themselves by modeling his cavernous helm. The headgear wobbled upon the average head and was prone to knocking the wearer off balance. No one, however, could brandish the iron mace with a single hand, a feat that Olaf conducted with self-satisfied ease.

For now, however, their weapons of choice were stowed away in favor of pickaxes and rope.

"We have little more than a week's rations," noted Morin, an archer. "It seems as if my quiver will be needed for the hunt."

Borgund's Pass seemed to Leif a mere cleft in the rock, beckoning none from a distance and seemingly stumbled upon by its namesake. Its general trajectory ran parallel with, rather than into, the mountainside. In fact, it bore a strange likeness to a steep staircase hugging a skyward wall on its right side. Opposing it on the left was a solid parapet formed from a short outcrop of stone. Aside from this, the erratic changes in grade reflected the irregularity of the natural world. The sun's rays dipped here and there, rendering traversal of the pass a game of shadows.

It was curious, then, to glimpse a flickering light deep in the recesses of the dark.

"What's this?" said Harald as he felt with his hands along the mountainside. He seemed surprised as the rock face folded inward. "It's some sort of cave. I see firelight beyond."

"That someone would choose to live here," said Leif with bewilderment, before his curiosity got the better of him. "Harald. Olaf. Morin. Archibald. You come with me."

The men lit their torches. The flicker of light was actually a reflection off the wall of the cave, for the tunneled path wove inward like a knotted and contorted tree root.

"Who could dwell amid this foul odor?" asked Morin. Indeed, the musty air had lingered for some time, suffering from decay and want of ventilation, and the walls were covered in some sort of wet grime.

Morin's words had been heard, for the men heard a strange laughter: old and female. It was a staccato cackle that echoed through the tunnel and then broke into a deep beastly drone.

"That's my cue," said Archibald, who specialized in espionage and thievery but not necessarily bravery. He turned to leave. Olaf, however, caught hold of his shoulder. Archibald was short in stature and quick on his feet, but the giant's grasp was unyielding. Archibald whimpered from his capture.

"Quiet," said Leif. "Are you a man or a boy?"

"Look," said Morin. He swept his torch over the rocks. Upon them were markings.

"Runes," said Leif. "But what do they mean?"

"Fools!" said the female voice from within. "The runes speak of your perilous fate. Why do you seek the mountains of the undead?"

"Undead?" asked Archibald. "Nobody mentioned that sort of thing when I signed the expeditionary contract."

"It's a trick," said Harald. "She plays with our minds for some foul purpose."

Another staccato cackle burst forth, this one more amplified.

Though the men's progress slowed with caution, the narrow cave walls began to diverge toward a rounded chamber. It was filled with tapers, lit to reveal a tabled assemblage of plant roots, herbs, and the remains of small animals. An ancient woman reposed on a projection of the rock and studied the men. Her aspect was repugnant with mottled skin, tortuous sinews detached from bone, and swollen eyes filled with a beastly blackness.

"What do you seek?" she asked.

"Silver," answered Leif.

"The short one bears a map," she said. "Show it to me."

They looked at one another.

"You heard her, Archibald," said Leif.

Archibald placed a quivering hand in his leather satchel and gathered a folded document. It was frail and weather-beaten with tears along the folded seams. Not trusting a handoff, he tossed it to the witch. She unfolded it and placed it on a stone ledge then bade them to gather round. Archibald stayed put while the others obeyed.

"The lode you seek is here," she said, extending a long pointy finger that was gnarled at the knuckles. Leif saw that a few miles beyond the western boundary of the Myrkur subrange was a crevasse. "In the depths of Mount Draugskund."

"Thank ye, good woman," said Leif as he extended a gold coin.

"Save your petty offering," she replied with disdain. "I have no need of it here."

"Petty?" Perplexed, Leif slipped the rejected coin back in his satchel. They had what they sought for. There was no desire to linger, so the men turned to leave.

"All is not as it seems," she warned.

"How so, old woman?" asked Leif with some annoyance.

"You will attract in accordance with your number."

"Attract whom?"

"They will come."

"Confound it, woman!"

"The draugr," she rasped.

Leif looked at his men with their blank faces, all of them foreigners to these alpine lands. "Who are they? Some long-lost clan?"

The witch exhaled a long-winded laugh. "You will see."

Olaf seemed to be losing patience. The folds of his studded leather hauberk stretched and cracked as he leaned his immense torso forward to study the witch's unsightly face. "The commander asked you a question. I advise you to answer him."

She ignored the giant's threat and cast small animal bones into a shallow reed basket. "Bal shalmeh! Minas mort uther!"

Something like a sonic wave blasted Olaf from behind, dropping the old woman's would-be intimidator to his bulging knees. The force of the blow shocked Leif, who had never seen the giant felled.

The magic lingered. Olaf gasped in horror as his skin and sinews rotted off the bone in rapid succession. A black smoke gathered, billowing around and through the giant's bone structure.

Archibald shrieked like a child and ran out of the cave.

"Olaf!" said Morin.

"What have you done to him?" asked Leif.

The witch cupped her hands and once again cast the bones. "Vitae remoth!"

The giant exhaled the evil substance within him with a pronounced gasp. A black vaporish smoke left his mouth and nostrils as his sinews and skin reemerged. Revived, Olaf stood upright and looked as he had before, as if nothing had happened.

The woman's odd laughter returned. "Your fate is not ensured by strength of arms. Return to the fjord. Descend and live."

"We bid you good day," said Leif, bowing, but not listening. The team hurried out of the cave.

Fear drove the reassembled team of forty up Borgund's Pass with great haste. By any other means, Leif would not have been able to expect such progress. Late that afternoon they reached a forested plateau, surrounded by the higher peaks of Myrkur.

"There!" said Leif, pointing at the easternmost peak,

which seemed covered in a gray-green shroud of mist. "Mount Draugskund. We'll establish our base camp here in this forest. We must build and build quickly. Stone will take too long to quarry and erect. We'll build palisades hewn from the felled timbers."

They set to work.

Leif oversaw their progress as the immediate environs were soon deprived of tree cover. Progress was steady but not fast enough to shelter the team by the time the sun departed. The men, hungry and tired from their arduous journey, feasted upon the provisions brought from port. With satiated stomachs, many succumbed to fatigue. Several of their more energetic members agreed to stand watch as the others slept.

A peaceful, restful night passed in the frigid confines of Myrkur.

They emerged from their heavy slumber at sunup and ate a light breakfast of salted fish. Afterward, the felling of trees resumed. This went on for a several hours before they broke for lunch.

Leif arose from his seat in shock as seven unexpected visitors appeared in the encampment, bearing supply bags swollen with loaves of bread. "Lord Connaught?"

"Yes?" The long-shanked lord, accompanied by his attendants, walked into the encampment with a satisfied air.

"You fool!" shouted Leif as his men sat there, seemingly dumbfounded by their financier's appearance, and perhaps even more by their commander's reply.

Connaught's face shook with fury. "I might have met with a better reception by those among my employ! Did you know that I have hung men from the mast of my ship for less?"

The ground was not yet frozen, and the snow cover was manageable enough to allow for some ease of movement. Connaught breathed the pleasant air. A breeze filled his nostrils with the scent of spruce and fir.

Leif was irritated to have his expeditionary authority preempted, but if any resentments lingered, he did not show it. The men muttered among themselves, seemingly amazed to have their employer, a lord for that matter, facing the same dangers alongside them.

A quiet, workmanlike mood settled over the camp. Three separate fires were started and managed by one of the soldiers. All remaining hands bore the tools of carpentry, and the encampment and its palisades were erected with haste.

Once construction was completed, Connaught turned his men to the hunt for the replenishment of their provisions. The archers, led by Morin, proved as able in this exercise as they were reputed to be in battle. The carcasses were cleaned, and what was not immediately cooked was salted and set apart to be cured.

"Well said, well said!" announced Connaught, though none of those surrounding him had drawn the breath of speech. His voice, filling the air with a cloud of vapor, echoed off the higher faces of the mountainside. He listened for a response, but not even an animal emitted an answer.

"Femund and his superstitions," he said with haughty surety. "The natives at port, who could have this land for themselves, have been led astray by their own cowardice."

Connaught now felt sure of his footing here in the mountains of Myrkur. All it took was someone well provisioned and bold enough for the task. Now he could turn to plunder, which would be the envy of the European kings.

Despite his self-confidence, Connaught knew that silver mining was an involved process. The ore often proved elusive, and once discovered, it had to be mined from the depths of the rock. From there, the smelting process was incorporated to separate the impurities from the pure precious metal. This required a significant investment of labor and materials, and the portability of the latter seemed questionable. They might be forced to carry the ore back to port, and with a downslope course of mountaineering, how much weight could one man carry in his sack?

"Men! Come hither!" shouted Connaught. It had been a rather dull, monotonous afternoon for those in the encampment. Now with their interest piqued, they assembled around the fires.

"Today we reconnoitered a large cave in the depths of Mount Draugskund," said Connaught. "Olaf! Bring it forth."

Olaf carried a misshapen object the size of a loaf of bread. He held it aloft for all to see. Its darkened aspect seemed to indicate the presence of lead, but bound to this matrix was another substance. From a cloudless sky, the sun's rays illuminated a gray metallic substance.

"Hundreds, like this sample, are within our means to readily access!" said Connaught with obvious joy. "The legends, at least in this respect, are true! The wealth of this region is ours to claim!"

A steady murmur arose in the encampment, accompanied by the lively eyes of greed, for each of the soldiers and laborers would receive a half-percent cut of the total valuation. Leif's contract, however, called for an additional quarter percent.

"Tomorrow we will begin to extract much more!" said Leif. "Timber shoring will need to be built inside the cave, so the carpenters will come with us."

As evening set in, fermented beverages were passed around, and an abnormally large ration of wild game was cooked on a spit for the assembly. That night, Morin stammered up the ladder of the lookout tower to provide the watch.

Connaught had commanded that the entire forested plateau and its surroundings be explored. This had been done to his satisfaction. No fortress, whether manned by the living or the dead, had been spied. The palisades encircled the encampment in a series of wooden spikes driven side by side into the ground, daring any assault from without.

Connaught gazed out of his cabin from within the protection of the fortifications. Some men were still carousing by the firepit, but most had turned in to the shelters with their bedded bunks of timber stacked three persons high.

A steady wind was bringing in a cold front, and snow was beginning to accumulate upon the ground. Ultimately this would result in a thick blanket.

Morin's post was at the peak of the encampment, and the ladder drew Connaught's gaze. He wanted to see the view.

"Lord Connaught?" asked Morin upon his employer's ascent.

"Morin. I could not bear to see you enjoying this view alone."

Morin did not seem to mind the company. "'Tis a fine night, sir. The white powder forms something of a moat about our encampment. Any tracks would be clearly seen."

"Aye."

Connaught, feeling warmed by his most recent beverage, looked absentmindedly beyond the palisades. "Anything of note?"

"Well, sir, my eye is sharp when sober, but do you see that patch of ground some thirty yards yonder?"

Connaught watched as Morin pointed out the location. A small boulder was encircled by snow. "Aye."

"Is it me, sir, or did it just move?"

"Nay, your drunken mind plays tricks," said Connaught.

"I'm much obliged, sir, I'm sure."

Although both felt tipsy, together they leaned out over the half wall of the lookout tower. Morin laughed, followed by Connaught, as if enjoying an unsaid, private joke.

"Nay," repeated Connaught. "We're but swollen with drink."

Then it moved.

Morin rubbed his eyes and strained to look. "There, sir, see?"

"Aye."

The snow had been displaced with dark earth piled upon it. "Just some burrowing creature," said Connaught.

"There's more, sir. Look!" said Morin.

More earth had been displaced. Connaught saw what looked like lumber lodged in the hole.

"What is that?"

"Should we go out, sir?" asked Morin.

They descended the ladder. Archibald, Harald the blacksmith, and a miner were the only stragglers left, still enjoying themselves before the fire.

"Archibald!" said Connaught. "Come with us."

"Sir?"

"Are you not the thief?"

"By repute, sir, but not by commission."

"I care not what you have stolen before," said Connaught. "What we need now are your skills. Harald, open the gate!"

"Aye, sir," said Harald as a narrow wall of palisades mounted on iron hinges was thrust open.

"Come with me," said Connaught as he grasped a torch.

Morin and Archibald followed their master outside. They walked toward the boulder.

What looked like a wooden chest sat in the depression where the ground cover had been stripped bare. The top was open, and in the lunar light of the full moon, Connaught could see a metallic substance.

"By the saints!" declared Harald, who had followed them out. The chest opened with ease, and inside was a cache of pure silver.

Connaught was astonished. "There must be a smelting works somewhere."

"We scouted the whole area," said Morin, spreading his arms wide. "Nothing escaped our notice, sir."

"Perhaps a gap in the mountain, a fissure we have not yet seen?"

"No, sir," said Harald, "'tis not possible. We reconnoitered it all."

Connaught looked about. Though nothing was stirring, and despite his pragmatic nature, something made him uneasy. After all, this was a treasure trove, and unguarded troves were inconceivable. "We'd better not linger. Best to get this to our camp."

The chest was heavy, and the men struggled to get it to the gate. Harald placed his fingers in his mouth and whistled for someone to let them back in.

Harald had overindulged a little. A handful of sleepers arose from the shelters and wandered over to see what the commotion was.

Connaught surveyed the change of expressions as eyes gazed at the open chest, which was placed by the light of the fire. Murmuring gave way to shouts and laughter as the shelters emptied of their remaining occupants.

Connaught joined in their revelry. Leif seemed of one accord with the other men in light of the unexpected fortune of the expedition.

"Did you hear that?" asked Morin.

Connaught laughed and playfully pushed the archer in the shoulder. "Hear what? You are not at your station."

Morin bore a sober expression. "I heard the clanking of iron on wood."

"Well?"

"Sir, listen."

Connaught heard the same and looked about. "It must be one of the men."

The noise started to Connaught's left, but seconds later it moved behind him.

"It's to the right of us now," said Morin after another pause. "It's encircling the camp."

"Sir," said Archibald, rushing up. "Someone bears swords outside."

"They rattle them against the palisades," said Connaught, who was confused as to how to interpret his own observations. "Somehow, men, and I do not know how, we have company."

"Who dares to disturb the lands of Myrkur?" said a strange voice from outside. It sounded old and decayed but beholden of great power.

Connaught stood transfixed as his men froze in their tracks. The rattling could now be heard all around the borders of the encampment.

"Stay your course!" said Connaught to the others. "This is why we built fortifications!"

He could feel a tug on his furs. It was a tug from the smallest member of the encampment. "Look!" said Archibald, who appeared as if a frightened child with nowhere to run.

Connaught saw a cadaverous person, followed by others, walking through the wall of timber with the eerie powers of a ghost. Their blackened skin seemed bereft of its natural elasticity. The epidermis had shrunk to a thin murky glazing about the sinews and muscle, like the exposed features of a mummy.

Yet they moved and spoke.

"You have trespassed upon the domain of the draugr!" said the first to enter the encampment. Connaught looked about in haste and saw some two dozen others of like form following behind.

The revenants were each attired in warrior's garb, consisting of a dilapidated cloak and rusted chain mail. The mail opened at the neck and was secured there by a braided bronzed torc; the head was crowned with a helm of iron, and a gilded broadsword was secured to the waist with a cracked leather belt. The broadsword gleamed in the moonlight as if forged in the bellowed fires of the pagan gods. And yet this untarnished instrument of death with its luminous reflection seemed at odds with the overriding stench of decay of the bearer. The ghosts somehow seemed to have a foothold in both the supernatural and natural worlds.

"The judgment of trespass is death!" said the revenant.

Connaught glanced at Leif, who nodded to Morin. Morin nocked his bow with an arrow from his quiver and let it fly. Rather than passing through ghostly mist, the tip lodged itself in the chain mail upon the revenant's chest. The being tore the arrow out, and a blackened liquid oozed from the wound.

"It can be destroyed!" said Leif.

Connaught hesitated, not knowing what they were up against, but he was encouraged by the impact of Morin's missile. "Let's surround them, men!"

The expeditioners seized their weapons, whatever could be readily obtained, and surged toward their would-be assailants. Connaught maneuvered the men to seal off the left and right flanks, pinning the revenants in a narrow space some five yards from the palisades. The draugr stood their ground, neither moving nor exhibiting any sense of fear. Their swords hung at their sides even as the men's outstretched weapons advanced the attack.

"You should have listened to the witch," said their leader as he pointed a skeletal finger fringed with a faint outline of discolored flesh. He seemed older, if possible, than the others—and more regal. A long gray mustache drooped over a thick, nested beard, and his helm was plated with gold trim at the brow and chin.

Connaught studied this strange being in confusion. "What witch?"

"The one on the mountain pass," said Leif. "She warned us not to go farther."

"And yet you have said nothing of this before?"

"Now you must die!" said the revenant. It engaged a grizzled soldier named Thorne in swordplay consisting of swift, heavy strokes and defensive parries to thwart the soldier's every thrust. Connaught watched intently, gauging his next plan of action, which hung entirely on the outcome of this game of death. He needed to know just what they were dealing with. With outstretched hands, he cautioned his men to hold their ground.

The other revenants stood surprisingly motionless as their leader fought on their behalf.

"I daresay the head can be severed," said Thorne, who seemed to have an arrogant sense of humor. "Would it then reattach itself?"

The revenant said nothing as Thorne swung his sword between the upper recesses of the chain mail and the base of the helm. His swing was true, but rather than decapitating his enemy, the sword severed the air. The revenant stood there with the wry smile of a face long acclimated to the grave.

Connaught looked on with awe, but his mind was alert.

Morin had proven their existence in the physical realm, had he not? What then was the trick to their reversal from the natural world to the spirit world?

Thorne seemed to recover from his shock to make a counterthrust, followed by another. A third offensive, however, found its way into Thorne's abdomen. He stood there teetering, his arrogant countenance giving way to shock and vulnerability.

Connaught glanced at the revenant. He had not seen it before, but in its mouth, a twin set of protuberant teeth gleamed like ivory. The revenant descended like a ravenous beast, its teeth puncturing the dying soldier's neck, depriving the man of precious blood and accelerating his descent upon the snowy ground. It would be the man's last descent. Although Thorne's eyes were open, they ceased to reveal any living aspect. The revenant licked its teeth with a cadaverous tongue as the men gathered in shock around the carcass.

Rage might have been the usual emotion upon seeing a fallen comrade, but this was erased by the dominant emotion: fear. Connaught could see the nervous twitch of the neck in some men and the involuntary shaking of swords and other armaments in others. None, it seemed, were in their right mind. How could they be? How could the rational mind make sense of what had just transpired?

Femund had tried to warn him back at Harfagr's Landing.

"We thought your kind were no more than legends," said Connaught as he addressed his foes. "We thought these lands were abandoned. Forgive my archer. Forgive my swordsman. They were merely defending our encampment. Will you not treat with us?"

"Vogg does not treat with those who would possess his silver," said the leader.

Connaught swallowed hard. He studied the fresh blood

upon the revenant's decayed lips. The legends of vampyres were true. In one swift stroke, his cynicism had been thrust aside. "And what if your possessions were returned?"

"You have been judged by the draugr," said Vogg. "You and your kind must die."

Olaf closed in with his Morning Star mace.

"No, Olaf," said Connaught, but he was too late.

The heavy mace swung about, only to cleave the night air.

Vogg seemed amused at his assailant's folly.

Connaught caught the giant's forearm. It felt like rock. "They transfer, somehow, from the physical world to another," he whispered. "We cannot strike when they are ethereal. We must learn when to strike. Look for it, and when you know, tell the others."

The giant nodded.

"Sir? Look," said Morin, pointing at the oozing wound in Vogg's chest. The feeding had stimulated something. The parched skin with its deathly hue seemed infested with maggots at the wound site. Rather than devouring, they secreted an oily white substance, and the rotted epidermis closed about the puncture.

"In death, they yet heal!" said Connaught.

"Strike them down!" said Vogg.

The entirety of the encampment engaged with their attackers as the night air filled with nervous shouts and the strained grunts of combat.

Connaught fought alongside his men, but it was important for him to be strategic. He dropped back, allowing others to fill the space he had left void, so he could observe this enemy from a tactical standpoint.

The draugr made strategic use of their transient ghostlike state. Connaught observed that this was a defensive maneuver and saw that when they were ethereal, the draugr could not strike their opponents. Moreover, from the last point of impact, namely, the clanging of swords, there was a time lapse in this transition.

"Listen, men!" yelled Connaught. "You have three seconds from the last point of contact! Three seconds until the man becomes a shade! Strike quickly! Strike repeatedly and true!"

The men seemed to listen. Olaf managed to decapitate one of the revenants with the sheer force of his mace. So had Leif, with the help of Harald, after severing the legs of a revenant, and then the head, with a broadsword.

Despite these minor victories, Connaught's men were succumbing to the enemy in alarming numbers. Morin and Archibald has been killed by the sword of the undead. Thirty others had fallen in quick succession thanks to the superior strength and swordplay of the draugr.

Olaf. Leif. Harald. They remained, among a depleted core of survivors.

Connaught continued to study his enemy. Save for loss of limb, the draugr could heal from their wounds whether they be from an arrow, a sword, or a bludgeoning instrument.

"Strike their heads, men! Strike their limbs!"

Olaf succeeded in felling another draugr. Meanwhile, Leif and Harald, despite a valiant effort, received mortal wounds and lay upon the snowy ground. Connaught could hear the burbling of their breathing as phlegm mixed with their own blood. But the draugr did not consume their life force.

"Olaf!" said Connaught. "Behind you!"

Two revenants leapt upon the giant's back as three others provided a frontal attack. Swords plunged into his flesh, and the giant dropped to one knee.

Connaught engaged with a revenant and sliced off its sword-bearing arm. He looked to his side and, seeing the fallen giant, grew dismayed.

The remaining men of the encampment were felled. The ground was strewn with the corpses of the newly departed. The campfires lagged from inattention, and the windswept chill was having its way. The hidden peaks, shadows of immense stone washed by the moonlight, felt like somber spectators.

Connaught glanced at the silvery treasure in the open chest. It seemed of little import now. What was the use of wealth without the partaking of it?

The remaining draugr, not much reduced in number, encircled their prey and stared into his feverish eyes. Connaught saw their decayed faces. They reeked of the grave. He thought he had been left alone among the living.

Connaught, in his anguish, regretted the entire venture. Although a man of purpose, he was not yet so hardened of heart. He hated the needless loss of life.

His enemies surrounded him.

"What can I do?" asked Connaught. "Will you not treat with me? A trade of some sort?"

"Those three," said Vogg, ignoring him as he pointed to Leif, Harald, and the giant. "Quickly now, before they draw their last breath."

Six revenants split off from the others as they surrounded the three fallen men.

Blood was spilt, and to Connaught's surprise, it was the blood of the victors. The revenants severed their forearms with filed fingernails, and the red substance that poured forth was forcibly indulged upon the lips of the fallen.

Of course, thought Connaught. *They must replenish their ranks.*

New pledges—pledges of the grave.

Connaught faced their leader. "And what of me?"

"Death," said Vogg with outstretched finger.

The verdict had been spoken. A broadsword was swept back for a full strike.

Is this the end of it? wondered Connaught as his eyes blinked between a living awareness and the onset of death.

Flakes of snow pelted Connaught's face, which was pale and distraught. A hundred questions, a hundred memories, raced through his mind as he gazed up at the sky for the last time. He could sense that cold, damp blade wielded by an agent of darkness only a mere step behind. His neck considered the blow. His breathing was rapid and vacuous.

And then a strange breach appeared in the snowfall. Connaught could see it in his peripheral vision. It was a discontinuity, like a gap in cloud cover, except that this was a clearness in the midst of the powdery precipitation.

The air inside the encampment parted like a seam, revealing a strange being from a wicked realm. For all the monstrosities of the draugr, there was no greater hideousness than this hell-like fiend.

Connaught's executioner stepped back. "Malsadus?"

"This one must be set free, Vogg."

The fiendish voice sounded otherworldly to Connaught, who yet struggled on the precipice of his mortality. He had seen the caricatures of devilry, the drawings and sketches of men, yet he could not have surmised that such abject evil could assume physical form.

"He trespassed our lands," said Vogg, who seemed defensive.

"And yet," said Malsadus, "I have use for him."

"Our ways demand that another life shall be forfeit."

"And you shall have it!" said Malsadus. "The lands of the north will soon teem with the countless fallen. The ground will be covered in corpses, a feast of which you and your numbers shall partake before the vultures arrive. I offer you thousands for the price of one."

Vogg bowed and said no more.

Connaught considered this curious serendipity of circumstance. It was almost awful. There was nearly as much dread in facing this Malsadus as there had been in awaiting the strike of the ghoulish headsman.

"You have been granted life, Lord Connaught," said Malsadus. The fiend seemed to enjoy saying *lord* as if it knew of the schemer's invention.

Connaught swallowed hard. "Yes, my liege."

"Then mark this moment well. It is *I* who saved your life. It is *I* who am your master now."

Connaught glanced about. He marveled at the vampiric revenants, who moments ago were about to murder him and acquire his blood. They stood motionless as if at the singular mercy of this strange new presence. The encampment reeked of sulfur, which Connaught had not noticed before.

"What would you have me do?" asked Connaught.

"Well now," said the fiend as it unfurled a maniacal smirk, "I would have you meddle in the affairs of the king."

CHAPTER XXVII

A Conversation
in Secret

Helsborg District, Near the Eastern Wall of Mithrendia
Nightfall

Swaths of torchlight swelled to reveal the surrounding walls and ceiling. They illuminated a rounded chamber about five yards in diameter with seats carved from the walls.

"Why must we meet here?" asked Darrig, who had disguised his newfound wealth with the well-worn remains of a dusty old cloak. With his hood cast aside, he addressed everyone on familiar terms. "It takes half a day on foot."

"I still say we should have ridden by horseback," said Roald with a scowl.

"I'm sure you gentlemen, given your exploits in Wolf's Hollow, can well afford an inn before your return home," said

Sigismund, the bailiff of the Duke of Mithrendia. He was a tall, slender-built man with puffy eyebrows that often twitched when he spoke. "Certainly His Grace the duke would have preferred to play host, but Castle Brygge is under constant watch by the king and archbishop. Mounted men, of course, attract attention on city streets, so we are much obliged at your sacrifice to arrive here this night."

"What? No secret passages to the duke's abode?" replied Roald in jest.

Just then Catherine whispered, "The castle is surrounded by a moat."

"One might burrow a tunnel," said Friar Carboni, "as my ancestor did here."

"Your ancestor?" asked Catherine in astonishment.

"Aye," said Carboni. "My great-great-great-great grandfather—I know that is a mouthful—was a Venetian ship merchant. As the story goes, he grew tired of the Adriatic pirates and Venetian politics and moved his family here, to the far north. At the back of his new estate, he dug a secret grotto deep in the rock for private reflection and refuge. After he and his family died, vegetation grew over its entrance, and the grotto lay in ruin for some time. A boy playing in the underbrush is said to have rediscovered it, and since then this place has been expanded many times over, forming the catacombs of this city. Many who cannot afford a proper burial have laid their loved ones to rest down here."

"What happened to your family?" asked Catherine, who regretted the question almost as soon as she'd asked it.

"Plague," said the friar. "Fourteenth century. It wiped out the Carboni name almost entirely, including everything my ancestors worked for. I am the last on my father's side, whom I never knew."

A story of death given utterance in a place of the dead.

No one said anything as the shadows of their somber faces performed a lethargic, rhythmless dance on the torchlit walls. Courage and conviction had brought them all here because the living were at peril.

It was too dangerous to meet in the original chambers of the grotto. Thieves and violent personalities were not the only ones known to lurk behind the dark corners of the catacombs. It had taken about twenty minutes to reach this obscure location from the entrance, and only Carboni knew the route through the endless maze of carved limestone. Seven corridors branched from one, and these gave way to dozens of others. Some pathways turned, crossed one another, or terminated at walls of solid rock. Others opened into small rooms such as this, where the air was stale. To lose one's light source here was a virtual death sentence, apart from being discovered. That, of course, was something they had taken pains to avoid in coming to such a remote location.

The occupants gazed at one another in a mutual attempt to calm their lingering fears of insecurity. The room was quiet save for their uneasy breathing.

Catherine marveled at the transformation of these men. She did not know the bailiff well enough, but she had studied the others. Carboni was a widower, a renegade friar, and an alpine recluse. Darrig and Roald were men she once had distrusted given their singular focus on the accumulation of wealth.

Something about them was different. Something had changed. Carboni had emerged from his drunken binges with an optimism he had not formerly possessed. Meanwhile the two knights, who had declined to share their haul from Wolf's Hollow, had provided a generous endowment to the wife and children of their fallen comrade Bjorn.

Catherine had insisted on accompanying her friend Carboni

to this secret meeting, whereas her Rhymer companions had remained at the castle. There was a tighter bond between the two orphans, but even beyond this burgeoning friendship, she had felt a vague notion that her attendance was necessary.

Sigismund spoke first. "Since our last unannounced inspection, our printers have managed to assemble two hundred fifty broadsheets for distribution to the public."

"Marvelous. And how do you manage it?" asked Carboni.

"It's too dangerous to keep the movable type set in position," said Sigismund. "During the last search, they practically tore the shop apart. So we must do it at night with the shutters closed."

"And the printing presses cannot be moved to the castle," said Catherine.

"Because it is being watched," said Sigismund, seeming to anticipate her words.

"What does the text contain?" asked Catherine.

"A Northmoorlandic translation of Luther's New Testament," said Sigismund. "Some key passages at least."

"How it has come to this is beyond me. We have reached such a sorry state of affairs," said Carboni, "that one must risk his life for the people to have any religious freedoms at all."

"I saw the most recent burning of that helpless man," said Catherine. "Why the perceived danger? Why should the nobles and the prelates think in such violent terms and act with such cruelty?"

"They fear that the people will challenge their authority," said Sigismund, with a heavy sigh, "once they hear for themselves what the scriptures say."

"But that appears to be more of a clerical problem," said Catherine, "rather than one that should trouble the nobles."

"Ah! But the nobles share a common interest with the

prelates," said Darrig, "and that is to hold onto their wealth and vast estates."

"Consider the practice of simony," said Sigismund. "A nobleman has two sons. The firstborn stands to inherit. And the second? Buy him an ecclesiastical office, and he can live luxuriously off the profits of the diocesan lands attached to that office, as well as the tithes of the poor. That is how it is done these days."

"And what of nepotism?" grumbled Carboni. "Remember Pope Alexander VI? Bribed his way to power. Had his enemies assassinated. Installed his son Cesare Borgia as a cardinal while he was still a teenager."

"We all know what enraged Luther," said Sigismund, looking round at his captive audience. "In Germany, there is a Dominican friar named Johann Tetzel who is in charge of the sale of indulgences. Get this: Tetzel advertises with a slogan that goes, 'As soon as the coin in the coffer clings, another soul from purgatory springs.'"[5]

Roald had been quiet during the discussion as he seemed preoccupied with the corridor beyond. Catherine watched as he sprang from his seat to the edge of the portal.

Darrig signaled for the conversation to stop. Catherine listened as she heard Roald's footsteps recede down the passageway.

Roald returned some moments later. In the lingering light, Catherine could see the whites of his eyes. He seemed anxious and pensive.

"And?" said Darrig.

"We've been eavesdropped," said Roald.

"By whom?"

"I know not. There must be hundreds of chambers like this. Someone followed us here."

CHAPTER XXVIII

An Ambush

Børgman's Bluff, Off the Northwest Coast of Mithrendia

Lord Connaught gazed into the placid waters of the Firth of Jutlanger. Reticent winds and the subtle luminance of the sun's early rays presented a mirage of tranquility. Nature and humanity worked in concert, or so it seemed, under the camouflage of man's artifice. Seagulls squealed and laughed along the embankments of the bluff, while vultures began to swoop in from the mainland to devour the fallen.

The garrison, if it could be called one, had been eliminated after thirty minutes of engagement. The ill-supplied troops had long escaped the notice of the Crown, a fact not lost on Connaught in his scheming and maneuvering.

He had learned that Børgman's Bluff was considered a

dead end post. It served the nation's defenses with no clear function save for a lookout.

A lookout for what? Pirates and foreign navies almost never ventured this far north, not when the end game, the prize, was a walled city known for its impenetrability to coastal assault. Its walls eluded long-range cannons, and if a warship were to come within range, it would be pummeled until floating debris was all that remained of its hull.

"For the mainland to be so heavily defended, it's a wonder they did not apply the same treatment to the fortifications here," said Captain Dunman. He leaned upon the misshapen stone parapet of the modest battlements and studied their foe in the distance.

"The king must think the distance is too far for artillery," said Connaught.

"And for conventional military planning, my lord, he'd be right."

Connaught looked at him with a knowing smile. "Convention is not what we brought here."

"No, my lord. Frankly, what we are attempting to do is unheard of."

"And yet we are taking an enormous risk in trusting that cannon manufacturer Gustafson."

"Aye, sir," said the captain, looking back at his employer. "An act of faith, it is."

"Reverently spoken, Dunman. Like a true devotee."

Connaught was not a spiritual man, and his engagement in the Black Mountains was something he had strived to eliminate from his memory.

"But I watched his demonstration," said Dunman, "as did you, and I think we are in range, my lord."

Connaught scanned the northern wall of Mithrendia with admiration. Its height, its armaments, and its constant watch by ambulatory patrols of guards was nothing short of excellent. He turned to his captain. "We watched Gustafson fire into the bay. There were no marks to judge distance by."

"Aye, it is difficult to quantify. But I'd wager my full wages that these bronze beauties are up for the task."

Connaught studied his recent purchase, which had been transported from his ships and positioned on the ramparts.

A new species of cannon had been bred on the mainland and therefore, in a sense, under the very nose of the Crown. Yes, the Crown's spies were everywhere, but they could not be everywhere at all times. It was apparent that their eyes and ears had not yet discerned the output of Gustafson's factory. Here, twelve of his finest products, hulking cylinders of cast bronze, gleamed under the burgeoning sunlight.

"They'd better be," said Connaught. "We had to ration other supplies just to bear the weight of this cargo on board."

"Aye," said Dunman. "They be wee heavy. Modify the hull with large timbers, we did, just to carry the cannon in halves."

The cannons were spaced some twenty feet apart. Connaught and Dunman approached the nearest unit. Connaught rubbed his weather-beaten hands on a small joint located near the midpoint of the shaft.

"The fore and aft sections of the shaft are internally threaded and screw together," said Dunman. "A technology borrowed from the Turks."

Conditions for an invasion of the bluff had been fortuitous. An early scouting report had spied a cove on the northwest corner of the island, and as it happened to be, this cove was visible neither to the mainland towers nor to the ports of the Grand Sweep. Furthermore, the ships had arrived under the cover of nightfall, aided by a southerly wind.

Connaught glared southward at the great bulkhead of

stone rising from the rocky cliffs. "They say that those walls are impenetrable."

"We've got balls of stone and balls of iron," said Dunman. "Grapeshot and case shot. If there is a wall we fail to breach, sir, we'll soon fire over. As long as Gustafson's calculations are accurate. The shot will prove especially lethal as it peppers the city streets."

Connaught was pleased with his choice of captain. "I like your spirit, Dunman. If our men had half your conviction, the wealth of Mithrendia would soon be our spoils of war."

"Aye, my lord, and so it will be if the infantry you have spoken of execute their part."

"Lord Berbery assures me that he has a plan."

CHAPTER XXIX

Ghost Stories

Only a week after my escape from Berbery, I found myself in another castle with another view from on high.

This time, however, my stay was not one of incarceration, though I had been warned of spies hiding in dark corners. They lurk near the drawbridge, they say, sniffing for any scent of heresy in these days of grave suspicion.

I have heard stories here in Westfall. A petty squabble between neighbors, in this perilous climate, escalated into a matter of a grave concern. I say grave both in a figurative and literal manner, as false accusations run rampant. One merchant, having been deprived of a few yørn in a business transaction, accused the other of Lutheran sympathies, and the authorities swept into action. Any damning evidence, if there really was any, was collected later. They are not immune from falsifying evidence to suit the Crown's purposes. I speak nothing of the transaction as the authorities were less interested in common justice. What the Crown demands is complete and total obedience, that is, the loyalty of the heart to the king's rule and the devotion of the soul to the king's religion. Any pockets of disobedience will be rooted out and eradicated under the pretense of treason. Treason, of course, demands a death sentence.

I then am a guest of the greatest heretic in the land. This heretic, however, wields immense power. There is strength in the walls of Castle Brygge, and the Duke of Mithrendia ranks second only to the royal family. In every other way save religion, he has been the close friend and ally of the king, and so this uneasy discordance has been allowed to linger for now.

Although my tortured mind ponders upon such weighty matters, the mundane activities of the outside world allay my fears. My window affords a view of ordinary people, not shape-shifters. In the snow-laden streets, beyond the stagnant and icy waters of the moat, they scurry about their daily tasks in their thick cloaks and high-legged boots.

I should not linger here in my loose-fitted bedclothes. The air is decisively cold as the morning sun dips here and there behind a cumulous cloud.

I hear something and glance back some twenty feet at my oaken chamber door. There is just enough of a gap between its base and the stone floor that I can see the faint outline of shuffling feet in the corridor. They say that a ghost wanders the halls at night. I have yet to see the apparition, but it was described to me as a tall, dark figure with cryptic features that defy description save for a bent back. Its malice is feared as it has been known to choke people in their sleep. Certain chambers that it favors in the east wing, therefore, lie abandoned. The duke is a pleasant and generous man, but his ancestors were not all reputed to be of a favorable disposition.

This one, believed to have lived in the fourteenth century, is the one the household staff call Owengärth the Mean.

I think that it is difficult for some to believe in ghosts without having witnessed the evidence oneself. Perhaps the veracity of another's story can be trusted, or for the curious researcher, maybe the sum total of documented reports is enough to be convincing. Some like me, however, must see to believe. I had to see an object levitate. I had to hear the unaccounted-for sounds of footfalls upon the vacant floor. I had to feel the hairs on my arms rise up as if charged with static electricity. Back home, in the United States, I had to witness the brand-new batteries in my flashlight drain entirely just before the manifestation. I had to know that a disembodied entity, a faint apparition, was watching me— watching my every move.

I too was a skeptic, before my eyes were opened.

My presence in this foreign land almost seems ethereal. Fear and exhaustion marked my first weeks. Along with it came the temporary loss of my identity, its evolving recovery posing a menacing threat. Then there was my convalescence in Castle Berbery, followed by an inconceivable escape, only for me to come to recognize my wounded existence in abject poverty.

Despite the ghost's reputation and the aforementioned spies, I have found my room here in the upper turret of the western wall to be a place of security. My fire is warm enough when I sit near the brick hearth with its pleasant herringbone pattern. My canopy bed is cavernous and comfortable. The drafts are not as difficult to bear with as those at Castle Berbery. By Northmoorlandic standards, I daresay my accommodations are a source of luxury.

However, what I cannot escape from is an increasing sense of loneliness. The Scotsman and the Welshman, who were entertaining and colorful during our journey from the east, said their goodbyes not long after our arrival at the castle. The duke and duchess were cordial and receptive, but I see them only briefly and on occasion. Ben and Mary are always fighting or avoiding one another, and I barely know the other two undergraduates. The orderlies of the Pictish-blue-liveried staff here are friendly enough, but we rarely get past pleasantries to go into any depth of conversation.

What I have found then, in this absence, is a burgeoning friendship with the duke's library. I have explored the castle, and to my reckoning this is the heart of it. The castle consists of four round turrets that flare off from a central square-towered keep. The upper platform of the keep serves a defensive purpose, but the lower floors house the gallery, reception room, dining hall, kitchen, and library. The library rivals Berbery's in size, but it lacks, perhaps fortunately, any nefarious works of the occult. It is a vast rectangular room with a central mantel and fireplace on the north wall.

Here my academic nose has found its way back to the accustomed smell of the printed page, or in this case parchment, my first love. After dressing for the day and breakfasting, I arrived in my place of comfort, where most days I was left alone.

"Professor?" asked Mary.

I was too distracted at first by the copious volumes of literature and learning to hear anything. I perused one title after another of bound materials with childlike enthusiasm, making a clear sweep across the west wall.

"Professor?"

"Hmm?"

"Have you ever seen a ghost?" she asked.

I glanced up at her with a frenzy of excitement. "Can you believe how many original works and painstakingly hand-copied manuscripts are present here in this very collection? Mr. Combs, our university librarian, would be spellbound by such an ostentatious display of historic materials. This collection alone would be worth millions."

"Professor?" Her voice did not indicate that she shared my enthusiasm. In fact, she seemed out of sorts. "Have you ever seen a ghost?" she asked again.

I looked up from my reading. There was something different about her, something compelling. "Yes. Yes I have."

"Really? Tell me about it."

It was a point of idiocy now that I recall it. Here I had been looking for companionship, and when she had arrived, my mind was adrift on less important matters.

Mary, however, surprised me. She circled around and swept in between my sternum and the shelved volumes, which were within my arm's reach. It was a cloistered fit. I was cut off from my monastic-like perusals and contemplations, and the lonely bachelor in me reawakened to the pleasant distraction of a very attractive young woman. I could feel her warm breath about me, and I could smell a pleasant fragrance in her hair. I have to say, it was a bit intoxicating.

"Ah!" I said. "A Northmoorlandic American, which indeed is a rarity. And a very beautiful one at that."

Mary offered a coquettish smile. "The duchess's ladies-in-waiting helped me with this. What do you think?"

I glanced at her attire, clearly the envy of a guild of dressmakers to the nobility. A close-fitted bodice of scarlet embroidered with the duke's insignia drew a tight rectangular border about her bosom and heaving shoulders. The sleeves, however, alleviated any want of circulation. The outer sleeves opened like the folds of a robe, and the loose-fitting inner sleeves terminated with a small lace ruff around each wrist.

This is where any resemblance to Continental, or even

English, style ended. Northmoorlandic women reportedly shunned milliners and their fashionable headpieces unless the wintry chill dictated otherwise, and even then they preferred hooded robes. Their long interwoven braids betrayed a fierceness that was emblematic of the wild, swirling nature of their native windswept moors. I had seen much of this on my journey to Mithrendia.

"I think you look stunning, Mary," I replied. I could hardly help myself. The indisposed bachelor, the bow-tied academic, crumbled inside the depths of my heart. *Could she really desire me,* I wondered, *with my graying whiskers and aging build?* I felt once again the passion that had been long been vanquished, and I wanted to sweep her up in these long-forsaken arms.

But should I? I quickly calculated our difference in age and put it at some twenty-odd years.

She had always been beautiful, but today there was a radiance about her. As Mary stood there before me, my eyes took in the ensemble. Her raven-black hair reached her shoulder blades, rather than the customary length to the small of her back. A torc, fashioned by a goldsmith into a braided rope pattern, encircled her olive-skinned neck. A Celtic torc, a symbol of power and beauty, symbolized her radiance.

Mary, I thought, *you should not have done this. You stand too close to me.*

My will, such that it is, wilted in her presence. I extended my hands to her shoulders and brought her to me as her cheek rested against the hollow of my neck. The embrace of another person sent waves of warmth cascading through the depths of my soul. At that moment, I realized how utterly starved I had been for an emotional connection.

Perhaps we both were at the same brink of desperation.

After a prolonged silence, I pulled my head back to study her face. Her cheeks were tense. Her green eyes, which exhibited an exotic Middle Eastern hue, were downcast. She repressed a sob.

For once, Mary, so full of unbridled vibrancy, seemed at a loss for what to do next. I could see that she was hurting. I could see that she was confused.

It was then that I knew. I took a step back to give her room, to give myself room.

"Is it about Ben?" I asked.

She nodded.

What was this momentary flight of fantasy? Why had I not thought of Ben until now? How selfish of me!

This journey so far had taken a toll on all of us.

"Where is Ben?" I asked. "I have seen less of him these last few days."

"Playing the historian," she said. "It's as if he is living in a fantasyland and cannot get enough of each moment. He is always listening to the duke and his courtiers, taking down each minute detail every time they draw breath."

"And neglecting her," I said as I studied Mary's face, "who ought to be his first priority."

She seemed to manufacture a smile, but only for a moment.

I tried to reassure myself that as far as this brief rendezvous was concerned, nothing had been done that could not be undone.

What we needed at the present moment was a diversion.

I returned to the central desk, which housed a decanter and two small goblets. "Now, about these ghosts! By the way, would you like some wine?"

"Yes."

I poured out a little wine in each goblet and handed one to her. After completing this task, I found a large armchair by the fireplace and sat down. I then beckoned her forward. Mary sat down in the chair across from me. A fire roared from within the fireplace with its projecting marble hearth, sculpted in reliefs of Viking ships and sea creatures of Norse mythology.

At least we were in my element, surrounded by walls of welcoming books. With that assurance, I regained my composure. She seemed to gauge my recovery and settled comfortably back in her chair.

"Would you call it a singularity? I mean, for those who have seen a ghost?" asked Mary.

"A singularity?" That was an interesting notion, I thought. "Do you mean a remarkable event that is believed, but only by some? Such as Moses and the parting of the Red Sea?"

"Maybe not that rare and dramatic, but yes," she said after a brief laugh.

"I gather then," I replied, "that you mean that the appearance of ghosts is rare in that some people have never seen them. Which, of course, aids in the general skepticism about them."

"Yes."

"In my experience, ghosts act of their own accord and seem to make the choice to manifest when an energy source is available. Their presence can be detected with equipment sensitive to the electromagnetic spectrum, and therefore science has a documentary and investigative role in the ghost-hunting business. You need not take it all on faith. Those who wield these tools often know where to go to find ghosts. Mostly I'm thinking of places that have an extensive history and have experienced some type of trauma. Old hotels and sanatoriums and battlefields."

"Then how do the dead become ghosts?"

"I cannot say for sure," I said. "But if you are asking for my opinion, then I would say that most people upon death move on as spirits to the afterlife, to a place with God or apart from God, to a place of blessedness or one devoid of such blessings. But some linger on here for a time."

Mary glanced at the fire. "But what makes these ghosts linger on?"

I sat up in my chair. "I have found that in many of these cases the individual was subjected to a sudden, unexpected death. However, in my interviews with clairvoyants who can communicate with the spirit world, a refusal to accept one's physical death appears to play a part. The departed linger in familiar surroundings, such as their home or the place of their earthly demise. Consequently, they reenact their earthly roles irrespective of the passage of time."

I stood up and returned to the decanter. "Would you like another?"

She seemed not to have heard me as she sat there lost in thought. I took solace in observing that her face no longer bore the signs of grief. "Professor?"

"Hmm?"

"I have not yet shared with you what happened back home on Halloween."

"Yes?" I replied.

She related an experience in the Alfred P. Bias Lecture Hall at Rhymer with notions of ghosts and a black swirling mass.

"And you say that you were the only one in the lecture hall to see these apparitions?" I asked, almost incredulous.

"Apparently," she said with some irritation. "Unless someone else was too cowardly to admit it. Everyone mocked me, especially Professor Morley."

"I am sorry that you had to experience their censorship,"

I replied. "But you mentioned that the two ghosts played with a spectral orb that looked like a miniature basketball?"

"Yes. Do you have any explanation for that?"

"Well, the gymnasium is only two buildings down from that lecture hall. Hmm. Wait!" I surged from my chair and began to pace the room.

"Yes?" she replied anxiously.

"Back in the 1970s, there was a freak accident involving two basketball players."

She seemed to follow my pacing about with interest. "What happened?"

I stopped for a moment and leaned on the back of my chair. "There was a gas explosion at the physical plant, which back then was located next to the gym. Two players had stayed late that night to practice their free throw shooting when it happened."

"How terrible!"

"Yes," I said. "Deprived of life in the prime of youth. Tragic indeed."

The conversation broke off for some moments as I searched the library for a volume that might be useful to our topic. The ceiling was lofty, providing ample space not only for books but also for artifacts of expeditions, presumably into the moors and alpine regions. I saw large maps and samples of ore, as well as mountaineering tools and mining supplies.

My mission to procure a suitable resource for discussion was unsuccessful, but by now the awkwardness of that tender moment with Mary was fading from my thoughts.

"Have you ever seen a black swirling mass?" asked Mary, blurting out with her usual frankness. "Blacker than black, maybe seven or eight feet tall?"

"No. I have never seen the like."

"After the two ghosts left the auditorium, this black mass

swept through the room and then went out onto Chestnut Street. It left a foul stench like burning sulfur. But that is not all. Shortly after it left, explosions occurred outside."

"My word!" I said as I started pacing again. "I had no idea! I had already gone through the portal."

Mary remained composed in her chair. "When exactly?"

"The thirty-first, you say? It had to have been a week prior to that."

"Did you arrive in the moors?" she asked.

"What moors?"

"What moors?" she repeated with a quizzical expression. "The heart of this island is covered in moorlands."

I rubbed my forehead in exasperation of my own ignorance. It was my nature to be well-informed, and I hated the helpless situation that constituted my arrival in this country. "I woke up in this castle tower overlooking a rocky gorge the prisoner of a Lord Berbery."

I filled her in on the rest of his story.

"This, then," said Mary, "is the evil that the servants here speak of. They watch for some outbreak of werewolves."

I sat back down and looked at her with candid solemnity. "I'm afraid it is coming. Berbery is planning something sinister and maniacal."

"This is disturbing," said Mary. "Perhaps Abelard will help us."

"Once more, I am left in the dark," I answered. "Who is this Abelard?"

Mary related her tale of Wolf's Hollow.

"He really is a vampyre?"

She nodded.

I already believed in shape-shifters and ghosts. Why not make it a triumvirate?

"This Abelard seems to wield immense powers," I said. "Perhaps greater than that of the shape-shifters I witnessed."

"There is good in him," observed Mary. The vigor had returned to her face. She seemed possessed of purpose again, which did well for the color in her cheeks. "He seems to fight against his very nature, against his own instincts."

"Unlike Berbery," I answered. "Berbery embraces the evil that he has become, and he calls himself a god!"

Mary stood up and placed her goblet on the desk. She seemed very graceful in her determination as reflected in the way she walked. *Ben is a fortunate man,* I thought, admiring her, *if he would only get his head on straight.*

"What would you say about the black swirling mass I saw in the lecture hall?" she asked. "Was that a ghost?"

"I cannot say, but it does sound more sinister. What did you say it smelled of?"

"Something putrid, like burning sulfur."

I pondered for a moment, gazing upon the embers of the fire. "Brimstone!"

"Brimstone?"

"This is mere conjecture, Mary. Burning sulfur, in biblical terms, is called brimstone. It symbolizes divine justice, like that which rained down upon Sodom and Gomorrah. It also characterizes the lake of fire, where the devil and his minions will be cast at the Last Judgment."

Mary seemed surprised at my hypothesis. "Okay?"

"What if, in this particular case, the black swirling presence left a trace of its ultimate destiny?" I asked. "Like a sensory footprint?"

Mary looked pensive. "What are you referring to?"

"In my opinion, such as it is, that swirling black mass was a demon, a fallen angel. The two ghosts you saw were human; the mass was inhuman. A ghost can levitate something lightweight, like a teacup, or even a miniature basketball, whereas a demon can levitate something heavy, like a refrigerator or even a human being. You mentioned that a terrorist attack immediately followed its appearance. Somehow, I think, this powerful creature was orchestrating something diabolical through foolish minds of flesh and blood."

"Or did you mean to say 'The devil made me do it'?" answered Mary with a sudden defiance that surprised me. "That age-old excuse is a copout, and it is sheer fantasy. It is no better than the hogwash spouted out at the Salem witch trials."

"No, that was not my intent," I replied. I must admit, I enjoyed her fervor, and she possessed a powerful intellect for debate. "I am convinced that those terrorists acted of their own accord. They were merely drawn into the snare."

"How?" she asked. "Have you ever heard a demon speak to you?"

"No."

"Have you ever had a demon influence your thoughts?"

"That's the catch," I replied. "It is difficult to know. How can we perceive that our own thoughts, even if on rare occasion and for a brief moment, might not be our own? It seems almost automatic to think otherwise, to cling to that notion that we are and remain in full control of our own faculties. But if this influence you speak of is possible, if it were true … how covert and cunning on the part of the instigator, that is, the tempter, for the power of suggestion seems authored by our own minds! It is the perfect camouflage for the saboteur."

Mary muttered something about the eerie mist of Wolf's Hollow. Despite some prodding, however, I could not get her to elaborate, so the conversation reached a point of stagnation.

I took all of this into consideration. Ghosts and demons.

Portals and destinations. The five of us, four students and one faculty member, had been sent here to Northmoorland for a purpose. But to what end?

I thought about what we had collectively experienced. Catherine and Matthew, I did not know well, but they had at least shared parts of their stories with me.

We all had been hunted from the beginning. I had been incarcerated, while they had been attacked upon arrival. What could we modern dwellers offer that these sixteenth-century people did not already possess? The progress and superiority of twenty-first-century society? Arrogantly, one might say yes, but then again, the terrorist attack at Rhymer rung hollow with such notions.

I was at a loss. I struggled to process our purpose here as I circumnavigated the room many times over. Mary seemed to watch me from the center, observing in silence and saying nothing.

Even under her scrutinizing surveillance, the answer finally settled upon my mind like a lucid dream.

"We have been brought here to learn the ways of these people in this age of reform," I said. "More importantly, however, we find ourselves placed in the midst of their struggle. I have met Berbery. You have met Abelard. Gather your friends, Mary. We must help the Northmoorlandic people through what is coming."

CHAPTER ✖✖✖

Nightmares

Catherine Latimer's Journal Entry
Castle Brygge

Since the night of our discovery in the catacombs, I have kept to the castle. If spies were able to reach us in that dreary, forsaken place, they certainly could find us in Westfall and the Marches. We were fortunate to have escaped with nothing worse than having been eavesdropped on.

It seems that everywhere we go our lives are at risk. Sometimes I picture my first days at Rhymer, before that first explosion, before I witnessed the powers of darkness. My concerns back then seem petty by comparison: making friends, keeping up with my classes, and stretching a dollar as far as it would go. That seems nothing like the constant anxiety I feel now.

Nevertheless, I recall having a helper. I think of the quiet voice who aided me in my escape to the professor's basement, where I met my new friends. Even before I began this journey, I was not alone, but who was it who whispered to me, and how? Was it a ghost? I have not received an answer.

The nightmares have been occurring almost every night. Armies, weapons of war, and corpses carpet the battlefield. In their midst are monsters and demons.

They come for me.

Something calamitous is going to happen soon. I can feel it.

Last night I lay in bed, tossing one way and then turning another. Hours passed. My knees moved into a prenatal position. My careworn eyelids finally closed in the black of night.

Golgotha, Place of the Skull, Jerusalem
AD 30

This dream makes me shudder.

The time and place are foreign to me at first. Nevertheless, I seem to be a witness to these events as they unfold.

It is midmorning in a dull brown landscape of sparse vegetation just outside the city walls. I see a man in his thirties, olive-skinned with dark hair and beard. He has been tortured to the brink of death. Each stroke of the lash, with its flesh-shedding efficacy, is apparent on His back. His beard has been torn in several places, and I see a crown of thorns with puncture marks along His forehead. The Roman soldiers force Him onward as He carries a heavy burden of timber upon His weakened back. He collapses on the ground under this immense weight. They must help Him reach the top of the hill.

Spectators have gathered to revel in His fate. He is mocked

and despised, most of all by the religious leaders and the soldiers. "Hail, King of the Jews!" they shout to disparage His name.

The soldiers set an assembly of two timbers upon the ground while a narrow hole is dug. The longer timber has been bound with a crossbeam near the top, and the tortured man is laid upon these beams. His arms and legs are stretched across the crossbeam and main timber. I can hear His agony as they drive nails through flesh and bone. The cross is lifted upright, and with a sudden jolt, the vertical timber is socketed into the hole in the ground.

Two convicted thieves are also crucified, one on His left and the other on His right.

It is difficult for them to breathe. The chest needs to be raised up for the lungs to function in order to stave off asphyxiation, but at what price? The pressure points are at the nails. With any movement, shock waves of pain surge through the body.

The agony of the condemned lasts for hours, sometimes more. It's an ingenious and cruel form of execution perfected by the Romans.

I hear mumbling and groans from those among the spectators who do not agree with the religious leaders. They say that the man in the middle is innocent. As this man is being crucified, He says of His executioners, "Father, forgive them, for they do not know what they are doing."[6]

The crucified man on His left hears this and mocks Him. He does not understand, but the one on the right responds differently: "Jesus, remember me when You come into Your kingdom!"[7]

And Christ replies in excruciating pain, "Truly I say to you, today you shall be with Me in paradise."[8]

Not purgatory, but paradise.

Christ, who died at Golgotha, would rise again on the third day. I went to His tomb, but He was no longer there.

I woke up agitated and wrote down what I had witnessed. The mocking, the agonies, these remind me of what I saw at the burning.

I returned to bed. Sleep was elusive for a time, but my mind, after so much tumult, began to dream again.

I saw a child, an angelic young girl, with long braided hair. She stood beside me barefoot and in white bedclothes. I saw her light a taper and heard her whisper, "The people who walk in darkness will see a great light."[9]

What light?

"Jesus is the light," said the girl. "He is the Son of God—He says, 'I am the Light of the world.'"[10]

"Northmoorland," the girl added, "will soon see for themselves that His words are true. They will hear His words of love: 'You have heard that it was said, "You shall love your neighbor and hate your enemy." But I say to you, love your enemies and pray for those who persecute you.'"[11]

"Lord," I whispered, "the Church has become worldly."

To my surprise, I heard Him answer, "My kingdom is not of this world."[12]

"And what of those who act falsely in Your name?" I asked. "What of the cruelties of those in power?"

I heard Him say, "Not everyone who says to Me, 'Lord, Lord,' will enter the kingdom of heaven, but he who does the will of My Father who is in heaven will enter."[13]

My dream takes me to a vast cathedral. I see Archbishop Otta leading Mass in flowing robes of the purest white.

He conducts the affairs of his ecclesiastical office with the greatest solemnity.

I also hear that he keeps devices of torture in his home. One of these is so strong that it can crush the rib cage. Another encapsulates the leg; pegs are hammered through a slot into the bone of the shin. It is said that he reads scripture aloud in Latin before the torture is administered. Confessions and recantations are almost always secured. The archbishop declares that he would destroy the body in order to save the soul.

How thoughtful.

"Is this Your way, Lord?"

"Come to Me, all who are weary and heavy-laden, and I will give you rest. Take My yoke upon you and learn from Me, for I am gentle and humble in heart, and you will find rest for your souls. For My yoke is easy, and My burden is light."[14]

"Why then is there such misery? Why do we suffer?"

"This evil world is broken," replied the little girl, whose words seemed wise beyond her years. "It is cursed because of sin."

"There is none righteous, not even one."[15]

"Cursed is the ground because of you."[16]

"For all have sinned and fall short of the glory of God."[17]

"Nevertheless," the little girl said, "Jesus won't leave or forsake those who love Him."

I heard Him say, "In this world you will have trouble. But take heart! I have overcome the world."[18]

"Have you heard what the apostle Paul wrote?" asked the girl. "'For I consider that the sufferings of this present time are not worthy to be compared with the glory that is to be revealed to us.'[19]

"We aren't alone," she said. "Jesus suffers with us too. 'He was despised and forsaken of men, a man of sorrows and acquainted with grief.'[20] 'Surely our griefs He Himself bore, and our sorrows He carried; yet we ourselves esteemed Him stricken, smitten of God, and afflicted. But He was pierced through for our transgressions, He was crushed for our iniquities; the chastening for our well-being fell upon Him, and by His scourging we are healed.'"[21]

Before she leaves, the little girl with the angelic face asks me, "Do you know what the name Jesus means?"

"No."

"It means 'the Lord saves.'"

"Why do we need to be saved?"

"Because we cannot save ourselves. Only God can do that. Only He can wash away the stain of sin. But we can choose to accept Him or not. He doesn't force Himself on us."

If only the Church would attempt to remember that.

"For God so loved the world, that He gave His only begotten Son, that whoever believes in Him shall not perish, but have eternal life."[22] "That if you confess with your mouth Jesus as Lord, and believe in your heart that God raised Him from the dead, you will be saved."[23]

Finally, I heard Him speak once again in my dream. "Do you believe, Catherine?"

What is my answer?

I wake up. It is morning. Despite the chill outside, the sun shines its embracing warmth from a cloudless sky. I can feel it from my window.

I also feel a deep, restful peace. Such a difference from last night.

CHAPTER XXXI

An Affront

Lord Connaught retrieved the post from his coat pocket and reread the communication. It apparently was written in Berbery's own hand, and it carried precise instructions.

"Is it time, my lord?" asked Captain Dunman.

"Nearing."

The sea bellowed and swooned in a ragged affair of successive undulations, but far in the distance nothing could be seen stirring upon the northern ramparts of Mithrendia.

Lord Connaught fought against his instincts to instigate. He was not one for this lying low sort of affair. He was intent on an offensive, and he wished to attack soon.

Børgman's Bluff, for that matter, had long ago worn out its welcome. He knew that the sailors were bored and anxious for action of some sort—any sort. Playing cards only captured the attention for long, and the cache of rum had already been dispensed with. Exploration of the bluff, which had been achieved, wielded little information. Those areas observable by mainland had been scoured by the night, and the shielded parts by day.

There was little to be said for this island save for the hidden entry cove on its northwest corner and the meager fortifications that had become the men's temporary abode. The cannons had been positioned and were aimed at their prospective targets. They lay hidden under drab gray covers, matching the surrounding battlements and eliminating any reflective sheen that might be perceived from afar.

All that could be reasonably done had been done.

Connaught was fidgety. Everyone was fidgety.

A sailor approached Connaught, who was in his new quarters reviewing maps of the mainland coast. "A dinghy, sir, has been sighted. Should we apprehend it?"

Connaught could not hide his excitement as he rose from his seat. "Does it bear a marker, a flag?"

"Aye, sir. Handheld, for it has no mast."

"And what does its standard contain?"

"Four quarters, it does, though I cannot yet make out the figures."

"Not anything?"

"Well, sir, it appears to be a dragon in the middle."

Connaught recognized its source. "Let it alone. That dinghy is our signal."

Connaught exited his quarters and walked into a grass courtyard, where he ascended a stone staircase to the upper fortifications and artillery. Dunman was providing the watch, and a few sailors loitered about their captain.

"War is upon us, gentlemen!" said Connaught. "Raise the covers and load the cannons!"

The sailors gave a shout and rushed to their positions. Gunpowder and projectiles were loaded with eagerness.

"At my signal, unleash hell!" said Connaught.

He scrutinized the north walls of Mithrendia, which bore some initial markings of activity, as guards moved about the ramparts. There was a routineness to the rhythm of their movements.

"Now it is time to see what Gustafson's offspring can do," said Connaught. "Are the cannons elevated to the appropriate angle?"

"Based on our initial calculations, my lord," said Dunman. "Some trial and error should be expected, however, as we confirm our range and hone in on the target."

The sailors, having prepared the artillery, looked back at their commander with anxious faces.

"This is the moment, men, when we make our mark!" shouted Connaught. "The Norse gods glare at our artillery. Aye, Odin watches from afar with jealous eyes!"

Some speak of greed or lust, but Connaught's ravenous appetite had found the source of its avarice, which was not money, not land, and no, not even the captivating desire of women, but the ability to inflict his will on the lives of countless others—he, the man formerly clasped in fetters while rotting away in some ghastly incarceration of the Pale; he, the man saved from death at the hands of the draugr; he, the lone survivor of a failed mining expedition in the Black Mountains.

A man of destiny, Connaught had a miraculous knack for survival, and conquering Mithrendia was his most worthy aspiration.

"Fire!" he yelled.

The battlements of the bluff swelled with the blinding, billowing effects of smoke. The mass bombardment overwhelmed the sailors, sending many to the ground in shock. The cataclysm of Gustafson's weapons of death overwhelmed the senses as shock waves reverberated like pulse vibrations through the chest and belly.

"Did we hit the mark?" asked Connaught upon his recovery from the blasts.

Dunman waved his hands to dispense with the dense cover of smoke. He leaned over the battlements and peered into the unknown distance.

"Well?" asked his commander.

"We have hit their wall," said Dunman. "Though we are about five yards low in our trajectory, we have inflicted certain damage."

"Gustafson is a genius!" shouted Connaught.

"Aye, my lord," said Dunman. "Based on the carnage after the impact, we have only to adjust our angle of fire. These cannons are clearly capable of achieving our aims."

"Make your adjustments, Captain!" said Connaught. "If only I could see the looks on those Northmoorlandic faces. To see their complacent arrogance succumb to fear with the knowledge that even the walls of Mithrendia are able to be besieged!"

Return fire from the mainland dumped its utter best into the waters of the firth well short of the bluff. Connaught laughed. The defensive barrage, which appeared reactionary rather than rational, stopped almost as soon as it had begun.

Guards scurried along the northern wall of the city as if trying to adjust tactics. Their unknown foe had achieved the unthinkable from a forsaken outpost.

"Our north wall is being attacked, Your Majesty," said the commander of the Fifth Garrison.

The aged king rolled out of bed and for once leapt to his feet like a youthful soldier. "Attacked? At Butcher's Gate? You must be joking."

The king rarely granted an audience in his private chambers, but failure to give an immediate report of this nature would constitute a breach of fealty. His chamberlain had done well to let the commander in.

"Nay, Your Majesty," said the commander, a rugged veteran cloaked in heavy furs. "We are being bombarded from Børgman's Bluff."

"The bluff? Impossible!"

"A thousand apologies, Your Majesty, but it is so. Whoever has taken the bluff wields artillery that we have not yet seen."

"How?" asked Alfarin. He rushed across the immense royal chamber as dragons and griffins leered at him from rugs covering the stone floor. The north window afforded a view beyond the Grand Canal, and on most days he could make out the hazy ramparts of the northern wall.

"We know not, my liege. Perhaps some genius artillery maker from the Continent."

Alfarin's mind raced with an endless array of scenarios. "Continent? It cannot be the emperor's troops this far north, can it? Or Francis? Henry? What damage has been wrought?"

"We do not yet know who," said the commander, "but their range is unprecedented. The first wave struck five yards below the castellated walls. The second wave destroyed the quarters of the northwest garrison."

"Destroyed?"

"Aye, Your Majesty. We've lost a hundred men, no doubt."

The king thought of Purgatory, his most beloved artillery piece. Despite its famed ability to inflict lethal force, it could not possibly reach the bluff. Its sole function was to bombard the isthmus if any invader dared to breach Butcher's Gate, and this function it did with unparalleled prowess.

Alfarin glanced back at his wife. From their bed, Queen Toriana looked at him with a steady gaze of stoic observation. Quiet and cool, her mesmeric emerald eyes seemed to dissect their current predicament with characteristic precision. He took comfort, in moments of distress, in relying on her steady nerve and unyielding presence of mind.

"No armada has been sighted?" asked the queen. She had not yet lifted the covers, but her pillows were stacked high, and she seemed to recline on her throne.

"Nay, Your Majesty," said the commander. "And that is the puzzling aspect of this assault."

"Send forth the galleys from Arengärd," said the queen. "They can fight the bombardment with recompense."

"Aye, Your Majesty," said the commander, bowing with reverential respect. "A fine countermaneuver."

"How's that?" muttered the king.

"Cannon of that range could hardly be that maneuverable," observed Toriana. "Not like our smaller cannons on board the ships. As our navy nears the bluff, we will have the advantage."

Although the enemy held the high ground in such a scenario, the queen's resolve seemed to calm the king. As he continued to scrutinize the Norsetown district from his window, he weighed the merits of her recommendation and found it worthy.

Alfarin nodded. "Have the galleys circle the island from both sides. We fight on two fronts. The westbound fleet will destroy the enemy's ships in the cove. We will cut off their supply lines and starve them if necessary. Give the lord admiral his orders."

"Yes, Your Majesty," said the commander, bowing, before he left the room.

"Their affront cannot be one done in isolation, Alfarin," said the queen, "for they cannot invade. I suspect something else. I suspect a trap."

"What do you perceive, my love?" asked the king.

The queen arose from bed, wrapped her fine figure in woolen blankets, and strode over toward her husband. "This bombardment, though it appears to be a success for our adversary," she said, "is merely a pretext, a diversion. We must determine their next move, for that is where the hammer will strike. I suspect Berbery in these proceedings."

"Berbery?" said the king, flabbergasted. "We hardly know this fellow. How can an upstart from the eastern reaches command such artillery, and so far west of his estate?"

"Perhaps he is in league with a naval man," she answered. "The bluff can easily be taken by a ship of warriors."

Alfarin grew irritated with this discourse. "And where would he find such a naval man for hire?"

Toriana glared with eyes that seemed to look through him. "Every year you allow Harfagr's Landing to remain ungoverned, my liege. It remains a port of schemers and profiteers."

Catherine Latimer's Journal Entry
Castle Brygge

Although we are sequestered here inside these fortified walls, news from outside travels fast.

Someone, some shape-shifter from Berbery's encampment, found an access point to the catacombs below the great east wall of the city. The Fifth Garrison, though formidable, was bypassed, and Mithrendia has been invaded.

We have also heard of bombardments from Børgman's Bluff, and though the location of the foreign cannon is outside the range of any weapon in the king's arsenal, it seems that the northern assault was a diversion. The main front of the attack comes from the east, out of the Forest of Andia. They march through the Helsborg district en route to the Grand Canal and beyond to the royal palace in the Glenhorne district.

If the reports are to be believed, the king and queen face a foe beyond reckoning. Arrows tipped in wolfsbane may be the city's best defense. Every door, every window, of every home is shut up and braced from within. The families do well to remain indoors for the werewolves subdue almost any infantrymen who encounter them in combat.

God bless our archers.

"Report?" asked the king from the high spot of his throne room. The timbered ceiling rose some thirty feet above, allowing twin thrones, accessed by staircase, to tower above all. One seat of scarlet satin stood empty as the queen was attending to the royal guard and their fortifications of the palace.

Two hulking sentinels, blond-maned and armed with halberds, had admitted the commander of the Fifth Garrison into a nervous chamber of diverse chatter. Advisers spoke among one another, arguing strategy and soliciting any news of note from the far reaches of the kingdom.

"By the looks of things, my liege," said the commander with an arresting voice that otherwise quieted the room, "the lord admiral has turned the tide at Børgman's Bluff. He fires at will upon the fortifications from the west and the east. The enemy may possess cannons of superior range, but soon there will be no one left to fire them. They will make a fine addition to your artillery cache."

"Splendid!" said Alfarin in a momentary break from decorum. Artillery was his passion, almost a childlike passion, and his greed for armaments filled him with visions of cast iron and bronze. He had not yet noted the solemnity of his guest, even as the sunlight, peering through rectilinear fenestrations of stained glass, cast conflicting shades of red, green, and gold upon the man's face.

"All, however, is not well, Your Majesty," said the commander.

"Oh?"

"Our north wall has suffered heavy damage in the interim, and the streets of the Norsetown district have been ravaged by cannon fire."

The king grew irritated at this interruption of his revelry. He looked at his commander with grave suspicion. "As a boy I walked those streets of Norsetown with my father the king. Its fortifications are my family's dynastic legacy, our gift to the kingdom. Ravaged, you say?"

"Ravaged, Your Majesty. I wish I could give you better news."

The king had never taken bad news well. He did not possess the cruel temper of Henry VIII, and seldom did he flame the passions of rage. Nevertheless, stoicism was not in his arsenal, and he had never mastered the art of self-possession. In short, his emotions were ever conspicuous, even from upon high. With sunken cheeks, he looked as though he were laden with flesh of pure lead.

The king pondered this ominous report in his heart as his wife entered the royal court.

"Make way for the queen!" announced one of the hulking sentinels.

"More trouble, Your Majesty," said Toriana as she ascended the stairs with cold deliberation. "Berbery has done far worse than we could have imagined. This feigned usurper, this upstart, has breached the east wall. Rather, he has circumvented it."

"Circumvented it?" The king gasped.

"They found a hidden entrance into the catacombs."

Alfarin arose from his throne and descended the steps in fury. The frightened courtiers parted to give him room as he paced about with agitated thoughts.

"After all these years!" shouted Alfarin, "Those idiots have dug too far with their maze-making and skullduggery! I should have sealed that place up years ago!"

"That is not all," said Toriana, who now held the high ground with her usual composure. "Berbery's troops march on the royal palace as we speak. They will be here in a few hours."

"They dare to march here?" asked the king.

"Thousands of shape-shifters."

The king felt his knees weaken as he leaned back against the stone tracery separating the panels of stained glass. Far above him and the glass, stone reliefs of imposing fortifications and war-making machines conveyed a sense of royal power in ordinary times. They also conveyed a sober message, namely, to check the sure-footedness of any foreign ambassador entering the king's presence.

These, however, were not ordinary times.

The king thought he heard the sound of muffled weeping from a few members of his court. He turned to face the queen, but his countenance was one of bewildered frustration.

"Thousands of werewolves? A single member of their lot sent my constable and gaolers into a frenzy!"

Catherine looked on as a winged creature of otherwise human proportions descended upon the ramparts of Castle Brygge, which housed a large population. This creature settled upon the castellated walls, crushing a block of stone into fragments and dust. The decayed skin, bulging with sinews of nocturnal muscle, bathed in moonlit iridescence. The eyes were the color of blood as the vampyre had already fed.

The people remained ignorant of such things. Catherine could hear the curses and screams that the creature's sudden arrival had elicited. The people might have stampeded into the private quarters of the castle had the duke's personal guards not stood in their way. Among these knights who provided the night watch, several drew swords and converged upon the unwelcome guest.

"You fools!" said the vampyre, glaring at them as they advanced. "You dare challenge me?"

"Stand down, men!" shouted Carboni, who was among the dense crowd of refugees on the moonlit terrace. In fact, the friar had been instrumental in rallying residents of the western Marches and Westfall to accept the duke's offer of protected shelter. Now these people were poised to turn on him. "Folks? Folks? Listen to me! Our great ally has arrived!"

"Are you crazy?" said Allister, along with an ill chorus of patrons of the Blue Griffin.

"I could use a pint right now," said Seamus as he reacted in shock to Abelard's presence. "Before we take the vampyre on, you know?"

"Aye, a draught would do," said O'Gregory. "Nay, more than that, I wager."

"Next round is on the house," said Marley with the same scowl he wore in all moods and on all occasions, "if we survive this sordid affair."

Carboni walked up to the new arrival. "You are welcome here, Lord Abelard. The people do not understand the honor you bestow upon us with your presence."

"How do you know me?" asked Abelard as he studied the burly friar.

"My name is Carboni, and I know your friends," said the friar, bowing with as much magnanimous grace as his stature would allow. "Catherine, Matthew, Mary, and Benjamin. They are my friends as well."

"Are they safe?"

"The duke has granted them shelter here in Castle Brygge," said the friar. "They are lodged in the family's private chambers."

Abelard seemed most pleased. "I had lost track of Catherine, to my great dismay. Where is the duke?"

"Somewhere about the premises," said Carboni. "There is much to be looked after with such an influx of people."

"I knew some members of the Carboni family," replied the vampyre, "before they were taken by the Great Plague in the year 1350. The original builders of the catacombs as I remember. I must say that despite such tragedy, it is a good and worthy name to bear."

"I'm not sure what good that name has done me, but I thank ye all the same," replied Carboni. "Me forebears built the catacombs that the enemy has used for his assault on this city."

"Built, yes," said Abelard. "But their later extension under the city walls was not your family's doing. I have seen the maze and marked its progress over the centuries."

While listening in on their conversation, Catherine had been observing the crowd of people who stood in awe of the visitor. Their exclamations and curses had dissipated to a low murmur as they sized up the place and the rank of this Abelard.

"Did the friar say 'lord'?" asked one of the curious townspeople. "Lord of what?"

"He is the Lord of the Heights," answered Darrig, who had assisted Carboni in the roundup of citizens. "The master of Wolf's Hollow. He is the greatest of his kind."

"Lord Abelard is an honorable vampyre … I mean, person," offered Roald with a grin. "Once he quenches his thirst."

Catherine made her way through the crowd to Abelard, who embraced her like a daughter. Despite the intended warmth, it was the cold embrace of a cold-blooded creature, through no fault of his own.

"I wondered if I might see you again," she said with some emotion.

"My lady," answered Abelard, "do you not remember my mention of the Night of the Draugr?"

"Yes."

"It is upon us."

"Berbery, too, is upon us," said Carboni with noted concern.

"This army of werewolves," said Abelard, "does not know what is coming out of the south. This Berbery is no student of history; otherwise the fool might have heard of the prophecy!"

"You must be referring, me lord, to the draugr," replied the friar.

"You know this?" asked Abelard.

"They have been my life's study in the alpine regions," said Carboni. "I fell wayward of me vows years ago and decided that I might do more good far away from my order. I have seen their movements. The draugr march upon these lands now."

"I have not met one so informed of their whereabouts and doings as you," marked Abelard.

"Thank ye, me lord."

The vampyre nodded. "And where are the duke and duchess? I would like to speak with them."

One of the knights, with a nervous stammer, answered, "I can take you to them, Your Majesty."

"Your Majesty?" answered Abelard. "I have not been called that for a hundred years at least. Nevertheless, young warrior, lead the way."

Catherine Latimer's Journal Entry
Castle Brygge

I make these notes in haste as the events of the night are relayed to me through informants of the duke.

A logging company that floats felled timbers downriver from Donegast's Range to Glenhorne in the center city has been deprived of its stock-in-trade. One might attest to the power of magicians, but how could fifty logs simply disappear?

I asked, and there is a suitable explanation for this strange incident. The timbers have been stolen—by Berbery's shapeshifters no less.

Moving large timbers, apparently, is best accomplished in werewolf form, whereas the practice of general carpentry and its wielding of tools requires the skin and bone of a human being. The shape-shifters have allocated the timbers for parallel poles, and the decking of the executioner's scaffold at Cuidaffe Green has been confiscated for crossbars.

In short, the grounds of the royal palace have become a makeshift workshop as Berbery's army builds siege ladders.

The royals, I hear, have countered with fire and pitch. Fire-tipped arrows rained down upon the lycanthropes as cauldrons of boiling pitch were dumped from the battlements onto the assailants. Howls of torturous pain could be heard as the werewolves met with more resistance than perhaps they anticipated.

Will the royal palace stay the course until aid arrives? And if the royals survive, will they renew their persecution of those Protestants who defend them? Despite the burnings, we all remain united with the Crown in a joint purpose.

CHAPTER XXXII

The Night of
the Draugr

A belard left Castle Brygge to go see Berbery, whose men were encamped at Glenhorne. Thousands of shape-shifters carpeted Cuidaffe Green like a plague of locusts, rendering the verdant green to scorched earth between the eastern wall of the castle and the Grand Canal. Abelard could not know the thoughts of the royal court, but given the overwhelming superiority of the foe, he determined that they could not be of anything other than imminent doom.

Abelard knew of the palace's history. One of the early Northmoorlandic kings had been given a sketch of the Tower of London, and hearing of its formidable reputation, he announced construction of a fortress at once. The result was Castle Grimdelag, a formidable opponent of the siege tactics of medieval warfare. Castellated walls some ninety feet high outlined a rectilinear central keep, and corner towers soared another thirty feet above.

The advent of cannon technology, however, had negated the long-held advantages of such fortresses. Nevertheless, Berbery's army had brought no artillery, only the powers of the werewolf. Berbery had brought no siege towers either, only site-built ladders. Success would come down to the point of entry. If he could breach this awesome tower of rock, then inside it he would find the soft underbelly awaiting total annihilation.

The night air was thick and heavy as Abelard flew about the ramparts. Blood saturated the land with the remains of the brave defenders of the realm. Two battalions of the Fifth Garrison had abandoned the city walls for direct combat, but the result was a massacre. Abelard had watched these developments during his aerial approach as the soldiers' superiors ordered a wide-swathed separation from the enemy to lessen casualties and unleash the archers. Although he desired to join their numbers on the field of battle, he knew that he must first help secure Castle Grimdelag with its halls of kings. A headless realm was one ripe for overthrow.

When Abelard arrived at the royal grounds, the fortress was already under siege. Timbered ladders of a length beyond reckoning were swiveled from the ground to the very height of the battlements. Large iron pivots with inset spikes, apparently prepared beforehand by a smithy, burrowed into the main logs, which ascended like a ship's masts. These hinged pivots also clamped the heavy timbers, allowing the ladders to be unfolded in sections to their full length. The shape-shifters accomplished this unfolding with winches and ropes. With their prodigious strength, the werewolves, by way of manual exertion, secured the base of any one ladder at the angle of incline until the massive assembly came to rest upon the tower walls. Then their numbers began to climb the rungs.

Even with these fearsome developments, Abelard managed to catch the attention of the royal defense. The guards, liveried in the royal colors of azure and silver, turned to address the strange being who walked upon their battlements. From within their pointed helms overlaid with thick nasal bars, Abelard could see the terror in their eyes. They saw a being from the crypt, a being whose decayed skin shone mysteriously in the moonlight.

A few of their number rushed forward with outstretched swords to subdue the intruder. This, however, was beyond their capability. The very breath of their adversary repelled them like a fierce gale.

Abelard waved a spindly finger as if to say, *Do not waste your life pursuing me.*

As proof of his powers, the vampyre grasped hold of a ladder and flung it from the castle wall with great violence. Several wolves perched on its rungs fell back as the ladder swung toward the earth. Its falling timbers became a weapon of war, rendering those earthbound, and those unfortunates in its path, casualties of war.

Even werewolves could be felled by trees.

The tower guards stood motionless, staring at Abelard in awe. They had just seen him crush a stone battlement in his fingers.

"Would you like to see more?" he asked.

The guards parted to make room as the vampyre walked along the edge of the ramparts. Abelard picked the large-timbered ladders one by one and thrust them to the ground. What seemed unconquerable, this assault of werewolves, teetered upon this point of vulnerability.

Abelard could see that a werewolf was nearing the crest of this last siege device.

I have not had this much fun in decades, Abelard mused. Indeed, Wolf's Hollow had become stale from disuse. None but the disembodied dead and the walking undead lingered there. *Not since the dynastic disputes of the Crown in 1474, have I seen such action, when the Duke of Donegal needed my assistance to stave off civil war.*

The werewolf approached the last rung, but it was not met by the horrified faces of soldiers. Rather, it was greeted by a monstrous vampiric face, emerging from the darkness behind the castellated parapet.

Abelard grinned at the werewolf.

The predator, so used to intimidating, recoiled momentarily. After a few moments, the wolf recovered, now surging with anger as it swept a fierce clawed arm at the vampyre.

Abelard could have dodged the assault with ease, but he chose to stand his ground. With eye-bewitching speed, he caught the arm of the beast midstride and arrested its momentum.

The astonished wolf grasped the ladder with its other paw as Abelard twisted the first arm into an uncontrollable position. The ladder twisted off the wall, warping the rungs and snapping them off one by one like a cascade of falling dominoes. The twisted wreckage collapsed upon the green, bringing an end to the eastern wall siege.

Abelard recognized their leader, Berbery, as the werewolves wasted little time in regrouping. *Their next target is the south gate,* thought Abelard. *And if they breach it?* It would be the end of Alfarin's dynastic line.

Abelard was thinking of the king's welfare, but the feeling was not mutual.

"Seize him!" said Alfarin, having spotted the intruder. The

king was covered in his best chain mail and breastplate. This assemblage of metal bore the essence of strength and vigor, but within Alfarin, Abelard saw a man on the decline. The skin and the muscle held no vestiges of the once ruddy youth, and a cadaverous likeness was settling in on a careworn face.

"And arrest your protector?" asked Abelard.

The men tried to obey their king's orders, but they were only able to surround the vampyre while maintaining the distance of an arm's or a sword's reach.

"Seize him, I say!"

They would come no nearer.

"You would do well, Alfarin," said Abelard, "to desist from this nonsense. I came to the aid of your father at his succession, when your family was upon the brink of civil war. The Duke of Donegal, that is, the eleventh one, would not have succeeded in staving off the coup were it not for me."

"This cannot be," said the king. "That was half a century ago, and yet you look so ..."

"Young?" said Abelard. "I've heard that before."

The king studied this intruder with awe. Abelard had a sense of what Alfarin was thinking and of what he saw: youthful vitality coupled with the visage of a wise sage, including the fullness of face of a mature man, and all within a monstrous frame of pale, arrested decay.

"What are you?"

"The fiend of your nightmares," replied Abelard. "And yet I have not come for you."

The king took a step back, in obvious awe. "Then what have you come for?"

The queen, by now, had reached the side of the king. She glared at the vampyre. "You yet live!"

"Aye," said Abelard. "Are you disappointed?"

She glanced over the ramparts at the wreckage of Berbery's encampment. "Nay."

"At least you recognize my contributions."

"Well now," said the king.

The captain of the royal guard appeared before them, almost out of breath. "The werewolves are launching a massive timber at the front gate. I fear it will not hold out for long."

"There is no time to get acquainted with one another, Alfarin," said Abelard. "What is the quickest path forward to the other side of the portcullis?"

"I will show you," said the queen.

Quick was a relative word as it took some minutes to descend from the ramparts and reach the castle gate. By then, the massive portcullis had just fractured into three pieces, and the werewolves, led by Lars and his superior, a centurion, were overwhelming the royal guards.

Abelard recognized the centurion's rank by a bald area as marked by a branding iron upon the shoulder. He surged after him and gripped the werewolf's shoulder as his spindly fingers grasped chin and nose. Claws swiped and lacerated Abelard's arms, but the vampyre fixed upon his adversary's face. He clamped the mouth shut and twisted the head farther than its natural limits. The bones snapped, and the centurion dropped dead upon the floor of the candlelit entrance hall.

Lars, however, was the deadlier foe. He attacked the vampyre from behind.

This ambush proved surprising. Lars grasped and pulled upon the vampyre's giant wings where the sinews and connective tissues attached to the back. Abelard's powerful lower body managed to retain a firm balance, but his torso bent backward. It felt like fire raging within his winged joints. Abelard had not seen such force from a shape-shifter, not once in a span of three hundred years.

However, the vampyre was cunning and had fought in many battles. He leaned even closer into Lars, using his ambusher's weight as a support. Like a catapult bent back almost to the point of snapping, he unleashed a leg drive that exploded from the stone floor. His arms pivoted overhead like a spring-loaded pendulum as he struck a third werewolf in the head and crushed its skull. This action allowed a partial disengagement, but Lars still gripped one wing and gouged Abelard's back with an onslaught of claws. It felt like a scourging, the beginning of thirty-nine lashes by leather straps tipped with filed bone.

Abelard swiveled around and struck Lars in the shoulder.

Meanwhile, other wolves were beginning to flood into the lower chambers of the castle. There were too many, even for Abelard. He thought of the prophecy.

The Night of the Draugr.

A green mist about chest level appeared outside the damaged portcullis. It did not enter the gate but rather converged into convoluted forms, forms that swept through the castle walls.

"Vogg!" said Abelard as the draugr emerged with their leader. The halls of kings reeked with the decay of the undead.

"Trouble, I see?" said Vogg with bitter sarcasm as he and his revenants raced past the besieged vampyre into the king's lair.

Abelard did not find such a greeting to be unexpected. Black Mountain vampirism disdained the Continental variety, no matter how many decades it had dwelt upon this Nordic island, no matter how Northmoorlandic Abelard had become.

He knew that they hated him for other reasons than this.

The draugr rested in the coarse, worm-infested soils of the earth; he dwelt in a great castle of nobility, partaking of a refined existence.

They possessed the ability to overwhelm mortals, but Malsadus had empowered Abelard with vampiric strength beyond reckoning.

Some of the draugr were more advanced in age, even centuries older. It was an accepted axiom that the powers of the vampyre grew with the passing of years. Nevertheless, Abelard swelled with the strength of two millennia.

That was being tested now.

Abelard could feel Lars's massive arms as they unfolded and wrapped around the vampyre's shoulders. Under this constrictor-like grasp, Abelard dropped to one knee.

Abelard considered his predicament, but it was difficult to concentrate with such profound stress about his upper torso. The werewolf buried its teeth in the vampyre's neck—a fitting reprisal, and a bit of irony to a vampyre.

The werewolf might kill me in this position.

Despite Lars's grasp, Abelard was able to swivel his arms upward with the elbows tight against his sides. The werewolf's grip loosened as the vampyre reached both arms behind his head, well over his shoulders. Rather than grasping the air, he grabbed hold of Lars's upper back and flung the werewolf overhead into a castle wall. Lars hit the wall with ferocious speed and collapsed into unconsciousness.

Lars was powerful, but not this powerful. The vampyre could have destroyed him in a single follow-up thrust, with one swipe the werewolf's head removed from its body.

Abelard, however, was preoccupied. He raced into the innards of the castle to engage the other trespassers. He was less concerned with the revenants as he observed their skirmishes. The draugr were more interested in lycanthropy than the Crown. They combed the castle, searching to engage any werewolf that crossed their path. These engagements were brutal manifestations of vicious powers: the swordplay of revenant vampyres, those warriors of the undead, pitted against the powers of an apex moonlit predator. With knifelike claws and backbreaking strokes of power, the werewolf was capable of sending a revenant to a second death.

Regardless, the draugr overwhelmed the werewolves because of sheer numbers. The werewolves inside the palace were destroyed, but not without heavy draugr casualties. Supernatural as they were, the revenants could not engage in bodily contact without a return to a corporeal state, leaving the heart and neck vulnerable. The werewolf excelled at targeting the latter, as did its vampiric adversary.

Before Abelard could catch up to Vogg, the revenants who remained sped outside, through the eastern walls, to battle Berbery and the bulk of his army.

The only remaining vampyre was Abelard. He assisted the guards with some temporary bracing of the portcullis before he met up with the king and queen in their locked throne room. Hundreds huddled before the high thrones of their monarchs. The people seemed no less astonished at Abelard than at the other unwelcome guests.

"Your stone walls are no safeguard against the revenants of this world," said Abelard. "But the draugr have taken the fight outside. They have not come for your scepter, Alfarin, but for revenge on those who would abandon the old order of our ways."

"They are gone then," said the king.

"Aye, let them destroy one another," said Abelard, with a bitter tone of remembrance.

"And yet the vampyres of Myrkur abandoned your rule long ago," observed the queen with a stoic countenance. "It seems that Your Lordship is a solitary one these days."

Alfarin looked at his wife in bewildered awe.

Anger kindled in Abelard's breast, but he would not allow

this beguiling youngster, this shrewd queen, to unsettle him. "Why were you surprised to see that I still live?"

"I have heard of the master of Wolf's Hollow," said the queen, "though I wondered if the legends still held sway."

She is indeed beautiful, and a bold character, thought Abelard, *one who might bend a dynastic king to her will.*

"And now that you have seen me," said Abelard with subtle sarcasm, "do you find me a heretic?"

"You are a monster!" she answered.

Abelard fixed upon her mesmerizing emerald eyes. Those piercing orbs, which coerced in a bewitching way, and dictated the decisions and the words of others.

Over Abelard, however, they held no sway.

"You call me a monster," he answered. "And yet you burn your own people!"

The courtiers, though scared, murmured in surprise at this outsider's authority to question the Crown's ways.

"We would have no more of that, if you did wish it," said Alfarin, who seemed unnerved after all that he had just witnessed. "I hate it all."

"Alfarin!" said the queen.

"And yet you have signed many death warrants, Alfarin," said Abelard. "The stake is a slow and cruel death."

"I, I did," said the king. He poured himself some wine and emptied it in a single gulp. "I hear their tortured cries in my dreams."

"You sacrificed your own judgment for hers."

"But Toriana is my wife!"

"And you are the king!" said Abelard. "She did not inherit your father's throne."

The king nodded as if ashamed.

After centuries of study, Abelard understood the coarseness and the subtleties of human nature. He could explain to these royal people the error of their ways. He could intimidate or threaten. Still, he could not change their character. That was the province of the heart.

The choice, then, was to remove the king and queen from power or let free will take its course. If he took their lives or imprisoned them at Wolf's Hollow, the people would rally around the family, and then reform might be swept away with the wind.

Furthermore, it was said that their eldest son, Orin, had a temperament like his mother's. Orin, of course, was next in line to the throne.

Abelard searched his heart. As a supernatural being, he could see glimpses of the future. The dynasty was rotting from within and would not last. As a natural being, he saw that while the people were their subjects, the king and queen were also subject to their people. If there was sufficient outcry against their policies, the king and queen would endanger their rule by not listening to the public.

The king's flushed cheeks seemed to have regained their composure as Abelard's words sank in. He sat upright in his throne and addressed the visitor to his court with a firm voice: "I thank ye, Lord Abelard, for coming to our aid in this time of peril."

Abelard bowed.

Toriana, who seemed to bury her anger with a face of composure, said nothing.

Abelard had achieved his purpose here. To the astonishment of the guards and courtiers, the vampyre flew through the east wall of the throne room and into the tumult of battle.

Abelard's powers included seeing things from afar. His

eyes were like those of an eagle. As he wrestled with his thoughts, he caught glimpses of the action on the battlefield.

Berbery was not difficult to spot. He had the maniacal quality of one with an accursed nature mixed with dark magic. His eyes glared with a knowing alliance with evil. His fur had a blacker texture than that of the others, and there was more girth to his muscled shoulders and back. The tips of his ears extended upward in elongated tuffs. His serrated teeth seemed enlarged beyond those of the other beasts on the battlefield.

The ranks of Berbery's army were dwindling. Berbery stood some thirty feet from the canal as the draugr hemmed the shape-shifters in against the outer bank. Cuidaffe Green, known for its verdant grasses and the fullness of its foliage, had become like a muddy bog set in a wasteland. Fires ravaged the trees as smoke billowed over the outstretched boughs, and thousands of arrows punctured the ground and the backs of the fallen.

Abelard could see that traction was poor. When Berbery turned to face the giant, the Morning Star mace was upon him. Before he could step aside, it had crashed into his shoulder and sent him writhing to the ground.

Berbery's bodyguard, Svein, surged into Olaf before the giant could reposition his ponderous weapon of war. Olaf staggered back as the wolf bit and clawed at his flesh, and his blackened veins streamed forth from the lacerations.

Olaf's plight, however, did not go unnoticed. Retribution was swift. Two swords were thrust through the back of the Viking bodyguard, and Svein slipped down to the ground. The blades were dirty, already stained with the blood of other shape-shifters that had been finished off by Leif and Harald. With one final stroke, Leif ended Svein's existence as well.

Abelard, from fifty feet or so away, dispatched one

shape-shifter after another, while Vogg walked into the company of his newest three draugr. At least Abelard assumed they were new as he did not recognize them, and he had never seen one with such immense size.

"This is the one?" Vogg asked as he gazed down at Berbery. Berbery snarled in anger, but his garbled breathing was like the breathing of a person with deep wounds. "The one who drew the shape-shifters from their abode in the Black Mountains?"

"This is the one, my liege," said Leif.

"Destroy him. Eradicate this foul Berbery."

Berbery's army had been decimated, though much the same could be said of the draugr's. As Abelard surveyed the Glenhorne district, it seemed a tomb with bodies of the Crown's men in their leather hauberks or chain mail; bodies of the shape-shifters, rendered human in death and devoid of any ornament or armor; and bodies of draugr reduced to skeletal remains, their rotted flesh having disintegrated into piles of dust. Cuidaffe Green, the site of state executions, was accustomed to countable corpses. Tonight, however, the sheer numbers and the stench of death overwhelmed it.

Berbery was not about to carpet the field with yet another of the slain. He rose to meet Leif and Harald, countering them both with a ferocious assault. He arrested the thrust of Leif's sword in midflight and struck off Harald's head with a single swipe of his free arm. Despite the deep gash in his paw, the werewolf wrestled the sword away with brute strength, before decapitating Leif with his own weapon of war.

Only one from Connaught's expedition to the Black Mountains remained, but he was the greatest warrior of them all. His anger had been kindled, and his passion burned with the fire of retribution. Berbery did not see the Morning Star mace until it was in full swing. It descended upon his head, and this time its aim was dead on.

Abelard was now about thirty feet away from his target. Although engaged in fighting, he saw this upstart lord of the east, this Berbery, sidestep the blow of the Morning Star mace. Berbery rammed his body into the chest of the giant as Olaf fell and somersaulted backward onto the moonlit grass.

Abelard was now some fifteen feet away. *If I could but reach him in time,* he thought.

Berbery was upon the giant before he could regain his ground. The werewolf arose from the torso of the fallen to deliver a killing stroke. Predator and prey had exchanged places, and yet neither knew what was coming. Abelard had only to leap upon Berbery's back.

Vengeance, however, is a precarious commodity. Vogg's ax fell like the blow of the headsman. Indeed, Berbery had not seen it coming. His headless body collapsed upon the very spot where the gibbet of the king's justice once lay. The tufts of the ears mingled with mud as his blood coated the ground. His blood seeped through the permeable blackened soil before his conquerors, all vampyres, could lap it up. It was a final consolation, if only he could have witnessed it. Lord Dominus the blasphemer, the departed, was no god after all.

Abelard was gravely disappointed in his old lieutenant's delivery of the fatal blow. It had come from Vogg, the revenant who once had dared to defy his master. Abelard had long desired to do this deed himself, to punish the one, this power from the east, who dared to subvert the established order that had been set millennia ago.

That order, however, had been subverted well before Berbery's arrival. Vogg had broken away long before Abelard replaced the shape-shifters under his command with dire wolves. That was long before the thunderous halls of Wolf's

Hollow were deprived of their revelry and Abelard's companions had been reduced to ghosts who haunted the corridors.

Abelard was willing to overlook the past as far as his old associate was concerned. This long-standing grievance had petrified and become of lesser account with the sands of time. Tonight he was in forgiving mood, outside of Berbery.

Olaf was regaining his ground as Abelard approached.

"It has been a long time, Vogg, my old friend," said Abelard.

"Olaf!" said Vogg, with some alarm. "Stop!"

Olaf did not hear his master in time. He moved against the intruder and swung his ponderous Morning Star mace.

The mace descended upon Abelard like an avalanche of rock. The spherical bulb with its protruding tricornered spikes would split the head of the master of Wolf Hollow's open with a single thrust.

Its aim was true; the acceleration of its mass could not mean less than a sure kill.

But its iron shaft was met by a grip of steel.

Olaf recoiled in shock. This weapon, too heavy for others to handle, had been taken from him. Yet Abelard was examining his mace as if it were a delicate flower.

"Do not destroy him, Abelard," pleaded Vogg. "Olaf is my best warrior."

Olaf, still visibly stunned at such inordinate strength, backed away from Abelard. The giant had never met his better.

Abelard, though annoyed, did not seek vengeance on his attacker. Olaf, he knew, was merely protecting his master.

Now the giant had a new master.

"Why did you desert me?" asked Abelard. "Did I ever dishonor or mistreat you?"

"No, my liege," said Vogg as a gentle breeze swept through the plains of war. The moving air lifted up his mustache and beard, a playful and living sentiment for a body of the grave.

"And yet you dwell in the Black Mountains, in the heights of Myrkur. Those lands are filled with an evil pestilence of diabolical origin, as they were long before you entered that domain."

Vogg lowered his head in disgrace. "It was Malsadus who tempted me to have an army of my own."

"Malsadus," said Abelard. "I should have known."

"What would you have me do, my liege?"

Abelard knew Vogg well. Such penitence was the substance of fear now that Abelard had the upper hand.

"I would have you depart from Mithrendia," said Abelard, "never to return. The prophecy has been fulfilled. Berbery is dead. Go back to your mountains. Take your army, what is left of it. I release you from my service, not that you ceded to my authority before."

Vogg bowed to his old commander, who took flight.

"Draugr!" shouted Vogg. "We go home. To Myrkur!"

Abelard circled the theater of battle, surveying the damage so as to determine what could be summarized about the night's proceedings. From high above, he saw it all.

The remaining draugr feasted on the corpses of the fallen before seizing their precious rings, their pocketed coins, and their forged weapons as booty. Upon hearing their master's call, the army of revenants left the Glenhorne district smoldering in ruin.

Meanwhile, Berbery was no more, and yet a small remnant of his army remained. The moon was drifting to the west with a couple of hours remaining before its banishment below the horizon. The wolves needed shelter, or rather a stronghold, from which to coalesce and centralize their source of power.

Castle Grimdelag had proven difficult to siege and subdue. The werewolves, now under Lars's command, had tested the breach in the south gate and found it sealed. Moreover, the archers of the Fifth Garrison and their poison-tipped arrows were once again within firing range. They marched on the palace with resolute courage.

Another castle had been scouted to the southwest. This one, though formidable, was more assailable than the king's abode.

"To Westfall and the Merchant Quarter!" Lars shouted. "Mithrendia will yet be ours!"

Abelard knew his next destination.

CHAPTER XXXIII

Castle Brygge

atherine had not heard a report in the last few hours. The refugees at Castle Brygge were hungry, and the duke's stores were being depleted of their meats and grains. Sweat-soaked cooks scrambled about the vast kitchen, stoking the fires and stirring boiling pots of stew. Meats were sliced, as were potatoes and carrots. Barley was fed into the cauldrons, and loaves of bread were placed on wooden carving boards.

Catherine, Mary, and Matthew had been assisting this humanitarian operation by ferrying supplies to the kitchen and carrying out the prepared foods to distribute among the refugees. It felt like the Blue Griffin all over again.

"Sir Matthew?"

Matthew gazed upon the delightful source of that pleasant feminine voice. She was a fair, freckled young woman with long curls of auburn and inviting brown eyes.

"My lady?"

"Madeline and I saw you at the market. Your head and your hands were bound, but we knew that the stocks were not worthy of your presence."

"Shouldn't you be out fighting, werewolf hunter?" asked Madeline, her raven-haired friend. "Kate here says that a knight has better things to do than serve food to strangers."

Catherine knew that she had underestimated her friend, as no one, not even she, could have anticipated Matthew's fending off a werewolf.

"Is there a werewolf left to face?" asked Matthew, his face flushed with the pleasure of being recognized. "Then again, I would much rather serve you fair ladies."

The two women giggled like schoolgirls. Catherine exhaled a hearty laugh before she could cover her lips. Matthew hardly seemed synonymous with the kindled flames of romance, but here in Mithrendia, his prospects were proving to be quite stunning.

Carboni was standing nearby, but Catherine could tell that his mind dwelt upon more pressing matters. She maneuvered her way through the restless crowd to see if he had heard of any news.

"The duke's informant has told us that Berbery is defeated," said the friar. "The draugr are leaving. The prophecy has been fulfilled, and the streets of Westfall and the Marches may soon be safe."

"How do you know this?" asked Matthew.

"Lord Abelard."

"He is here?"

Carboni nodded.

"Where?" asked Catherine.

"He meets now with the duke and duchess. I will take you to him."

"And what of the werewolves?" she asked.

"This is where the danger still lies," said Carboni. "Berbery's army has been decimated, but some two hundred werewolves remain. They march, or rather sprint, on all fours toward Castle Brygge as we speak."

Darrig and Roald appeared to have overheard the conversation. It was not like such armed men to be cloistered, doing nothing. Other brawny clansmen from the western Marches loitered about. They seemed bored and out of place.

"They march upon us?" asked Darrig. "The wee heavies are getting restless. They are pinching for a fight."

"Aye," said Roald. "Darrig and I owe them one. The point of our swords, says I, for Bjorn's sake!"

"Those were dire wolves," said Darrig.

"Werewolves, dire wolves; what's the difference?" replied Roald. "They're all evil. They should be hunted down and slaughtered."

"I know of your great prowess as adventurers, Darrig and Roald, but this foe is far superior to the four-legged creatures you have yet seen," warned Carboni. "The clans would be better served from within the castle walls."

"Cooped up inside like frightened children?" said Roald.

"Unlike the draugr," said Carboni, "the shape-shifters cannot transport themselves through solid rock. This castle harbors us, protects us. We would do well to fire upon their numbers from the ramparts with poison-dipped arrows."

After serving them food, Mary, apparently tired of the crowds, retreated into the domestic quarters of the castle.

Based on their recent conversation, Catherine had learned of Mary's meeting with the professor in the library. Catherine had been pleased to see a restoration of Mary's confidence, but once again her mood was one of descending darkness. Mary's passion was for her lover, but he had seemingly cast her aside.

Ben, in this time of heightened emergency, was nowhere to be found.

Catherine had become acquainted with her friend's disposition. Mary had invested two years with the young historian, and in this foreign place and time he had deserted her.

How, then, could this circumstance rear its head at a time of war? How could Ben act in such an ambivalent manner when one should rally the troops and protect those that he loves?

Catherine had seen the professor in the corridor beside her chamber door and shared her concerns.

"Poor Mary," said the professor with obvious sympathy. "I know where he is. Let me see to it."

Professor Porter caught his protégé by the elbow as the duke, the duchess, and their entourage exited their interview with Lord Abelard. In the process, the professor secured Ben's meticulous notes, scribbled even to the edges of a piece of parchment.

Ben seemed shocked by such an unsuspected academic theft.

"What are you doing, Professor?"

"Helping you, Ben."

"By stealing my work?"

"Not stealing. Merely confiscating, at least until you regain your senses."

"My senses?"

The corridor before them seemed dark as though the household staff had not attended to the torches along the walls.

"You have not been yourself," said the professor. "You neglect your friends, and Mary in particular."

Ben flashed with apparent anger. "With all due respect, Professor, Mary is none of your business."

"Ah, but she is! She met me in the duke's library recently and divulged much personal information that I did not ask for."

"Then I must ask that you forget about what she said and leave us to our own affairs!"

The professor softened. "You are right, Ben. I should not invade your privacy. On the subject of Mary, I will withhold my opinions."

Ben gave a subtle nod.

"Nevertheless," said the professor, "I must admit, in the academic sense, that I am surprised by you."

Judging from his subdued disposition, the professor's protégé seemed quite put off by this remark.

"I have done everything according to the ascribed methods of a professional historian in these circumstances," said Ben.

"And yet that is precisely where you fail," said the professor.

"Whatever could you mean?"

Ben had seemed cool and confident as a graduate assistant, relaxed enough to bounce that stupid ball off the walls and floor of the secretarial chamber of the professor's meager basement office. But here, the young man had been driven by some unseen and unyielding determination as if bent on making his mark. Indeed, it had changed him, and not for the better. His carefree zest for life had been replaced by a hardened edge.

"You record the lives of others," said the professor. "That is, their history, and the history of this island nation. Which, in and of itself, is a fine thing to aspire to do. But your devotion is extreme. You forsake your own life in the process. There is a balance to these sorts of things."

Ben would not engage in eye contact with him. "Perhaps I am focused on something far more important than the mundane details of my former existence."

"Like following the duke around like his personal dog?"

Ben appeared to be particularly irritated by this remark. "I cannot keep precise notes without remaining in the duke's company. Can you imagine what the professors in our department might do to have such an opportunity as this? Can you imagine the uniqueness of my dissertation?"

"They will not understand, I'm afraid," said the professor with some melancholy, "if we are fortunate enough to return to Rhymer one day."

"What are you saying?" asked Ben.

"Time travel, Ben. Who in the academic community would possibly believe our story? We would have better luck convincing the patients in a mental ward or the clientele of an opium den."

"You cannot mean ..."

"Mean what?" asked the professor. "That your work does not matter? In ordinary times, I would not insinuate such a thing, but these are not ordinary times."

Ben appeared dull and reflective, which angered the professor.

"Wake up! We are about to be besieged by the remains of Berbery's army. By two hundred werewolves!"

"Yes?"

"Do something about it!" shouted the professor. "Be a part of the answer."

The professor followed as the young historian walked

to a north-facing window. They could see the enemy fast approaching with savagery as the werewolves killed the soldiers and civilians in their path.

"What do you have planned, Professor?"

"A fair question, Ben. I am no warrior, as you know. I love my library, rather the duke's library. But today I step across the threshold, from my sanctuary into the unknown. I am prepared to go to the end in fighting these foul beasts, in helping our friends. Will you join me?"

Ben began to pace about the room, his gaze upward, while his fingers fumbled and fidgeted about as if playing an imaginary piano.

"Well?" asked Professor Porter.

Ben stopped for a moment and turned to face him. His countenance seemed resolute, and his fidgeting had stopped.

"All right, Professor. Let's send those foul creatures into the abyss."

The master mason's residence was shut up with the servants Markus and Gilda secured inside. William McCormick, his daughter Adaira, and his apprentice Erik had left to join the regiment, and that regiment marched on Castle Brygge. Rather, they marched past the duke's fortress in hopes of engaging the enemy before they could lay siege on the castle.

Erik had been tactfully antagonistic toward Adaira's presence in this urban theater of war, as had her father. They preferred her to remain safe within the boarded-up confines of home. But Adaira was a Northmoorlandic woman, and she had insisted in participating with the archers. Her overtures were incessant. Having been granted an opportunity beforehand to exhibit her skills before the regiment, she had proven capable of marksmanship.

That skill, however, needed to be honed. Practice required time, a precious commodity that ceased to be in supply with the sudden invasion of the city.

Erik worried about Adaira, almost to the neglect of his duties, as he marched in a distracted rhythm with the third row of infantry. A mere thirteen rows of armed men separated the archers, who were marching in back, from direct engagement with the enemy.

That said, the street-lined shops provided protection of their flanks as the formation of troops swelled to the full width of the thoroughfare. Shop owners peeked now and then from their dwellings on the upper floors. Elsewhere, cracked-open shutters slammed shut.

The regiment stood alone in its defense of the streets. Only the torches mounted on sconces from the walls of abandoned shops provided any assistance. Light and prayers formed the sole civilian contribution. Lapping flames licked the air as if in anticipation of an engagement.

With flared nostrils, Erik could smell the enemy before he sighted the werewolves' advance. A foul odor, that of a wild, wet dog, played with the anxious mind, and the men seemed on the precipice of abandoning the formation. Erik's instinct, like that of the others, was to run, that is, until he spotted someone familiar. Although he had not yet seen Lars in werewolf form, Erik recognized the eyes. Bearing a strange redness, these were the eyes of one who had almost plunged Erik headlong into the depths of the quarry.

"Lars!"

His adversary had once more become a leader.

Lars led a contingent of shape-shifters, perhaps one hundred in number. Nevertheless, one hundred werewolves were like a legion of men on an open field. The regiment had swelled from its modest beginnings to a troop of some two hundred fifty, but this was an insufficient assemblage.

The tight urban quarters and the regiment's disciplined formations would have to make the difference. They had to. There was no other option if they were to be victorious.

William, bearing an iron helm, spear, and shield, led from the center of the first row. "Our enemy approaches! Phalanx formation!"

Erik held his pike aloft. He, like the others, had to be diligent around his comrades. The Merchant Quarter lay closest to the mountain meadows bearing wolfsbane, and the pikes had been dipped in the poison beforehand.

The wolves drew close.

"Ah, the master mason!" said Lars in a thunderous voice that sounded, if such a thing were possible, like an articulate snarl. "I will avenge myself this night and cast your family into the utter darkness of Hades!"

McCormick seemed to ignore him as he barked orders at his infantry. "Maintain your lines! Courage! Discipline! Together, and only together, we will defeat this foul enemy!"

Erik said a prayer for Adaira and her father as he braced for battle. Some of the werewolves charged the front line as others sprang over the initial rows into the depths of the formation. Forty men were mauled, but the pikes of their comrades were numerous. Many hit their marks, and those marks were fatal.

The werewolves seemed to be astonished at the number of fallen, but their hatred kindled a mounting counterattack.

"Re-form the lines!" shouted McCormick. "Re-form the lines into the testudo formation!"

Erik was disappointed given the success of the phalanx

advance. However, he considered that the defensive testudo formation would help protect Adaira.

"Archers," said McCormick, "unleash your fury!"

Gaps in the rows of infantrymen closed. Rectangular shields were lifted to form a united, protective barrier like the hard shell of a tortoise. Still, through a small gap in cover, Erik could see a dark sky breached by a flood of arrows. These, too, had been dipped in wolfsbane. The howls of the recipients told of their effectiveness.

Despite their losses, the enemy lingered. Erik could hear the wolves who had evaded the initial thrust, and they were enraged. The beasts drove wedges in the lines, unleashing their fury upon the warriors and stripping away shields. Once exposed, the men were an easy kill. The slapping of shields and the scratching of their metal surfaces seemed like a torrent. Erik struggled to maintain his composure. He wondered, almost helplessly, about Adaira, but it did not seem that the wolves had advanced to the infantry's rear guard.

Meanwhile, arrows stained the night sky with their kinetic shafts of wood. They flew through the air like schools of fish in a swift-moving current.

Erik studied these missiles almost distractedly until he was swept back by a crossing blow, but his breastplate prevented a fatal swipe. His attacker moved on, and Erik regained his footing. Realigning with the others, he overlapped his shield with those of other soldiers to ensure a united front. Pikes poked through small gaps in the shield cover.

Through a small gap in the overlapping shields, Erik could see the master mason. McCormick, who had evaded Lars's first charge, grasped a sword from his belt to face the counterthrust.

"You avoided your fate before," shouted Lars, "but I will yet be the death of you!"

McCormick parried the first stroke, a crossing left, but Lars swept his arm back and landed an overhead blow. McCormick's helm bore the brunt of impact. He dropped to an unstable knee.

Lars snarled and was set to pounce, when a rain of arrows fell ahead of what had been the front line of the testudo formation. He leapt to avoid the lethal barrage and dove on top of McCormick.

McCormick had placed his best and most courageous men in the front lines. Erik had noticed a breakdown of discipline in the lines behind him. He glanced back and could see Adaira nock and then release a succession of arrows. She had evidently spotted Lars and was raining her fury in his direction.

Lars ripped off the master mason's helm. The beast leaned down to gorge himself upon the blood from McCormick's exposed neck.

Even the disciplined front lines were losing their position after yet another assault of the werewolves. There were too many men separating Erik from his master, and Erik felt powerless to help. Laden with emotion, Erik looked back at Adaira, who could see that her father was in grave trouble.

"Father!"

She nocked another arrow and let it fly.

Erik followed the arrow's trajectory, but not without breaking his concentration to look for his master. He could see the beast breathing its foul warm breath over McCormick as Lars's teeth descended upon the older man's flesh.

From Erik's point of view, Adaira's arrow had launched a bit off target, but the wind pushed it to the left. It drifted almost with unending patience before beginning its descent.

Erik's chest heaved with an involuntary convulsion. His master, lying prone and vulnerable, was at the point of death.

McCormick, seeming to ignore the oncoming threat, rotated his head and strained his neck in a frantic search. He appeared to locate his daughter through the throng of soldiers. "Adaira?"

Adaira answered. The arrow found its mark in Lars's back. The beast flared with contemptuous fury before slumping over his former master.

The remaining werewolves, having seen their fallen leader, found a narrow alleyway branching off the main thoroughfare. They swept through this alleyway much too quickly for McCormick's infantry to trail. The regiment had to find contentment in their isolated victory.

"Adaira?" asked her father as he rolled Lars's hulking body off his chest.

Erik rushed to join her and his master. They surged, arm around shoulder, in a collective embrace.

After expressing their familial affection, Erik and Adaira helped McCormick to his feet.

Together they studied the werewolf.

As it sank unto its earthen demise, the bestial fur receded into the pores, revealing the muscular frame and long shanks of the former quarry master.

Together they studied the man.

Erik could sense that each of them had something to say about Lars, and yet after having been in the heat of battle, their lungs were heavy. Their actions had spoken for them.

Lars had been like a wild sojourner laying waste to any accommodation and trampling upon the gifts of love and fellowship.

In the end, the enigma, that riddle of darkness, had been felled by one who once adored him.

Abelard had missed the initial skirmish in Westfall, but he approached Castle Brygge from overhead just as sixty werewolves made their assault on the front gate. With sunrise nearing, the wolves had wasted no time in crossing the icy moat.

In an hour, the wolves would return to human form, and at that point they would need the security of a fortress and a warm fire. In an hour, Abelard would seek his diurnal rest, though he knew not where.

Several wolves climbed the raised drawbridge. Gnawing like rats, they sank their teeth again and again into the coarse braided ropes.

A flurry of poison-tipped arrows rained down from the battlements at the pack of wolves across the moat. Archers from the Marches assisted the duke's best marksmen, and together they picked off a dozen of the attackers.

The drawbridge was nearly flush with the castle walls, and owing to the oblique angle, it did not afford a clean shot from the battlements. Some archers rushed to the lower floors to target the enemy from the windows.

Meanwhile, the wolves kept gnawing as strand upon strand tore away, until the wooden drawbridge dropped into place with a tremendous thud. The unbridled screams and wails of the refugees within the castle pierced the walls as Abelard descended from his flight.

The landlocked wolves, now furnished with a causeway, rushed above and across the stagnant waters of the moat. Several of their number had managed to carry a large timber, some thirty inches in diameter, all the way from Glenhorne to Westfall. Others joined them as they positioned the ramming device a few yards from the portcullis.

Abelard thought of Catherine and her friends. He thought

of the unarmed townspeople inside the castle. They would be fodder for the wolves if the latter were to breach the gate.

Abelard descended upon the drawbridge, positioning himself between the timber and the portcullis. The wolves salivated at the chance to crush the vampyre with their collective strength.

Abelard sensed their rage, but their utter disregard of his authority fueled the fury that welled within him.

"You will soon recognize your master, you dogs!" he shouted.

His adversaries answered with action. Fifteen wolves charged forward with the ramming device as they pinned the vampyre against the oaken gate. Abelard could hear the iron chains, reinforcing the gate from within, rebound and clang against the portcullis.

The vampyre could also hear the duke's men clamoring inside as the duke shouted, "Brace the wall!"

The men apparently went to work as Abelard could feel the vibrations of braces shoved against the interior side of the door.

There were pressure points now on both sides. The wolves snarled and howled as they pushed the timber into Abelard's chest. He could feel his sternum compress, which caused his breathing to become difficult.

The bulky log, however, was wider than Abelard's shoulders, allowing him to grip the sides. The vampyre pushed with all his strength, and fifteen wolves moved backward against their will.

Once Abelard's arms locked out at the elbow joint, the wolves attempted a counterthrust, but the vampyre's strength was unyielding. He gazed beyond the ramming device to the outer banks of the moat and saw the lethal assault of the arrows.

He did a quick scan of their numbers. There were some two dozen wolves left, including those attempting to pulverize his torso against the duke's front door.

Abelard had bought additional time for the castle archers. Suddenly, however, the arrows ceased to fly.

What was happening? Had they run out of the poisoned missiles? Abelard could hear shouting overhead from the battlements as warriors abandoned the castellated walls and jumped into the frigid waters of the moat some twenty yards to his right.

First Darrig. Then Roald. These men were followed by some of the duke's men and by warriors from the Marches.

The others surprised him. Ben. Matthew. Professor Porter. And Carboni? The friar's fall made a great disturbance upon the tranquil waters, but even he descended with an iron claymore.

Abelard was amazed at their courage and foolishness as several werewolves rushed to meet the men along the outer banks. He needed to disengage somehow to protect those who would otherwise be overwhelmed by the foul beasts.

Keeping his arms locked, the vampyre slowly slid his left hand toward the center of the log's end, before his right hand maneuvered to grasp farther out along the shaft of the timber. Trying to grip a twenty-foot log from its end was not advisable. His opponents in this contest of strength and will were many, and they had better leverage on the siege weapon.

Carboni's group was approaching the outer banks from the murky waters of the moat. Other armed men apparently had dropped from various points along the castle perimeter and now raced around the banks from both sides to engage with the wolves.

Abelard released his locked arm and patiently allowed the timber to converge on his chest. His muscles were becoming fatigued. The werewolves, sensing a turn in their favor, strained to overpower him.

The vampyre planted his feet against the portcullis and swung the immense log to his left. Abelard released his grip as the timber splashed into the water with those wolves left of the log in tow. Those wolves on the right staggered near the drawbridge as they attempted to regain their balance.

The vampyre stepped to his right and jumped off the bridge, spreading his wings and flying to the outer banks. Ben was just emerging from the water when a werewolf standing above him delivered a death stroke.

The claws burrowed into Ben's cheek. His attacker's arm, however, was deprived of its momentum by a pale hand of spindly outstretched fingers. The enraged vampyre swung his free hand and relieved the werewolf of his head.

Abelard stood between his friends and the onslaught of wolves. His attackers were formidable, but they were no match for the ferocity of his power. Whether in terms of speed, strength, experience, tactics, or wisdom, all lycanthropes who encountered the aged vampyre found themselves at a disadvantage.

The fifteen beasts that remained seemed to hesitate. The goal was entry into the castle or some secluded location, and their powers, like the vampyre's, depended on the waning moonlight. They were running out of time.

Abelard glanced back over his shoulder. "Why did you enter the theater of battle?" he asked with a perturbed tone. "The castle walls were your protection."

Carboni, shivering and drenched to the core in his dark tunic, answered for the others. "Nay, my lord, you are our protection. Foolish as we are, we could not see you facing these foes alone. Our arrows and spears are spent, and idle waiting weighed upon our consciences. The four of us are no warriors," he said, looking at the Rhymer men, "but we wanted to help if possible. Look before ye. Darrig and Roald are accomplished men-at-arms, and they can help you dispense with these foul beasts. So be the other wee heavies, the gladiators of the Marches."

Abelard looked at his friends and at the other warriors, the latter of whom had hemmed in the wolves from the near and far approaches of the thoroughfare. "So be it as you will. Gather the arrows and spears that missed their targets, for their tips still bear the mark of wolfsbane. You need only puncture the skin of the werewolf for a kill."

The wolves did not wait for the scavengers to arm themselves. Unlike the castle, the adjacent shops and dwellings, though three- and four-storied, were half-timbered and therefore more suitable for climbing. Abelard could see the wolves scale the walls in quick succession and then disperse in various directions upon the slate-tiled roofs.

As Abelard took flight, he gained a better view of the thoroughfare. He glanced back down at Carboni and the others. "The regiment is coming. Direct their archers' attention to the roofs. I will hunt these foul deserters, these renegades of Berbery, one by one!"

The battle had moved away from the castle, but from a window in the upper gallery, Catherine had seen something turn back.

She and Mary had been calming the refugees, especially the frightened children, when Catherine saw movement from afar. She raced across the wooden-planked floor, dodging sculptures and wall-mounted breastplates and swords, to catch a better glimpse.

What she saw made her spring backward.

The wild-eyed beast galloped upon all fours and leapt from the edge of a roof. She could see its rage as it surged over the entirety of the moat before landing at the sill of her window. The diamond-paned glass shattered, revealing the head of the predator.

"Mary!" she shouted as she surveyed the sixty or so persons in the gallery. "Get everyone back!"

Mary, having just delivered the last of the bread, had a silver serving plate in her hand when the intruder made his entrance.

No one present needed prodding to respond to Catherine's command. Women stampeded toward the inner corridors as they scooped up screaming children and overwhelmed the exit ways. Some of the escapees, heedless to caution, became lodged in a human pileup within the constricting space, causing others to lose their balance upon impact. They tripped over one another upon rising and then scurried away.

In the end, Catherine and Mary were left alone with the werewolf, which was having difficulty squeezing its broad shoulders through the fenestration. Additional shards of glass crashed upon the floor and spread at their feet.

The wolf, seeming to observe the rectangular dimensions of the opening, twisted to make room for its upper torso.

It seemed like a rabid dog, its teeth gnashing in an almost uncontrollable fury with snorts and snarls that sounded hellish and reeked of putrid flesh.

The beast began to writhe its way through the window. Catherine glanced at Mary and, in desperation, considered what to do.

Catherine lunged for the wall to retrieve a sword from its mount. The weapon felt heavy and unwieldy in her hands. She thought of grabbing Mary by the hand and rushing to another chamber, when she heard a loud impact.

"Mary?" she shrieked.

She heard it again and dropped the sword.

Catherine turned to track the commotion. That is when she noted the odd weapon.

"Mary?" she repeated just as her friend blasted the assailant with a swift whack of the silver serving plate, followed by another and another.

"You foul, disgusting hound of hell!" shouted Mary with unbridled passion, which Catherine later surmised was the culmination of weeks of pent-up anger.

Luckily for Ben, Mary had found another victim. Contact with the silver had left burn marks upon the epidermis. The force of the blows stunned the beast for a moment. Then it began to rage, its belly still upon the sill of the window, as Mary smacked it once more with a downward thrust of the tray.

Catherine glanced beyond, through an adjacent window, in time to see an arrow take flight.

The arrow struck the beast in the buttocks. It howled without ceasing as its body flooded with spasms. Then without warning, the head slumped.

Catherine gazed at Mary, still heaving from the exertion. Mary just stood there, inhaling perseverance and exhaling tenacity, as beads of sweat coated her warm cheeks and even bedewed the dark bangs upon her forehead. Catherine had never seen Mary with such a sense of prepossession, especially since her seeming abandonment by the one she loved. The two exchanged glances of friendship, of enduring companionship in a time forged by trial.

Having taken stock of her friend, Catherine looked upon the fallen, rendered a corpse by that curious archer below.

It was no ordinary archer who had let that arrow fly. That person, bearing a bow and standing on the outer banks of the moat, was a young woman with flowing blonde hair, wearing a grin of satisfaction.

The archer was soon joined by the Rhymer men, along with Darrig, Roald, and some other warriors of Westfall and the Marches.

Catherine could hear their enthusiastic conversation well considering the broken glass. The ebullient crowd seemed like long-lost friends reconvening in prosperity after years of hardship.

"Have all the other wolves been slain?" asked Carboni, still drenched in his rustic tunic.

"Aye," said Roald.

"Three shot down by arrow," said the professor as he looked graciously upon Adaira, McCormick, and Erik, Adaira's betrothed. "Thanks to our young sharpshooter here and this fine regiment."

"Aye, me lads! One by ax, a twain by sword, all tainted with wolfsbane," noted Abilach, one of the large kilted warriors from the Marches, otherwise known as a wee heavy. A hearty red-bearded friend of Darrig and Roald, Abilach had once been served by Catherine at the Blue Griffin.

"And the rest by beheading, thanks to a certain vampyre," said Matthew. "Although until today I had never heard of beheading a person without a machine or weapon. And of course Lord Abelard fed off the last one, at least what was left of its neck." Matthew seemed to pause to consider this strange and morbid concurrence. "Nevertheless, personally, I enjoy flooding the furry kind in the Grand Canal."

"We all know of your worthy exploits, laddie," replied Abilach.

Carboni winked at Catherine, not that he seemed to enjoy

Matthew's descriptions, but like everyone else he was in a joyful mood.

Darrig shared what appeared to be a private joke and then pointed toward the dangling carcass in the castle window. "Won't his next of kin be put to shame when they hear that the last of Berbery's men died from a blow to the backside?"

The victors let out a hearty laugh.

At that moment, Mary poked her head through the window and seemed to recognize Ben. Catherine could sense Mary's relief at his well-being, but Mary's spirit remained unabated.

"Mary!" shouted Ben. "Are you unhurt?"

Mary stared down at him but said nothing.

"Mary?" said Ben.

The fighting men began to laugh.

"She must be yours?" asked Abilach.

Ben nodded while seeming to sheepishly accept the ribbing of his compatriots.

"You mean *was yours*, you fool!" shouted Mary.

This brought the victorious warriors to an obnoxious roar.

CHAPTER XXXIV

Our Lady of the Forest

A belard with his hawklike senses and preternatural awareness had seen it coming.

For others there had been little forewarning, but for the guards who stood watching the sea from the north wall, there had been much.

All was quiet, inordinately quiet for a waning night such as this.

Connaught's cannons had stopped their destructive barrage as there was no one left to fire them. The lord admiral's men had done their work, and the waters of the firth had faded under a dense white cover.

The vampyre hovered in flight over the city. A thick fog rolled in like a ghost ship before the first rays of dawn and carpeted Mithrendia in a mysterious silence. The fog lingered, casting eerie sentiments among the populace, who could not help but wonder if some evil yet remained. How so? Few burghers left the sanctity of the space behind their locked doors and their boarded windows as they awaited some sign of assurance that the battle was over.

Although the sun's illumination was not yet apparent, Abelard knew of the upcoming hour. In his mind's eye, he found Mithrendia already licking its wounds and burying its dead. Those of a less superstitious nature were the first to leave their secure nests, and they were awestruck by the immensity of the battle and the carnage it had wrought.

The grounds of Cuidaffe Green, once the site of the age-old practice of trial by ordeal, and later a site of more conventional executions, had long been a curious combination of the grisly and the immaculate. Its once pristine grasses and manicured shrubs were laid to waste and covered with corpses. The place of the Crown's justice was rendered a makeshift cemetery, as were many of the city's fields and parks. Majestic oaks and elms oversaw the work of mass interment like watchful chaperones as shovel tosses of earth darkened what was once verdant and pleasing to the eye. Overflow graves were dug even farther afield, beyond the city walls.

Those among the living, already exhausted from the tumult, attended to their duties with grief and wailing. Strangely, however, the combatants, whether friend or foe, could not always be discerned. The former images of the draugr and the shape-shifters had vanished, leaving rather ordinary anthropomorphic remains and dust. For human they were, and human they remained in death, lying side by side with the other fallen. *The other fallen* being the city dwellers who never knew a personal transformation into a creature of the night. Yet here they were, the intertwining of good and evil, strewn together, so common to the human condition.

The living attended to this macabre scene as if it were the aftermath of the plague.

Nevertheless, the spirits of the living thrived in their pain. Public grief turned to joy as residents of Norsetown, Helsborg, Glenhorne, Westfall, and the Marches roared in celebration while hailing the victorious dead.

The enemy, vanquished. The city, to be rebuilt.

Abelard, flying over Westfall, realized that his work here was finished. His home had become a tomb. From his forgotten fortress he ruled the draugr and the werewolf with a hollow scepter. He had dwelt in those halls for too many years alone, a vile predator and a servant of devilry. It had taken a vulnerable yet brave young woman, almost a victim in his arms, to wake him from his brooding existence and to reawaken his heart. For Abelard swore that she was a descendant of his beloved. For the first time in over a century, he reconnected with what he once was. It was a vivid and stirring recollection. He remembered the good that had been lost and the evil that had filled the vacuum.

There would be hell to pay for such sentiments.

Abelard was exhausted when he descended upon the battlements of Castle Brygge. There he met Carboni, who had been assisting the departing refugees as they descended the staircases. With the advent of the first rays of the sun, Abelard felt the shadows of the stone turrets most welcoming.

"The powers of darkness scheme, yet the outcome does not always fit within their preconceived notions," said Abelard. "Their plan was fulfilled, but only in part. The rest was thwarted."

"Ye speak in riddles, me friend," said Carboni. "I know that your ways are both mortal and immortal. What do your immortal senses behold?"

"I fear there will be a reckoning."

"With them?"

"Aye."

"And they will call ye to account for what displeases them?"

The vampyre nodded.

"And what now?" asked Carboni.

Abelard gazed at the arrested decay of his own arms and fingers. "This body has not aged in three hundred years, yet it carries the weight of the centuries. The companionship of darkness does that to a man."

Carboni seemed to understand. "Aye. It erodes the soul."

Abelard nodded.

The two stood there for a moment, watching the refugees pass.

"Catherine is well?"

"Aye," said Carboni. "She assists the duke and duchess with the refugees below."

"Good."

"And ye, me friend?"

"My work here is finished," said Abelard, turning his somber glance upon the friar. "They come for me, Carboni. I know not when. That is, I know not when if I do nothing. Nevertheless, I know a means to antagonize them."

Carboni seemed curious. "Draw them into a fight?"

"Aye."

"How so?"

Abelard sensed that this reckoning would involve two sides rather than one. However, he feared one side more than the other. "I must reach consecrated ground, though my kind are repelled by sacred objects."

"Are ye sure of this, Lord Abelard?" asked Carboni.

"I am."

Carboni seemed to consider the finality of Abelard's words for a moment.

"Then let us proceed to Our Lady of the Forest," said the friar with excitement.

"Us?"

"Aye, me lord. I would not miss this reckoning, as ye call it, for anything. Besides, ye will need one in holy orders such as I. Me betters, sir, ye could certainly find, but perhaps not with me knowledge of the alpine regions and those who dwell there. If this be ye burden to bear, then I will help as I can."

The fog was lifting. Abelard noticed a shift in cloud cover high above. The shadows would assist him in his trek home. The vampyre bowed before taking to flight.

"Into the west, Lord Abelard!" shouted Carboni. "I will meet ye directly, though I cannot travel with your surreptitious speed!"

"And yet," said Abelard, "you move by daylight, when the vampyre must rest. Look for me upon the darkening of twilight!"

Catherine could see that Mary was in no mood for travel.

Ben would have liked to have gone, but his uphill climb to salvage something, anything, with Mary was just beginning.

Professor Porter also stayed behind to assist the duke and duchess in apprising their tenuous situation with the queen and the archbishop now that the cries of battle had ceased, now that the common enemy had been vanquished.

Catherine, however, had insisted on coming, as had Matthew. Indeed, Carboni would not have been able to shake them had he tried, quite unlike his pals Allister, O'Gregory, and Seamus, who in victory returned to their usual seats of consumption at the Blue Griffin. That victory, of course, had been achieved apart from their effort, but for years and pints to come, no doubt, they would add their rousing, colorful commentary to the story of the whole affair.

The three travelers left Castle Brygge by midmorning, after a light breakfast of what was left of the duke's rations. They exited the southwest gate of the city, wandered through the outskirts of the western Marches, and abandoned civilization for the alpine meadows.

After crossing a pleasant brook, they lost sight of the earthen trail and relied solely on the friar's sense of direction. The soft-padded meadows of the hills and dales gave way to rocky outcrops and heavy growths of forest, which were accompanied by a steep grade. Fir and spruce trees of majestic heights covered their path with cold shadows, harboring islands of alpine snow. Catherine, though tiring, kept pace with the burly friar, who moved well for a large man.

Matthew, meanwhile, who had grown accustomed to long walks through the city, was a traveling companion without complaint. He had adapted well to this foreign land and time, beyond Catherine's expectations, and he seemed to have abandoned that peculiar habit of looking in his pockets for a cellular device. His courage surprised her, as did his awareness of others. His face no longer bore that distracted glance when he was spoken to, and he was quite capable of engaging in extended conversation.

For now, however, all of them were quiet. Catherine could hear a faint rustling in the background, but a slight breeze accounted for this, so she turned her attention to other thoughts.

A few minutes later, she heard something else. This time it was the snap of a twig.

In actuality, there was a fourth member to their party. A black-hooded person skulked about some thirty yards behind them, hiding behind trees and brush. Nevertheless, Catherine spotted him and whispered her findings to Carboni.

"I have a notion as to that one," said the friar in response. "Let him follow if he must."

Even as their westbound journey assumed a southerly aspect, the skulking pursuer kept his distance while keeping apace. Although Carboni's calm assessment reassured Catherine, she could not shake this intruder's presence from her thoughts. She kept track of him here and there, with subtle glances over her shoulder. It was an irksome annoyance, piled on top of other worries, not the least of which were the aftermath of a concluded battle, the precarious state of religious reforms, and the nebulous fate of this evening. She thought of Abelard and of what might happen to him just as they arrived at a small clearing in the forest.

Beyond the gravestones was a stave church. Its longitudinal axis ran east to west, providing an immense backdrop to the memorials of the departed.

"This is what we seek," said Carboni.

It was nearly twilight, but the languishing rays of the sun still afforded a suitable viewing. Catherine saw a magnificent post-and-beam structure of heavy timber with an ascension of sloped roofs and clerestories, one after another, shrinking laterally while towering into the sky. The siding consisted of vertical planks with carvings of Celtic crosses, and its shingles were like thousands of wooden scales sheltering its underbelly from the annual burdens of winter. Timbered dragons' heads, a pagan leftover, flanked the church's gabled ridges, and a copper weather vane, still bearing its unblemished color, crowned its uppermost peak.

"It's gorgeous," said Catherine.

"Can we go inside?" asked Matthew with some eagerness.

"Of course, me lad," said Carboni.

The church had a modest floor plan of two dozen pews that were bisected by a central aisle and overlooked by a lofty balcony. These afforded an intimate view of the altar and, beside it, a raised pulpit, three-sided, built over an inverted dome of ornately carved wood. Here communication on the earthly plane rose to the ears of the divine. A cavernous ceiling soared almost to the uppermost peak of the roof, allowing an orator's words to be lofty and of profound intonation. Even the whispers of the visitors, by comparison, seemed vibrant and extensive.

Catherine noted few windows. Portraits substituted for fenestrations around the perimeter and served as portals for spiritual reflection. She lit one of the tapers and gazed at the oil paintings of saints and the renderings of biblical scenes. The central piece in the back of the church featured a pietà with Mary grieving over the body of her crucified son Jesus.

On the side of the nave facing the graveyard, there were five portraits with faces depicted according to the artist's eye: a central portrait of King David; to the right of that, portraits of Samson and Jonah; and to the left of it, portraits of Rahab and Mary Magdalene.

"Who are these people?" asked Matthew.

"Persons, some of great ability and achievement, who also struggled with their shortcomings in life," said Carboni. "But they ultimately held on to their faith."

Catherine wished to reflect on this, but now was not the time. The trio walked back outside. In their absence, the hooded person had maneuvered his way to the church and stood peeking behind a corner.

"What of the draugr?" asked Matthew. "Will they come tonight?"

"The draugr dare not walk upon consecrated ground," said Carboni. "Ye need not be concerned—"

"Nor can I trespass this sacred land," interrupted another from afar. "Every crucifix, every baptismal font filled with holy water, has been like poison to my soul. I cannot suffer it, though I might wish it otherwise."

"Lord Abelard," said Catherine.

"Lady Catherine," said the vampyre with a preferential bow. "Somehow—and yet given the odds, how could it be?—you seem a relation of my Eleana."

"I cannot tell you," answered Catherine, "for I do not know myself."

The vampyre lingered beyond the outskirts of the gravestones that dotted the elevated area at the south of the church property. "I can come no closer."

Yet with distance there was proximity. He seemed emotional, if ever such emotion, which she thought he felt, could be discerned in that pale face.

"That you, all of you, would come here for me fills my heart. However, I fear that I have unnecessarily placed your party in grave peril."

He seemed to catch a prospect of that hooded figure lurking behind the corner of the timbered sanctuary. Catherine and the others turned to look as well.

"Hello there!" shouted the vampyre.

The clandestine figure would not answer.

"Indeed, you have placed them in grave peril," said a foul guttural voice that issued from an unmarked place that somehow was near. "For they see the unseen realm, and they will suffer for it!"

Catherine saw, at last, that familiar seam of clear air rip open as before, revealing another dimension and the fiery foe she had beheld in her former life. That familiarity did not comfort her. She stepped back, the tips of her fingers bracing the outer timbers of the church for support.

This time the fiend appeared with several others, each as grotesque and twisted in evil as the speaker. They towered over human beings, and the very air seemed charged with their overpowering will and their malice.

"Malsadus," said Abelard in a resolute tone. "I knew that you would come. My powers have grown, I daresay, for you to bring five more of your kind."

Catherine studied their hideous faces, which were clouded by black smoke that swirled about them, coalescing here and diffusing there but never presenting a clear visage of their countenances. They were neither human nor beast, but perhaps some abomination in between. They stood on two legs, and yet their faces were those of horned creatures, like the goat men of the pentagon graffiti she had once seen on a city street back home. Only Malsadus, who stood a head taller than the rest, presented a discernible face, one seared and scorched by flame. It was the ravaged face she had seen in the depths of her nightmares.

Before, on Chestnut Street, Catherine struggled to comprehend what she had seen. Now she knew that these were demons of the abyss.

Matthew fell to one knee beside her. "I've seen these things in graphic novels," he whispered. "And fantasy games. But they aren't real. They cannot be."

"And yet I see them as well," she answered.

"The mind struggles to acknowledge what the eyes have seen," whispered Carboni.

"Do you mean that you have seen them before?" asked Catherine.

"Aye," replied the friar. "Well, only one of their number. But I saw it as clear as any other thing I have beheld with mine own eyes, in the midst of an exorcism. It had manifested to claim the pour soul it had possessed. These are perverse and unscrupulous characters. Be on your guard."

Abelard remained where he stood, scrutinizing, as Catherine watched the demons sweep across the cemetery.

The friar spoke with sudden rage. "You dare trespass upon sacred ground, you fiends of the dark?"

The arch-demon, Malsadus, turned to face Carboni as the burning smoke coalesced about its humanoid form. "I have walked where I wished and trespassed where I may for millennia before you were born, you fool!"

"Such insolence!" thundered Carboni. "Your pride borders on blasphemy!"

Malsadus and the other demons laughed in wave after wave of what sounded like successive torrents of water. Their very presence bespoke of great power. Catherine could not help but feel that she and her group were hopelessly outmatched by these beings of the underworld.

"Millennia?" asked Matthew, who was still hunched over on the ground. "Can this foul creature have hidden itself from human history for so long?"

"Yes," whispered Catherine as she massaged her friend's shoulder. "My mind struggles with the ramifications, of what it means."

Carboni ripped the necklace bearing the crucifix from his neck and held it aloft. "I revoke thee, abominable spirits, in the name of ..."

One of the demons diffused into oblivion and coalesced around Carboni before he could invoke the name. The friar grasped his throat in apparent agony. Gasping for air, his torso shook in spasms as his eyes bulged from the strain. Catherine reached for him, not knowing how to fight his oppressor, who threw her to the ground with unyielding violence.

The impact on her upper right arm and shoulder was

excruciating. She wanted to lie there, but circumstances dictated otherwise. Matthew helped her to her feet by her left arm, and she looked desperately at Abelard for assistance. In society, the vampyre was the epitome of power, but before these creatures, and in this environment, Abelard could not summon his full potency. He seemed helpless, an outcast, standing beyond a hidden barrier that prevented his passing.

"You speak well of yourself and your power, Abelard, but I know your weaknesses all too well," said Malsadus as smoke swirled about his face. "Just as I exploit the weaknesses of these flesh creatures."

Catherine and Matthew had instinctively stepped away from Carboni or, rather, the overpowering entity that oppressed him. Still, Catherine could hear the friar gurgling as he tried in desperation to invoke the name. She could hardly bear the sounds of his pain as the demon prevented his vocal cords from articulating any sounds other than coarse grunts.

The demon had also broken Carboni's crucifix. She had not considered wearing one of her own, as the vampyre was not her enemy.

"Did you wonder, Abelard, about the artillery assault upon Mithrendia?" asked Malsadus. "I know that you saw it, there upon the firth, in your mind's eye. For I have given you that power."

"I may," said Abelard in a point of defiance.

"I took that fool Connaught's soul," said Malsadus, "from what remained of his char-burned body, there upon Børgman's Bluff. He was a plotting, ambitious sort who lusted after a glorified name. He will be remembered in history's annals, though he will think little of it in the fires of hell."

Abelard seemed to hesitate. "And Berbery?"

"Berbery," the arch-demon replied with satisfaction, "is held in my everlasting grasp. His ignorant heart now knows the domain of his hidden master in Hades. There in the smoke of his chastening, the once mighty overlord has an eternity to ponder his demise. He knows his conqueror, as should you."

Catherine continued to watch from afar, between nervous glances at the suffering friar. She could not discern what the vampyre was thinking or planning, but she saw that Abelard seemed to be studying the crosses guarding the graves of the dead.

"Their lives were short," said Malsadus, "whereas yours has been long, Abelard. Nevertheless, the hour has come. Your time is at an end. You have outlived your usefulness."

"Come with me," said Catherine, grabbing Matthew's hand. They ran into the church.

"What?" replied Matthew.

They had reached nightfall, which was casting its shadows across the sanctuary. The lit tapers were few.

"We must find something, anything," said Catherine as she grasped one of the tapers. "Look around. We need a cross. Holy water, if you can find it."

"Well now," said a contemptuous, screeching voice.

Catherine stopped for a moment and looked back at the hooded figure who had just entered the church. The face's features were undiscernible in the shadows save for a hooked nose.

"A renegade friar and his heretical friends," said the intruder, "doing who knows what mischief to Our Lady of the Forest's sanctuary and grounds."

Catherine, with frantic movements, continued her search, before finding a crucifix behind the altar. "We have no time for your false accusations, Canon Pious."

"A barmaid and a tavern lackey stealing from the altar, I see. Ye have traveled far from the Blue Griffin, have ye?

Stepped up in the world too, eh? Nice accommodations now in Castle Brygge, the house of heresy."

"Don't you see what is out there?" thundered Matthew.

"See what?" replied Pious. "A mendicant friar, a stain upon his order, in a state of convulsion? Too much ale and liquor, I gather. Gives ye the shakes, does it not? And that tall, pasty-faced fellow standing out beyond the gravestones—another Lutheran, I suspect." He rubbed his hands greedily. "This will be a fine report that I deliver to the archbishop. I see the rack in your future, or perhaps the archbishop will have a more ingenious torture in mind."

Catherine and Matthew glanced at one another with great surprise, the least of their surprise pertaining to his threatening words.

"And that is all that you see?" asked Matthew.

"I saw the three of ye all the way from Westfall," replied Pious. "And then that pale fellow joined the game. Must have come from Edelburg or the western woods."

Catherine wanted to remind him that he was outnumbered four to one, but she had no time for a verbal spat. Still, his seeming ignorance of the situation scared her, leaving her to question what she had just witnessed.

"We have no time to wrangle with you," she answered. "Let's go, Matthew."

Pious stood at the doorway, but Matthew thundered toward him at full speed. "Get out of our way, you worthless ..."

Matthew seemed to remember that he was inside a church and stopped speaking. He bolted forward with Catherine just behind him.

The hooded figure sidestepped them at the last moment, leaving a clear path for their exit.

Once outside, they were reminded of what they had left

behind. Catherine saw six demons, a vampyre, and a choking friar.

The demons had not waited for her arrival. One stayed with the friar, while four others, upon Malsadus's orders, surrounded Abelard.

Abelard fought to keep their spiritual fetters from entangling him. One demon bore an otherworldly whip of red flame, which swirled around, encircling the vampyre's torso. Abelard could not peel it off, but he was able to grapple with the demons as they crept up close. He overpowered the first demon, wrenching it to the ground, while pulling the whip wielded by the other. As the second demon drew near, against its will, the vampyre pummeled it with a barrage of strikes to the head and chest.

In the end, Abelard bore the whip in hand. He thrashed it about to keep the other demons clear of him.

"Your powers are as you say," said Malsadus. "Indeed, I have made you strong."

The arch-demon nodded at the third and fourth demons, who descended into the depths of the ground, while the first two flanked the vampyre on each side from a distance of some five yards.

With the demons' attention fixed upon the vampyre, Catherine and Matthew rushed to assist the friar. She held the crucifix aloft. "I command you to go, you foul being! Depart at once from this man!"

Black whiffs of smoke enveloped its face, but the demon thundered in laughter. The laughter swept and swirled about like a tempest of wind.

"More!" shouted Matthew, his hair buffeted by the gusts. Neither of them could hardly stand against the gale force. "You've got to say something more, Catherine!"

"I'm trying!"

"You're the one who went to parochial school!" said Matthew.

Catherine struggled to remember. She thought of the prayers she had learned in school. She thought of the nuns and their teachings. She recalled the words of the priest during Mass.

Something stirred within her. *Invoke My name.*

"In the name of the Father, and of the Son, and of the Holy Spirit," she said with a firm and strong voice, "I command you to depart from this man Carboni. I rebuke you, you evil spirt, in the name of Jesus Christ!"

The laughter stopped. The demon released its grip, and the friar collapsed upon the ground, gasping. Several deep and pathetic-sounding inhalations and exhalations seemed to revive him and bring about a more normalized state of breathing.

The demon, however, did not abandon its post without retribution. It flung its fierce arm about, sending Catherine and Matthew airborne for several yards, before they collapsed upon the ground. Catherine felt the agonizing impact on her bad shoulder and noticed three lacerations on the opposite arm, whereas Matthew, who seemed to take a hard bump to the head during his fall, lay motionless upon the grass.

"Seize him," commanded Malsadus from the center of the graveyard.

The first and second demons commenced another attack on the vampyre, who pelted them with the confiscated whip.

Catherine watched helplessly from the grass as the third and the fourth demons arose from the depths of the earth. They grasped hold of Abelard's legs as the others converged. The fifth, apparently enraged from Catherine's invocation, lunged onto the vampyre's back and enveloped him as the first and the second secured his arms from either side.

Abelard strained to fight them off, but they bound his wrists and ankles in fetters forged in the netherworld. Those fetters glowed with the flames of the abyss.

"Lord God, forgive me, for the evil I have done," said Abelard as the demons gagged his mouth with a cloud of the darkest black. He choked as this foul substance spread into the inner recesses of his body, rendering him mute.

With the vampyre secured, the demons shifted their focus.

"What about him?" asked the fifth demon. "The hooded one who is hiding in the church?"

Catherine, despite her preoccupation with the demons, had not missed the hooded figure standing at the door—the hooded figure who, no doubt, had seen her and Matthew tossed headlong into the air, the hooded figure who had slammed the door to secure himself inside the stave church.

"That fool Pious?" said Malsadus, with a self-satisfied grin. "He's already mine, and yet he does not know it. I have blinded him to our presence. He sees only what is happening in the natural world. He will remain in ignorance, as will Otta and Toriana. Those sanctimonious vipers will do my bidding."

The vampyre was incapacitated. Matthew was still unconscious, and Carboni had neck wounds. Six demons, including an arch-demon, stood on church grounds. *What more,* Catherine wondered, *can we do against such foes?*

She thought of what to say. With her injuries, she felt weak, so her prayer was but a whisper. "Lord God, Your power is greater than that of our foes. Will You not help us?"

Her weary head dropped onto the grass. She could see Abelard wince under the tightening grip of the fetters.

"Take him to the outer darkness of the deep," commanded Malsadus. "You are going home, Abelard. A realm of fiery brimstone and smoke will be your abode. There you will thirst for water. Not blood, but water. There you will thirst for relief from torment. There you will hear the sweet music of wailing and the gnashing of teeth. Hell's door opens to embrace you for an eternity. I bid thee welcome!"

Catherine was on the verge of blacking out when she saw them. She saw the illumination of shadows. Six figures of great light appeared like ghosts through the timbers of the stave church. Except these were not faint apparitions. They were resplendent beings in dazzling robes of an unearthly fabric. Vibrant hair flowed about their fair faces, which were youthful and unspotted and yet exhibited the wisdom of many years.

Something like sunlight glimmered and shone in radiance about them. Serene and full of grace, and yet fierce warriors of immense height, they were bearing golden swords and shields. A bluish flame the color of the afternoon sky wove around each blade like a braided helix. Convex, curvilinear recesses in their shields seemed to emit and store some ethereal concentration of energy on the surface.

The angels divided their numbers. The first one approached Catherine. She could feel loving hands placed about her upper regions, and yet the pain of her injuries ebbed to the touch. The lacerations on her arm faded and the shoulder healed as the angel helped her to her feet, then departed to assist the others.

Catherine turned to see a second angel gather Matthew from the ground. He awoke with eyes of wonder. For one quite capable of being chatty, Matthew was speechless. The angel smiled as if aware of his nature. Matthew stared at his rescuer like a curious infant.

A third angel assisted the friar to his feet and placed her hand upon Carboni's chest and neck. His breathing sounded normal again. However, his face bore shame as if the angelic light revealed the depths of his broken vows and the neglect of his holy orders. The angel seemed to acknowledge something else. She touched the widower's heart and placed her hand upon his face, which flooded with emotion.

The demons for their part seemed to allow this victory of sorts. They had come for their prize, and hovered around Abelard. There was a sense of dread in his countenance.

The angels now turned their attention to the demons.

"You cannot have the vampyre!" shouted Malsadus with fury. "He is mine. He made a deal with me!"

"Was it not you, Malsadus, who tempted the bandits to attack him in his youth?" asked a fourth angel. This one wore a golden sash across his chest and broadcast his voice like the flowing undulation of many waters.

"I rescued him and gave him a new life," said Malsadus. "It was I who made him what he is now."

"Are you claiming to be his savior?" asked the angel.

Malsadus seemed to become even more enraged at this reference. "Look at him! A decayed bloodsucking parasite taking what is forbidden by law!"

"Did you not make him this way?"

"A perversion of humanity!" replied Malsadus. "An affront to your God!"

"We have been sent to tell Abelard that his evil deeds are forgiven," replied the angel.

"His name does not belong in the book of life!" shouted Malsadus.

"And yet he will be given a choice," said the fourth angel.

"Not on my account," replied Malsadus as he and his demons prepared for battle. "Before this night is over, he will dwell in the fires of hell."

The vampyre remained bound with spiritual fetters. With his mouth gagged, the vampyre tried to cough, but the dark cloud appeared to seize his throat and cause torturous convulsions.

"Help him! He's choking!" shouted Catherine.

A fifth angel with silklike streams of waist-length hair shot a blinding light from her shield, and the dark cloud dissipated into the night air. Abelard gasped and cleared his throat of the contagion, but he remained bound.

"Do my eyes deceive me?" whispered Matthew. "Can this be?"

"Aye," said Carboni, clearing his throat. "A fight between angels and demons. And here we are in the arena."

The third demon cast his arm about, and a shrouded energy dispersed like a tsunami against the angelic host. They braced their glimmering shields against this spiritual weapon, and it ricocheted off into the darkness of the forest.

The six angels surged forward to fight at close quarters. They grappled with the demons as beams of light and swaths of darkness wrapped around one another. Catherine saw a crack of the demonic whip as flaming red descended upon the angels. Their defense was azure-blue flame, which unwound from the angelic swords and engaged the whipcord in midflight. This engagement produced sparks, which combusted in the night air and filled the cemetery with a low-lying cover of smoke.

The cords themselves traced pathways of boiling intumescence in the darkness. The churchyard pulsated with energy, leaving a charged scent, not unlike lightning coursing across a landscape. The flames of their warfare seemed as comets traversing the sky, but neither party could get the advantage over the other.

Malsadus surged into the fray to tip the balance. With a magician's sleight of hand, he produced a staff from the bowels of the netherworld, as if forged from molten rock beneath the earth's crust. It looked like a double-ended mace, studded with spikes and dipped in magma that oozed along its metallic surface.

The angels concentrated their shields with their pulses of energy on this weapon. Still, they could not overpower the arch-demon. The staff of the netherworld repelled their attack with swift and decisive movement. Malsadus punctured and pummeled the shields, which seemed to incapacitate the ethereal energy the angels had summoned.

"I fear for the outcome," said Catherine, standing next to Matthew and the friar by the southern wall of the church.

"Aye," said Carboni. "This arch-demon is more powerful than the rest. If there be some way that we might free Lord Abelard, that may tip the balance."

"But how?" she asked.

"I fear that I am at a loss," said the friar. "I cannot find my vial of holy water. My tunic was torn at the inset seam pocket, perhaps during the battle of Westfall."

"Without it," Catherine replied, "how can we unbind Abelard's fetters?"

The demons, with the advantage of the arch-demon, had turned the tide in their favor. No one could repel the power of Malsadus's staff.

Nevertheless, the arch-demon seemed ill at ease as something caught his attention.

"Your evil shepherding of this man is at an end, Malsadus!" thundered another voice. A seventh angel, a head taller and more broad-shouldered than the others, appeared from the stave church. His face was like burnished bronze, and his words were like thunder. He bore a platinum staff of such immense diameter that claymore blades had been forged and hammered from the shaft at each end. A light energy pulsed along the angelic staff, shifting toward one end and then the other based on the movements of the one who wielded it.

"An archangel," said Carboni in astonishment.

The staff of the archangel clanged against that of the

arch-demon. The force of the exchange drove Malsadus back a pace, but he rerouted the trajectory of his staff and drove the mace with an overhand blow. The magma-like substance flowed to the outer tip of the spikes.

The archangel met the stroke of the mace with his own staff, emitting electric sparks, and the forest rang like the clanging of a cast-iron bell.

With the arch-demon thus engaged, the angels wrestled with the demons until they pulled them away from the fallen vampyre. The bluish flame of the swords flared up, extinguishing the fetters, and the vampyre rose from the ground.

The archangel pushed his weapon against that of his foe, summoning a crackling of light energy, as the combatants struggled at close range. Catherine could see that the red-hot magma lingered a mere inch or two from the archangel's sternum.

Abelard surged to help him, but not before the archangel exhaled a fierce wind. The magma on the arch-demon's staff solidified like basalt.

Malsadus seemed stunned. He beheld his compromised weapon in his left arm. Seeing this opportunity, Abelard seized his old master's weapon with both outstretched hands. The vampyre, summoning all his power, ripped the staff away and bent it into a horseshoe. Abelard then cast its remains to the ground, where the archangel shattered it with a downward thrust of a claymore blade.

Abelard pummeled his old master with left and right punches from closed fists.

Before the arch-demon could retaliate, the archangel surged behind him and swept the platinum staff around the front of his enemy's torso. Bronzed fists extended beyond the arch-demon's sides and pulled the staff up to his upper abdomen. The light energy pulsed across the staff as the arch-demon shielded his eyes. The archangel had encircled Malsadus, who was now caught in an unyielding grip.

"You have no legal authority to do this," said Malsadus as he struggled with his bonds.

"And yet we do," said the archangel. "For the agreement was made under duress, and it has been revoked by the Lord of Hosts."

The angels surrounded the vampyre to protect him from any demonic counterattack as lingering smoke from the fierce engagement billowed about the trees. Sinister black masses of cloud swirled about the faces of the goat men, but they stood where they were, surrounding the angelic encirclement.

They had heard the verdict.

Catherine found a breach in their ranks and ran up to embrace the vampyre as Abelard looked around with obvious emotion. He exhaled a heavy sigh. There was coldness in his chest but earnest conviction in his manner.

"A man of God was sent to me once when I was young," said Abelard, addressing the heavenly host. "In my brash arrogance, I forsook his counsel and turned him away; and I became the accursed creature who stands before you this night."

To Catherine's surprise, Abelard knelt before the angels in supplication. She dropped to one knee with him, giving thanks to their rescuers.

The angels lifted them up. "Kneel not to us but to God alone. It is He who sent us as soon as He heard your prayers."

"What prayers?" asked Abelard.

The third angel, who had helped Carboni, laughed. "Do you not remember what you said before the demons muted your speech? It has been answered. Your trespasses against God have been forgiven."

The first angel added, "And it was Catherine who asked for deliverance from the fallen angels."

"Did you not know, Abelard," said the archangel, "that a second man of God was sent to you?"

The archangel glanced over at Carboni, who looked shocked at the recognition. Matthew, perhaps bearing an expression of equal shock at this assemblage of supernatural beings, stood beside him.

"So I have a choice?" asked Abelard.

"You do not," said Malsadus with the archangel's staff still pressed against him. "Your fate is sealed."

"Is not your master Malsadus called the father of lies?" said the archangel.

"And Eleana?" asked Abelard.

"She is home with us," said the third angel.

Catherine looked upon that decayed face, which shone with iridescence in the moonlight. But Abelard's spirit shone brighter. He bowed his head in what seemed to be grateful silence.

"To see her, Abelard, you must be born again," said the first angel.

"I am over three hundred years old," said the vampyre. "How can one such as I be reborn?"

"The sins that have been forgiven you were transferred to Christ at Calvary well before your birth," answered the first angel. "He, the Son of God, died willingly for you, and for others, so that you might live with Him in eternity. It is a gift, and those who accept it are spiritually born anew. Do you believe this?"

Malsadus and the demons erupted with gruesome, earsplitting sounds that Catherine could not bear. Poundings like heavy feet thudding upon timber planks reverberated in the churchyard. That was not all, though. She covered her ears, to no avail, as fiendish hisses and snarls penetrated flesh. These tortures, covering a wide spectrum of sound waves, were interspersed with bursts of hideous laughter. Acute pain surged through her eardrums as pulses of pressure built up in sonic waves.

"The Lord rebuke you!" thundered the archangel.

The noises subsided as the cemetery went silent. Catherine was amazed to see the demons obey as the hisses and snarls and the poundings ceased.

"Yes, I do believe," said Abelard in answer to the first angel's question.

The forest awoke with yet another noise, this time the harmonious collective shouts of the angelic host, as the demons writhed and twisted about like serpents. They scurried away in great haste into the depths of the earth. The archangel released his grasp on Malsadus, who took a last vindictive look at Abelard and Catherine before disappearing in the hidden seam of air.

Catherine observed the countenance of her friend. The iridescence faded, and the arrested decay returned to living tissue. The weight of the centuries seemed to fall from Abelard's tired shoulders. His plague of vampirism left him, taking with it its immense powers and its accursed wretchedness.

Catherine could not believe the transformation.

For a moment he was an old, old man with age spots, wrinkled skin, and a thin-haired scalp. Abelard had lost much of his muscle mass, and his frail back stooped over.

Three-hundred-year-old men, no doubt, are not long for this world.

"Goodbye, my friends," he said with a weak voice. With his last remaining energy, Abelard stepped onto the church grounds.

With some assistance from the angels, he lay down upon the grass and drifted to sleep.

His body stopped breathing.

"He's gone then," said Carboni. "Let him rest in peace."

Catherine knelt beside Abelard and wept. Matthew stood over her, rubbing her shoulder, as she had done for him.

"All is not over," said the first angel.

Just then, a curious thing happened. An ethereal mist like a bright vapor rose from the corpse.

Catherine gazed upon this mist as it manifested into a more definite form.

It was Abelard in the prime of youth again, pristine without any signs of decay. He glanced at his friends and nodded, but not with solemnity; a joyous grin arose on his face.

Abelard walked with the angels through the wall of the church.

Catherine rushed to the door that, some minutes earlier, had been ripped open by a fleeing Canon Pious. She looked inside the sanctuary.

"Anything?" asked Carboni as she glanced back.

"They disappeared at the altar."

"It is as it should be," Carboni said, sighing. "We have witnessed a miracle this night. And we have had a glimpse of an age-old struggle: a battle for souls."

This spiritual battle left something strange in its wake. There were no bodies or debris, no abandoned weapons or fortified encampments. Indeed, the churchyard seemed eerily quiet after such a finale. Aside from the stars and the moon, only the tapers inside the sanctuary gave light.

"Can we go with them?" asked Matthew.

"What, and lose your status as Lord of the Maidens?" replied Catherine.

"It is not yet time for ye, me lad," said the friar.

"Well, what happens now?" asked Matthew.

The friar clasped his hands together. "Have you not heard?" Carboni bellowed with rousing energy. "We have a wedding to attend! Our friends Erik and Adaira. After we bury our friend, of course. There are shovels in the back closet, as I remember. If we're lucky, that old casket may still be there. They like to keep an extra as the carpenter lives some miles away."

"It is strange to speak of a wedding and a funeral in the same breath," said Catherine, who felt an unusual concurrence of joy and sorrow.

"I cannot recall a burial that wasn't depressing," said Matthew with a cheerful grin. "This will be a first."

"I will miss our friend," Catherine said, sighing, "but he has been set free from his demons."

"Have you seen Lady Mary?" asked Ben after a meager dinner of stale bread in the duke's kitchen. Normally he belched after a repast, which pleased the cooking staff, but currently he had too little in his stomach to observe sixteenth-century decorum.

"The Lady of the Silver Plate?" asked Arnald, the young kitchen boy. "No, sir." As one of the cook's sons, and a curious sort of about ten, he recounted Lady Mary's thrashing of the lone werewolf to breach the walls of Castle Brygge.

"Yes, she is quite the fighter," replied Ben. *The wolf may be done for,* he thought, *but she has yet to finish with me, lucky fool that I am.* "Master Arnald, what do those of the house staff call me?"

"The amanuenses," said the boy with a shrug. "Don't ask me, sir, to tell you what that means."

"It's a clever term for secretary," Ben said, sighing.

Which means it came from the duke or duchess, he thought. *How fitting.* "They don't seem to recall me jumping off the castle wall, swimming the icy moat, and engaging with the werewolves, do they?"

"Oh, no, sir," replied Arnald. "Lord Abelard protected you from otherwise certain death."

"Well, at least I played a hand," said Ben with some frustration.

"I don't follow, sir," replied the boy.

"No matter. It's a phrase borrowed from the playing of cards. You'll learn about it someday."

The cockiness had worn off in gradations until little of it remained. Northmoorland could do that to a fellow. Ben had been confident, even arrogant, but he now realized that he had based his feelings on the wrong things. One could think well of himself, even supremely so, in a university basement. A quick wit, a top graduate school placement exam score, and a beautiful girlfriend had placed his self-assurance on high. Besides, he was tall, athletic, and handsome. His aspirations of publishing dictation of the duke's proceedings had seemed like the fast track to academic fame. That is, until the professor burst his bubble. Who would believe them if they returned home?

Why hadn't he thought of that before? A simpleton could have considered that conundrum.

On top of these developments, Ben had been rescued from marauders, had served as a lackey boy in a foreign tavern with a strange native tongue, and had sought refuge in a castle. These events had been humbling, but in the course of such events, he had lost sight of what mattered most to him: Mary.

Ben left the kitchen to search the gallery, the dining hall, and the library. He found the professor, of course in his usual abode of books, but Mary was conspicuously absent.

"Looking for Mary?" asked the professor as he lowered his latest read, an exposition on civil government.

"How did you ...?" Ben stopped himself in midsentence. "Of course."

He found himself running through the castle corridors, searching every nook and cranny in this never-ending fortified estate. Over three-quarters of the domestic staff were accounted for, at least to his reckoning, when Ben reached the corridor housing Mary's sleeping quarters.

"Shh," said the young maid as she closed the door to Mary's room. "She is fast asleep."

"At seven o'clock?"

"She's been a bit tired of late, sir."

Nervous sweat glistened from his brow.

"Why didn't I walk by here earlier?" he said almost to himself. "Fool that I am!"

"Shh!"

Ben was too keyed up to go to sleep himself. He thought of the Blue Griffin and of engaging the familiar patrons in conversation once again, but he couldn't go there now as Otta's men prowled the streets at night.

In his frustration, he thought of risking it anyway. He descended a spiral stone staircase to the lowermost level and approached the portcullis.

"My apologies, sir," said the castle gatekeeper. "The duke forbids any to leave at night, for their own safety."

"So be it," said Ben with some heat. He raced back up the stairs. He approached his bedroom floor, Mary's floor, but kept moving upward until exiting at the upper terrace with its castellated battlements.

"Do you need something, sir?" asked one of the night watch.

Ben surveyed the city in a panoramic view. Other than the numerous signs of burial and some damaged buildings, Mithrendia appeared as it had before the great battle. "It seems quite peaceful tonight."

"A bit uneasy, sir, if you ask me," replied the guard. "After the events of two nights past ..."

"No doubt," answered Ben. "To think that werewolves sprang about these streets ..."

Sleep had been difficult. Ben spent a couple of hours with the night watch before descending to his chamber. He read for another hour by candlelight, but he could barely comprehend the words. He felt worn out physically, but his thoughts strained without relief, seeking any means of reconciliation. If he could somehow make Mary see how he felt about her.

The thought of Mary leaving him left him turning his head this way and that upon a soft down pillow that provided little comfort. His nightclothes, for that matter, were soaked in sweat. When insomnia had held its sway for some hours, he opened his eyelids and noticed a strange green light emanating from the bottom of his chamber door.

He walked out barefoot to see what was amiss.

There in the corridor he found Mary, her dark hair flowing, unrestrained by braid or hood, as she stared at a strange green light that framed the ceiling, walls, and floor of the corridor. Upon seeing him, she turned to retreat into her room.

"Mary, forgive me."

She glanced back. "And so I should, you twit?"

His tone was for her ears alone, but her reply was the opposite. She'd spoken so loud, in fact, that she woke the entire corridor. Catherine, Matthew, Carboni, the professor, and several knights of the ducal staff came pouring out of their doors.

Ben saw that they had been summoned by her elevated voice. Nevertheless, they seemed mesmerized by the portal that lay before them.

"At long last!" said the professor.

Matthew dropped to his knees.

"What is this?" asked one of the knights, backing away.

Catherine embraced the friar, who struggled to keep his tired eyes open. "This is how we came here, Carboni, though I fear what we might find if we go back."

"If this be ye way home, ye must go," said the friar. "Though ye will heartily be missed. Aye, especially by me."

"Aye." Catherine saw those familiar convective swirls, those eddies of air, around a gilded frame illuminated by a strange green light. She looked back at Mary, who stood next to the door of her chamber. "Are you ready, Mary?"

Ben seemed to look back as well, anxious to hear her response.

"What are we waiting for?" replied Mary as she raced headlong into the portal.

Ben followed after her, with Matthew and the professor in tow. Once across the unseen vertical boundary, their likenesses were lost to those who remained.

In the end, it was Catherine left with the friar as the fierce knights of the castle had abandoned the corridor.

"I will never forget you," she said as she embraced her friend for the last time.

"When next ye see me," said the friar, "I suspect we'll have angels for company."

He kissed her upon the cheek. "Go now. May blessings be upon ye."

€PILOGUE

An Inquest

Catherine had not anticipated this.

Locked doors, of course, were no hindrance to disembodied spirits. Their former holding cell, the corporeal body, had long since been interred in the depths of the earth, and as ghosts they were free to penetrate stud wall and stone at their leisure.

Yet Catherine had seen it, or rather the aftermath. The problem pertained to the inanimate world—a manila folder to be exact.

A certain pair of basketball players from the 1970s were up to their old tricks. They preferred shooting to passing as most players do, at least those who shoot well, and those who only suppose that they shoot well to the collective disgruntlement of their teammates. Add a dunk and a rainbow jump shot followed by a regimen of behind-the-back lookie-loos and between-the-leg ricochets off the parquet to complete the picture.

Dr. Heiderberg had run out for lunch after his morning appointments. The waiting room was empty except for Mary's previous ethereal acquaintances, who remembered her.

With a prompting from the power forward, the point guard swept into Dr. Heiderberg's office and fumbled through some files. The appropriate file was procured, and with an affected *swoosh*, the file was slipped under the door to the power forward. The forward leapt over to deposit its contents on the waiting room table in the hopes that it would stand out among the fine homemaking, Crock-Pot cooking, and miniature golf periodicals that served as someone else's idea of entertainment.

The waiting room was never empty for long. The ghosts had left, and three of the living had stumbled in for their early afternoon appointments.

Catherine, though exhausted, was inwardly celebrating the return home as she seated herself next to the professor.

"Do you not know? Have you not heard?"[24] cracked Matthew as he addressed the disinterested young woman sitting behind the sliding glass window.

Behind the receptionist, a twentieth-century filing system remained en vogue. Hung on the stark white walls were dull metal shelves overflowing with hundreds of files, each tabbed with the first three letters of the patient surname. These files cataloged rank, serial number, and mental disorders of the human personality within a simple manila folder, recording the complexities of the human soul in a concise clinical diagnosis.

The receptionist smacked away the stiffened remnants of some cheap gum and handed Matthew a clipboard holding some documents. "You will need to fill out the first four pages."

Not even such procedural necessities could dispel Matthew's amusement. He broke into a mischievous grin. "Who has believed our story?"[25]

"Apparently not the psychiatrists," said Ben, returning to the seating area. With bloodshot eyes and a lethargic countenance, he looked worse for wear as one might expect after suffering through a gauntlet of examinations and cross-examinations in a dim clinician's office.

"But are we certifiable?" asked Matthew. "Can I have you Baker Acted?"

"Only if those standard-issue jumpsuits come in white," joked Ben. "The kind that bind your arms."

"How about orange? I prefer some color."

"That's for the city lockup. You'll need to commit a crime first."

Upon the day of their return home through the portal, their strange bedclothes had been immortalized. Perhaps it didn't help that the portal had disposed of them at a table in the middle of the campus food court during the busy lunch hour. Their peers at Rhymer, having seen the missing persons signs, considered that ownership of a cellular device gave them the right to snap unrequested and unappreciated photos of their cultural predicament. Within hours, the five had become social media sensations, and the general relief at their reappearance gave way to a curious mixture of amusement and suspicion.

"But am I to blame if they confine us?" asked Matthew as he sat down wearing a T-shirt, jeans, and a jacket with gel in his hair. The others had followed suit, reverting to their former ways and means. "Are any of you? I dare not discuss what happened to us, not even with an anonymous pseudonym online. All they have are those ridiculous pictures. We could say that we went to a costume party as a group."

"Hmm," said Professor Porter. "A fair point. And how then did this psychiatric nonsense befall us?"

"The provost, I suspect," said Catherine. "She has a clinical background."

"What, then, would have prompted her?" he asked.

"Or who?"

By virtue of their status as university employees or matriculating students, the five missing persons had been corralled by the administration. The president of Rhymer, after tearful well-wishes and hugs for the benefit of the television cameras, had quietly ordered a mandatory psychiatric evaluation.

"Let me guess," said Matthew. "Mary."

"Mary," repeated Professor Porter.

Catherine rolled her eyes and leaned her head back on the couch cushions. She had not returned to those violet highlights, and her short blonde hair was now midlength. "It had to have been Mary," she said with a dejected sigh. "She must have told somebody."

They all looked at Ben, who grinned but found it prudent to keep his mouth shut. After all, he was still in a state of limbo with his sweetheart.

Catherine glanced down at the tabled periodicals before seeing a certain manila folder atop one of the piles. She leaned over and read the color-stickered letters aloud: "A-U-G ... Mary Augustine!"

The professor retrieved the folder and flipped through its contents as Catherine looked over at the receptionist, who seemed uninterested in their presence.

"Guys?" said the professor. "Look at this."

The professor read off some scribbled notes in Mary's file:

Hallucinations with a medieval fixation.

Delusional thinking, including stories of time travel and barbarian hordes.

Paranoia about monsters and an inordinate fascination with lycanthropy.

Recommend sensitivity training at the local zoo, where they keep a relatively tame family of gray wolves. Perhaps a visit to the petting zoo?

Developing a wanton distaste for men.

"That last one pertains to me," said Ben with a sigh.

"Hey!" said an authoritative voice.

Catherine glanced over at the door, at the suspicious gray-bearded man staring at them. It was Dr. Heiderberg, apparently returning from lunch.

"That's privileged information," he growled. Secretive, scrutinizing eyes scanned each of them one by one.

Catherine had experienced enough drama as of late, and though her threshold for tolerating such things had widened, she still felt nervous.

The psychiatrist tossed some burger wrappers in the wastebasket and swooped over to confiscate his case notes. "You can't look at this. It's a violation of doctor–patient confidentiality."

"Then how did it get here on the table?" asked the professor.

"It was just sitting there, open," said Catherine. "How could we help but notice?"

"Something's going on," said Dr. Heiderberg with a cross expression upon his brow. He held the closed folder aloft. "Jan, did you see this?"

"No, Doctor," replied the receptionist, who for the first time seemed attentive.

"And why not?"

Jan stopped smacking her gum. She looked nervous and seemed to be cornered. "I had nothing to do with it, Doctor."

"Of course not," replied Dr. Heiderberg, "nor did you have the presence of mind to see something that should have been obvious!"

The psychiatrist, still holding the folder aloft, turned back toward Catherine and her friends. "Unless I find a suitable explanation for this, I'm holding you all responsible!"

"That is hardly fair," said Ben.

"It is utterly ridiculous," added the professor.

Catherine wanted to shout in anger.

"Try the door, my friend," said Matthew, motioning his head toward the far office, which bore a placard with the doctor's name.

The door handle was an anodized aluminum lever, the kind that swiveled up or down, and Catherine could see a keyhole at the rounded end.

The doctor moved toward his office door. Finding it locked, he fumbled angrily with his keys.

"Does it lock from the inside?" asked Matthew.

The doctor said nothing. As the door swung open, Catherine noticed the absence of a locking mechanism on the inside handle. It was also an interior office with no windows or other openings.

"Then how could we possibly have gotten in?" asked Matthew loudly as the doctor shut the door with an abrupt thud. "Did you give one of us a spare key? Do you think Jan let us in?"

Mary had been absent since her examination, which perhaps was for the best. Catherine had found her to be moody and easily angered since their return home.

Everyone, however, seemed a bit irritated now. Matthew

was tossing a small couch pillow aloft, Ben was nudging the coffee table with his feet, and the professor was fidgeting with the imaginary piano keys on his crossed-over knee.

"I'm beginning to think," observed the professor, "that every thought that is entertained inside that precious head of Mary's is given voice by her tongue."

"Why, Mary?" asked Matthew, as if she were present. "Why did you tell them anything from our collective experience?"

"Her session, in normal circumstances of course, would have been confidential, so some liberty of expression would be expected," said Catherine. "Nevertheless, I did not expect our story to be well received. I will go in there with a bridled tongue. Did you reveal much to them, Ben?"

"For the most part, I bored them with the procedural details of a professional historian." A subtle grin spread across Ben's face. "And yet there is a certain freedom in being branded as delusional, don't you think?"

"How could that possibly be of benefit?" asked Matthew.

"If I go out and do something completely irrational," said Ben, "who's going to change their mind? We've already been labeled by the fine doctor here, for if Mary is delusional, then so are we."

"If we divulge anything," added Catherine.

"We fought with monsters, marauders, demons, and psychotic churchmen," observed Matthew. "And this is our reward? To be labeled for life?"

"I heard whispers in the corridor," said Ben, "about hallucinations and posttraumatic stress from the shooting on Halloween."

Catherine stood up and stretched. She was tired of being sequestered, whether in a basement, a tavern, a castle, or even the waiting room of a psychiatrist's office. She glanced about the waiting room for something, anything, that could distract her from this frustration. The coffee tables were filled with other magazines about knitting, skiing, and Christmas cookies. Everything about the room seemed trivial compared to what they were going through.

Out of the corner of her eye, Catherine saw a book with black binding on a corner table. Nevertheless, the television screen, mounted on the wall opposite the receptionist counter, distracted her. It was airing a local news station. The news anchor, an attractive, middle-aged woman with wavy brown hair and bearing a stern face, was speaking.

"Look!" said Catherine.

> And in other news, students and faculty at Rhymer University continue to cope with the deaths of sixteen students, two facility maintenance workers, and an adjunct professor. This urban campus, still reeling from the Halloween terrorist plot, was rocked by Wednesday's police announcement, which revealed the perpetrators as a disenfranchised group known as Heks Myrkur. Six suspects, including three students, have been arrested, and the police are on the hunt for two more.
>
> Last summer, members of Heks Myrkur began defacing university property when administrators refused to sanction their request to conduct public séances and perform various occult practices on University Lawn. The cult was banned from campus at that time.

"And they call us delusional," said Matthew.

Catherine glanced at the others. "That name sounds familiar."

"Of course!" said the professor. "The Myrkur Range in Northmoorland,"

"What's that?" asked Ben.

"The Black Mountains," said the professor. "That terrorist group appears to have associated itself with the ancient occultist practices of the Myrkur Range."

"Their core members are practitioners of black magic," said an elderly person who had just entered the room. He wore a long-sleeved shirt and pants of black, and a long gray beard covered much of his white cleric's collar. "I have seen evidence of the remains of their satanic rituals in the basement of an abandoned building near campus. They are fools, summoning demonic beings of great power that they cannot possibly control."

"Monsignor Lewis?" said Catherine, rushing over to embrace him. She had only known him for two weeks prior to their departure through the portal. Nevertheless, there was something about his demeanor that reminded her of a certain friar. Not in looks or the consuming of ale, of course, but in his deliberate manner and resolve, and certainly of his knowledge of the powers of darkness.

"My dear Catherine," said the monsignor with a deep, gravelly intonation that seemed full of wisdom. Beneath his dark eyebrows were kindly brown eyes, but his countenance was firm and determined, like one used to battle.

Spiritual battle.

"I have not seen you at Mass since this sad event happened," he continued. "When you went missing, the parish of Saint Anne's launched search parties to find you and your friends. Many filed into the sanctuary to pray for your safety. When we received word of your safe return, we called the campus to learn of your present whereabouts."

"I'm surprised that they alerted you to our presence here," said the professor, "as they process us like delusional dunces with their psychiatric evaluations."

"Yes," said Catherine. "How did you ever find us?"

"Many of the parishioners of Saint Anne's work on this campus," replied the monsignor. "I was told by a certain bird that you might need some company today."

Catherine did not know of whom he spoke, but she was grateful all the same. She looked around at the others. The presence of a friendly person, a clerical friend, even one they did not know, seemed a welcome distraction and a relief.

So this is what it is like to be the Church, she thought. *Caring for one another and bearing one another's burdens.*

The friendship of the five had been forged through the fiery trials and tribulations of the North Atlantic in an era of reform. It had been a spiritual battle of sorts, for many back home doubted the existence of angels and demons, let alone ghosts. How could their peers at Rhymer be expected to believe or appreciate what they had witnessed?

Perhaps she could trust Monsignor Lewis with her story, Catherine though, as her curiosity got the better of her. She glanced back at that corner table. Noticing that the others were engrossed in conversation, she walked over to it.

The cover, obscured by months of accumulated dust, was nevertheless familiar, and the book was gathered into knowing hands. Catherine recognized it as one of a multitude of biblical translations, ranging from formal to casual-conversational, all written in English or any other native language. The language of the people. Whether borrowed or purchased, it was readily available to just about anyone who desired to read it or listen to it on audio.

How easily accessed now, it seemed, and even taken for granted. To gain that very freedom, often overlooked today, good men and women endured unspeakable agonies as martyrs.

ENDNOTES

1 Neil Grant, *Scottish Clans and Tartans* (New York: Crescent Books, 1987), 237.

2 Genesis 9:4.

3 Genesis 9:6.

4 James 1:17.

5 James D. Tracy, *Europe's Reformations: 1450–1650* (Lanham, MD: Rowman and Littlefield, 1999), 50.

6 Luke 23:34.

7 Luke 23:42 (NIV).

8 Luke 23:43.

9 Isaiah 9:2.

10 John 8:12.

11 Matthew 5:43–44.

12 John 18:36.

13 Matthew 7:21.

14 Matthew 11:28–30.

15 Romans 3:10.

16 Genesis 3:17.

17 Romans 3:23.

18 John 16:33 (NIV).

19 Romans 8:18.

20 Isaiah 53:3a.

21 Isaiah 53:4–5.

22 John 3:16.

23 Romans 10:9.

24 Isaiah 40:21a.

25 Isaiah 53:1a. The actual verse uses the word *message* instead of *story*.

Lightning Source UK Ltd.
Milton Keynes UK
UKHW010634100820
367987UK00001B/13